ALL THE
WRONG SIDES

ALL THE
WRONG SIDES

Mark Quinn

Library of Congress Control Number:		2022921188
ISBN:	Hardcover	978-1-6641-1848-5
	Softcover	978-1-6641-1847-8
	eBook	978-1-6641-1846-1

Print information available on the last page.

Rev. date: 11/23/2022

To order additional copies of this book, contact:
Xlibris
UK TFN: 0800 0148620 (Toll Free inside the UK)
UK Local: (02) 0369 56328 (+44 20 3695 6328 from outside the UK)
www.Xlibrispublishing.co.uk
Orders@Xlibrispublishing.co.uk
847537

DEDICATION

For Annie, my partner in life and love

Chapter I

Quinn had died in the night: first, the curtain had been pulled around his bed, and then the nurses and orderlies—quietly so as not to disturb the other patients on the ward—had lifted the body onto a trolley and wheeled him out of sight to where they go.

Mandy was tucking the sheets in at the end of a patient's bed. This man had spent most of the morning asleep, his breakfast things barely touched, so the nurse muttered animatedly to herself as she worked. It's hard enough as it is, but that makes it so much worse for us, when we don't know who to call, she was saying. She was thinking now about the empty bed, the one belonging to the deceased. I wish families could bear that in mind, she sighed.

I'll try to remember that, said the man in the bed, who was awake now. The nurse's uniform was bright white and baby blue, which reminded him of the pictures of his grandchild. They will hardly bring him over from England to see me here, now, in this state: a baby can catch things in a hospital. 'I haven't lost that yet,' the patient added, reaching for his temple with his fingers. He was not exactly sure what he had said out loud and what had remained in his head. I haven't lost my memory.

Perhaps he could make conversation with this one.

Mandy was pausing over her patient's notes, clipped to the end of his bed. 'Sure you haven't, Mr . . .'

'I'm just Frank,' he insisted cheerfully. 'By name, by nature.' Eilis had tried out *Francis* for a while, maybe a day, maybe the day she showed him off to her parents, but it felt to them both like she was referring to a totally different man so. His wife would be in later on to see him.

Mandy gave him a little smile. If she had perched herself on the side of his bed, it would not have come as a surprise to Frank; it was a good smile, one of those. But, of course, she didn't, she wouldn't. Perch on his bed. Proper nurse. Probably worried about the policeman looking at her from outside the ward. Frank was past worrying what people thought of him—those he might have worried about were dead already, or else not around. Frank, by nature. She lifted his wrist and brought her watch to her face and checked her patient's nature that way, recording his numbers in the notes. These went at the foot of the bed again, beyond his reach. That was her done.

This one gives nothing away, Frank thought. She reads his monitor and adjusts the feed into his arm and breezes past the subject of the dead man. She'll be back later of her own accord, but he can press the button hanging at the side of his bed if he needs anything in the meantime. Jeremy, or it might be Nicole, will be along. He'll have a nice lunch, they do good toast if he'd rather, there's a coffeeshop on the floor above if he doesn't like the tea they bring, one of his visitors can go there later for him. Will he have any visitors?

Frank still felt the touch of his fingers on his temple. I haven't lost that yet, he sighed, adding it to the list of things he still had. An orderly was stripping the sheets off Quinn's bed, preparing it for the next victim. Frank wondered what it was that had finally killed the man and whether anyone would be interested in talking to him about it. He'd keep his eye out. No doubt that policeman would invite himself in at some point. I'm keeping my mouth shut, said Frank to himself. I'm not about to start touting now.

Despite this, Frank fell asleep. If anything went on in the ward, he missed it. In any case, while the police were sorting out the business with Quinn, an officer was to remain on point and no one other than staff was to come or go.

ℰℋℐ

'Good girl for slipping in past your man there in uniform,' Frank said out loud to the chair below the window. He was talking to Eilis, his wife. She brought a bag of yogurt nuts and a two-litre bottle of 7

Up. 'They have no Lucozade in the shops,' she explained. The sunlight coming in through the window left her in darkness and, because he was buttressed by a pillow wall arranged like sandbags, he could not actually see her. Her voice sang to him from behind.

'They have. It's a sports drink now. Tennis players use it. I have read about it. Electrolytes.' Frank set the nuts and lemonade on the table that reached across his bed. This table was like a giant staple on wheels, pinning him in. It still had the things from breakfast, the tea he hadn't asked for, the porridge bowl with the curdling puddle of milk. 'This thing is a trap. Could you push it out of the way for me, love?'

She ignored him. 'You're in a mood. You need cheering up.'

'Not now, please, Eilis.'

'Why not? Everyone here could do with it too, they're so glum.'

'They're not glum, they are dying. People don't appreciate it, love.'

'Who doesn't? Who doesn't like a song?' Eilis looked around at the beds and patients, at their visitors and their life-supporting machines, as if she might find there an inspiration for a lyric, or an entire song.

'You can hum.'

That's what he always used to say when he wanted her to stop. She tried instead to cheer her husband up with pictures of their grandchild, in the arms of the handsome man who was their son. 'Do you think they will bring over the wee lad now? I so hope they do.'

'Over my dead body. That's what he told me, in so many words. Don't get your hopes up.'

'Did he not say he would come, now that you are? In here?'

Frank hummed the song he imagined was in her head. It was a habit he had, which helped him to think of his wife. 'They might have said something along those lines. Is that what you heard too?'

Eilis was already changing the subject. 'Who was that?' she whispered, pointing with her head at the empty bed.

'You don't know him. Mandy was cross at him for some reason. I caught the name, but it doesn't matter now. There'll be another along to take his place before long, I shouldn't wonder.' Frank had an imaginary stick with notches on it, and he fancied this helped him to stay alive. You'll outlast another few yet, the stick promised. He was in a better mood.

'Mandy?'

'Yes.' Frank flattened the creases from the bedsheets across his knees and lifted his fringe from his eyes. He knew how to tease his wife even now.

'Is Mandy what you call your nurse?' Eilis sat back, further out of her husband's sight.

'It's what she calls herself. I suppose too it's what her friends call her. We have only just met, so I haven't landed on a pet name for her yet, if that's what you're asking.' He sucked in his stomach, stretched forward his chin, a little cruelly.

'Don't get yourself worked up, Frank. You knew what I meant.' What did she mean? 'I mean, is she a good nurse? Are they looking after you properly?'

He performed a so-so with his head. 'I have a button,' Frank replied, lifting his hand to show. He had little left to say, so he let his wife fade away. There would be a TV room somewhere, he thought to himself. The provincial final would be showing, but only on RTE, and Frank was doubtful the City Hospital had an aerial for the Irish state broadcaster. Jeremy would not know, not with a name like that, but then again maybe he would. No harm in asking. Lunch would be first, he reckoned, they serve meals early in hospitals to discourage visitors from staying. They do good toast, he had heard. He would put it to Jeremy then, if he showed up, rather than waste a button-press now. Like his notch stick, there was a debit account for pressing the help button, and you wouldn't want to exhaust it too quickly.

'You would like that, wouldn't you?'

'What are you on about now, Frank?'

'Over my dead body, if it got the boy back over.'

'There you go, with your rubbish. Why would you say such a thing to me?'

'It's what you've been saying for years, Eilis. "You have it coming," you're always saying. "You should take what's coming to you." You are always saying that. You may get your wish yet.'

'I swear, it makes you happy just to watch others be miserable. Twisting my words like that. I wish I hadn't bothered with the yogurt nuts, now.'

Frank nodded, like his wife had stumbled upon some essential truth they could agree on. They both smiled.

'If I leave now,' Eilis reasoned, 'do you think maybe more of your visitors will show up?' She looked around for supporting evidence, recollecting what she had brought with her. 'I will leave those for you, shall I?' She meant the nuts and 7 Up. 'See, I do love you! It gets dry in hospitals. It's hot here already. So . . .' She had her coat over her arm. As she leant in to kiss her husband of forty years, the coat slipped onto his lap. She caught it but had to sacrifice the gesture of affection. 'So . . .'

Others did come to visit that afternoon: it was as if all his friends (and some were not his friends) had chosen just that day to come and disturb him. It was as well that, in a hospital ward, a day lasts all day, the time never passes. Otherwise, he would have had visitors piling up on top of each other, there were so many. Some more police officers were visible in the corridor outside the ward. Frank had nothing for them, so he pretended to sleep and they didn't disturb him. Easy enough to give them the slip, Frank laughed to himself. Jackson from next door had a query about his lawn. He was happy to do it, anything for Frank and Eilis, but it would have to be after Sunday now. That'd be marvellous. Lawn was a fancy word for the patch of grass at the front of their house. Why did Jackson feel, just because he mowed his grass, he had the right to a hospital visit? 'Seen much of Gloria lately?' Frank asked, watching his neighbour redden. Still, you would never catch Sammy on the other side volunteering to do anything as useful as cut the grass. Sammy and his friend Pat promised to set aside a gin and tonic for him at the pub. If you're allowed in your condition. I am not pregnant! How bad can G&T be for you, anyway—doesn't it have quinine? Coming from Sammy, that was a kind of thoughtfulness. Another one, Liz, came unexpectedly and left after twenty minutes of bewilderment. She looked well despite. She came alone because that was what she was nowadays, now that her husband had come off the road. He wasn't careful. 'James was so happy to be home,' she said. 'I knew it was a mistake. What was all that running for, for it to end this way, Frank?' When did this happen? Six weeks ago. Holy Jesus, Liz, I hoped all that had passed. Frank had two small pork sausages and an ice scoop of mash surrounded by a moat of gravy when his lunch arrived. Two penises, one bollock. Frank was unfussy with food. I could live okay in a hospital, better than most, I wouldn't starve.

Jeremy exclaimed that no one, in all the eight years he had been a nurse in this hospital, had ever to his knowledge inquired after RTE: 'It can't be all our patients are Protestants!' He said it in a nice enough, non-sectarian way and pledged to check. Two of Frank's cousins from his mother's side called in, or rather his cousin and her husband. Both could talk, and Frank let them because he hadn't much to say to them when he was well and even less now that he wasn't. A sister would have been more use. The peace process had been financially and otherwise advantageous for their farm machinery business, whatever otherwise meant. Good for them. They had tickets already bought for the All-Ireland final, so the County team had feckin well win the provincial today. Frank pointed out the mechanism of the back door. Come again, Frank? What 'back door', I've not heard about a back door. The competition was not a straightforward knockout. You mean we might lose and we won't have lost at all—what's the point of that, Frank? As he knows about GAA, Frank must come with them to the senior final in September—would he like that?—and Frank thought that at last his cousins were good for something, they were otherwise advantageous, and indeed, yes, he certainly would like that. Frank's customary source of Croke Park tickets was likely not still open to him, but he saw no reason to reveal this to his cousins with their farm machinery business, and certainly not now while there was a police presence. Dublin never failed to live up, and he would prepare his sandwiches and wrap his biscuits the night before just as he had the last time in '86. You're forgetting '95, Frank, are you not? That's unlike you. I don't forget, he insisted: I just prefer not to remember that one. His cousins prepared to leave. 'That'll be something for us all to look forward to.' Dublin—he knew it well—was a good straight drive, for the most part, especially past the border on their sleek European roads. The city itself was not necessarily to be entered, he explained, no need with the parking on the side streets just a walk away from the stadium. I can always stay over in a B&B, if it comes to that, I know of one I like. 'We are taking the Gresham,' they said. Good for them.

All of that happened. Somebody maybe should have stepped in and insisted the patient have proper rest.

Jeremy was as good as his word. No, the game wasn't showing live, but a friend in radiography had guarantees there would be an extended sports bulletin after the regional news that would have highlights. That'll have to do for me. Will you come and collect me, or will I need to press this? Good man.

Frank slept more. Hospitals always did that to him. Even if he were only visiting, the air inside a ward was like an expanding yawn. There was nothing for it but to slip under it and snooze. No one died this time; he missed nothing. His ears and nose remained alert to the beeps and stench. Cash, his very great friend, used to say that about him: Frank, you hear it all, nothing of any import ever gets past you. That was evidently untrue, for plenty went on that he never knew of or got to hear about, but Cash was always generous with this flattery, and Frank let him. Anything changes on your front, Cash, and I'll let you know—you need only ask. As if Frank was likely to hear of any such changes. He was well out of all that now, although he had recently travelled home to stand on the touchline with the other old guys. The chat there was all about the football, not the politics, as if Frank had been gone too long for them to trust him with that. An insider became an outsider after not very long: it was sometimes the very moment they stepped away. One time, one guy at a game asked him about Cash—where is he, is it true he is a big shot over the water—and he said he had lost touch. Was Cash the tout, the informant, everyone says it, do you think it? This same guy wanted to know: he was your friend, they say. They say he told the police about the thing, and then the whole thing went up. That's how it was? I had other better friends, insisted Frank. And that was that. The ball was punted forward, a point was scored, and the chat settled back into its one-line inanity. ('Is that Hughes boy the son of Declan Hughes?' 'Aye.' 'He can play.' 'Aye.' 'May he rest in peace.') That guy was a youngster really, never actually met Cash and barely even knew Frank, but there he was with his questions about Cullycreggan. Even now—when Quinn was out of the way so Frank was finally in the clear, and there was supposedly no politics left anymore, only peace—there was still plenty politics lying about back home. Frank knew.

'Frank?' That man nurse was leaning over him, smelling nice like a bath and not like a hospital. 'Shall I wheel you down now?'

Frank checked he was covered up. He had come without his pyjamas. 'Is it my scan already?'

'You had that, Frank,' said Jeremy. 'No. You wanted to watch the news, and the highlights after. I'll wheel you down now so you're ready. Do you want that still?'

I've had my scan? How did we manage that? Frank swung his legs over the side of the bed. He was ashamed of his legs. They were hairless and shiny and pink in a way he never expected a man of his age could have legs. They were not a model for how legs should be, not one he imagined Jeremy (even Jeremy) would envy. Frank brushed his fringe from his eyes. 'Help me into that,' he said to the wheelchair. 'If you know it, don't tell me the score,' he warned his chaperone sternly. You only watch highlights if you don't know who's won, or if you know you have won. The look on Jeremy's face was enough: he hadn't a clue.

The news was comical to watch. He knew one of the journalists, had seen her on the television before, funny where people end up. You can tell by the way they listen to their politicians, these other patients are all Protestant, fair-minded though they appear to be. They can't shake off their structural ascendancy even now when they have none. Funny-interesting. When politicians are universally detested, there will be hope for us all. One or two of these Protestant patients might even appreciate GAA if they are prepared to give it a go, but the peace is too fragile yet for that advance. Pity. No parity of esteem while we are still in the post-trauma phase. Would you hear me, to listen to me I could be my son! Some of their rugby boys would do rightly on a Gaelic pitch. I'll not voice that opinion outside of here.

'Did your team win, Frank?' That was that already.

'They did. Can't you tell just by looking at me?' Frank was walking back to his ward, trailed by his drip stand, having abandoned his wheelchair in the television room. 'See, I am celebrating!' No gin and tonic, however. Sammy and Pat would have extra for him. He would see if he could get someone to bring a proper paper for him tomorrow morning, to read about it at his leisure. Eilis would, if she remembered his regular order at the shop. Frank was a partisan where newspapers were concerned. He had picked up one of their tabloids in the TV room, which he could read in his bed only if no one was watching. Peace may have broken out on the streets, but people were still sectarian in their daily reading habits. That was his observation. As a rule, Frank didn't refuse to read their paper just because he was a bigot, but because, when he did read it, he never found anything in it he wanted to read: the stories were always about themselves. (Sometimes, he admitted, he felt the same way about his own paper.)

While he was away, a new neighbour had moved into the bed in the corner of the ward. This one had grey, matted hair and an omnivorous beard that ate up the whole of his face. A huge bulge protruded out of the side of his pyjama top. He lay on his side nursing it, having the look of a dog when it's been struck by a car. He was not dead yet, but his owners, caring insufficiently, had abandoned hope already. The man sighed with effort. Out of respect, Frank pulled his curtain round a bit before he opened out his newspaper. Kitty Shiels had been gaoled for three years in America for supplying guns to the boys over here. There's more scandal behind that story, Frank thought, and if I know that then so must they. That'll come out just at the wrong time, you wait. There was a different story on the front page. They had a name for the informant at the inside and top end of the paramilitaries, acting for the security forces. Insecurity forces. Ha ha. This informant up to that point only had a code name. The man's real name sounded like it should be selling you ice cream in Portrush. Such a lot of Italians had ended up in Northern Ireland, bringing their talent for sectarian violence with them. He was knifing people and planting bombs and the rest of it, all under the English noses—or worse, with their say-so—just so he could pass on to them information about Republican killing and bombing and all the rest. He denied it all. He wouldn't be selling a lot more ice cream if he hadn't denied it. Right there is a man who will need protecting, from just about everybody on every side. He can have one of these here hospital policemen, thought Frank with a chuckle. Informants were liable to lose their knees, and that's just the ones who went in for a little bit of touting. Was there a place on the planet that would take him (the ice cream man, or whatever he was) and hide him? Back in the day, there were countries, Frank understood, where you could go for a cooling off; there were boys even who took time out in England, if they reckoned England was far enough way. He knew some himself who had done that, some other than Cash. 'How do you know that, Frank?' Eilis would ask with deliberate ignorance, inviting no answer. Sometimes he did and sometimes he didn't know what would stir her. You'd know that too, love, if you ventured home more often and listened.

They were starving him from here on, it now transpired. Word came to him, a bit late to be any use. If he had known, he might have doubled up on the hot pudding at lunchtime. He had been advanced along the queue owing to a cancellation. Who cancels life-saving surgery? 'She died while she was waiting, I think,' said Mandy, who was back on. 'Or that does happen, whether it happened this time I can't be sure. But that's marvellous news for you, isn't it, Frank? The cancellation?'

Frank wondered who would take his own cancellation as good news. He seriously wondered: did his son have his own notch stick, tallying parental demises, playing the inheritance one-two? He should get balloons in and party food. Every cloud's. 'I am hungry already, Amanda.' Silver lining.

He would grab her while she was here. Mandy huffed, she didn't say anything, but Frank heard from that that she didn't like 'Amanda'. As 'Francis' was to him. Fair enough. It was worth testing her on it. 'Can I have yogurt nuts?' He spied the bag at the end of his bed. 'Mandy? They're only little.'

'Nuts is the worst. Nuts are the worst, rather.' Mandy confiscated the bag like she had just won the prize for best ward matron, and she secreted them in her tabard. 'They'll be safe there,' she lied proudly. 'Can I help you with anything else?'

Is this all necessary? He had been starved before, that was par for the course, one of those things you accepted about going under the knife without really understanding why, reckoning there were greater unknowns about surgery that were more worth bothering about. Mandy nabbing his nuts was fair enough too, as he would undoubtedly have eaten through the whole bag in the night. It was the protein in the nuts or the oils or the high-calorific content, one of those, all of those, but he knew, or he had read somewhere too, that nuts were as a matter of fact worst. Slow release. So she could have his nuts. So to speak—he'd make a mention of that to Eilis, see how she reacted. She snatched my nuts, Eilis, and shoved them down there, yes there. There's no call for that kind of talk at this time, Frank. No—Frank forced himself back to the point—was the operation *per se* necessary?

Mandy was reading his reading on his monitor at that point, giving nothing away as per always, meaning that, for sure, the operation was necessary. But did that have to mean that the operation had to come now, as in first thing in the morning? Didn't they recommend a bedding-in period first? His GP had said something like that, or perhaps he had imagined it, he was always reassured after he'd been to see her, his GP. A period of observation. He had hardly been bedded in here, just that one sleep overnight and the nap after lunch, and even that one had been disturbed by the beeps and Jeremy waking him up. 'Thank you, Mandy. Perhaps some water?'

'Water is fine, for now anyway. Not for the couple of hours before you go under, in case you vomit under anaesthetic. I'll bring you a nice jug of fresh in a while. I have these ones to see to first. Okay, Frank?'

Frank nodded surrender. He could hardly complain about the attention he'd had from her already. Run off her feet, like the whole NHS, barely fit to provide him with a jug of water. He could wait his turn, he had longer in him to wait than some that are here. At least he had family and friends around him to help, no shortage in that department, who could bring him news and some laughs. Eilis was pretty good that way, never left a gap in the conversation so to speak, without filling it with a song or something. She didn't bring his newspaper, however, that was an oversight, nor anything else to be getting on with reading. Just drink that he couldn't drink, and nuts that were the worst thing to eat. Not a book in sight. Maybe he should have stayed in the television room. There would have been something on he could have watched. Frank lifted out the newspaper he had hidden when Mandy had appeared. It had the same stories in it that his own paper would have had, and yet they weren't the same: the perspective was the other perspective. All perspectives are wrong, he realised. Funny. A politician was mumbling about decommissioning, as ever. When would they ever put *him* beyond use? Not that the politician was wrong, from his own perspective, from the perspective of wanting to humiliate the other lot; but from the perspective of wanting just to get on with peace and all that goes with peace, he could just shush for a bit. He was weaponising the deweaponising issue: he needed to do the opposite of that. Frank read that. And he read about the latest nonsense out of McCann's mouth and couldn't believe she was still being listened to after all these years. And still dangerous. A good thing his grandchild wasn't being brought across the water to see him here, his son wasn't wrong there. Frank took a mental note to try not to say otherwise. *Over my dead body.*

☙❧

The lights in the ward were dimmed to drop the hint to the last remaining graveyard revellers that they should leave. The room was big and dark and empty now, the machines humming and ticking in the way his stomach juices did when his tummy was also empty. He needed a shit, of all things, as if his body had spare food its gut still wanted to twist and cramp and expel. He knew the routine; this was not his first hospital overnighter. Things can go wrong on the toilet; it's best to plot it all out before leaving bed. He was sure enough on his feet, and there was the drip stand to cart along, which might act as a steadier should he lose his balance. The toilet was opposite the nurses' station, so there was no getting away from that—they and the policeman would all know what he was up to in there, the mere knowledge of which, unless he was absolutely confident in his bowel, could frustrate his. A watched kettle. There were handles and rails and all sorts in there, there was no excuse for falling over, but the light cord could be tricky to locate and then distinguish from the emergency pull. Then a red light would come on instead of the white one, and no amount of cool can save a man in an open-backed hospital gown from panicking in a red light. Best to plot it all then before leaving the bed. He gave Mandy at the station a little apologetic eye-roll on his way past: here I am, what can I do. Send for an ambulance if I don't come out in. What would be a reasonable time.

There were no untoward events in the loo. Mandy avoided meeting his eye on the way back. She let him find his own way into bed, mentally kicking off the slippers he had forgotten to put on. She watched him look under his bed, maybe checking for something. His bedside Anglepoise was lit. He fumbled for something at this bedside table then put his hands to his face. She hadn't noticed before that he wore glasses. Black-rimmed glasses that were fetching in the '70s. His fringe flopped over a lens. He was reading some newspaper he had picked up.

'Reading, Frank?'

'No, not really, not this comic anyway. But there's nothing better. I came in without a book, for some reason I can't fathom. I like reading, you know, Mandy? It's a thing that's stayed with me, that. Can't say why it is, my wife doesn't have it, my son does: more an affliction than an addiction, he says, and he might be right there. Certainly feels like an affliction now.' Frank hoisted the unloved newspaper up for Mandy to see. 'No offence.'

'None taken on my part,' she assured him thickly. 'Can't you sleep? Do you need something to help you off?'

'The only thing that works for me is whiskey, and you'd be sacked for offering me that.' He paused to check he was correct. While he waited, a warm sting suffused his mouth like a whiskey placebo. 'And I'd probably choke and die under GA, knowing your luck and mine.' Mandy laughed. 'You have a nice laugh, Mandy.'

'Thanks, Frank. That's a nice thing to say to a nurse.'

'It's a nice thing for a nurse to have.' Frank looked away, to make sure she didn't think he was a pervert. He had a habit of flirting with the wrong people, so Eilis said. You are always doing that, dropping wee compliments to set a person at her unease. It's a nice quality, and it's not at the same time. People can take it wrong. As you well know. Which is why you do it. 'I suppose you have a lot of paperwork on?' he asked, to change the subject.

'No. First time ever,' Mandy said without guile. 'I'll sit with you for a bit, if you like. I'll likely send you off to sleep before you know it.' Frank was nervous, the night before his operation, just as he should be, it was only rational. She laughed again, because he liked it and because it wasn't odd to laugh then.

'Other way around, more like,' Frank replied chivalrously. He wouldn't mind talking, as it happened. There was something about earlier in the day that had unbalanced him. He thought it had been the anticipation of the match, then the unexpected scheduling of his operation due to the person being cancelled, but it had happened before all of that. Quinn's bed had lain empty all day when there was bound to be somebody in need of it, and it must be bad luck at least to keep a dead man's bed on display in a ward like this. At the very least. But that wasn't it exactly either. Hospitals really ought to employ vetting over visitors, any bloody person can just wander in. It's not right that police officers are allowed to roam free like that. Murderers get better consideration. Maybe he was just nervous, as the nurse had figured. Where was the button to press for that?

Mandy was sitting on the seat his wife and other visitors had taken up earlier in the day, only she was still and unafraid of silence.

'Mandy, how good are you at keeping secrets?'

'Okay, with the ones I am allowed to keep. If it's a medical thing, I can tell you straightaway that I won't be keeping it to myself. Other than that . . . if there's something you need out rather than in . . . I'm as sound as a pound.' Mandy laughed again.

'That's good, Mandy. You keep laughing, that's the best way to go. Laughing, or singing, it's much the same—you can do both, whether you're happy or you're sad. Laughing suits you.'

Mandy was not laughing now. She knew it when a patient just needed to talk, as if listening was too painful for them now and it was better if they just filled the silence themselves.

'Do you know what an informant is, Amanda? Of course, you do, it's a simple enough word. Or tout? *Tout!* You can't say the word without spitting. Do you know what happens to a tout around here? No reason why you should, it's a thing we are not supposed to do any more, although I can tell you that history takes a long time passing in these parts. They're beaten, they're left for dead. But that's not the half of it, Amanda. The worst is that they are never forgotten: the smell on a tout lingers forever. Even if he can prove it was never him—he never passed on information to the police—even if he can pin it on an even guiltier man, he will still stink of it.'

The only light in the ward was seeping in from the nurses' station in the corridor. Most patients were asleep, apart from those kept awake by the sound of their own monitors.

You need to know from the start that the man I am going to talk about here isn't a bad person. In fact, in my opinion, he may be the best man I ever knew. But people died because of him. You might say the same about me, but that's another story and I am not half the man.

'I see,' said Mandy. She thought what else she might say or do. 'Do you need me to fix your pillows, then?'

'No, leave them, would you, Mandy?'

CHAPTER II

Jimmy Cash was Scottish. Saying that then was like saying now he was a hunter-gatherer. People from Scotland killed for food and lived in stone huts, or so we thought. Later, I learned that they built ships and hated each other for religious reasons much as we did ourselves, but, for us then, Scotland was exotic. I knew no one personally who had ever been anywhere other than Ireland. Shiels—our goalkeeper—claimed to have a second cousin somewhere in America, but he liked to tell stories that no one listened to. Jimmy was the exception. He added to the mystery by rarely discussing it so, in our minds, Scotland became a wide-open plain with occasional stone houses and Presbyterians. Jimmy had survived this somehow and come among us. One rainy playground day, we invented the game where Jimmy was captured by the staunchies, tortured and escaped but paid the price with terrible injuries to his face.

Everyone had a deformity then. Every child in the McHugh family had a crooked back because they never ate oranges. *McHugh! Stand up straight!* None of the rest of us had an orange to split between us, but we still didn't suffer the spinal curvature that Susie, Joe, and Sean did. Later, Sean—who could not curse if his life depended on it—was lucky to land a job that suited his disability, heaving meat in an abattoir. We all had our teeth missing. Children had given up sweets for the War, and they were rationed still for years after because somehow sugar was needed by the government to build the NHS, but, despite that, we still had our teeth missing. Medical science indicated there was a shortage of calcium in our mothers' milk, which was the biggest joke ever because the country was always full of cows. Our baby teeth dropped out, but the adult ones refused to come. Drink your buttermilk, our mothers would say, with the same urgency as *Grow up*, and *You need to start paying your way.* Eventually, our teeth came in time for us to leave home.

I was born premature: six weeks, ten weeks—Ma didn't like to say, to count back to the moment of most likely conception. In those days, there were millions of babies but no sex. It was enough to be told that I had *come early*, like it was a decision I had made by myself, overhasty. I didn't ask too many questions because, in those days, I didn't. *Cat caught your tongue?* people used to tease, not knowing half the truth of it. *What's that, Frank?* people would ask. *I didn't quite catch that.* I satisfied myself with the things I did not say to them and sang the songs in my head that I could not sing out loud.

Jimmy was cursed with an orofacial cleft. I know, Mandy, you will be *au fait* with the medical. His philtrum was off-centre and split, not the whole way up to the nose but enough to make the surgery they had given him less than totally successful. Maybe he had been carrying a gene for it, but neither of his parents nor his sister was affected. Affected in other ways, perhaps: Moira. Soft in the head. You will probably tell me off for saying so, but there it is: she was dropped at birth, some said, and she was never right again. Vulnerable, you would no doubt call it. He himself suspected he'd suffered an *in utero* virus and, when he was prepared to talk about his deformity—which, fleetingly, and only ever with me, he sometimes did—he discussed it as if his face was separate from himself. He thought of it as a malfunction or an engineering error, and he pointed at his wayward philtrum the way a Scotsman would a faulty bit of welding: he was ashamed of it for now, the poor workmanship, but that didn't mean it had to remain that way. Cleft (rather than harelip) was what he called it, because if to cleave meant to split apart, it also meant to stick together. Cleave, clinch, cling. Even illogic is a sort of logic if you are clever enough. He became an engineer.

Undernourishment is relative. You don't lack oranges, or sweets, if everyone does. My dad was a tall man in life, but I doubt he was ever more than five feet eight, and we buried him in a short coffin. I'm not big even now. We gave up bananas for Lent because there were no bananas to be got. If everyone is undernourished then, relatively speaking, no one is. We were all wee skitters without knowing we were. The other thing that we all had in common was that none of our fathers had work, those of us who had fathers at all. None of us examined the reasons for this too closely at the time, the more that we were grateful for the little we had. That examination did occur, later, among those like Jimmy who were never as poorly off in the first place. When Jimmy grew, he grew bigger than the rest of us—he must have been over-nourished—and we had to stop belittling him with *Jimmy*. Fr McCaul put *Jim* in our Gaelic football team. There were sixteen boys in the class, but one of them—Casey—never grew and had two legs in callipers. This meant that even McHugh was guaranteed a spot. *McHugh! Stand up straight!* McCaul would say every time. If Jim hadn't played, there would have been no team. 'Your face already looks like you have been in a good fight,' the priest said often, reasoning it would scare the opposition. Fr McCaul put him at left corner-back. 'You can't be goalkeeper: however tall you are—and you have inches on Shiels—you have to know something about the game to play in goal, and we are yet to discover that about you. I've never heard of a Scotchman who could play the game, but I will not be prejudiced just yet. We have only one natural leftie, Ryan, and we need him at corner-forward, where he can do some damage. 'Is that all right with you, Jim? Left back in the corner?' Aloysius Dynes laughed. O'Rourke laughed. Fr McCaul always spoke to Jim as if idiocy were his affliction and he therefore didn't get jokes. Dynes, my best friend, was always the first to join in. 'Frank, you can keep an eye on him at half-back, will you? You know what you're doing there.'

Fr McCaul coached the team and drove the minibus. It was the same minibus used by the scouts and the boxing club, both of which Fr McCaul also had a hand in. As parish priest, he had what he referred to as 'access to local contributions'. One such contribution had been the Pat's Pan bread van. Pat's had gone up in the world and opened a shop off the Diamond, so people would go to them for their baps and bakes, and not the other way around. Pat himself (his real name wasn't 'Pat', it'll come to me) stripped out the trays and shelves, but the aroma of bread was ingrained so, when his bread van became our minibus, our tummies would rumble on the way to every away game. The scent of a thing is millions of tiny particles of the thing itself lodging in your nose: that's the truth, and it makes sense sure enough. But the memory of a smell? I can recall that waft of a pan loaf in my nostrils as if it were there right now, yet it's not. That's a trick of either the memory or the senses. Maybe there's a doctor here who knows.

Smaller towns and villages—the remoter the better—are full of wee lads not left yet, who maybe don't even drink yet or chase girls, who practically sleep in their boots. Football is more of a religion to them than religion, everyday including Sunday. That's what it was like for us. Our wee town had four streets: they held hands in the middle to make up the Diamond, which had a pub on two of its corners, a chapel for Fr McCaul on its third, and nothing at all on the fourth. At one time, I remember, there was a horse that seemed to stand all the time in the Diamond weeing into the gutter like he was the town drunk. Is the word dray? Was that the type of horse he was? There was a wagon there, which would make sense if he belonged to a brewery and he was doing the two corners of the Diamond. Eddie! It just came to me: that was his name. I mean the horse. One time Eddie was there all the while and then, I don't know when, he was not there at all. The same as when they replaced McAllister's fishing, hardware, and sports store with a hairdresser's we didn't need until we got it. McAllister's children moved to decent jobs in the city, having no interest in tackle but glad of the wee bit of money their dad had come by, and McAllister himself took up a pew in the back bar of Suzy's.

The Pitches were behind the graveyard, which was behind the chapel. Fr McCaul, who complained bitterly about the puddle the cemetery was sited on, proudly lectured us on the natural drainage our fields enjoyed due to their sandy soil. Before the last ice age, our whole town—he meant maybe more than just the town: the county for sure and probably a chunk more than that—was all underwater, in the sea, as could be confirmed by the abundance of limestone in the quarry as well as the sandiness of the Pitches. Our bedrock was formed by the compression of millions of ancient skeletons. We could play and train in all weathers, meaning that, despite our disfigurements, we were fitter than all those boys in other villages who had to play their football on a bog. Our balls bounced higher, Fr McCaul told us without laughing. It earned us a few easy points a game. We ought to have had finer teeth and bones than the other lads too, given that the water we drank was strained through the calcium carbonate beneath our feet. That's how I see it.

McCaul made a speech a couple of years back, when he gathered us all together again: we were the best wee side he ever drove. We beat all around us, the year we took the County Shield. Carrycreagh, Dunaderry, Ardbog, Balnakerry, Skerrybeg. Ryan put away most of our goals—he was a nippy bastard—but the rest of us, even backs such as myself, knocked over the occasional point. Fox, McHugh, O'Rourke, Dynes, Quinn, Cash. Others, the names wouldn't mean anything to you. Tullymourne, Glencort, Michaelstown, Ballytor, Toberlough, Carntasie, Shesk, Beagh. We were in some places! Places where nothing happens but games of football. Some of them were good teams too: Michaelstown fancied themselves then as they do still and had their eye on the Shield themselves when they met us in the semi-final. Those boys drank their mothers' milk, and it must have been good stuff. Their forwards were like gods. Only O'Rourke on our side could have compared. One of them, I swear to God, he had muscles on his legs; he must have been cutting turf since he could walk. And there was one they called Simon—that's a standout name, not one of ours—and this Simon he had a tan, like a tan you can only get on the Continent. There's a difference between being ruddy, as we all were, more or less, and being tanned: you get ruddy from running around and working in the outdoors; tans are for people with leisure to sit down. That was this one, Simon. He played right half-forward and was thus up against Jim, and he gave Jim the runaround the whole game. He had him inside out, and, to be fair, he was starting to showboat before it happened. The boy Simon—I swear, he had a smirk on his face—dropped his shoulder and hand-passed the ball to himself right over Jim's head: pop, like that, and he ran on with the ball. But he sort of stopped to look around, to soak up the applause or whatever, and Jim, who had turned and kept running, clattered into this boy, their right half-forward with the suntan. His whole body (not just his body, his person) crumpled like a half-filled sack of loose sticks. I can hear the terrific crack of it even now. Is that what sound is, do you think? Millions of tiny particles of the thing itself lodging in your ear. Hearing a crunch like that leaves a bruise, it has an enduring impact on your eardrum. The boy was sick on the pitch before they carted him off with the bone sticking out of his leg. They hadn't it in them after that, we ran away with the game. There isn't a book, but if there were, that would be in it. We took Carrigbay apart in the final, I am told. I can recall nothing about it at all, as if the Michaelstown game caused such a massive neural disturbance it annihilated all else. Jim didn't even remember that much. Or, put it another way, he held a different version in his memory.

Fr McCaul collected in the money at home games. If you haven't seen it, you won't know what it looks like. Four or six men parade around the perimeter at half-time holding an edge of a big sheet like it's the Olympic flag, only instead of coloured rings it will have writing on it such as *For children of broken homes* or *For the destitute.* Anyhow, that's how I recall it, I might be wrong with the words. In actual fact, the money was not destined for the destitute, or not all of it anyway. Some of it went straight into the bread van or the minibus in the form of petrol. It never occurred to us boys that *we* might be the poor bastards the crowds were throwing their spare coins for. But it's a fact that Fox and Dynes had no fathers, that Mrs McHugh blessed her children with many different fathers, and that not one of us had any money. We suspected that Jim's family had money, on account of being from abroad, but, to be fair, we saw no evidence of that. McCaul fed us! That's right, I had clean forgotten. Every match day—and every other day we had training—Fr McCaul's maid, Alice, served us up a bowl of chicken and potato soup, which we ate, of course, outside even when it was raining. We thought at that time this was just Alice being kind, making up somehow for being Protestant—a sort of penance, even though Protestants don't do penance, am I right?—but that's all nonsense, I realise now: it was only Father paying for it out of the sheet money. Because, otherwise, we would undoubtedly go hungry. I am only realising that now, that's me: stupid. I think they still pass the sheet round at games, but that would be for other purposes these days.

CHAPTER III

Everything important that was going to happen had already occurred. This bit happened later. Jim Cash and his wife, whose name was Betty, were getting out. They would have been happier to leave without any sort of send-off. They had not gone out for drinks with friends; there was to be no photograph to preserve the occasion. Their only concession to celebration was to have booked a sleeper for two in the overnight boat to Liverpool. Betty was going with her husband, and she despised the line on her travel documents that made plain that accompaniment was her sole purpose. She was not emigrating as, or in order to, or for the purposes of: she was just going with, with her husband. She had all the wrong prepositions. Jim was aware of a general chronic resentment in her but, without crossing words with her, was unable to attach it to a specific cause. They failed to talk about the only thing that mattered. He understood only that his wife was frightened and allowed himself to believe that fleeing was the best thing for the both of them. He was also going for an additional purpose, emigrating to Rhodesia to supervise an extensive civil engineering project. To those who required an explanation—his sister, the embassy, the building contractor for the Housing Trust in east Belfast he was walking out on—that was the explanation he gave. Actually, he was leaving because he had been advised that his life might depend upon it. That, if they had discussed it, would have been something he and his wife could have shared. Jim might have told her of his own terror. His single suitcase had been packed as by a man in a panic. More underpants than shirts. Betty had travelled before: she knew how to pack. Her suitcase concealed the box of antidepressants that she hoped would last three months. 'Getting away will be your cure,' promised her doctor, a man who had married her friend and who was keen for her to leave. 'The whispers will stop. You can start again and stop taking these.' Cushioned around the pills was a precautionary supply of Kotex napkins. It had been suggested to her—by a woman who was somehow connected to another man from the Housing Trust who had worked before in Africa—that she would have her own maid. In fact, most probably, a maid and a cook. 'You will be treated like royalty, because you are white' was the warning. The Queen does not bleed in front of the staff. One must mop that up by oneself. Betty had rolled three cotton dresses—lemon, peach, baby blue—a hat, an umbrella, paper to write on and pens, and boots to walk in because she was desperate not to be bored. She hoped she might find a Dansette and some records to buy in Salisbury for she enjoyed music or, failing that, a sewing machine.

They did not expect their send-off party to be him, Frank. It was dark, the ferry was tucked into the dock, massive and wet and dumbly indifferent to the queue of lorries and cars filing into it. The foot passengers were penned into a demountable cabin, a single bar heater ineffective against the chill air, a fraying poster listing the items they must not take undeclared into England. A couple with their three young sons were their nearest neighbours, secretive or disciplined in their own unhappiness. The youngest child, about four, his face stained by recent tears, tried unsuccessfully to achieve connection with one of the strangers; he shrugged off his failure and reached for a book from the satchel he had been given to carry. Frank, perhaps expecting jollity, had a bottle of Guinness in each of his coat pockets and decided against sharing them now. Betty wondered at his audacity at being there at all.

'Good of you to show,' Jim mumbled so as to not draw in the other family. 'We never had a party, you know.'

'I know that,' said Frank, nodding his head, understanding almost everything. 'But I didn't want you just to go. Without . . .' He hoped that Jim would, just there, acknowledge that they had been good friends since childhood, that that counted for more than any squabble over recent events. Jim didn't speak, held shut his misshapen mouth, his cleft lip fixing his expression in incidental disavowal. 'Without saying goodbye.'

'We didn't want a party.' Jim inclined his head towards Betty: the decision to not celebrate was jointly theirs; or it was taken to spare her in particular. 'You needn't have come.'

'Yes,' agreed Frank. He needn't have. He shouldn't have. There were boys back home who, if they had known that Jim was intending to be here in this place and at this time—and was about to flee the country for *Africa*, for God's sakes—would have been here all right, and it would not have been to celebrate. 'Sure, it's only me, Jim. No one else.' The two elder brothers opposite, the ones that weren't the four-year-old, were keeping themselves entertained by giving each other dead legs, having to do it without attracting the attention of either parent.

'At least that's one thing,' Jim conceded.

'You didn't bring Eilis with you this time, Francis?' said Betty suddenly. She was sitting against the wall, somehow closer to it than the others. She would have blended into it if she could. 'I like Eilis.'

'She is . . .' Frank struggled to finish. He had not thought to suggest it to Eilis or to tell her that he had taken it upon himself to rise above all the scandal and rumour to see his friend one last time. Now was not the time to be in the company of Betty and Jim Cash if you knew what was good for you. Later, possibly, when less implausible stories had reasserted themselves as the more likely truths, then the two of them would be fine to show their faces again. *Sure, we always knew that that would never have been Jim's style, he was not a one for that. Betty was good for a laugh, not everybody's cup of tea certainly, but I bet not up to half the stuff they said.* Later, with charity, with times changed. How would Frank even have put it to Eilis? *I stand by my friends, I won't be found wanting.* That had not proven to be so. She would have been as confounded as he was to learn that Betty liked her or thought of her as something apart from him. 'I'll tell her that.'

'Do. I don't suppose we will ever see her again.' Jim now recoiled from his wife, recognising the mood she had slipped into. She confronted more than he was himself prepared to do, she spoke when it was not necessary to, and she said things that were hard afterwards to pretend had not been said. It awed him. But he didn't think Eilis deserved this treatment, even in her absence.

Betty came away from the wall and looked around her to gather the assent even of the neutral family opposite. 'It's true, don't you think? We will never see or hear the lovely, talented Eilis again. It's one of the only things I could regret about going away, now that I think about it.' She stuck out her bottom lip, like a grotesque impression of sad Marilyn Monroe. Her face changed, and she moved on. 'It does feel like the last time for us too.' She meant Frank and herself, including Jim too, although that was less clear. 'Tell me I am not the only one who gets premonitions like that. Not premonitions, just normal everyday feelings. Maybe I have not seen a person for a while—oh, an ex-boyfriend, someone like that, you know what I'm like—and I bump into them just like that, or even it might be a prearranged thing and it's in a hotel—and I look across at them (it's been a perfectly pleasant occasion, I have behaved myself, it's all lovely), and I can tell this is it: this is the last time we will sit like this or see each other in this random way, and it's such a pure moment I could cry . . . I could cry even now, not because it is you particularly but because a moment this pure and honest is such a precious thing and I am the only one noticing it. Or you and the other people do notice it but haven't got the heart or guts or soul or whatever it is to face up to it.' She knocked Frank hard on the chest as if to listen for the hollowness within. 'Not enough there, Frank,' she repeated, knocking. 'Not there.'

The three brothers were now all sitting on the ground, reclined on their fronts like on their living room floor, chins propped for television, quiet lest they be sent to bed. Their mother rested her head on their father's shoulder. It grew darker outside and just a little warmer inside.

'You have a bottle of something in your pocket, Frank. I can see it.' Betty would have wrestled it out had he not done it first. 'You have two! You really were hoping for a party. These people won't mind if you open them.' The father straightened himself under the weight of his wife's sleeping head, poising himself to defend his world. Frank cracked the both bottles open on the window latch and offered one to Betty, ready to share the other with Jim. 'Don't be a fool, Francis,' she sneered. 'When have you ever seen me drink stout from a bottle?

Give it to him.' She meant her husband. 'He likes drinking that way with other men. He's more forgiving of his treacherous friends. Aren't you, Jim?'

Cash acquiesced. The man with the family appeared to relax. No one took their turn to talk. Outside, the line of uncouth lorries gently penetrated the rear of the ferry.

'What do you have in there, Francis? Aside from your physical heart and your physical gut, what is there of you in there?' She was back against the wall, not caring who might listen or who might respond next. 'You have this marvellous, crystal moment in front of you, where all there is is everything you have ever experienced with the other person but nothing, nothing at all, ahead. Jim will tell me that *moment* is incorrect, that it implies a pivot where there is a before that is different, perhaps opposite to, the after. Jim is an engineer, he knows things like that, he is building roads from Salisbury to bloody Nyasaland, aren't you, dear? So scrub "moment" because I feel his correction coming. Let's call it an edge, I will call it an edge . . . or precipice or ledge or . . .' She faded, like she was bored all of a sudden or embarrassed by her inadvertent rhyme. Then she rallied. 'Edge is a perfectly good word. It sounds like "end", with something uncertain tacked on: a fall, a soft *g*, a cushioned landing, a thing you might recover from. Nothing, in other words, Frank, for you to be frightened of! You frighten too easily, don't you, pet? Not enough heart or gut. Jim's got more, much more, in him, which is why I am going with him to R . . . Rhodesia.' She could not say the word without laughing. She was giddy already. 'Well, Francis, what have you got in there?'

Just then, Frank felt that Betty must be right: this really was going to be their last time together. Oddly, when he had decided to meet them at the harbour, he had said the words 'last time' to himself but with no sense of finality. Last time for a while, last time for now; last time forever. He felt her punch against his chest, harder this time. It was too wet for the sandals she wore, he thought, too cool for the check cotton trousers so she hunkered inside her woollen coat. Her hair was heavily sprayed, and her eyelashes were unnaturally dark and alluring. Jim had let his stubble grow, or it was late and he would not shave again until after the crossing. It traced a line around his scar. His hair was antiquely curly and unlacquered. Frank took in these beautiful surfaces, knowing they were not the same as recalling the persons themselves, but knowing, too, that without conscious effort, he might lose even that much of them. He blinked and allowed them momentarily to disappear from beside him, taking with them also their sounds and their smells. In their place, the scent of the wooden framework of the shed he was in was suddenly pungent, that and the whiff of vomit left behind by a long-gone passenger. The family—the three boys, the mother, the father—all slept, the one breathing in the others' breathings out. Frank would stay alert for them. He had blinked, and they, his friends, were gone.

'We can stay in touch,' said Frank. It was not as meek as it sounded, and he found some courage. 'Rhodesia is not, you know, a million miles from here. They have civilisation! There will be phones and post offices, you can always get hold of me. I doubt I will be going anywhere.' Then, with slightly more courage: 'It might be handy for you to have someone here you can check in with.' He glanced over at the sleeping family and felt responsible for more than he ever had in his life. He wished Eilis was also there. 'I can keep an eye out for you, so to speak.'

Betty was already exhausted and said no more. 'At least that is one thing,' Jim admitted again.

Chapter IV

One November, back in the day, Aloysius Dynes stole the bread van and drove me and Jim Cash to see the famous Daytona Showband, who had come up from Dublin to play the Palm Beach in Slieveban. The Palm Beach was no such thing, with neither a palm tree nor a strand in sight. Slieveban has ideas about itself. A local man who sold carpets converted his warehouse—you know the sort of thing, yay high out of breeze blocks and pebbledash—he turned this warehouse into a licensed dance hall by putting a lit sign on the front and a mineral bar in the corner. I may be doing him a disservice. He certainly managed to pack out the venue any given night of the week, and Slieveban is no size, as you know, so he needed to draw them in from all around. Aloysius Dynes was a regular customer. I was not, and I assume Jim had also never been because Dynes only ever took Jimmy Cash places when I was there too. It was also the first time, to my certain knowledge, either of us had been in a stolen vehicle. The van still smelled of bread, though now it more often carried Boy Scouts and footballers. Aloysius had other designs on it that night.

'You two are to keep your ugly mugs well-hidden tonight, you hear me? Or else, don't let them be seen around me. Especially you, Jim. You're not to scare away the girls. I have a good feeling.'

I stretched my legs in the back, while Jim kept his eye on the road from the passenger seat. Aloysius was a good enough driver if you looked away and paid no attention to what he was doing, which was the same general approach the RUC seemed to take in those days. There were none of the vehicle checks or the where-might-you-be-goings that we later had to get used to. It was different, I imagine, at the border, but I will be honest with you, bar one time, I never remember bothering with the border in those years. That one time was with my father, so I can't have been older than about six myself. My father had a car, which most hadn't: I want to say it was a Standard Eight, but I can't be sure that was even a thing. It was black. He never discussed his business with me, but, as I understood from my mother, who could not conceal her excitement, the plan was for the three of us to smuggle maybe three boxes of jarred and tinned food over the border into Dundalk, where we would exchange it with a man for booze and cigarettes. I suppose those must have been cheaper in the South at the time. Since my folks were what you might you call practical abstainers, they never touched a drop themselves but had no objection to assisting others with their habit. The intention was to sell on the contraband alcohol and keep the cigarettes for themselves. The whole back seat of the car lifted to expose this cavity beneath. That's where my part in the crime came in. I was to lie asleep—or pretending to sleep—across the seat so that the customs officials going South and then going North again would not want to disturb me and so reveal our cache. You make sure you don't budge, Frank, said my da—the only words he shared with me about the whole conspiracy. I had a stuffed rabbit I used to help me sleep then (I can't mind its name; it'll come to me later, not that it matters), so when the time came and we approached the customs post, I brought this rabbit up to my nose like so and I would have been the picture of blissful slumber. Same going back up. The Southern Gardaí were a nervous lot. They had their eye out for gunrunning, which was definitely a regular pastime then. They had my mother and father both out of the car and asking them questions such as you can imagine: where are you driving from, where are you driving to, what has been your business, do you have a commercial licence, are you transporting any livestock or meat, what do you have in the boot. They open up the boot. They see me in the back too, they must have, and my mother starts up with this invented story about how terribly ill I was in Dundalk and how a doctor down there advised her to take me to see a doctor up here. Is there anything there under his seat, the Guard asked, and my father piped up with his best posh voice: No, that's welded down since the previous owner had a situation with it. The Guard said something about letting us

---

through this time, as if he would turn a blind eye to us smuggling guns just this once and no more. We were on our way and through the next town before my father breathed. Never again, he said.

I was stretched out again in the back, this time in the bread van. Aloysius was singing some song from the pop charts. He was an even better singer than he was a driver, and he knew every lyric from every song. I often wondered what girls saw in him—because he was not, by any stretch of the imagination, a good-looking boy—and that, I think, was it. He could make girls smile and make them see past everything else. 'You know you got me goin' now. Just like I know you would,' he sang.

Jim was watching every twist and shout in the road like his life depended on it. Where's the road off there take you to, he would ask; who owns that farmhouse; if that's an Orange Hall, does that mean we are nearly there. Did we know the name of the stream going under this humpback bridge; would the Daytonas be taking this same road, did we think. He was just excited to be going, but I guess we could have seen in him even then his eye for logistics.

The Daytona were some band, let me tell you. They wore Hawaiian shirts and sunglasses and could sound like the Beach Boys one minute or Bill Haley the next. I didn't know all their names then. They had a very pretty singer that we would like to have seen more of. They had one guy who seemed to play every instrument, whatever the song required. But their lead man was a star—Sean Hamill, we all knew his name already. He was better looking than many of the other show band frontmen of the time, and his voice could have taken him anywhere. If I am honest, for us the best part about him was that, although the Daytonas were a Southern band, he was from the North. As I say, they were famous, certainly all over Ireland, so what they were doing in the Palm Beach is anybody's guess. They were doing the Hucklebuck is what they were doing! And Frankie Valli and Frankie Vaughan and everything in between, which is a lot. We danced, the three of us, not caring that we were just boys with no girls. Aloysius had forgotten Jim was ugly, and I wasn't much better. He could dance as well as sing; he could have won competitions if he'd been bothered to enter. Watching him made me want to laugh, not because it was comical to look at but because he could move in such wondrous ways, the only appropriate reaction was to cry or laugh in admiration. Aloysius Dynes was only three months older than me, but he was the singer, the dancer, the driver—he was everything I still was not.

The band took a break midway for us to visit the mineral bar or to head back to our vehicles for the beer we may have stashed there. I saw O'Rourke from our team sharing a bottle of something with a local girl, and I was filled with envy. Envy is a kind of courage. You can want a thing, even quite badly, but without the spur of envy you can still fail to act. This is what happened. They put a girl up to sing against some pre-recorded drumbeats and chords. Not even a proper relief band. She had no chance, you would think; she was the one no one was there to listen to. But she looked like Clodagh Rodgers and could sing too, so more than a few turned from the bar counter to pay attention. She took a deep breath and entered a peaceful place, where the crowd there were all on her side. She sang *Yakety Yak* and one or two other numbers you wouldn't believe we could dance to. You don't hear songs like that anymore. (I've lost the tune of them now. They were the first I heard her sing, and it would be some comfort to me now if I could hum those stupid songs to myself. Don't talk back.) She came off, the Daytona Showband came on, and that would have been the end of it but for Aloysius Dynes digging me in the ribs, telling me over the noise of the Daytonas to have some courage and to go up to her. Dynes always got the girl, we picked up the scraps after him. That's the way it normally went. He was always meeting a girl after. After the match, after dinner, after whatever. After.

'You saw her first,' he said to me. 'You have your eye, I wouldn't want, I am. After.' Aloysius dug me in the ribs, and he stepped aside for me. I flicked my fringe out of my eyes and walked up to speak to the girl. That's how I met Eilis. All thanks to Aloysius.

It's unfair to suggest that the Slieveban carpet warehouse was the height of Eilis McClean's career. The Daytona Showband were well-known already and would become better known still so, to have supported them then was not nothing. Eilis got to sing in swankier venues after that, like the Mecca in Belfast and the Arcadia on the coast, places where it was fine for one side to mingle with the other. Some say that was less of an issue in general back then, and I would say they're right but only because our lot had not started making a fuss yet. The very fact that bands from the South could come up to the North and play The Queen in red, white, and blue halls meant it was okay for us to go too, so long as we left before the end. I wouldn't say I would be confident I could have identified someone from the other side in those days, not the way I would be pretty sure of myself now. No offence intended. I doubt we were any better at mixing during the day—we had our schools and our sports and our streets, and they had theirs—but, in the evenings. People my age say that, you know: we didn't mind our differences so much then. When that all changed, it all changed very quickly.

My account of it is that Eilis climbed into the back of the bread van with me that same night, and, for years, Aloysius Dynes backed me up on it, though what he might say now about it is not to be guessed at, God rest his soul. Eilis put about a different story that was more respectful of her dignity, which is fair enough. What's not to be denied is that the four of us—Eilis, myself, Jim, and Aloysius driving—travelled across the country, following every type of show band, dancing on all floors, for month after month, up to the Arcadia on the coast, all the venues in Belfast, and all along the strangly line of the border. Not, as I recall, over the border itself—that took another sort of organisation. Every time in Fr McCaul's bread van. Really, he couldn't not have known we were doing it, no matter we were always careful to fill her up with fuel. The more we convinced ourselves that the priest knew what we were up to, the more we were sure that no sinning was involved. Ah, but there was! I had to help Eilis get herself sorted out one time—I took her up to the city for that, although there were other places she could have gone. It was the best thing to do, she would agree now. She was able to continue singing and performing. The second time was worse than the first. She swore *never again* after that. She kept singing and her name went on the posters. There was a book that she appeared in. She could have sung with any of the show bands; she had it all. The bread van became her unofficial tour bus, and Aloysius Dynes was her driver. He was noticeably easier on the pedals and on the corners, like he had something valuable in the back. The more he took charge of the wheel and the road, the more Aloysius Dynes liked to think of himself as her manager. I think that is the only job he ever wanted for, unless I am mistaken, it's the only useful thing he ever did with this life. 'Look who is left back now,' Jim said to me once about Dynes, a couple of years later when he and I had moved up to Belfast. 'Left back and wasting his life.'

Aloysius may have been sweet on her, but he never took advantage and insisted she keep all her earnings. 'Eilis is the one who puts herself on the line each time,' Aloysius would say. 'She is the one who has to learn all those songs, sing her set or change it according to the demands of the ones who have pushed their way to the front. I don't think I could hold it together as she does. She is better, half the time, than the band she is meant to be playing relief to, and we all know it too.' Aloysius would say this, or one or other of us would, but always while she was changing out back and couldn't hear. I don't know why, it might have helped later if we had told her to her face. Talking was never my thing. Talking was Aloysius's thing, but maybe he was falling in love with my girlfriend, so talking to her was dangerous. Jimmy liked her music, he told me years later, but he was already getting into other business by then.

It's difficult to imagine all that now, it's easy to forget. When the show band era halted—as it suddenly did after the massacre—most of the old dance halls closed down or returned to their original industrial and agricultural usages, pubs got licences for music as well as alcohol, and Eilis picked up some bookings there. She sang Dusty and Sandy and even—you'll never credit this—some Clodagh Rodgers. She might have been something herself, but she will tell you I held her back.

CHAPTER V

When she wasn't singing in the clubs and bars of Belfast, Eilis was pulling pints in them. We were married by now. One time, she had a cleaning job in the hospital, and another time she was employed working on stands in the exhibition hall. Gradually, she sang less and worked more. She had many jobs, none for very long but none that she missed either. She would quit any job for a chance to sing.

'There's a breath you take in as a performer,' she explained in words to that effect. 'When you have learned all your lines, rehearsed all your steps, run through every move in your head; when all the props are in place and all the technicals are lined up; when absolutely everything is ready and it's about to be your time, there is an extra breath you take.' She paused, as if to take that breath. Then, 'You probably would not understand.'

'Try me,' I said. Would I ever have said that? Would I have instead said something like, 'No, you are probably right, Eilis'? Or would I have held my tongue?

'You reach behind the fear, Frank,' she said. 'You push aside the panic, because panic is self-indulgent, to a space, a wide-open space of calm and peace. Can you imagine peace like that, Frank?'

I suggested I could, or I admitted I could not, or I held my tongue. I didn't honestly know what she meant, but I know that she all too rarely reached that wide-open space of peace and calm.

'On stage. It's the most at home I ever feel,' she told me. And now I remember this was during a row, or these were parts of several conversations, and this time she had the boy on her knee and I would not have said *try me*. This was long after the show bands had quit and after she had stopped the singing altogether, and the most shocking thing to me at the time was that she said all of this in the present tense as if she was still going on every night. At home, on a stage, with scores of people listening and dancing and singing along. 'I am not allowed to feel that way any longer.' There, the reality. I remember looking at her and seeing just how beautiful she still was, with her blonde hair cut straight and short at the neck and her blue eyes sparkling beneath her tears. I mean, she wasn't old—we were not old then—but it still took me aback how amazing she was.

I was luckier in the city. After a few months on building sites where there was still labour to be had clearing bomb damage from the long-ago War, I got a job in the plant room of an American company that had just landed on our bit of planet Earth. They had accepted the invitation and tax inducements from the devolved government to build their factory near to the new Housing Trust development in that part of the city where only non-Catholics were welcome, but, being American, they had fancy I-have-a-dream notions, so an opening was found for the likes of me in the plant room. All my new colleagues were called Alan and George and Odette, you get the idea. I was on the wrong side, but never once did I have a problem with them, not even in the really terrible times like when Eilis and I and some of our neighbours had to clear our homes out under armed protection, me carrying an armchair on my head. Odette brought sandwiches in for us because she knew we had a baby. That was good of her but the sort of thing people still did then. And the company changed my title so that I was in charge of my part of the plant room, and that allowed them to say they had fair employment practices at managerial levels. That was good of them too. I kept quiet when they played their anthem on the Queen's birthday, and I took my holidays when they did because they closed the factory down for a fortnight every year around the Twelfth of July. I even played soccer with them on Fridays after work, although we went on afterwards to separate pubs. They said I was too short for centre-back, so they put me in the midfield.

Jim had also moved up to the city, where he was a student of engineering, and he grew a beard. I am sure I frustrated him with my ignorance, for he would talk to me about the need to decolonise our minds and how we should learn from the French Situationists and reclaim our spaces. 'We have to realise our majorities,' I think he said once, more than once. 'Imperialism is merely the creation of and triumph over false minorities. Women, black people in the States and in European empires, Roman Catholics here: they have all had their minds colonised and many barely recognise their own oppression or, worse, acquiesce in it when they do.' He meant me. He practised his critical theory on me, which amounted to a deconstruction of my default to tactical silence—that's what he called it. He said that, if people like me didn't speak up, we would not be heard by others like us, and we would go on assuming we were a minority. 'I am just keeping my head screwed on,' I would say in my own defence. That was already starting to be no easy thing.

⁂

Eilis and I saw plenty of Jim. He still came to hear her sing, and he sometimes brought his student friends along too, although it was clear soon enough that Eilis would not be providing the sort of psychedelic rock that they listened to in their own rooms.

'You should be listening to your big Scots friend,' one of them said to me, blowing French smoke in my face. 'How many of you work in that American company? How many of you live in that new Housing Trust estate in the east of the city?'

'How many of *me*?' I replied. This was a conversation we had on many occasions. I know what was said.

'That is a classic response,' Alec (or Sarah, or Dermot) said, moved almost to write it down as poetry. 'How many of me? That could be the slave song of all the oppressed! Jim, do you hear how your friend talks?'

'Are you an engineer too?' Eilis asked, I recall, obviously trying to change the subject.

'Of human souls only!' Alec said—this time, it was Alec. 'I am taking political anthropology, but I am really a writer.'

'Really?' asked Eilis, genuinely interested but blithely crushing him. 'Do you write stories?'

I did not much welcome being an item of interest to a political anthropologist. 'How many of me do you imagine there are out there?'

'Frank, there are thousands just in this city. Tens of thousands outside it. Then, if we are talking about the world, there are millions.' This may have been Jim—renamed by his friends the Scot. 'The greatest number of people are not privileged, are not in the ascendancy. They only have jobs or homes or political rights because they have—*temporarily*—been granted them.' Apparently, I was numerous and everywhere, alienated from myself by my default to tactical silence—that again: my failure to speak up for myself was also a failure to tell a story to others. 'Timidity is not neutrality,' Jim insisted. 'Timidity empowers the powerful, weakens the weak.'

'You should scream and shout and sing!' said the screaming, shouting anthropologist. I wondered then, did he do anything else.

'Frank won't sing,' giggled Eilis, and we both laughed. She laughed at me; I laughed at the rest. 'I've never heard you sing, have I, Frank?'

That was back in the days when it was possible for Eilis to say that kind of thing, and it was possible for no offence to be intended or taken—when referring to my songless days was not a comment on my mirthless soul. Those were the days when she still sang, even if less frequently than before, the days when she would have said of herself— even when working in a bar or wherever—that she *was* a singer. She never heard me sing because she could do that for the both of us. Of course, I *did* sing—'I *do* sing!'—along with her, along with her crowd and her—'I sing *along*!'—along with the favourites of the day, whatever was requested. I sang when everyone sang, because those were the sorts of songs she played. And when she stopped, I picked the song up in my head.

'So you sing other people's songs?' said the anthropologist, excited at his new discovery. Whole original theories opened up for him, I supposed, theories that could take the form of a poster or a street manifestation. I tensed, and, to his credit, I think Jim did too.

Eilis did not grasp the politics of the question—that's how it seemed to me in that horrible instant. I wanted her to understand that Jim's friend Alec was demeaning her, and at the same time, I wanted her not to rise to his provocation. She sang *only* other people's songs; she had no songs—no voice, therefore—of her own; she collaborated with her own oppression was what the little prick was saying. I wanted her to get all of that and then not respond to it: only then could she be his equal and then his superior.

'Walk on by.' That's all she said for a while. It was spoken with a smile, as sweet as always, and directed at no one in particular. If it was to me, it was a holding of my hand so I would not raise it. If it was to Jim and his friends, perhaps it was telling them that in her there was nothing interesting for them to study. Foolish pride is all that I have left so let me hide.

The tears and the sadness you gave me when you said goodbye. I am sure that was then, I mean I am sure that was what she said in the pub that time—walk on by—then and not later when it would have been uttered with bitterness. Then it was just a song that she sang because people asked her to. Walk on by, she said to the clueless, French cigarette-smoking anthropologist who had asked her if she sang other people's songs. It was genius.

This thought only comes to me now. To sing the songs that others have written: that is the epitome of empathy. Did Alec and Jim even know the books they read and quoted from, for surely in there, there must have been something about giving voice to . . . amplifying the sentiments and concerns of others. How much easier it is to scream and shout and sing simply what's in your own head, the little that there is there. It is genius—it is *politics*—to mobilise the cares of another person. Eilis was a show band support act, and then she was a clubland singer in a shimmering dress, and every time she moved. I think this only now. I am so many decades too late.

⚬⚬⚬

The brick through the window had a note attached pointing out the mistake that had been made when we had been accommodated in the new Housing Trust development. Eilis was not there at the time, which is why perhaps she focused more on the brick—what brick, what do you mean they threw a brick—than on the fact that we needed to clear out immediately, grabbing anything of use or value that we could carry. She was working in a city bar; I was minding the baby in front of the telly. Tommy Cooper. Terry the neighbour had warned us, coming to the door after his boy had knocked us up, penny for the guy. As it was a new development courtesy of Thompson

Builders, Terry explained, there were pallets aplenty to build a sky-high bonfire, and the locals were keen to establish a new tradition for the area. Terry said enough of this to make himself plain; he was too kind and gentle a man to make it any plainer. The new tradition was simply to be the age-old papist-bashing tradition brought to life in this new estate. I was to understand that nothing personal was intended by this; indeed everyone was agreed that there was absolutely nothing that we as a family could do about our condition; in fact, Terry had been given the green light to offer us fair warning. I said nothing to Eilis. She went off to work. I sat down in front of Tommy Cooper with the boy and a brick came through the window. Just like that.

Eilis carried the boy in one arm and a stuffed suitcase in the other. I found that, by balancing her grandfather's armchair on my head, I could still manage the second case. In the olden days, we might have had a donkey, and we would have been better off. There would have been a cart too, so room for bedding and some kitchen utensils, a small quantity of books even: the things that refugees call valuables and which we had to leave behind. A cart of such things would have been a basis for starting the new life, for I have read that homes founded on wheels can be stable even when pulled by a donkey through a modern city. Carts have their downsides, however, and our cart would undoubtedly have gone up in smoke. A spark from the sky-high bonfire, a curling flame alighting on our mobile home, and we would have been the guys on the blazing woodpile. The night was black enough for people who didn't want to not to see. For people who did not want to see . . . A thousand pairs of eyes were turned away. Two or three other families had the right sort of idea, having loaded up the cars they were lucky to have. The police made sure they had safe passage out, past the big brown sign of the Housing Trust. I am certain the police felt proud of the job they were doing, ensuring the cleansing of the area occurred without bloodshed. We had no car, alongside another small number of misallocated families, and the police protected us until the last occupied house was well behind us. Gentleman Terry had placed a call for us, so Jim Cash came and picked us up in a car he borrowed from a friend he told nothing about this to. To whom he told nothing. Detty—Odette, from work—brought in sandwiches for us. It's awful what those people did to you, she said, even though those people were her people too. Eilis' regard for her grandfather's armchair, the valuable family heirloom, did not survive long its displacement to the house we rented in the Embankment area of the city. A mattress would have been better loved. We got some new neighbours: Sammy next door, Gloria some doors down.

The Embankment is near to the university, isn't it, with a windy walk through the botanical gardens to the pubs where Jim liked to go with his friends. These were not pubs where Eilis sang, for they served a more radically class-aware clientele than would ever likely be seen among the Markets men in the Rose. The Markets men in the Rose bought their wives a martini and joined them in a singalong to Petula Clark. The pubs where Jim—the Scot—drank with his friends served Italian coffee during the day.

'They look down on my shoes,' said Eilis once, complaining I was taking her to one of these places again. 'I'm oppressed by my shoes, they reckon. I can't even remember how.'

'Heel?' I said.

'Heel or no heel. I am either confined by gender stereotypes, or— if I refuse to be—I am self-repressed by insisting on my individuality. Sarah said that. She actually might have put the words in a different order, how would I know, I'm only stupid enough to wear flat shoes.'

I told her she wasn't stupid. 'I know I'm not stupid!' Then she walked into a giant pampas tree. She struggled to disentangle herself, because it's wild stuff, pampas. It's a grass, I know, before you try to correct me. If the stuff that was growing in the botanical gardens was a grass, I must be a grasshopper because it had grown as high as the glasshouse itself. Those guys are meant to be horticulturists—maybe Seamus thought that Paddy had planted the thing with precautions, tying in the roots, bagging the stems, lopping the tops, but neither Paddy nor Seamus nor any other botanical Mick had read the tag (maybe it was in Spanish). So, by now, after a usual wet summer, the pampas had grown unconfined, grown beyond whatever purpose had originally been planned for it, exotic still but in at most a domestic sort of way. Eilis walked into it, and its long feathery blades paddled their load of rainwater on her.

That was the time we met Betty. I forgot that, I thought she must have been among the group before then, but Eilis insisted forever after that it was then, and we were in Jim's student house, not a pub. 'She never spoke to me the whole time,' she said. That must mean that I don't remember the first time. I thought I did. I thought it was in one of those bars and the men were drinking coffee when Eilis and I arrived, wet from pampas, and Betty was not drinking coffee but had a long glass of wine in her hand, pink with ice. She was wearing a length of coloured glass beads—plunging is the word—plunging in a way that suggested a precipitous opening in her front. She wasn't wearing shoes at all, and the nakedness of her feet made imaginable the nakedness of the rest of her. Maybe she didn't speak—maybe Eilis was right—but I am certain that she *made noises*, noises that said she was bored or angry or. Let me think.   She was in the wrong place.

Eilis and I agreed on that part. Whether it was a house gathering or a pub, whether she was in boots or her stocking feet, Betty was always a flower planted in the wrong garden. We had heard that she was Jim's girlfriend; he had told us himself on an occasion when it was just the three of us. She worked at a hotel in the city, they had met when he was there for a family wedding, she was studying something vague like art or tourism but either had quit or was in the process of quitting, she was eight or ten years older than the rest of us, she agreed with abortion but had not had one herself, she had spent the summer in Yugoslavia. She was from Newcastle or thereabouts. We knew all of this about Betty from the very beginning, which is why perhaps our recollections differ about the first moment. The glass beads that hung around her neck: she bought them in Central Europe or she made them in college—she told us, she never told us, one of us never gave it a second thought. She hung on every word that Jim spoke without hardly ever seeming to agree with him. She would lean in, not miss a thing, understand everything, and then destroy it all as lovingly. She dismantled him and made him stronger, and to us it seemed he didn't notice.

We arrived at Jim's house, the front door was open, someone we didn't know was squatting on the step with a book I recognised. We climbed past her to the living room, where we found Jim and half a dozen others, including Betty, distributed haphazardly like litter. Jim leapt up immediately, interrupting whatever it was he had been talking about and, placing a brotherly hand on my shoulder, guided me to a low-slung armchair in the corner where Eilis could perch on my lap. 'Are you okay there?' he asked, like he wanted us out of the way but not out of the way. 'Yes,' we said, because that's what we would have wanted too. Someone passed me a bottle of beer over Eilis' shoulder.

Maybe Jim had given us his seat. He was talking and, because he was standing, it had the character of a speech. He made an effort to keep their eyes on him, lifted upwards now and not just at the level of the rest. From our angle, there was something altered about him, even from the last time we had seen him the week before. Above his beard, his harelip was more pronounced, unevenly splitting his face. Actually, it was more as if the cleft was where two separate faces met, both belonging to him. I still recognised the little raggedy boy who had arrived in our town out of nowhere, who grew out of his football shorts and kissed the girls in the back of the bread van driven by Aloysius Dynes. The other face was newer, stranger, a touch more handsome maybe, and with it he spoke about representation and gerrymandered wards. The two sides of his gerrymandered face joined at the lip. It was not a speech, of course, because everyone here agreed with him more or less. Eilis and I kept ourselves quiet, and, as usual, Betty held off commenting and offered only interim ahems.

The strategy of watchful disengagement has run its course. The logic behind it—Blaseau, I believe, called it late Gandhian, in that it bore recognisable elements of passive resistance . . .

That's it.

A refusal to take up seats in the chamber or posts in junior ministries. Tactical non-voting. This is a hard strategy to hold to—is it Kappstein?

Ahem.

. . . because it calls for complete discipline in the ranks when, in reality, there are no ranks because we have by definition no organisation.

No way!   Ahem.

But the logic was sound. When defeat is engineered into democracy, it is not democracy. When, in a contest, only one outcome is possible, it is rational not to engage in the contest. This is what

McCann, in our conditions, has coined minoritarianism—that is, embracing the status of the inevitable loser—the underdog in common parlance—and bearing all their grievances and witnessing their claims. 'Holding and watching', she calls it.

Minoritarianism.

Holding and watching has served a purpose because, incontrovertibly, we have justice and we have evidence on our side.

Yes!

But McCann herself says it is high time we shifted strategy.

. . .   *Ahem?*

We need to find the correct path for our condition, as always. The black nationalists show one possible way, and the insurgents of the Maghreb.

We have our own history, Cash.

There is that. March through our past into our future!

Who said that, Cash?

I said that.

Ahem.

The point is we have borne grievance and witness for long enough, we have been watchfully disengaged past the patience of many of us.

Ahem . . .   Is that you saying that too, Cash?

Maloney, McCann. Maloney, in the Law Department . . . you have read his reports for the IJL, the Irish Justice League?

. . .   *Ahem?*

Jim did not attempt to cite these reports from memory. He pulled a pamphlet from a bag he had strung across his body, bus-conductor fashion, and looked for the faces of those who were still interested. He found Betty and Eilis and, behind Eilis, me. Judging by the numerous turned-up corners and underlined passages and generally battered appearance, he had read and shared this Maloney pamphlet many times. He had even on the blank front page etched the letters *I, J*, and *L* in green ink (in upper case and lower, side by side and in a vertical line) and thereby engineered a prototype logo. He knelt among us.

Using the government department's own figures, he told us, the IJL have worked out that a family in the minority community has a one-in-six likelihood of being allocated a Housing Trust home within eighteen months of application; the rest have a two-in-three chance.

Adults who identify as belonging to the majority faith are much more likely to cast their vote and are four times as likely to have additional ballots through business ownership.

Ahem.

Minority areas are under-represented. It takes on average three thousand more people to elect a councillor from such an area than it does in a neighbouring ward serving the other community.

Gerrymandering.

That's it, Eilis. Remember, all of these figures are already known. Have the misfortune to be born under the wrong god and you are less likely to go to university, have a job, or live in your own home, more likely to be in prison or die of a bronchial condition.

I coughed there, in order to be funny.

Ahem.

I think we exhausted him by not saying anything. Anyway, he stopped.

Ahem. Betty politely, devastatingly, took her turn. May I? she asked. Was his *yes* a nervous yes? I didn't think so. The way she fingered her glass beads put me in mind of a snake charmer: he agreed with every criticism she laid at him.

I think your numbers might be wrong, Jim. I know that they are this other man's numbers—or from the IJL (she regarded his design)—but I suspect they have been counted up the wrong way. Now I am not political like you, so I am not able to tribalise my analysis as nicely as you do.

That was her exact phrase: tribalise my analysis.

You see, as I see it, you have got your majoritarianism in a twist, and that McCann woman really ought to know better. The majority community is not what she thinks it is. They are not all ascendant. Privilege, luck, being born under the right god (as you put it) can also be a trap.

Of course, a trap. Yes.

The company boss with his two votes: he keeps a wife at home depressed and abused. He is scared of her lest she gets out and spills all his beans. She embarrasses him by not behaving reliably, no matter how conditioned she is or how hard she tries. Naturally, she cannot work. The bruises would show in daylight. Luckily, there is plenty for her to do at home where she spends the immensity of her time alone. She has children, if she manages to get that right. The children they have dress for church on Sunday and stay in those mental clothes from Monday to Saturday. Nobody knows they are there! They are driven mad just preserving their status. The government department does not have statistics on them, so the IJL can't campaign on their behalf. But in any fair world, they would be counted among the oppressed. Don't you think? Those abused women don't vote, and they as sure as hell are not represented. Those children are strapped tight to the bus driving them to a great education and a superior job, you bet they are. And their hair will be as neat as their religious views. Not a hair out of line. Are you holding and watching out for them?

Well, yes, there's that.

This might have been where Jim got his 'false minorities' theory. As I say, Betty blew him apart and made him stronger. If she did it while we were there, she surely did it while we weren't. I would say there was no performance about Betty. Sure, the way she dressed and the way she spoke had an effect—I won't deny she stirred me—but none of it was scripted or rehearsed. If it had been, she would surely have, at least occasionally, selected a different performance, one that would have done her more good.

∂χ∂

Jim persuaded me to go to a public gathering where McCann was speaking; Betty and Eilis both had better things to do. I think I must only have heard her speak once, and her first arrest must have occurred shortly after it; but despite this, I don't recall what she said. What she spoke *about* is clearer to me, although there is a chance that I have simply reconstructed this from other broadcast comments she made over the ensuing years. She adamantly refused the path of armed resistance; she wanted nothing to do with the men and women who were disinterring guns from old campaigns; military engagement was a shortcut to our defeat. She raised cheers for saying all of this, while the room we were in was lined with men all dressed alike, who could have sloped arms at the click of her fingers. Apparently. Her innovation was the mobilisation of the ordinary woman and man. She wanted them to use the weapons they had already legally at hand: their voices, their labour, their boots. Go on strike! March! Sit in! She urged us to identify what I think she called administrative and economic targets. Do you know, it is hard now to remember what the activists were saying then, at what point it turned from one thing to another, who had—if anyone had—the idea to make us start killing each other instead. It was not then, but it might have been soon after then, and it might not have occurred in a room full of witnesses.

We have got to do something. I swear that Jim had no greater plan than that.

CHAPTER VI

Girls played games on the Pitches with controlled violence. A few more stones were added to the graveyard at the normal rate. Eddie the dray was put into retirement. The older men drank in Suzy's, while the younger men stood around outside it, and Fr McCaul tried to interest them in something more constructive. McAllister joined the men in the bar after his hardware store was taken over and his children emigrated to Belfast. Nothing had changed, but everything was about to.

First, they laid the service roads for the construction trucks. Then they dug the utility trenches for the gas, the water, the electricity companies to put in their pipes. Then the builders themselves arrived, driven in from all around in their buses. The builders were Thompson Builders. They wore uniform blue overalls and tattoos, and after work they drank in the Adair, which is where their buses picked them up. Some people in the town felt that the quality of the houses they built must in some way be influenced by the church they went to: the staircases would be somehow narrower, the windows a wee bit meaner. That was pure prejudice. In one year, the initial row of Thompson Houses was finished, and Betty and Jim Cash moved into the first of these. The early months and years of their marriage were played out to the accompaniment of crunching earth movers and clattering scaffolding. The second and third row of houses were to be larger than the first, with garages and front gardens and second bathrooms. Nothing mean about them. These took longer to build, and Thompson—the man, the company—triggered a clause in the original contract to demand more payment. The twelve half-built houses then became an irresistible playground to the children of the town so that Fr McCaul had sometimes to be told he had insufficient boys to make up two packs of six cubs. The little brides of Christ, too, could be found there, making pretend homes in the pretend homes. Here is our kitchen, and here is our through-lounge (as if they knew what one of those was), and there (they indicated through the naked rafters) are the three/four bedrooms. Boys—they forbade the girls—found a way up the stairs that weren't yet stairs and sat with their legs dangling down through the gaps in the joists, pretending their testicles were at risk. They held races across the bottomless bedroom floors, balancing like tightrope walkers. The more daring thing would have been to have met and played with a child who actually lived in a Thompson House. It did occasionally happen. *My daddy says I should feel sorry for you, because your type is not as good as our type. Oh, I didn't know that before. My mummy says you can't come to our house, because it's new and she sleeps in the afternoon. Do you know the lady, Mrs Cash—I hear the grown-ups say she sleeps with other men in the day. What's a through-lounge?*

Sometimes, Jim Cash drank with his old neighbours in Suzy's, and sometimes he preferred to go with his new neighbours to the Adair, on the second corner of the Diamond. Either his views had changed again since leaving the city, or he was infiltrating them. 'They are not what you think,' he would say in one bar and then in the other. 'They want the best for their families, like anyone. They are all minorities.' The men in Suzy's were inclined to disagree. *It's dangerous talk like that that can lose you friends, Jimmy.* 'Jim.' Jim. 'You should make more of an effort to get to know them.' *Not got that lovely wife with you, tonight?* He had tried but failed to lose the Scots he had reacquired while living in the city. *Is that a Protestant accent you have now, Jim?* Jim was in Suzy's that time the police raided it. *Look who is left back now.* It was a Saturday night in November and therefore probably a religious occasion, and the manager—or, more likely, the manager's son Declan—responded spontaneously with a lock-in in the back bar. Only those already in could stay in, and only the initiated could tell from the street view that drink was still being served. O'Rourke was there with a handsome new haircut. Quinn was there getting drunk. Aloysius Dynes was there with a harmonica, displaying a skill with it that Cash was not previously aware of.

'When did you learn that, Dynes?'

'Same time you learned engineering, Jim. Scottie. Maybe you can play us something later?'

'Sadly, I have no party pieces. But I could probably fix that bread van for you.'

That, for some reason, was seen as a provocation on the part of Jim Cash—Aloysius was known still to be very attached to the beaten-up van he once, many times, stole from the priest—but calm was restored by the unlikely person of Declan, the manager's son. Water helped down the whiskey. Aloysius applied his mouth again to the mouth organ, and any misnotes were drowned out by spirited rebel hymns.

The lovely Betty has her sleep to catch up on, I wouldn't wonder.

O'Rourke laughed at his own jokes and glanced at reflections of himself. Quinn grew quieter and more dangerous. The chat turned to others' business and to current affairs. Catholic ladies in a crystal factory, even those whose put on accents could cut glass, were being kept out of what a management man had called the 'public-facing jobs'. ICTU had entered the fray. A battery hen farm in Balnakerry was being investigated by the safety-at-work people, even though it was the monks who owned it. The Brothers were keeping tight-lipped about it. In the shipyard, no Catholic could rise above a certain level unless they had a skill that no Protestant had, might have, or might acquire in the not too distant. ICTU had invited themselves in to that one too.

Is the Irish Congress of Trades Unions legitimising the economic gerrymander of the NI statelet by talking to it, thereby delegitimising any argument they might seek to make before they have even sought to make it? Do they do more harm than good by turning up in their potato-smelling suits and banging on the doors of the bowler hats? Should they feck away off? Is it better for workers to barricade themselves in and keep their bosses out (one drunkard asked—it may have been more than one), or for them to set up a picket outside and stop others from crossing the line?

That's a question of symbolic ownership of the means of production, that is.

That's why I asked it, you eejit. We occupy the premises because they are in a sense ours. We say, so to speak, dislodge us from this place if you can, but you will have to lay siege, and we have our supplies with us: we dare you to take from us that which we have decided to take possession of. Or—and this is the other option philosophically— we stand outside the gates and say, we are here and physically able to work, but we are refusing you our labour, and we are denying you too the labour of others. All we are to you is our labour, that is the only part of us that is ever yours and, even then, only if you pay us appropriately for it. Which of the two is it?

That's easy, you have answered it for yourself.

I don't think I have. I am torn. I want to say, by my labour I own the machinery and the building and the profits and the rest of it: they are mine, because without my labour, the machinery and building are idle, and the profits don't accrue—they only *exist* as a consequence of the work I do. On the other hand, I am more than that which I can produce: I am more than the sum of my working parts. My labour is a time-limited thing, available by the hour and at a cost. Both are true, but both means of protest are not available at the same time: I cannot be both outside and inside. (That was a lot to say while drunk.)

'You should stay in bed, if they aren't paying you to be in!' That, I believe, was Quinn.

'Non-participation is not a viable option,' said Jim. Not when there are workers prepared to get out of bed for less. Non-participation is worse than apathy because it is a deliberate act of self-denial. And, when a community stays in bed, the other lot gets up and raids the kitchen cupboards. 'It should be us doing the raiding. Us, who have no cupboards or else nothing in them.'

'That's fighting talk, Jimmy Cash,' said someone that Jim did not recognise. At first, he thought this was Quinn too, but the voice came from a dark corner of the bar. 'That sounds like talk that likes the sound of itself. Are you sure that's you talking?'

'It's not just talk, if that's what you're driving at.' Jim chose that moment to shift his own philosophy. That moment, that sentence. (Maybe it was the whispers about Betty.) He did it by himself, with no encouragement from me. He had forgotten already his neighbours who drank in the Adair. The shift, in theory, may have happened earlier, among his student non-conspirators in the city or at that convention where, to their horror, the Communists and the nationalists found themselves in agreement. But the point of this moment was that it was then that his philosophy became an action. A highly specific action. He agreed on an impulse to meet the fighting-talk man alone.

ତ୍ରଠ

By sheer force of wounded feelings, Aloysius got his bread van back on the road. The van was more or less his now, the scouts being too few in number since the Thompson Houses were nearly built and the football team taking a back seat because of the disproportionate number of girls being born. The men in Suzy's put it down to the calcium carbonate in the water when they weren't putting it down to their own sons' lazy sperms. 'It's yours to have if you can get it going,' Fr McCaul told Dynes, waiving off with his hand any thought of tax or insurance or legal possession. 'In return for the odd occasional favour, of course.' Aloysius had the body he always had as a child, so when his hair began to thin, his arms and legs refused to thicken in the way he thought a man's limbs should. The girls he ought still to be going out with were now married, or on the way to being married, so the ones he did entertain in his van were younger sisters. He carried on like this until the boys outside Suzy's put a more or less permanent halt to it. No more of that dirty carry-on, if you know what's good for you, Dynes. Message heard, Dynes drove the bread van further afield, and everyone was satisfied with that arrangement.

The Protestant women of the new housing development quickly formed themselves into a firm, impenetrable knot. They commanded their children not to play with the local children, no cowboys and nurses, no going down the Pitches or dangling from rafters in the half-built houses.

But those are our houses, Mammy, nearly built for us, aren't they not?
Play hopscotch with your sister, Wesley.

The state provided buses to take the children off to their state schools in Ballykill, and the Protestant women never knew what they got up to there, so much the better for all concerned. Betty was, and was not, a Protestant woman. She may have been born one, but she could never be one: her choices of clothing, husband, and distraction all placed her outside the knot. Her hair would not fit into such a tight bun, and she could not possibly use that same mouth to pray to a vengeful god—not the mouth that, if the rumours were true, and sure how could they not be at least in part, the filthy cat, at all times of day. Betty heard these rumours like everybody else did: in Pat's Bakery, in the Mace, not from her husband, on her walks into and out of town, not from her children (as she hadn't any), in the Adair when she went for a treat with Jim. While many others pretended not to believe them, Betty had to pretend not to hear them. Where were the soldiers who were reputed to call in on her when Jim was at work, and who were the RUC men? Conveniently, for those who believed the rumours (or didn't but spread them anyway), a man in uniform rarely comes supplied with a name. Lance Corporal Philanderer or Detective Sergeant Cantkeephiscockinhispants is name enough. There was no denying that Betty was unhappy and lonely, so there was no denying it. In the long mornings and longer, languorous afternoons, Jim away and working late, the house done or not needing doing, the not-children not playing, what Betty got up to in her own head gave what was in all those other heads a run for their money. Tut, ahem. Chance would be a fine thing, she thought and thought. She turned in her bed and heard again and again the mortifying click of the man closing the back door behind him.

Fr McCaul, smug that he had picked up on certain rumours, missed what was really going on in the town. 'Morality is both a collective and a personal concern.' He had read from Paul's second letter to the Ephesians and from the Gospel according to Luke and had reached the point where the congregation were as captives before him. 'As a person must know right from wrong, so must a people.' Fr McCaul always read his homily from scripted notes, the better not to fluff the carefully balanced lines. A people must know when to act, when to condemn, when to put a halt, and oftentimes it falls to an individual, on behalf of the people, to take such an action and to make such a condemnation. A whisper is little better than a silence, so as the silence must end, so must the whispering. Fr McCaul was pleased with the words he had written the night before and which he had already spoken once at the earlier Mass, because he felt certain they spoke to the general at once. He meant to improve the moral quality of his flock, not just his sheep. Cash, on the other hand, sitting with the seat empty beside him, felt sure the priest was sending a message to him. Your face already looks like you have been in a good fight.

✿

He had agreed on an impulse to meet the fighting-talk man alone. I was not there, you understand.

'Why are we meeting here?' Cash asked Patrick Ryan. He recognised him now. He hadn't seen Ryan since their school days and the days playing GAA when Ryan scored every goal.

Ryan looked around at the crooked gravestones, at the grass soaking his shoes, at the entrance to the church that, despite the weather, he refused to stand in. 'Did you expect an office, Jimmy?' The rain rapped on his hood like drumming fingers, so Cash ignored the 'Jimmy', though he knew it was meant to demean him. The greasy grey sky broke a window over the Pitches behind him, letting the sun crack through to the girls smacking camogie.

'I never got the hang of that game—I mean hurling,' admitted Cash to no one in particular. 'Why was that?'

Ryan answered him anyway. 'It's 'cos you're a Scotchman,' he said sagely. 'It's not born into you. No instinct for it.'

The basic unit of this game is to whack a ball away out of your hand with a stick before fifteen men can stop you, a hit-and-run or be-hit game. 'You might be right.'

'I am right, otherwise you would never have married a Protestant lassie. What was that even about. But setting your non-Irish instincts to one side, you have been telling anyone with ears willing to listen that you are a Republican and are itching to action.'

'"Itching to action": I don't think I ever said that.'

'Would you ever shut the fuck up? I don't need you correcting my English just 'cos you're more a native of it than I am. Did you or did you not tell or imply or otherwise indicate to a room full of bastards at Declan's lock-in in Suzy's that you were impatient, keen, not to say gagging to take up the fight?'

'I said something about non-participation not being a viable option.'

'That means what I think it does, does it?'

Cash nodded uncertainly, uncertain that Ryan understood him, uncertain about his own meaning. 'It means what it says.'

'Right.' Ryan then glanced about him, as if a straggling Mass goer might be emerging from the chapel or a corpse might be eavesdropping from behind or beyond a grave. 'Right, well, I can sort you out there. And I hear you know McCann and acquired some technical skills up there in Belfast.'

'I don't know McCann. I have met her. Not even met her, I have seen her.'

'Close enough.'

They drove to Slieveban and then beyond Slieveban to Cullycreggan. Ryan drove like he only had need of two of his wheels at any one time. Both men knew the roads well already, but, anyway, the closer they got to the border, the slower Ryan drove and the more attention they both paid to the roadside, the hedgerow, the verge, the places where men might hide devices. Cullycreggan was more a place marked on a map than existing in reality: it had no houses to speak of and only a hut to drink tea in and buy milk and turf from. Other than that, it was a road over to the South, with a customs border manned by bored men. Ryan said that on Saturdays when, for some reason, the crossing was busier, the customs officials were joined by proper RUC. That would be their target. Today was Saturday. Ryan and Cash sat in the hut with their tea, Cash watching how Ryan watched the road.

Over there is a caravan being towed up from down South, on its way to Rostrevor, I'd bet. A tractor with stinking whatsitsface, silage. That boyo in the flatback will have red diesel, unless I am very much. Oh, ho, ho, just waved through, did you see that. Three, that's an odd number of policemen in that. Would that minivan with the band, remember them, be off to Slieveban, do you think. One the other way, a family for Dun Laoghaire, I'd be willing to guess, with a roof rack to boot: that'll be a load for the customs man to check. No meat, no poultry, no fertilizer, what else are we not allowed to take in and out of our own country. Are you watching this, keeping your eyes peeled. Is there nothing, only tea in this establishment, nothing other than that to keep us looking innocently occupied. Have you fruit bread? That's mighty kind, we'll have a slice each, yes, with butter, and I will have jam. Cash will get this one, won't you? (Sorry, I should have used another name, maybe she will think I said 'cash'.) Holy shite! They're heading over this way.

Where else would the police be heading for a cup of tea?

Well, you can shut up for one.

They're gone. I thought they would never go. Have we seen enough, do you think?

What were we here to see anyway?

You are fucking useless, you are.

Driving back. 'Frank has a car, has he not?'

'Frank has a. He's in Belfast with Eilis.'

'The singer.'

'What of it?'

'He can drive us. A Saturday will suit him as he will be off work, and no one will suspect. You will ask him.'

'Will I?'

'I say "ask". You tell him to be ready. The Saturday after next will give you time to put the device together too.'

'I haven't said I will.'

'Well, you can go and fuck yourself. You're doing it now whether you like it or not. What do you need for it?'

A moment. Another moment.

'I don't need much, it won't take much, I have what I need, or I can get it from a supplies firm we use. Listen to me talking, like I have any notion how to do this.'

'Good man.'

'Frank won't like it. Frank has a child.'

'There is nothing for him to do, just drive us there and back. I would do it myself but obviously this car will be marked now, you can't be too careful.'

ଚ୍ଚ

Frank disagreed before he agreed and then finally disagreed.

What's Ryan up to these days, Jim?

'I can't tell you for sure, Frank. He's one of those this-and-that types, I think. He will fit your kitchen or scrap your car or tarmac your drive. Do you know, now that I have said that, he might be one of those cowboys that Betty got in that time to do our drive. *Irish*, she said they were, whatever she meant by that (I assumed she was talking southern, like a gypsy traveller), but now, now that I come to think of it, he was one of that gang. Oildrum, turning the tar, you know the way they do it, and then spilling it out like sick and spreading it all over what was the drive already. A perfectly good drive, mind you. Don't stand there, or there are these planks you can step on if you must, how else am I meant to get out of the house. Weeds! In no time. Those weeds with the wee white flowers start poking through all over. Betty says we got a good price, *what can you expect*, she was that embarrassed, as well she might. Ryan's a bollocks. And he knows nothing about laying a road.'

But you are doing this thing with him anyway, this thing you aren't at liberty to tell me about?

'Frank, for your own good, I wouldn't tell you. The less you know the. But he's a crazy head, without a shadow of. Drives like a loon. He will kill himself before he gets around to anyone else . . . you did not hear me say that. That said, he says far too bloody much. He sees himself as a cell leader, and the one thing everyone knows about that is that you don't tell anyone else who anyone in the cell is. He is only playing at this. It's like he is trying to get the attention of McCann and the boys in Belfast or Derry, *see me what I can do*, and he's got it all wrong. Just my luck, to fall in with. I need you with me, Frank.'

Frank asked him: Is this what you have been aiming at all this time, Jim? It's a bit small-fry minor division for you, I would say, would you not? Scum of the earth style, sleekit even, if I have understood correctly what the plan is; not cricket, if that's a thing. I thought there was something else in store for you, a principled stand somewhere with TV cameras watching. You could be at the head of one of our marches—with your friend Maloney and the Heroes of Ireland League, them boys—maybe take a dignified brick in the head. I could see you doing that, Cash, that would be right for you, you have the face for it already. I would stand with you then, beside you, no moral compromising in that one.

'Kind of you, I will remember the next time I need someone to mop my bloody forehead. So, I agree, we are not writing history chapters here, there'll not be a place for us in the annals, but doing nothing—I have said it countless before—is morally compromising. Let's not have that one again. I have decided already, I am doing my bit of the thing and no more, Ryan will do whatever he is planning to do (I daren't ask more, he would probably tell me), and all we need from you is to drive. You can do that, Frank. You love to drive, so you tell me. C'mon, Frank, you'll never have to again.'

Frank surrendered too easily: Stop doing my head in, you're doing my head in. Jesus, I will do it, all right, not that I'll be doing it with any enthusiasm or glow in my downtrodden minority heart. Christ, this is a fuckup of a place, if this is anywhere near the right thing to do. You just need me to drive you and him and. Whatever it is you are there to deliver. Down to the border.

'Cullycreggan.'

Cullycreggan. That's it?

'And back again.'

Yes. I suppose that would be in the contract.

'No contract, Frank. You'll not be getting paid for this. Although, maybe you can get your petrol back. That would be fair. I will ask.'

Don't.

'So I won't bother asking. That's easier. No involvement really at all, hardly a scruple to be contemplated, not even a receipt. The whole thing is easier for you, just saying.'

You asked for this. I did not.

಄ಚಿ

An army patrol passed through the town. Nobody was really sure if that had ever happened before, the newspapers weren't saying, and so they were somewhat welcomed on account of the novelty of it all. To have a juke at the Diamond and a nosey around the Thompson Houses, they sent the soft-bitten ones to the town. The hard-bitten ones were needed for proper defensive/offensive duties in Belfast and Derry and the actual border. The softies had no hair on their faces and not much grey matter between their ears. They were jumpy. They jumped at a run-of-the-mill fight going on outside Suzy's to do with Declan barring a man for hitting another man who had hit Declan himself. The fight resembled more an altercation between the legal types, debating the obvious conflict of interest involving the bar manager's son. But the army men jumped anyway and put old man McAllister against a wall. That was unnecessary. McAllister was an old man implicated in nothing whatsoever. Jumping and letting off a round of their bullets was also an unnecessary response to seeing one of Fr McCaul's mitching Boy Scouts hanging from the rafters in one of the nearly-houses. Not even hanging from his neck but from his hands, but this here softie Brit fired off his gun at nothing in particular. Lucky for that at least. Bullets flew past the wee boy, through the floor that wasn't there, and smashed the window that hadn't been installed. (Thompson inspected his contract and the Crime Prevention Act and successfully sued the Northern Ireland Office for damage to property. The small print described property as 'any construction built, nearly built, in the process of being built or not built'.) The wee fella hanging from the rafters nearly died of a heart attack but was otherwise unscathed and was supplied with a good story the next time he went underage drinking. There I was, minding my own business, just hanging about as you do.

Cash built an explosive device. He got explosive material from a girl who worked in the office in the quarry who made the cement that was sold to the construction firm that did some of the building for the Housing Trust where Cash was an engineer. He had the wire, he made the switch, he rigged up the timer and trigger. Mad Ryan put in a request for shrapnel. For Cash, that was a step further than he wanted to go: up to that point, he had been an engineer; now he was a murdering bastard. The construction firm that did some of the building . . . the construction firm that had imported from Greece a hundred boxes of bolts that were no match for the nuts they had imported from Poland . . . the construction firm was happy to have its nuts and bolts off its hands, no questions, and Cash found a way of packing his bomb tight. He would have liked to have been Edward Fox and taken his kit into a forest to try it out on a watermelon, but that's where firearms are different. The bits worked apart; whether they worked together, they would have to wait and see. Mad Ryan was happy with that. Let me see that, he said. Let me see that again, do that bit again, I want to see the order it goes in again. What happens if I do this? *Don't do that!* Ha ha! I'm a mad bastard. *That you are.* What did you say?

The soldiers marched through the town again, and this time they were not at all welcome. They made Aloysius Dynes open the back of his bread van, and then, because they didn't find what they were looking for, they demanded he lift the bonnet. *They say you are always tinkering with this. An unusual interest in engines, wouldn't you say?* Nobody said that to you. It would be unusual if I wanted to shove my cock in the exhaust, but that's not a thing here in Ireland, maybe it is where you're from. I'll start the engine if you like. See, it doesn't work. Hence, the tinkering. *And you say you have no papers proving this is your van?* It's not my van—it's Fr McCaul's, it's the parish van. *And he just lets you drive it?* He lets me drive it if I do the odd errand for him, not that that is any business of yours. *Be on with you.* Dynes saw the back of them and played an anti-English air on his harmonica. The girls beating seven shades out of each other on the Pitches caught sight of the squaddies and decided to launch all the sliotars they had at them, over the graveyard, past the chapel, onto the Diamond, where soldiers from the Second Regiment found that in Ireland it could rain leather balls. A legitimate target.

ᘒᕼᘎ

Eilis had had her hair done at Collette's. Collette had a bulging breastbone from her emphysema and was fussier than she need be. She took far too long over it, talked too much shite between gasps for air, and was inclined to keep cutting as if only that could keep her standing. You had to keep your eye on her. Still, Eilis was happy with the job, board straight cut sharp, evenly blonde. Swedish-looking, she would say to herself, though not to anyone else (if anyone asked). She jerked her head the way she would at a microphone to check the move and sway of it in the mirror. Class. It didn't matter that this was her biggest booking in forever how long, she would do her own make-up. She didn't understand women who could let other women loose on their faces. Only she knew the jaw stretches and looks to the sky she needed to make sure the slap filled the cracks. Not that she had any, or many, wrinkles, even after childbirth. In the facial department, if not exactly everywhere else, she could still hold her own. Stop talking to yourself as if you are old already, she used to say to herself. But she couldn't tell herself to stop talking about her age without talking about her age. *I'm not even thirty!*

The Daytona Showband were playing the Panadol tomorrow night in Belfast, and Eilis was the support act. It wasn't called the Panadol, it was something like that, she called it that as it always gave her a headache singing there. It made no sense, but it made her laugh. We had no other name for it, even after it stopped being a joke. 'Wasn't it the Daytonas I was playing when we first met—you and me and Aloysius and Jimmy?' Was Jim there? Aloysius Dynes was for certain. 'Your old Blarney about Dynes stepping aside, for you to chat to me.' It's true, he did, he put me up to it in a nice way. 'What's he even thinking that I would have been interested in him for? That wee skitter.' There were plenty who were interested in him then, however hard it is now to credit it. He was/is a good man in his way, Aloysius, as you well know. He was practically your manager in those early days, without a thought for himself . . . 'To be fair, you're right . . .' booking your spots, driving you left and right and all over. 'No more about Aloysius Dynes.' No more about Dynes, agreed. 'I have no desire to have him on my mind, if you don't.' Mind? I don't mind. Eilis wrapped a feather scarf, what do you call it—not a boa— around her neck, snowy white, its frondy fingers touching her lips. Fffl. That's going to annoy her. One of those sacrifices. She looked amazing, and she thought so too.

'So, obviously, you'll stay in with the baby. And I'll be needing the car. I could take the bus, but you'll hardly want me to.' Eilis knew that Frank disliked it when she took the night bus home. The night bus was unreliable. The night bus was prone to being hijacked, burnt out, and pushed across the road to deter the army. Still, he seemed put out; she had a sense for these things. 'Or I could take a taxi back if.'

'No, no, no, that's.' Frank was nodding out the words he wasn't saying. 'That's.'

'Did you have plans, Frank? It's not as if this hasn't been in the calendar for about a year.' Eilis pointed downstairs, through the hallway, into the kitchen, to the back of the kitchen door where she kept a calendar that, evidently, at that moment, her husband knew nothing about.

'No way a year, Eilis. You don't have to exaggerate.' She heard him pass the blame to her, just like that. 'I may have had plans, inadvertently, yes. Nothing I can't.' She watched him nod again to fill in his blanks. 'I'll need to make a quick call, that's all.' To someone, he wasn't saying who. Probably Detty.

'Odette?'

'No fucking way, Eilis! Forgive me. Jeezzz, no, no fucking, why'd . . . ? I can't believe you sometimes.'

'Okay, then, not Odette.'

'Odette? Why'd you even think that?'

'Sandwiches.'

'Sandwiches. She gave us sandwiches once. Is a person not allowed to be nice? She was being nice.'

'Okay, then.'

'I was meeting Cash, if you must know.'

'I don't have to know. Jimmy?'

Frank nodded. She could see she had hurt him. Jimmy was the most normal, innocent person for her husband to be seeing on a Saturday evening. Cash now, apparently. With or without sexy Betty?

'You never said. Betty there too?'

'Sorry, I should have put it on the,' Frank pointed through the bedroom floor to the kitchen, to the back of the kitchen door. 'Calendar. No, Betty is. Actually, I don't know what Betty gets up to these days.' But he had heard.

'Just the boys. There's always tomorrow night. I won't be out two nights on the trot.'

'Yes. No. I'm not bothered, to be honest. Can we keep that one open?' The father of her child went down the stairs, along the hallway, out the front door to go two doors down to ask the neighbour there for the lend of her phone. Borrow. Gloria was the one with the phone and the bedroom slippers. He often did odd jobs for her in return.

⊙⊙

I place a couple of calls. The second is to Quinn, the taxi driver.

⊙⊙

The baby was more of a toddler now than a baby. It could feed itself a banana but still needed help with a spoon: about that old. He was a he, despite the woollen tights Eilis dressed him in. He hated those woollen tights even then and would hate them years later in the photos. I fed him banana with a spoon, and we watched TV. It was dark outside. Outside our house was always darker than most, something to do with the river.

I dropped the spoon when the *News Flash* flashed onto the screen, and the toddler cried. The boy did not like the news, especially local news, not even then. He couldn't read, but he recognised the shape of the *News Flash* words, rushing forwards, pushy, in a hurry to get on with the bad stuff, looking the way swear words sound. One or other of us—Eilis or me—would always say, 'Oh no', upset that our programme had been interrupted, nervous about the bomb that had gone off or was about to go off or hadn't gone off because the security forces had got there first, alert for names of people or places that we knew or cared about. The boy sensed all of that in us and was triggered, just as now, crying—no, wailing like he was the whole tribal village in mourning. He wailed now, bawled and hollered, ululating or doing that rattling thing with his tonsils. He was the emergency—I thought that, if he didn't stop soon, I would need to get him to A & E—that I almost missed the real one. Oh no.

I picked up the spoon. There were no pictures (just the white italic *News Flash* curse on the night-blue background). Whoever was on duty in the newsroom read the words that the RUC press people had given them, sketchy at this stage, less information than anyone who truly cared would need, enough information to titillate those who were into that. The tour bus belonging to the popular Southern show band, the Daytonas, has been damaged in what is believed to be a roadside bomb. Police have not yet released details of any casualties but local reports. No one has yet claimed. The RUC have set up a special. Relatives should. I searched frantically, with banana fingers, for a pen and paper to write down the hotline number. I stumbled to the door, meaning to ask Gloria for a loan of her phone again, then remembered the baby. The baby was still crying, well, of course. I could leave him there in front of the telly (the News Flash was over, he would settle.) That did seem the best idea—what could happen to him in the time it would take to make the call. But, how long the call would take was anyone's business, I might be hours, I didn't know how these things worked. Gloria, Gloria was not the babysitting kind. 'Up! Come here you with me!' I said to the boy, all jolly seeming, like we were off on an adventure.

Gloria had seen the interruption to her programme too. She had been watching *The Eurovision Song Contest*, of all fucking things, so she was already in a funny mood. She grabbed the boy from me at the door and swapped him for a piece of scented paper on which she had written the emergency number. 'You can be so useless, sweetie,' she said, I remember. I remember all the details from then of all the things that are pointless to recall. The banana on my fingers, Gloria with her lavender paper and yellow bedroom slippers, her bright red handset looking like it belonged in the Kremlin. I remember phoning the number and thinking for a long time it was the wrong one. Gloria's number and mine were the same, I checked, no mistake our end, but it rang and rang. 'There will be a lot of people trying to get through,' said Gloria, irritating me with her lack of tact. There would be a lot of people trying to get through because it was an enormous fucking disaster: this, bluntly, not a consolation. Gloria put the news on. They were now carrying pictures from the scene, so I could look at the people not picking up the phone. The toddler played with a cat on the sofa. I remember thinking, I didn't know Gloria has a cat, she must call it her pussy and think of herself like Mrs Slocombe. I was thinking this as lifeless bodies were being carried through the living room on stretchers. The phone rang on. The longer I held, the further to the front of the queue I was getting. It worked that way in my head. Gloria was uttering her own words of condemnation, getting in ahead of the politicians, Republican bastards, and I am unanimous in that. The television pictures jerked. The cameras tried to pick out some debris on a field. The reporter repeated the phrase from earlier about the roadside bomb.

'Gloria, where are they?'

'They are all a bunch of friggers, is what they are.'

'Are they not in Belfast?'

'Legitimate targets, my arse. Excuse my French. Cover that wee baby's ears. Wee fuckers messing with innocent folks' fun.'

'That's them just over the border, Gloria. Did they say where they crossed the border?'

'I'd bomb the lot of them to high heaven, if I got my chance. May God for.'

I hung up, shutting Gloria up in the process. I called directory enquiries and got them to connect me through to the Panadol. There was pandemonium there, naturally. Someone, a wee girl, rushed off her feet, I ought to have asked her her name, confirmed for me that Eilis was there and was safe, and promised to let her know I had called.

('I will get her, if you like, Mr McClean.'

'No, you must be needing this line for other callers.'

'It's really no trouble. Eilis is a great favourite with the staff here. I can fetch her no bother.'

'No, really. I'm on a borrowed line myself. And the baby has just started. Please let her know I called.'

'I promise you, I will.')

I thanked Gloria for her phone, and she assured me it was her pleasure. 'Frank, it's nice having neighbours like you and Eilis around. In times like this. Sometimes, I think I wouldn't see anybody if it weren't for this telephone.'

You're a good neighbour, Gloria, I assured her.

'Will you be needing the telephone again today, do you think, Frank?'

I said I didn't think so.

'Because, what is that? Is that three calls you've made today, Frank?'

I'm happy to pay, Gloria.

'What were those calls you were making earlier, Frank? Were they about this business? I have ears, Frank! Would you mind telling me who you were talking to?'

Of course not, Gloria. He was an old friend. I needed a favour off him.

'And the other call?'

No, Gloria, there was no other call.

I put the baby to bed and waited up. Eilis would be on her way, but the wee girl at the Panadol will have told her I called, so she would not feel she had to hurry back: she could hang around the hotel, do the things there that might be useful to do. There would have been punters who turned up, expecting the Daytona Showband, who might still demand their night's entertainment. Surely to goodness they would not make Eilis sing in front of them, on a night like this? But tragedies like this were ten a penny in the day, don't forget. You couldn't put it past them. How else were the managers of entertainment venues to make a living if they threw their hands up every time their top billing were massacred? Don't look that way at me: that was the reality back then. The RUC would right that minute be giving the Panadol the once-over, sniffer dogs, bag searches, background intelligence if they had any on the staff. If no one had phoned in a warning and all else was dandy, that would be it: the hotel would remain open. Eilis would sing. It turns out that is what they made her do. Poor love. If you ask me, that's what.

I waited up. The normal news came on again, and the local news and an extended bulletin. There had been another explosion, somewhere near to the border, apparently only catching the boyo who set it. Among the Daytonas, Sean Hamill, Davy Black, and Seamus McDowell were all dead, Cynthia Sorley had life-altering. Seamus McDowell was only nineteen and could play every instrument, they said. He was from Clifden in Galway. There's a plaque to him there even now, if you check. Davy Black was the fat one, the drummer, may have been blind but I may have remembered that wrong. Dark glasses. Four wee daughters, distraught. Sean was the star, though. He could have played Vegas; he had the looks and the talent. Genuinely. Any songs they played of their own, he wrote. He was the only one from the North, Derry or outside Derry. Never married, for whatever reason, but had a string of you know. He could do that falsetto thing that Gene Vincent used to do. None of these names mean anything to you. If they hadn't have died, you would know them yet.

The baby woke up again and, like before, cried in such a way as I could not console him. The news had unsettled him, his ma was not home (which could not be a good thing), he had to put up with me not knowing what I was up to. I sat on the floor with him, I rocked and sang to him, I stood out the back door in the wee yard and let him grab at the washing line. On the Embankment, our bit of Belfast was darker than in other parts—there was no row of houses opposite, just the windy, stinky Lagan. You get a better view of the night in the dark. In the day, I would stand there with the boy watching the boats from the rowing club row one way up the river, and, if we stood there long enough, we could watch them row back past us in the other direction, having gone exactly nowhere. I had the boy sobbing on my shoulder still, now more of a regular tragic moaning. I looked up to the sky, which was deeper now, going further out and beyond. I fancied the constellations formed bends and corners and that the darkness was a road past them, on and on, deeper and deeper to infinity. One star (I saw one star when I know there are billions) guttered in that way they have, it shimmered like it was being seen through water. Then, I thought, this star is crying. Crying because my boy was crying, because a tragedy had happened, crying for Eilis, who had been made to sing. Crying because I was.

By the time Eilis got home, the boy was asleep again, and I knew I had not killed the Daytonas. I came down from upstairs when I heard Eilis let herself in.

'Hi, love.' I could have sat there for three nights and not worked out what I could ask her or say to her. Eilis had already kicked her shoes off in the sitting room and shed her glittering bomber jacket and feathery scarf. She was in the kitchen boiling the kettle for hot water. I was standing by her grandfather's armchair, spying on her in the kitchen past those coloured plastic hanging strips that used to be everywhere then. She shook her hair away from her face, like she does when she is performing, and, with those plastic strips and the harsh fluorescent light, for a moment I was in the wings watching her on stage. She was humming to herself. Years later, I would know that was a hum to stop me from talking to her. I didn't know it then. I tried talking to her, off stage, from the sitting room—about the wee lad, Gloria—but she hummed away. She was having a strip wash. She rolled her stockings off first, set them in two conjoined rings on the draining board. She spun her skirt around to unzip it and let it fall to the floor. She bent slowly (in pain, in age?) to pick it up and drape it over the seat of the breakfast stool. Then, roughly, she tore at the buttons of her blouse, suddenly or again angry at something in her head. The hum became a grunt, and I stopped trying to talk. She poured the steaming water into the basin and, with a flannel, scrubbed first her face then her armpits, working her way down until she reached her feet. One foot at a time kicked up to the sink, she applied the flannel meticulously to each toe and between each toe. She wanted to be clean, or she wanted not to leave her stage. She was humming again and drying herself, and, for a moment, I interpreted this as happiness. Please, can she be happy, I thought. Happy to be alive, to have me and our son, to. If that can't be enough, I. If she can't.

She lay in bed beside me and kissed me goodnight as usual. She turned away.

'Are you all right?' Yes.

'Did they make you sing?' Yes.

'I thought, when you didn't come home, it must be that.' Yes.

'Was it a good crowd? I mean, were they good to you?' No.

They wanted the Daytonas. When they heard that the band had been attacked, they still wanted the Daytonas. Maybe they didn't realise.

'I called you. Did you get the message?' Yes.

'Some wee girl, out of her depth possibly. Did you get the message?' Yes.

'You understand, I couldn't stay on for you to come to the phone. Gloria. As it was, I had been trying for ages.' Yes.

'I had been calling the wrong number, the one the police gave out for people near the scene. Then I realised, you were at the Panadol, not near the scene.' No.

'For a moment, I thought you might have been with them in their bus. Stupid. I must have lost my head there. The boy was.' Crying.

'Are you all right?'

Sometimes, when the boy cries, the only thing that will do is his mummy. You know that. He's all right now. He knows his mummy is back.

'There was a newsflash. Then, on Gloria's TV, they had pictures. They were in a field, by the side of a field, the bus was. The bus was in the field. Bits of. You didn't see that?' No.

———

'I couldn't hold for you to come to the phone. Honest. And I knew you would be occupied there. The wee girl didn't say, but I knew they would make you.' Sing.

'They shouldn't have made you. I can't believe they made you.' Sing.

Sean and Davy and Seamus. 'Cynthia Sorley, your friend, is.' Eilis gripped the bedsheet or gritted her teeth. Maybe she wanted me to stop. 'Injured, badly. But not.' Dead.

'Thank God you're safe.' Eilis lay completely still beside me, emptier even than the sky above us then. 'I didn't know at first, but when I recognised that their blown-up bus was beside a field, so couldn't be in Belfast, I knew then you weren't.' Dead.

'Yes, that's right. And you had the car.' Yes.

Not me. I didn't have the car.

Eilis needed the car. Legitimate.

So I hadn't driven. I didn't go with Ryan and.

Whatever it was wasn't me. Quinn had taken over from me, he said he would do it. Even though we weren't friends. My car was needed elsewhere, legitimately, is what I had said. So another man had driven to Cullycreggan.

'There was another explosion, near the border.' Ryan and?

'They are saying it killed the boyo who set it.' Who is Ryan?

'Do you understand? This was not the one that got the show band. Same time, different place. Cullycreggan.' Who is Ryan?

Ryan is a mad eejit from the town. It was all his doing. Even Cash had little to do with it.

It?

It, the.   It was all in Ryan's head, I doubt Jim knew much about it. He told me nothing. Ryan's the one. But he got Jim to construct a device.

A bomb.

They were to go to Cullycreggan with it. Me too. But you needed the car.

What are you telling me?
They planted a device by the road.
A bomb. What are you telling me?

Why are you telling me, Frank?
'Thank God you're safe.' Next door, the boy started up again with the crying, and it filled the empty night.

CHAPTER VII

Ryan, I am pretty sure, would have been doing all the talking. That was the like of him, never steady. The fact that the driver beside him was not Frank—not me—would have unsteadied him more. He ought to have called it all off there and then, the integrity of the operation compromised. Any other Saturday, I could have been the driver; any other Saturday, Eilis would not have been supporting the Daytona Showband at the Panadol, she would have been at home with the boy, and she could have quietened him during the newsflash.

'Easy round this corner,' Ryan might have said. 'We don't want the van in a ditch before we even get to the border.' They would have slowed a bit. I can see Ryan's knee bobbing recklessly, bouncing the device on his lap like it were a baby and not a homemade bomb.

What would he have made of what he saw as they came into Cullycreggan? Did he imagine the RUC had all taken the border guards for a cup of tea? 'Where are the fuckers?' he would surely have cried. 'What the fuck has happened here?'

I wonder, could he have called it off then? Then, I realise, the choice was not really his to make. The jerry-built bomb on his lap, the device rigged up by Cash out of bits no one would miss, was about to explode in any case. It was simply a matter of which moment. It might have been when Ryan decided to rip into the stand-in driver, taking his fury out on him until the both of them were blasted to smithereens. Then, or another moment, while the two idled in the van waiting for security personnel to turn up and die in the explosion with them. The moment is indifferent. If Ryan had planned to cradle the device and lay it gently by the side of the road, just on the border post where guards and police chat amiably, then his plan was thwarted. The security personnel had not shown up, had been called elsewhere, had sat longer with their teas, had heeded a warning to stay away. They were not there. It was just Ryan, his silent driver, and a bomb that would choose its own moment to go off.

෨෪

The Republicans had their hands full dealing with reprisals from the Daytona Showband affair. They issued a statement through local radio that the Daytonas had been targeted for their connivance in the economic prosperity of the showbiz industry, or some such drivel. Nobody bought that. The economic prosperity of the showbiz industry was just about the only thing people here could agree they were in favour of at the time.

Betty and Cash fled for Rhodesia for good reason, and no one but me saw them off: that was for good reason too. I was their last friend. The funerals were over; the RUC were content that the Cullycreggan case required no investigation worth its name and quickly shut it down, justice having been seen demonstrably and lethally to be done. Ryan, the bomber, had mishandled the device and blown himself up and was now in a locked box six feet under. The driver too. The Republicans were too embarrassed to claim responsibility for anything. But, in short order, they began their own internal investigation for how Cullycreggan had gone so wrong, and soon enough they would lay their suspicions on likely touts. Why—unless there had been a tip-off—had no security people been caught in the blast? The border, at that post, was on a Saturday typically busy with guards, customs officials, and other uniformed personnel. They weren't all off watching the Eurovision Song Contest with Gloria. They must have had prior information. McCann's boys started sniffing around about the few people who were known to be aware in advance of the plans for Cullycreggan. They weren't at that point interested in me, so that left Cash. Cash had run his mouth at Suzy's and got caught up with Ryan, who got him to build a device. But when Cullycreggan happened, Cash was nowhere to be seen. Change of plan. The boys had questions for Cash, so Cash got out. They were never likely to drop their interest in him after that. I may have been the only person alive who knew that Jimmy Cash was not a tout.

Which is why I was there to see them off at the ferry. At the dock, we shared the couple of bottles of Guinness I had smuggled in. To my surprise, Betty was very sweet about my wife. They were not that dissimilar in many ways. I am not sure Eilis ever gave Betty a proper chance, preferring to heed the whispers that she had a different man in uniform for each day of the week. Eilis could be funny with women as far as I was concerned. Just your type, I can hear Eilis saying, as if Eilis herself wasn't. I remember Betty had her hair up for the journey that night. There was a time when travelling was an occasion, and you would always dress for an occasion, especially if it was an overnighter in a sleeper cabin. Now, I can barely picture Jim himself as he was then. There was the harelip, of course, some mix of accents—part Scottish, part Irish—handsome in a peculiar way. Although the demountable lounge of the Belfast-to-Liverpool ferry might well have been the last place I would set eyes on my friend, I didn't manage to take in all of him. I wonder how far the whole picture is distorted when you alter or remove a detail, a fact, a word.

He wrote to me from Salisbury. His letter had a red stamp in the corner: white guy, a Jesuit, I suppose, with a one-room school building behind him and some tropical-looking foliage; with its *par avion* label it had been flown in from a million miles away. The white government there had declared their unilateral independence from Britain already. 'That's no joke,' he wrote. 'This lot have their own definitions of "minority": the white population here is vastly outnumbered but behave as if they have always had power, and always will. They might be wrong on that last point.' He asked after Eilis. He was sorry she had more or less stopped singing. 'When I heard about what happened to the Daytonas,' he said, 'Betty and I straight away thought about Eilis. We sat up all night talking about it. The pictures on TV, we found ourselves looking for Eilis. Just awful.' Then he said something about Betty listening to records on a Dansette she had picked up in a Salisbury market. He complained about the rain, as it must have been pouring down at the moment he was writing that particular letter. That's what he did: switching from one subject to the next, connecting unconnected thoughts like he was talking to himself or to a confessor he dared reveal only fragments of his sins to. And I noticed a peculiar affectation in his handwriting, like he thought copperplate did not sufficiently express his personality. Anytime he wrote an *r* or an *a*, he used a capital letter. Do people do that to reveal or to disguise something, do you think?

'We have this maid—you know, I don't know who pays her, she might be a slave, heaven help us—her name is Maisie. The maid is in the contract, with the job and the house and the car—she watches me like I can't be trusted—she could be right! Betty has her eye on her too.

'You wouldn't believe the heat here—check where we are against the Equator. But then it rains and you think the earth, the Earth, will be washed away. But the most exuberant flora, Betty says it's bougainvillea—Maisie rolls her eyes. It's the way we say it. The gardener says Yes, miss—we have a gardener!—young guy, seems to spend his days resting on the pole of his rake or repairing the fence, and I won't tell him off for it because, like with the maid, I don't know who is paying him.'

And then, getting to the point. 'I am in charge of building the main road out of the capital to Nyasaland.'

Cash was in charge of building the main road out of the capital to Nyasaland. Whether that was the whole thing, just some section of it, or some part of the management of the project was never clear to me: Cash assumed I would not be interested in the details. The precise layering from sub-base to base to sand to asphalt; the geology of the subgrade it sat on and the means of levelling it off (whether by dynamite or a legion of men and pickaxes); the route it took around, over, under, in ignorance of, or despite topographical features: the details. All he said about it was that Betty had suggested he recruit a team of Irish gypsies to do the work. 'I spend 90 per cent of my time just trying to get men, equipment, and tar all in the same place at the same time,' he said. 'I am more a general than an engineer.'

'And I thought I might miss politics—the moves you have to shake if you want to build a road around here!—especially one that links the capital to one of the homelands. Douglas, you won't have heard of him—nothing happens here unless he is in your pocket, or you are in his. What's the phrase?'

I hadn't heard of Douglas, but Central Library had the *Economist*.
I was half-expecting to find Jim's name in one of those library books
or magazines, playing a bigger role there than mere road builder. Cash
would be right at home smoking a cigar on a veranda, mixing his
martini with politics, fixing a deal before all the pieces were in place.
There, in the profiles, was that man Douglas, the prime minister's
factotum with a gold-ringed finger in every pie: he could make use
of Cash, I began to think. Douglas was a Scot too, by heritage. That
was a connection for a start. Officially, he was minister for homeland
affairs, meaning he had charge of all relations between the capital
and what they considered the tribal areas. As much as possible, as far
as I could work out, this meant ensuring that the indigenous people
maintained their bloody rivalry with each other, equipping them with
just enough guns to keep themselves down and the minority whites
in power. These guns might come from the Israeli government, the
South Africans, or any mercenary outfit that could be paid to take a
side against sub-Saharan black nationalism. Douglas also had a hand
in roads. Connection number two with Jim. He bothered himself
with the location and direction of them, and with finding from
overseas the money to pay for them. Despite, or perhaps because of,
the wholesale appropriation of state assets, the Salisbury government
was an economic basket case already. That's what the *Economist* in
Central Library told me.

'There is any amount of labour lying around here—I arrive at
the office in the morning, and there is a polite line of men, some
with their own tools—but, and I am ashamed to say this, the bosses
must be white. It's the law: a black man cannot have authority over a
white. And, even if they do have the commanding presence, which,
boy, they do, there's none of them with qualifications—from what I
gather, they can become priests in their churches and teachers in their
schools—not unlike home, come to think of it! Any change on that
front at home by the way? I won't hold my breath, but you will keep
me informed, as you promised, if things shift. Here, skin tone is God.'

(Mandy, would you mind? That cup of water, thank you. Skin
tone's not our problem, is it? Although some would say. Do you know,
maybe it's just my imagination, but did the British Army never send
any of their black soldiers over here to us? They do have black soldiers

in the army, I know; I have seen adverts, but I wonder, did they have a policy of not sending them? That's not me being racist, because you will have worked out by now that I have not much time for any British soldier! You gotta laugh. I remember one time—obviously, more than one time—but I mind this one time, I was driving the boss, the *American* boss, for some reason we were outside Newry, I guess we were coming back up North, in a bit of a hurry as always, and there was an official roadblock – army and RUC – and this young guy, I would say maybe twenty if that, I remember he stuck his head through my window, gun pointing first so it was by my right ear (I hated that), wanting to know the usual, where we were going to coming from, and I noticed . . . as I say, no more than twenty years of age . . . he was shivering, not from cold—there was a line of sweat along the blond hairs on his chin—but from fear, and he smelled that sweet shit smell. I am not saying he had. But the wee critter was scared out of his pants. White guy too. Maybe he'd just been posted. Wonder if he lasted.

Anyway.) Where might Douglas go looking for such qualified, commanding white men? Rumours were that he searched for Aryans of Nazi persuasion in Argentina. He scouted for Broederbond trekkers in South Africa, and he waylaid Orangemen loyalists who were building the segregated housing ghettos in Northern Ireland. These were the types of places he assumed he would find the folk with the skills he needed, and none of the scruples.

'I'll say this: you can turn yourself into whatever you want here, if you are the right colour—the maid would have a different view. Betty says Maisie inspects her knickers for bleeding, she has to go—make yourself a millionaire or pretend to be one, but do it quick because, I tell you, this place is about to blow. Betty is playing golf now—I bet you didn't know they had enough grass here for golf—there's a ladies' club.'

If Jim Cash left the country because he wanted not to be Jim Cash (and Betty wanted not to be Betty), Rhodesia was the sort of place one could live in disguise. Or none of that.

'But none of that. How is Eilis?'

Not so good, but there was no easy way of telling Jim that. She is not playing golf with the ladies. 'Eilis has more time now to herself. She busies herself with the house and the boy, more the way I think she has wanted to all along but couldn't because of her.' Singing. There are things better kept to yourself, you feel. That may not be a medical opinion. 'You know how Eilis always liked to glam up and.' Look her best: she was still sitting at her dressing-table most evenings, straightening or curling her hair, doing her make-up, like 'she would like nothing more than to go back on stage', whereas in reality she was putting on her armour. Is armour a weapon, or is it always only a defence? I am sure she was assaulting me with her mascara; in her head, she was applying it to her eyes against my will. She was wounding me with her bloody lipstick, shaming me with her blusher. Am I taking this too far? The full made-up, defiant face. It's your fault, all of this, she was saying into her mirror to the husband she saw behind. What was she contemplating in the mirror? You scarred poor Cynthia Sorley for life, she was thinking. No one will listen to a face like that trying to sing to them. You knocked the song out of her, as surely as you did for Sean and Davy and Seamus. May God rest them. What if I had been there too, did you (do you) think about that? Your bomb killed them in a country lane, but it may as well have been at the Panadol. Limbs everywhere, Frank, d'you hear me. Bloody mess. And they were just about the one good thing. Now, none of the show bands. There aren't any. There's no. There's. And there you are, with your, pretending you have nothing to do with, as if nothing has, like you want to go on like nothing. Maybe you should have run off with Jimmy and Betty Cash.

She said none of this to me out loud, but I know she can't get past the Panadol, even though in her rational moments she knows we (and especially I) had nothing to do with it. She has rational moments, and she knows we had nothing to do with it. I have my rational moments too. But, for a time there, I did think that perhaps maybe I had suffered a blazing memory-erasing headache.

'Do remember to send our love to her,' Jim wrote. 'So many of our favourite memories of the old place are of times spent with you two. Betty still says that Eilis should have cut a record.'

Should have. Time past; time passed. Should have, never did, never will. Eilis did not (does not) have the gift Cash seemed to have for self-invention and reinvention. However much make-up she applies. Jimmy was a wee Scotch boy and could not play football, but

Fr McCaul gave him a position, and there with his ugly face he pulled on a shirt and he was our most fearsome defender on the Pitches. Just like that. I can hear the crack yet of when he broke the leg of the Michaelstown showboater, Simon with the suntan. Felled him like a sack of loose sticks. But Jim lost all memory of that, as if he had had his own blazing memory-erasing headache, as if recollection was no longer useful to the man he now wanted to be. I can hear it yet: that cracked bone is in my ear still.

❮❯

Around the time that Ryan was recruiting Cash to the Republican cause, Douglas was talent-spotting racial supremacists in Ulster. Easy pickings, you would imagine. Cash was not among them, but, in the Housing Trust, he knew plenty others who had been tapped up by the outreach department of the Rhodesian government. You will be treated like a king, your wife won't have to lift a finger, tax-free bonuses and benefits. Cash had no plans to join them, but a thought can rest in your brain—taking shape quietly and selling off your property—waiting for its moment. Then Cullycreggan happened. Once he was not immediately kneecapped or arrested or even questioned, Jim decided to cash in his three strikes of luck and take the job: project manager for Nyasa Communications. The Housing Trust were sad to see him go and sorry they could not throw a party for him, but, as they were 100 per cent state-owned outfit of the government in Northern Ireland, and Rhodesia was a pariah with whom we did not do business, then surely, he could understand? Have an ashtray. You can work your notice as annual leave. Stay in touch.

I imagine Jim landing in Salisbury airport with all the wrong clothes. Nothing makes you feel more out of place than having a suitcase of clothes designed for another climate. I remember now a bottle-green sweater he liked to put on for Suzy's, corduroy trousers he wore to death; all of his apparel was made to perspire in. If they were put up in a hotel in the capital, pending their removal to a villa in the suburbs, Betty would have taken advantage of the hiatus to kit out her husband and herself with clothes more suiting of the setting. Linen cotton damask muslin cool polyester. The reinvention—really just an adjustment—would have begun straightaway. Like switching from drinking beer to gin would have been the sensible thing, because gin has quinine and this was Africa after all.

The club where they drank with other colonials (or expats, as they preferred to call themselves)—what was it called? There were Dutch there and Americans as well as South Africans and Brits, so it won't have been the Victoria or Balaclava. That last appeals to me, though, I must say: yes, let's say it was that. Now in the right clothes, Betty and Jim took their seats at the high bar of the Balaclava and ordered cocktails. Somewhere, they had learned how to do that, knowing the names and the mixes they liked, what to sling before dinner or after. Maybe sophisticated Betty knew from her hotel days. The Balaclava was not some dingey hole as it would have been if it were situated in East Belfast, with portraits of a young queen, rosy cheeked, above the dim optics. This Balaclava was sun drenched, was as much an outside bar as it was inside. It had waiting bar staff with crisp white shirts and little black aprons. The floor was black-white-black-white chequered. I can't imagine a beery bar towel or branded mirror, but that's not to say they didn't have them. The patrons—experienced and fat, or skinny blow-ins—played international versions of poker and bridge for huge pots of money. Jim and Betty played too, not sure about whose kitty they were blowing. Jim had the faces for poker, you would have to say, crooked and inscrutable. Their poker conversations and their normal conversations would all have been about money, the money they had and the money they were aiming to get soon. I wonder how long it would have taken Jim to break into and then manipulate their venal conversations.

Fifty.

Fold. Fold. I'm out.

I will see your fifty and raise you . . . what have I got there, Sal? . . . I'll raise you another fifty.

You, with the face, can join in next hand. Can someone vouch you?

His name's Cash. He's with Nyasa.

Nyasa Communications? The Danny Simms' laundromat?

Cash! We like that here! Carloads . . . no, freight-loads of cash, isn't that right, Piet?

Timetable in my breast pocket, Brad. Just so I always know when to expect my next wagon. Told you many times, Piet. You just have to let me know when you want me to cut you in.

Not my own master on that one. Mr Douglas would not like me going freelance.

I hear the PM's man compensates you well. So, are you seeing my raise? Go on. Sal wants another diamond.

Danny Simms? Who is that?

If Sal wants another diamond, I should not like to get in the way. In fact, I happen to be aware . . .

Of course, you are, Piet. Diamond Piet. Ruby Piet. Which is it now?

Danny Simms is your boss.

He's not the one I report to.

She. She is the one your boss reports to. She is your boss, chum. You had better learn that quick.

Did you offload that Soviet shipment on . . . which one was it?

Nkomo. Yes. He and his boys like a Kalashnikov. Have you seen him?

Specimen!

And who's *her* boss?

That's the right question: you *are* learning. Draw a line from any of us here, and soon enough it will end up with Mr Douglas. The minister. Danny Simms works for him. She's the one who makes him look good.

The one we're really scared of!

Ha. Ha. Ha. Ha.

Douglas is the man who has his hand on the money tap, but without Danny Simms, there would be no tap at all.

When do we meet her?

Is this your good wife? (Betty.) Betty, it's a total pleasure to meet you. I like you already. Yes, I imagine Danny Simms will introduce herself to you at some point. Don't expect an entourage, she travels light and fast.

Betty, if you play golf, I need a partner. Hi, I'm Sal.

I wish you weren't supplying guns here: you are pissing in your own tent. Nkomo, Mugabe, they are bad news. Sell to Tambo's lot instead, make a good clean fight of it in South Africa.

MK, *Umkhonto we Sizwe*. Did I say that right? Don't worry. The Spear of the Nation are valued customers. Their problem is taking the merchandise off us and getting it back over the border. I haven't found a secure way yet to do it myself.

I could help you out there. Hang on, you, Cash: your Nyasa Communications set-up must have experience with nervous border guards.

I wouldn't know about that.

Ha. Ha. Ha. Ahem. The Balaclava has no ears, chum.

Is that the sort of operation Danny Simms signs off on?

Oh, yes. But she likes a man who can show initiative. Do we think our man Cash, here, is an initiative man?

I will match your raise.

I'm definitely out.

I've not played, Sal. Is golf hard?

Betty, darling, it's a walk in the sun.

※

Or none of that. Danny Simms was tall and slender, at ease with a belt of shell cases across her shoulder. Scrub that: she was stumpy and officious, ordering the world from her desk. The *Economist* sidebar, which referred to adjutants and enablers who did Douglas's bidding, didn't picture Danny Simms or even confirm her sex.

I was lucky to catch that piece in the *Economist* that time: the Central Library lost some of its windows when the *Belfast Telegraph* offices next door were hit, and my mate the librarian shut the shop for the rest of the day. However.

I don't see how Cash, with his role there and his personality, could have avoided Danny Simms.

This will be how it went.

'Funny place for a Catholic from Ireland to show up.'

Cash scrambled to stand up from behind his desk. 'Yes, miss. Northern Ireland actually, miss, ma'am.' (Scotland, he might have said.)

'Simms. Simms is enough. Ireland . . . whatever . . . the world doesn't give a shit for the distinction, right? You're Cash, right?'

'Yes, miss . . . Simms. Yes, that's right.'

'And you already know who I am, right?'

'Yes. Simms.' (He would have sat down if he was told to.)

The Jim I knew would not allow that to have been the first impression he gave: he would not have been caught napping behind his desk with a mess of drawings and broken pencils. No. It went like this.

The initial approach would have been from him, a forensic report on the shitstorm that was the Salisbury to Nyasaland road-building project. The wrong sort of workers, with the wrong grade of hardcore, in the wrong place at the wrong time. 'One could almost believe it was not in fact the intention of the ministry to complete this highway.' He might have dared that to provoke an invitation.

'Funny place for a Catholic from Ireland to show up.'

Cash was on-site, the drawings in his head, supervising the demolition of a village. 'Simms? Cash.' He offered a handshake. 'Scotland, actually. But point taken. Can someone here fix you a cup of tea?'

Funny place for a Catholic from Ireland to show up. The fact that Jimmy was less Catholic and less Irish than the rest of us is no explanation: it would be a funny place even for an Ulster Protestant to be residing. It's a long way to run away to. He must really have wanted those tax-free benefits.

'You think we don't want to build this road, Cash?'

An open-backed truck, its tyres as hard and high as a man, filled with the women and children of the village, passed between them, giving Cash the chance to collect his thoughts.

'I think that Nyasaland does not exist—it's Malawi. I think perhaps you are building a road because that's the best way of scattering populations like this one. I think maybe you are scared of these children and these women, though I can't see why.'

'What were you doing when we found you, Cash?'

'Building houses.'

Ha. 'You would rather be doing that here, right?'

'I knew what I would be doing here.'

'It doesn't sound like it. Think: what do men fight for? They fight for their wives and their sons and their daughters. That's reason enough to build this road through their towns.'

An excavator, white and rusted around its cabin, its claw raised was at that moment pulling down the wall of a school room. A priest, a black man, was doing his best to stand in its way, while at the same time he was shooing some children away from harm. 'Away! Away!' he was crying, to the white men in the hard hats, to the children with no shoes.

'This. This will make the men fight. They will kill for this.'

'You're afraid for your life, Cash, right?' She laughed at him. As if people here had several lives and one was easy enough to spare.

Away! The women and children being driven away in the open-backed truck must have been roped in, because none climbed out despite their screaming. Engine pain and gear grinding and groaning of fallen masonry drowned some of them out. 'Away!' shouted the Jesuit. Where were the men, cleared away before Nyasa Communications arrived there in the form of its engineer?

'It's terrible to watch this, right, it's a tragedy what's happening here. These people have been brutalised by colonialism. It has fucked them, right? It's in their heads!' She jabbed her pointing finger at her temple, like a spear. 'You would not be human if you did not cry. The Brits . . . !' She said it like it was a disgusting thing she needed to be rid of. 'The Brits brutalised these people and raped this country. It's still a beautiful country, Cash, when you look.

'But look at them now. They stand by while their school is demolished and bleat as they are evacuated. They have been *lessened*, Cash, right? You would not allow this, I would not allow this, but they *allow this*. That's what it really means to be brutalised.'

Funny place for a Catholic from Ireland to show up. Unless he had a different plan.

◎⋈◎

'I wonder often, Frank, have they forgotten about me entirely back home?' The letterhead on the paper was a hotel in Bloemfontein: Danny Simms was moving him about. 'Does anyone in Suzy's give even a second thought about big Jimmy Cash?' They do, still. 'Does anyone wonder where Betty and I flew off to?' They do, some do, after a fashion: where did those effers fly away to, asks Quinn, asks O'Rourke, ask others. 'Would they even bat an eyelid were we to walk back in?' It's still too early for that. Don't walk back in yet if you value being able to walk at all. 'Remember, you said you would keep an eye on things for me.' I did: you're better off staying where people trust you, wherever that is. Bloemfontein is South Africa, no mistake, which is no way the same as Rhodesia. I never got to ask him about that because, though you may sleep there and have a breakfast, a hotel is not a home, so no letter of mine was ever going to reach him there.

'How's the wife? I hear you ask. She has all the time in the world to do whatever in the world she likes, but she still appears bored.' Betty maybe played a bit of golf with her friend Sal. I have in mind those sprinklers they use to keep the grass green, where the pressure forces the water around in rotating Ys and most of it evaporates in the arid air before it can land. So this water, precious to life—the force of life—pent up in a pipe, bursting to get out, is just pissed into the sky in a pretty arc.

ᘎᘏ

'You're actually the smart one in this household, right?' (I am imagining a conversation between Danny Simms and Betty Cash, perhaps at a party thrown by the latter in honour of . . . What could that be? A stretch of completed road, a birthday, a successful trade with MK in South Africa.)

'Is that what Jim tells you?' (Betty was usually straight to the point, but I imagine, on this occasion, she would be cagey around her husband's boss. And that alone . . . God! That fact alone would make her miserable.)

'Your husband has never mentioned you, beyond the fact that he has you here with him in Rhodesia. That's good, right? He has betrayed none of your secrets.' Simms would have taken a sip of her drink at that point, looking over the rim of her whisky tumbler at her hostess so that the kiss of her glass veiled the bottom half of Betty's face. 'Actually, you are something of a mystery.'

Betty was used to being thought of as mysterious, less so to having it remarked upon in front of her: the power it usually conferred upon her was therefore denied her in the one instant. Her mystery was somewhat now a petty thing, a girlish thing to be kept in a locked box, fluffy, dismissible. She folded her hand. 'Jim is the one with the secrets.'

Neither woman wanted to discuss those. It was Betty's turn to fill the gap with alcohol. Hers was a dry gin topped with chilled tonic, which she trickled down the long neck of her glass into her waiting mouth. It barely hesitated before continuing its languid journey down her throat. She looked around the room—*her* room, her *living*-room—noticing that no one was missing her, and no one was missing her infamous guest. Did they even know that this was Danny Simms? People in threes or fours were gathered around their drinks or tiny bowls of exotic nuts and candies prepared by Maisie. Betty looked back at Simms—maybe at her shortness, the roughness of her hands, the wayward tufts of her sandy hair—wondering what kind of marvellous woman was she at all. Did she sleep with other men or other women or Jim? If I were a bit stronger or weaker, would she want to sleep with me? Would I be her type? Betty laughed a little drunkenly into her gin. Simms would know where to find her, if it ever came to that.

Simms had first looked at Betty as a way of looking at Cash, but in the three minutes she had spent with this strange woman, she had entirely forgotten the husband. Pretty, dressed cheaply, but (what would she, Simms, know?) not unfashionably. Maybe ten years her husband's senior. The most impressive thing about her so far was the fact she felt no responsibility for filling the silence between them. There were a hundred clichés available to the hostess, from surface pleasantries to well-mannered justifications for walking away, but this Cash lady grasped at none of them. She pities me! Simms realised: she takes me for the lonely one. I meet people, I reorder their lives, I return to my hotel room in a place I barely remember, and I am alone. On a different plain, that's *this* woman too! (Simms edged back an inch, the better to recalibrate her sight.) She is also in the business of disruption, and she also cannot recall what it is to be at home. 'Jim is the one with secrets,' she said with—what was that?—pride. Pride is too self-effacing a word, too little me. She meant something else when she said it, something approaching possession. Jim may have his own secrets, but he is also the vessel in which this woman has lodged her own.

'Cash is no dummy, but you are the bright one, right? No need to answer, I can tell.' Then, because she judged that they understood one another: 'How are you not entirely crushed by the dullness of this existence?'

This was an insult, an attack on her husband and on their choice to flee Ireland. But in the state that she was in, Betty took the slap for an advance, an effort at flirtation from this weird woman, and, because she knew at that moment how vulnerable she was, how prone she was to disgracing herself, she opted to withdraw. 'My apologies, Miss Simms. I must allow you to join more stimulating company.' She departed miserably, feeling she sounded like a flustered Victorian. But not to Simms, who was left standing again alone: she believed she had got the measure of her employee's wife.

   ◦◦◦

'No thank you, love,' Betty would say to Cash when he offered for her to stay with him in the provincial hotels he was sent to—with their strong alcohol and British food. 'I will keep myself busy here.'

He thought she was bored. He thought she was paranoid about the maid, making up tales about how she inspected the bedsheets and stole from the jewellery box. On the contrary, Betty was learning from Maisie how to cook with local ingredients and making clothes on her sewing machine for the gardener's nephews. Cash did not know about that, so he could never tell me, so I am no wiser either. Betty went in for animal rescue, for all I know.

I see the car parked on their driveway, the car the company gave them along with the maid and the gardener when they arrived but which they barely used because Jim was chauffeured everywhere. I see a Mark 1 Ford Escort in white but wonder, was that in production yet while they were in Africa? Its lines—bonnet to roof to boot—would appeal to Betty, tracing out a mountain amid rolling hills, a Mount Nyangani perhaps. She was not a driver, but she could learn (and, for certain, I know that later she could drive), and the car would be calling to her, with its promises of rocky adventure. A car will do that; a car sitting undriven is ticking with potential, looking every way out of its windows, willing to go anywhere; a parked car is not a corpse. The young gardener taught her, I think. He, according to Cash, had time on his hands, and driving, like gardening, is in essence a person putting their faith in processes—natural, mechanical—they hardly understand. He would have put on a shirt to be her teacher. She, close to his scent, opened a window or closed it. (I apologise: I cannot picture them driving without imagining some sexual encounter between the two, despite having no grounds at all for supposing that. I am prone to the racialised stereotype, unable to place an indolent black man near an idle white woman without there also being sex. I know it's wrong to think this, but if the thought is in my head, what can I do? All these thoughts are in my head. It may have been gentler than sex, I tell myself: laying a hand upon a hand on a gearstick or steering wheel, a kindly admonishment or laughed-away blunder. Then again—the thoughts again—there may have been intercourse of the type to get the gardener sacked. For, unlike Maisie the maid, he was not given a name in Cash's letters.) The windows were open because, in Rhodesia, it was always hot. The sun blanched the road a pale yellow and baked the clay of the roadside houses to the same colour. The white Escort kicked up a cloak of ochre dust so that, but for the engine noise, the driver and her partner might have moved around anonymously.

When she could drive alone, she took the car outside of the city and to all corners of it. If Sal, the lady golfer, knew where she was going, she would tell her not to go there. The library, here, had books showing mountain ranges and waterfalls and ugly bulbous-headed birds; Betty may have ventured afar, but I doubt—maybe it's just my own timorousness—I doubt she would have dared stay away from home overnight if alone, if not in a safe bed, if not at least with her husband's vague knowledge. There would be practical reasons for her to take the gardener with her. Even brand-new company cars can break down, let me tell you, and Betty was no mechanic. Salisbury, Sal will have warned her, was wild enough when you moved outside the domains of the white administration and the colonials' communities. 'Wild' might have been a Sal word: what would I know about that? That's possibly my racism rearing its head again. I need to watch myself, thinking that the place would be wild just because it would be unfamiliar. So not 'wild' as such but, in the final analysis and given the state of affairs as there was then, not entirely safe either. 'Wild' as in unpredictable and hard to read if you are a woman from Northern Ireland. A funny place to show up. Sal, I am guessing, would also have her views on the gardener and the Balaclava would too.

Simms (if she ever said it) was right about this: Cash was no slouch, but Betty was the bright one. Remember how I said she would perch on the sofa in Belfast while Jim gave his political lectures, aheming away, making him sharper? I know they say that a blunt stone can sharpen a blade, but the metaphor does a disservice to the stone. Betty was book-learned, and she was aware of the world. She could have been a spy or run guns or traded diamonds, or she could have set up and run a school or a business or a human rights group. It is incredible to me that she did none of these things (or none of them to my certain knowledge) so that anything I might have invented along the way seems more true to me than the likely truth.

This gardener needs a name now. I will call him Joshua, because I have associated him with Nkomo. Nkomo, Mugabe, Lumumba, Kaunda, Tambo, Mandela, Kenyatta, Nkrumah. Names together like an epic poem to me, melodic and exotic and unlockable. What do I know if books is all I know? Joshua's face glistens remarkably with the heat, sweat patching his paramilitary fatigues. There is a Kalashnikov, one among the guns run to him, among the guns he is running southwards. It is not just 'he'; there is an operation much larger than 'he' because, despite what Simms might have said, they would not in the end allow themselves to be brutalised. Let's say Joshua is supplying Umkhonto we Sizwe, Spear of the Nation, the youth wing of the ANC. An uprising in South Africa is good for morale, and business, in black Rhodesia. Joshua should despise this white Irish lady, occupying this vast near-empty house, ignorant of the abundance of jacaranda in her garden, fearful of the maid Maisie, punished by the sun. But driving a white lady, his boss, admits him to parts of the country that he would otherwise need the pass for, and she seems reckless about her own safety. And, he has noticed, she doesn't ask all the questions she is entitled to ask.

Danny Simms says to Jim Cash, 'The world turned against the white government here when we dared to declare our independence, with only the Nationalists in South Africa standing by us. So why would we smuggle weapons across our border to their enemies? Not for the love of the black man, no! But if the ANC terrorists can strike a blow against the white government there, perhaps the world will sit up and see what we are up against here.'

Jim Cash said to himself, 'The black people in southern Africa work every farm and every factory but run or own none of them. They are diverse and scattered so that, though they surely know it not to be true, they can be counted a minority by their enemies.'

Betty said to Sal, *apropos* of there being no black people in the Balaclava, 'Why are there no black people in the Balaclava?'

Jim Cash recollected to himself, 'A person must know right from wrong, so must a people. A people must know when to act, when to condemn, when to put a halt, and oftentimes it falls to an individual to take such an action and to make such a condemnation.'

Betty said to Sal, 'I am not fucking my gardener. He is teaching me to drive. I would like to invite him here for a drink, just to see the reaction on your and everyone else's face.'

Jim said to himself, weapons that could bring down a government in South Africa might do the same in Rhodesia.

Jim Cash said to Danny Simms, 'Jesus, I will do it, all right, not that I'll be doing it with any enthusiasm or for the reasons you gave. Christ, this is a fuckup of a place, if this is anywhere near the right thing to do.'

And to himself, Cash said, 'This is a funny place for a Catholic from Ireland to show up.'

ⱺⱦⱱ

Mandy says, 'So, what did Jimmy do? Did he . . . ?'

Well, that's hard to say for sure.

'That's hard to say for sure because, naturally enough, he wasn't going to tell me! I do know that Tambo for the ANC was able to get hold of a cache of weapons and get them into South Africa from Rhodesia. Douglas always denied having anything to do with it; I never saw anything of Danny Simms but a name in the *Economist*. I do know that road to Nyasaland was never built.'

Mandy paused before

CHAPTER VIII

she spoke again. 'You can't always get what you want.' She shifted the pillows behind Frank's back because she could see he looked uncomfortable. Her sudden movement, and banality, made him pause. She was only a nurse after all; what was she to know of Nyasaland and Oliver Tambo and all that. She was only young, without a worry for that sort of thing. In his day, apartheid in sub-Saharan Africa was not a million miles away from the Troubles here, even if they were about a million miles away. People wore badges and refused wine. Mandy had missed out on all that, which was a good thing overall. But what was she talking about?

'How do you mean, Mandy?'

'Just like I said: you can't always plan for what happens. But you don't want to hear from me. What about Jimmy?'

'No, Mandy. Your turn. You've had me talking too long as it is. I need a rest, and I'm parched. I had some sweets in my locker, but someone stole them. You wouldn't pour me?'

'Just a wee sip, Frank, remember. Nobody stole your sweets, Frank. Remember, I am keeping your yogurt nuts in a safe place until after your.'

Frank eyed her suspiciously. 'I never had you down for a thief. Those other ones, maybe, but. They've taken everything. Where is everything, you? What happened to all the things that Eilis brought in for me?' A rage of spittle had formed in the corners of his mouth, and tears spilled from his eyes.

Something had slipped in her patient's mind; she instantly recognised the symptom, the suspicion. Some people came into hospital with it, and, for others, hospital brought it on. Hospital wards, with their day-long bedtime and night of constant noise and light, were engineered for disorientation. She drove people mad; she had seen it often. She settled herself to the front edge of her chair, as if she had a storybook wide open on her lap and said, with the softest but firmest voice, 'Do you want to hear me now, or do you not? It's your choice.'

Frank remembered that he was thirsty. He was sure one of the women had brought sweets to him today, and now they were gone. He sipped from his plastic cup, and it settled him. 'You go on ahead. I may rest my eyes while you go on. Sorry about all that just then.'

Frank pushed back gently into his pillows, dropped his eyes, and allowed a smile to rest on his lips. It would be okay to let someone else do the lifting for a bit. What age was this one, Mandy? Same as his son, or thereabouts, it's so hard to tell what with even men wearing face cream. Where had they hidden his clothes? (Peculiar sort of hotel, this.) Who is this Nicole she is talking about?

'You had Nicole earlier, blue cardigan, gave you your meds. You commented on her legs, so Jeremy had to have words with you, do you remember. She is very sensitive about her thighs, you ought not to have said anything.'

No, doesn't ring a bell. Jeremy, I recall: my football man. 'Did I make her cry?'

'I'm saying nothing, as I'm worrying that you'd think that was a good thing. Nicole is a cracking wee . . . Well, she is a cracking nurse—taught me everything. It's sad to see her like this.'

Frank agreed that it was sad, though he could not for the moment recall this Nicole. He could try to bring her to mind, or he could sleep. Mandy had a nice laugh, and she had a soothing voice.

The origins are hazy. Like a million others, Nicole trained as a nurse in Ireland and then beat a path to England. They must have lain on special boats and trains back in the day, because it seems almost every girl from here who couldn't type did that at some point. Perhaps the English admired our hospital corners, who the heck knows. I have three aunties that did the same, mind I think one of them was a cousin not an auntie, and her 'stay in a hospital' was to have a baby rather than to be a nurse, but you get my point. Nicole was one among many. What do I remember she said about that time? Her landlady was a bitch, God forgive, there were French letters everywhere to be bought but not to be used. This was in Newcastle. French letters is what we would call Durex, which is a perfectly fine thing for a girl or boy to have on them nowadays—everyone should carry them . . . you can't be too . . . don't die of bloody ignorance—but in those days, it was practically illegal from the way Nicole tells it. But I think she meant she had to sneak boys past her landlady if she wanted one in her room. Looking at Nicole now, you'd hardly credit it, but you know what they say about Irish nurses then, and, according to Nicole, it's all true!

Apparently, her landlady was thought a good landlady because she allowed her in at all: many wouldn't have an Irish one. Did they think we had three legs!

'No. That's just the Catholic nuns.' (Frank was not yet asleep.)

All those Irish girls over there keeping the NHS going, and all those Irishmen building English roads and so on, yet they had a reputation for idleness. And fighting. Drinking, yes, I am sure that prejudice was accurate enough, but Nicole is a good wee worker even yet, and I'm sure she was then too. Likes her white wine, mind.

She is in this room in Newcastle that she can't have you know in, because her landlady will bang the floor or kick her out or worse. *Our* Newcastle, in County Down, is a lovely seasidey place—as you are bound to know—but I don't get that impression of the one in England, at least not from Nicole's telling of it. Shipbuilding and industry and trouble on a Saturday night, and cold and wet all year round.

Like Belfast. (Frank, by now, was more asleep than awake.)

I suppose you might say it was not dissimilar to Belfast back then.

Her job was in one of the brand-new NHS hospitals, with beds to spare and ward nurses tripping over themselves. I doubt such a time ever existed, but there it is: that's the way Nicole tells it. She preferred it not too quiet, so was happiest of all in A&E where there were plenty of broken ankles and stabbings to keep her busy. That's the way we are, Frank: who wants to have to deal all day with mundane lumps and bumps? Compound fractures and knife wounds give you something to chat about later over your white wine and kebab. As it was plush, they would get all the Newcastle United boys in who had been crocked on a Saturday, busted knees, broken toes, concussion. They had their share of players from Northern Ireland in that side. I'm too young to know, my dad's a regular at Windsor Park, Nicole had her eye out for them probably too: Davy Craig, Willie McFaul. Would that be right?

No answer.

One of them, she said it was (which means it was probably not one of them but another she couldn't name). Let's say, he broke his leg and he was in A&E, in the cubicle one on from where Nicole was treating a burn. She is funny, the way she tells it: *oooh, aaah*, she goes mimicking his yokel accent, screaming, *Mammy!* You get the picture. As I say, many of us are happiest in Accident and Emergency amidst the screaming. Whichever one—we will call him Tommy for the sake—Tommy is weeping buckets, Nicole is done with her burn, and it's otherwise a quiet night, so she pops her head around the curtain to see if she can offer any assistance to a wounded footballer. As you would. Footballers had no money then, but they had nice legs, Frank. Only think of Geordie Best. I probably shouldn't be going on like this, but you're asleep anyway.

I'm awake.

Nicole moves in once the strapping is done and painkillers have started to take effect. Tommy may be delirious, but she is happy enough to have got him chatting about something other than his broken leg. 'Talk to me, Kathleen,' he cries. 'I'm not Kathleen, I'm Nicole,' she says. That kind of thing.

'Where are you from, Kathleen? No, don't tell me!' This is where it starts. I'm from Northern Ireland like you, she says. Of course, you are, anyone could tell that, no need to tell me that, but where *in* Northern Ireland? No, don't say! On like that.

'You're from the east of the city, would I be right, Kathleen?' I'm not Kathleen, she says, but apart from that, you're right enough. 'I'm good at all that, accents, I can often tell.' Aye, but no good at names, she says to herself.

'Off the Upper Newtownards Road. I'm not wrong, I know I'm not.'

'Practically everything in East Belfast is off the Upper Newtownards Road, Tommy, so that's no great shakes.' But she is probably quite impressed by this time and leaning in, I would say. I know her.

'You're from Dundonald.'

'I am.'

'Dunlady Road.'

'I am!'

'Number 34.'

'How the fuck?' (Excuse my. Nicole has a tongue on her.)

'Your brother is called Sammy and your ma's a dinner lady.'

'You can't tell all that!' she shouted. Nicole smacked him on the leg before she remembered where she was, but he was so dosed with painkillers, it didn't matter, and he just laughed. Turned out brother Sammy was a goalie, and they had played five-a-side. Of course, Sammy had mentioned his mother was a dinner lady, because that's the sort of thing you mention.

'How did you know I was Sammy's big sister?'

'Because you're pretty, and everyone knows Sammy's big sister Kathleen. I mean, Nicole.'

That's how Nicole tells that story, and I don't think she's lying. They got chatting about home. Tommy wasn't long after arriving in England, was in digs himself, and was missing his mother's cooking. It undoubtedly did not help that he had just had his leg snapped. In short, he was miserable, and he made Nicole miserable, and that night she got back to her room and decided she was going to move back to Northern Ireland. She did not mention if she managed to smuggle Tommy past her landlady or if she even tried. Stairs might have been a problem for him. She came home, and shortly after she was married.

Well, things don't always turn out as you planned them. 'Biggest effin' mistake I ever made' is how big Nicole likes to put it.

Frank shifted his position as if he were uncomfortable with his nurse's language. It wasn't that; he was asleep still. It was the plasticated coating on his piss-proof mattress. He kept sliding to the bottom of the bed on his slippy sheets. Mandy pulled and tucked, and it was better again.

Nicole let a broken-legged footballer talk her into coming home here and getting hitched, and she can't let it go. It's true, when she went for senior ward assistant whatya-whatever, she never got it (Jeremy did), but in her head, that was all down to her having discontinuous service: 'They can't stand that I nursed overseas' is how she describes her stint in Geordieland. 'Just because I saw a bit of the world before I stopped all that and settled for here,' she says. Nicole can be a bit up herself, though I love her to bits: it's not as if Newcastle *is* anywhere, but that's the way she goes on.

Will she leave?

She might. She left her husband. She did that to focus on her career and because he was a bastard to her. Good on her for that. That probably took a bit of courage. So she could well leave. But I doubt it.

'Will you leave?' Now Frank was awake. He found himself again towards the bottom of his slippy bed.

Probably.

'Explain that one for me, would you, Mandy?'

There's get-up-and-go people, and there's sit-down-and-stay people. Nicole, for all that she got up fifty million years ago and went to Newcastle upon the centre of the universe, she only had to meet one wee Paddy with nice legs—one of them broken—before she hightailed it back home again. That's not oomph: she lacks a surprising amount of oomph for a divorcee. Which was exactly her feedback when Jeremy got that job over her. She moans like the devil about Northern Ireland being a societal wasteland, about how the Belfast scrawns have Hurricane Bloody Higgins to look up to as an athletic icon, our actors can't do Shakespeare, unless we are talking Kenneth Bloody Branagh and Shakespeare didn't write one-man shows, our restaurants serve seven types of chicken and seven types of potato and—if you're lucky—one type of vegetarian, which is hidden in the international/ gay section of the menu, and the politicians compete with each other in the useless Olympics. One half of our population won't support our football team because the team are not Irish enough, and the other half won't support them because they're rubbish at football. When we stopped killing each other, we started killing ourselves: we are experts in suicide, really good at it, come round here any night of the week for a lesson. To celebrate our contributions to world terrorism and naval disasters, we are making theme parks out of the Maze prison and the *Titanic*. We are morbid, inward, backward, and suspicious. This is all you get from Nicole. Never do you hear her say a word about the good side of things.

Frank had the need for drugs by now; his head was spinning. 'What would you say the good things are?' Mandy tugged at the sheets from under him, like why was he changing the subject?

Not now, Frank: try to keep up. We are talking about my good friend Nicole, and the downer she has about everything and everyone and how you might as well not plan for anything because nothing will come if it.

ɔ⁄ɔ

Frank was beginning to think that these were as much the views of his own nurse as they were of her colleague.

My son tells me I am mad for wanting to live here. He says I am mad for remembering news headlines and sick for wanting to. He is of an age now where I have to put up with such opinions, and, in any case, he might be right. I am always listening out for the news. He says I am paranoid, I have a condition. He means this in the clinical sense rather than the humorous one. And he thinks it's not just me. How many of me do you think there are, I ask, and he says that just there is a classic symptom. He says we are trapped by inertia, that in the end we must want the life here however bad for us it gets. He lives across the water. I have never been.

You have got to be mad to live in London, I say, not meaning the same thing. He sent me a photograph of the view from his office. He works for one of those City firms so he says his job is as safe as houses. But, if you ask me, how can you work at that height and not lose your head? They are literally in the clouds. The photograph has him in it, holding the wee boy—take-your-baby-to-work day—like he is saying all of this can be yours one day. The Thames, the Tower of London, Tower Bridge, the rest. I have never been. There was a message in there for me, for sure. Don't try to suggest I should do anything different with my life, because this is what I have here. I put the picture on the fridge, and then I put it in a frame and placed it on the kitchen window ledge beside one of me and Eilis. I look at it and then look out the window into the yard where I put up a slide.

It was a pity that Mandy and his son didn't know each other. Come to think of it, maybe they did! That wouldn't be so peculiar: she was clearly a person of advanced views, was probably only volunteering here for now as they obviously had a shortage of people trained to chat to the residents. His son also hated home, said that once—more than once to his face: I hate here.

(Do you remember that time you lost me? His son asked. And that toy VW Beetle I used to have?

We never lost you, son. You wandered away.

Maybe so, he admitted. I was getting some practice in.)

It turns out, I am the one who is hard to live with.

⊘⊙

It would be a shame if Mandy left, now when things were meant to be looking. 'Aren't things looking up for young people, you know, here?'

Mandy was at that moment checking her patient's temperature and heart rate. A bit hot, a bit fast, within range. Would you like to lie down for a bit, Frank, and catch a proper sleep?

'No!' Why would she think that? 'I asked you a question!' Maybe she was confused by *here*. 'Didn't you hear me?'

I heard you fine. Hold your, steady your horses. No need to take that tone with me. Things looking up for young people? By here, you mean here, I suppose?

Maybe, I can't say, I'm not an economist, if that's the word I want. Where should I start? The hoped-for peace dividend has yet to fully materialise, and, for now, the public sector is still over-dominant. We are subsequently too vulnerable to setbacks in the political sphere: if you will, power sharing and wealth creation are too closely aligned. Now, you would not want to come to me for fiscal advice, but the girls here say that now might be the time for the North to slash corporation tax to bring it into near-parity with the South and thereby level the inward investment playing field. We can build ships and planes and buses and trains, but we need to give the Japanese and Canadians incentives to come here: they have their own scenery; they'll not be over-impressed by ours. Our creative industries aren't looking too perky either. We've always had our share of poets and guitarists, but (this view is my own) they have for too long been trammelled by our dis-integrated education system: our artistic outlooks are embattled, besieged when they need to be embracing. So long as we continue to send Seamus to his school and Diane to hers, our singers will continue to sing songs about walls. The world out there has heard enough about walls already.

Like I say, I am no economist.

(You know, you are welcome here any time, his son had told him. Even Mum would like that. But you'd have to be dying for me to want to come back and see you at home in Northern Ireland.

Well, you are the name on my donor card, I say to him. So stand by.)

Frank had let his face turn away from the nurse. His mouth had fallen open, drool was drooling onto his pillow, yet he was still not asleep. Invisible little hands were churning his stomach, for hunger, for fear. Was he being kept here against his will? That nurse keeps tucking in the sheet at the end of the bed, trapping my feet like she plans to torture me later. When did he consent to being held here? If he had not agreed, who could have agreed on his behalf? He could not remember, though he felt vaguely sure that someone—maybe he—*had* agreed to his stay here. Here: that word again. He wanted not to think too hard about that; he preferred for now not to recall too clearly. There was something too massive about knowing that, and it had to do with the little hands churning his stomach. It was more important for now to know who had stolen his sweets and where his clothes had been taken to. Mandy said she knew, and he was not to worry. All the answers were contained on the board clipped to the end of his bed, which (he knew, without trying) was beyond his reach. So, if Mandy were to leave, how would he ever know what was going on? What hope was there for here without Mandy? She was the key to so much: to how he was here, to how he would leave here.

Will you leave?

Probably.

Explain that one for me, would you, Mandy?

I met a man recently, Mandy said, moving to lean against the darkened window behind Frank's bed. I was with Jeremy, walking in Botanic Gardens as we do sometimes when our shift finishes at twelve. Jeremy is my friend. We are not into each other. He's more like a little sister to me, though he hasn't started stealing my make-up. You would not believe the scrapes I have got him out of—I had better not say. I love the Botanic: there is a plan to the layout of the flowerbeds, but still they are a chaos of blue and pink and yellow and purple. You get a big stretch of sky above the Gardens on any given day, but on that day it was the clearest, palest blue. The brightness of the sky cast a uniform shade over the grass beneath, so the green was as dark as the sea. A little girl, wearing a startling red and yellow T-shirt, was all alone on a blanket on the grass having a one-person picnic, the purest concentration of happiness I have ever seen.

Anyway, this man I met. He was sitting on a bench, near the Palm House, feeding the birds with bits of his lunch. The birds were grey, but I don't think they were pigeons. Even though it was hot, those massive pampas were wafting breeze at him as if they were being operated by an invisible punkah wallah, so he was the coolest person in the park. And he was wearing a grey suit, with an off-white shirt and charcoal tie, and because he was rather young looking, he could have been one of those boys you spot in your class photograph whose face you've forgotten and whose name you are sure you never knew. Young looking, I would say his *face* looked young with no lines and no trace of facial hair, and his *body* was young looking in that he was slim and he could stretch forward to feed the birds without stooping. But he had old-man hair—still black but curling like muffs around his ears and patchy up top. When we got close to his bench (we wanted to sit), he looked up and suddenly gave us the most beautiful smile you ever saw. That was the surprising thing: that was the whole reason I am telling you this now. Spaced-out people can smile, and babies and simpletons can smile, and that can be beautiful: this was not one of those. This was like he already knew us, would know us better still in the future and that absolutely everything in the world was going to be okay. I thought maybe he was a patient (Jeremy said the same later), or he was famous and unusually humble. Whatever, I was sure he was in love with me. Did I mention he was Asian?

He stood up and said he was pleased to meet me, as if he had been expecting me. Evidently, I thought, he assumed we were someone else, someone he *had* been expecting. He was an academic from the university or a curator at the museum or a horticulturalist or aviarist. But Jeremy and I were nurses, both still in our nurses' uniforms, so no way could he take us for any of those things. He was simply excited to see us, specifically me. I can't say at what point it was that he took my hand in his—it was there before I knew that it was, and I made no effort to withdraw it because it felt natural that a stranger from India should be holding my hand by the pampas outside the Palm House in Botanic Gardens. Even Jeremy did not find it weird at the time, though he did when we talked about it later.

'Is he a magician, do you think?' Jeremy asked me when we were alone in the Studio restaurant in Stranmillis later. 'Misdirection, sleight of hand. I must say, he is not sleazy the way magicians often are, with their slick hair and greasy sleeves: he is clean, and he has the best teeth I ever saw.'

He called me Amanda like it was the name of an Oriental jewel, *amundah*. This jewel was jade or ruby, lost, mythologised, looted by invaders, and secreted by tribesmen. *Amundah.* There was no way of correcting him because he somehow had more knowledge of such things than I. He was a grave robber or an archaeologist or a smooth-talking conman. I agreed to meet him another day, alone, and in the Studio restaurant, Jeremy gave his blessing. 'Good teeth: he may have money' was Jeremy's take on it at that time. I am Amundah, and he is Raj. He said his name was Raj, but I don't think it is: that's just the name he reckons I can pronounce. Raj is a good enough name (imperial, majestic), but it's not his name if his name is Rajesh or Ramesh, Raghav, or Rajiv. Does he think I could not handle it if I knew his name was Raahithya, a wealthy man? Or I would be crippled by irony to learn he was Rudra, the reliever of pain? 'You are my balm,' he says to me, leaving me to guess at the pain he wants me to nurse him through. I have to say it irks me that he doubts me over such a small, important thing. I looked those names up. I might start calling him Ray.

I know a great deal about Raj-Ray aside from that. He is studying agriculture here so that he can inherit and run his father's wheat farm in Uttar Pradesh. He has a sister, who idolises him, and a younger brother, who cannot abide him. His mother is very wealthy, very bored, and consequently very fat. His father cannot wait to die. Raj is due to marry Riya when he returns to India, but Riya hates his guts (preferring the younger brother, I suppose). She advised him to marry an Irish girl, as a way of breaking the arrangement, and that's what he wants to do too. I'm the Irish girl he wants to marry. He has a car. I don't: I live in the city and there are buses to everywhere I need. Raj won't take a bus. He says, where he comes from, people who ride the bus don't inherit their father's farm. I say, where I come from, nurses take the bus and I am a nurse. He says that he loves that I am a nurse—I am his balm. We drive in his car, and now I have been to places that I have never been to before. We went to Newcastle—*our* Newcastle—which is amazing, by the way, with the beach and the mountains, and Raj even sang an Irish song about it, badly but at least he knew it. I didn't. He parked the car on the beach. I think Raj does not trust sand: I took his shoes and socks off him and rolled the legs up of his trousers, and it was like he was a man who wanted anaesthetic before encountering nature. How do you manage in a field? I asked him, but he insisted that earth was a different matter: the shore is a shifting thing, he said, seductive but unreliable, not the ground beneath your feet but the crumbling edge of the world. One should hesitate before one leaves firm ground. I forced him; he did it for me. The sand is soft, it tickles, I said. It, a grain, is organic matter reduced to its smallest seeable form, stretched out on a plain for our pleasure. It was warm, I took some clothes off to sunbathe, and Raj removed his shirt in an act of courage. His body surprised me. It wasn't scrawny the way I had imagined an Indian man's body to be. I watched *Gandhi* when it came out. His shoulders were sloped like the Mournes, his stomach rippled like a beach after the tide. And it was brown. People would notice that. Every ploughing season and every harvest since he was a child his father had made him work the family's fields after long days at school, until he ended up with the body of a labourer and the mind of an intellectual. The disjunction embarrassed him. I told him it shouldn't. I told him I loved him.

'So, will you leave?' Frank was forgetting his selfish reasons for wanting Mandy to stay with him, moved by the love story of Amundah and Raj.

Probably not.

'Explain that one for me, would you, Mandy?'

Because there are get-up-and-go people and sit-down-and-stay people.

'You said you were the former!'

I did? I did. But chatting to you here this evening has made me realise how much I would miss if I upsticked to India.

'It has?' But that didn't make any sense. All Frank had talked to her about was murdering showmen and gunrunning for terrorists, and Jimmy Cash was the only one among any of them who had made anything at all of his life, and to do that, he had had to leave the country, so why was Mandy here saying that it all made her pine to stay at home when she should have been hearing the opposite message like his son had? A short while ago, he was desperate for her to stay; but since then, he had heard that things were not necessarily looking up for young people here, and a person of her acumen and acuity ought to make her own way in the big wide world. You would have to be mad to want to stay here, here.

'You ought to go.'

'I don't want to go.'

'You have nothing to lose.'

'I have everything to lose.'

'You love him?'

'I love him.'

'You could be happier there.'

'I could be happier here.'

'But where, after all, is here?' This question slipped Frank's mouth before he could haul it back in. Here ought to be the easiest place to know. It has to be wrong not to know here; but where, after all, are his clothes if he is in the right place?

'Here is where I am. Here is always where I am, it cannot be anywhere else.'

'You cannot be there?'

'*You* can be there, but I can only be here.'

But I only sometimes know where I am when I am here. I might be on a boat, in a cabin, comfortably in bed like it was my bed but on the move, going somewhere I can't see where because the windows are dark. Or I might be in a hospital bed—the very definition of an alien, unwelcome, *there* place, for all that it has a comfortable mattress and warm blankets just like home. She says she is a nurse, which is why she is here. But that does not explain why I am here. I am slipping again.

'Is it important that you love him?'

'It's not important that I love him. It's important in the end that I love someone, I suppose. It doesn't have to be Raj.'

'But you do love him? I remember you said you did.'

'I did say that. I said it ten seconds ago. I said it to him. I did at that moment. I do at this moment. Love has its moments. Moments like that are pure and honest, and so precious I worry that I am the only one noticing.' Mandy was still standing by the darkened window, behind her patient's head propped as it was by pillows, as much then his invisible visitor as his nurse. 'Maybe you can't trust something like that.'

Explain that one for me, would you, Mandy?

A moment like that can be pure and honest, but it has a hard shape too. A moment is a point, a pivot, a triangle with before and after tilting up tilting/ down; a moment is ambivalent, it really doesn't care what happens next, it cancels itself out and has precisely no bearing on the outcome. All that love invested in moments is not to be trusted.

Raj and I were walking along the Embankment, here in the city, and it started to rain. Sometimes, I think in Belfast that the rain comes straight from the River Lagan, streaky and sulphurous. Wherever I am, rain is just rain but when I'm in Belfast, I see it as *Belfast* rain. Then I catch myself on. This day, it was raining hard, my umbrella was busted as always, and my jeans were sucking the puddles up from below. So I was feeling good, and I said so. 'I love the rain!'

'This isn't rain,' he said, insulting my city's rain, sticking his hand out from under his own busted umbrella as if he had only just noticed. 'We wouldn't call this rain in Uttar Pradesh.'

I tried to say that rain was the same, scientifically, wherever you are.

'You can only say that because you have never experienced monsoon,' he said. 'A monsoon is like the ocean turned upside down. The drops, when they hit hard ground, bounce so high that they fall again as rain. Indian rain is Indian water, holy from the Ganges, profane from the sewers. The rain smells of *us*, our bodies and curries and chutneys, of tea, of rice, of my father's wheat.'

For some reason, this was a moment. From this moment on, it mattered that we were from different places: I was here, and he was there.

You are a farmer, I told him. You study this subject. You know this is nonsense. Or only poetry. He didn't know, or he wouldn't know it. Rain is just evaporation and condensation; a raindrop is a million water droplets from a cloud. Rain is magic enough without having to belong to anyone. There is no special Belfast rain and no special rain in Uttar Pradesh—just sometimes more of it.

I'm not sure love can outlast too many conversations like that.

That sounded true enough. To Mandy, it sounded true enough. To Frank, it sounded like a fairy tale of rubies and magical rain.

For a second, less than a second, sleep grabbed him and pulled him under. It took all his power to pull himself to the surface again.

'Mandy. Mandy, that's your name, yes? Mandy, I am scared.'

'I know you are, Frank. We can keep talking if you like.'

'Mandy, you ought to go.' You don't need a footballer or a farmer, but you ought to go.

CHAPTER IX

Footballer or farmer or anyone at all, you ought to go. You're right, Mandy: it doesn't matter if you love Raj, just that you do love someone.

'You can't always get what you want, Frank.'

You can't always get what you want, that's true. I am scared, Mandy. Do the people here really know what they are doing? Do they know what to do with me?

'You've nothing to worry about, Frank.'

You don't know the half of it. Is there news, have you heard any news today, can you get the news here in a hospital? Was that man arrested yet? That man that killed that man?

'What man, Frank?' Mandy glanced involuntarily at the police officer sitting, possibly sleeping, on the chair in the corridor. 'You watched the news earlier. Then you watched your match. Jeremy looked after you there.'

He did, he did all right. No bombs today, if I recall. There was my cancellation. And that other man in the bed we forgot about: they haven't got the man who killed him, I can say for certain.

'There's not been a bombing for a good while, thank God. The old boys are the peacemakers these days.'

If you believe that, you. I've not had my letter in the post from McCann, formal cessation of hostilities towards yours truly. Still check my kneecaps, and under my car, every day. They can still drive you off the road, when you're not careful.

'Did they ever . . .'

You know what they did with touts. There *was* a thing on the news about that, now I remember. The British ran their super-tout right to the top of the Republican movement, till he was directing operations and informing on them at the same time. He was big fry. I'm not talking about big fry, I'm talking about the small fry, the type of fry that doesn't make it on to the news—not now, not then, not even when you do your damnedest to get it on the news. Wee touts, wee scallywags without the common sense to realise they'll get caught. See a man round here with a finger missing and you'll know why. You know why anyway, it's in your line of.

'Why are we talking about touts?'

Ryan, let me remind you, was a loudmouth. When Cullycreggan blew up in his face, everyone in Suzy's—and, I assume, everyone in the other bars and private places where these things are discussed—knew what he had been up to, and mention of Jim's name was not far behind. Jim was the brains behind the device, and the device had been a dud, so what kind of genius was Jim? Genius enough not to have been at the scene himself, genius enough to catch the boat to Liverpool as soon as. Suzy's knew about Jim because Ryan was a loudmouth. *I have wee Jimmy,* he would say, *you remember from around here, Scotchman, got himself an education and now he's fixing me a bomb to put where his big mouth is. Has a high opinion of himself, if you ask me,* he would tell all and sundry in Suzy's. *I sure shut him up when I showed him the job I had in mind!* Who else did they know about? Did they know about the driver? Rather, did they know about the *intended* driver, me? Or (may he rest) did Ryan take that nugget to the grave with him? In which case, only Cash knew about me. Jim Cash never uttered a word: that's certain. So, why did I have to start looking over my shoulder? And under my car and in my post and.

'Didn't you say you had got a man called Quinn to do your driving for you then? You called someone called Quinn?'

What's that, did I say that, did I tell you that, you better watch who you tell that sort of thing to. You could get a body into difficulties.

'I didn't mean.'

That's all right. There *was* a Quinn, yes. Quinn never really went away. And he could have a mouth on him too, so, yes. Yes, there was that to contend with. So checking under the car and the van and so on was just common sense from my point of view. What we did next is on our own conscience only. Let's just say that Quinn is himself no longer in the reckoning. He's another who opened his big mouth once too often. Paid for it in the end, you might say. Which also begs the question: Who, Missie, is paying for my time here? I am not tight, but I don't recall booking this, and I would have comments to make before I paid a cent of my own money. For one thing, they've given me a plastic mattress like you'd give a child you didn't trust, and these pyjamas—I have since discovered—have no arse in them. What's that about.

'It's a hospital, Frank, you daft eejit. Nobody pays! And I sincerely hope you have no complaints about me?'

No complaints from here about you: you are the good one. You know when to keep quiet. Hospital, yes, I know, they want to open me up. That's why for me the restaurant is shut, why I am being starved.

'Were you threatened, Frank? Did they say you were an informer?'

I'm going nowhere. You go if you want to. That was how Eilis reacted every time I mentioned putting all of this behind us. I thought maybe an extended holiday, a cottage out of season over the border, something cheap, I knew a man. Even when the boy was born, she could not be persuaded. Often a drive out, but no further. *You should take what's coming to you* was her view, as if I deserved a kneecapping. She just took my wanting to leave as another attack on the singing career that she wasn't having. The States, we could go there: they love an Irish accent in the States, I said, they love an Irish girl who can sing. She did think about that one, for all of five seconds, and then it was back to You need your head examined, you never stop running, you never mind what or who you leave behind. *You just wish you had gotten away with Jimmy Cash when he did. As if they would have any need of you over in Africa!*

📖

Going with Cash was never even. I doubt if Betty would. That wasn't. Eilis had gotten the wrong end of that one. Though she was right about Africa not being the sort of place for. For me. The Republic, maybe; America at a push. Instead, I was doing the worst sort of job for someone who, to save his bacon, needed to check under his car and look over his shoulder: I was a driver for Robert Tubby, as in private driver, as in the American technology firm I was working for all along, as in Bobby Tubby. You might remember the name.

Well, you should. Mr Tubby was a gent, of course. He could chew the face off of any man in the company, crush them under his fag-stained Chelsea boot, humiliate them until they smelled and their pants were wet, but he was never anything but kindness itself to me, and to Eilis for that matter. He would send over tins of canned pork to us, especially imported from America, like he thought we were all still fighting the War. In fact, I'm certain he did think that. He had all his food imported because he was under the impression that we were all too poor to have shops. How that man ever ran a business, I'll never know. He had fought in the War . . . Italy . . . Monte Cassino . . . '44 . . . shitstorm, I doubt he ever recovered. He gave us sweets for the boy, like he was a GI still. All that hollering at other people, that was the PTSD, which we had no name for then unless you could call it shellshock. Bobby Tubby's wife—always just 'Mrs Tubby'—was herself a victim of the War because she was a victim of him. The car was like a home on wheels. Aside from a chilled cabinet he could keep Coke in, he had a car phone he could use in the back, which he used to shout at Mrs Tubby while he was on his way home to her. He would catch me glancing at him in the rear-view, and he would do that head thing that men do when they expect no comeback for beating on their wife. 'You gotta see my wife to believe her, Frank,' he would say. 'Small, like a hamster, quivering black eyes. Never stands up for herself. Your wife like that, Frank?' No, sir. 'No, I bet she ain't, I bet she ain't.' I bet she gives as good as she gets, your wife, he went on. I was driving on the Shore Road or in Ligoniel, or someplace like that, eyes on the road. I bet you your wife can stand up for herself, am I right, no don't answer, I know the answer. Mr Tubby didn't have to be told much he did not already know. Eyes on the road, me. I told him that Eilis was a singer. 'We Americans love an Irish girl who can sing,' he said, offering no examples. You'd love to hear Eilis sing, I said, then wished I could take it back because what if he actually did want to hear her, where should I suggest he go, which particular Belfast dive should I direct him to? But he dropped the subject; of course, he did, it disgusted him.

'Disgusted him?'

Is that too strong, do you think, Mandy? He was a Howard Hughes clean freak. He was the CEO of a tech company that sucked the dust out of the very air for fear it would interfere with the circuitry. My duties with the car included polishing it outside and in, and he always sat alone distantly on the back seat. I think even the word 'singer' evoked for him smoke and ash and, who knows, fluids of the kind. The man was a freak. *He ate his pork from a sealed can.* He was easily disgusted. He liked me as a driver because I wore gloves in all weathers.

The car was a Rover (or it was for most of the time I was driving him). You'd think he would prefer an American, but Tubby was an oddity all round. When I wasn't driving him, I was allowed it for my own use. That was never an official perk, never written down anywhere, because to do so would have involved completing tax declarations and insurance disclaimers. It was never in my name. I had it, I kept it clean, Tubby was never kept waiting. Lovely car to drive, a Rover, smooth and quiet when it wasn't breaking down. God protect me if it ever broke down with him inside it. *What's this? I can't sit here! What have you done? Who's that approaching us out there? Get us moving again!* You'd never believe this man liberated Italy. Maybe it's the price you pay for liberating Italy. I mean, maybe you can't go through extraordinary experiences like that and expect to be normal at the end of it. This stuff affects you—you know what my son's views are on the matter. He thinks we're all mad, but psycho-mad not just bonkers-mad, your uncle pissing his bed in the night because he has literally no one in the world. He ate pork from a tin. Bobby Tubby would only take a piss if he was at the firm or in his own house. We could be at a meeting in the Northern Ireland Office, for example, and he'd be twitching, I could see from the side, he always had me in the room with him not to say anything, but just in case he started twitching, *I'm twitching* was his way, his way of saying he needed a piss and I had to get him out of there and back to his office sharpish. *I'm not going there, I know what's been there.* He'd be quiet on the way back, not reading his papers or talking, conserving his energy, keeping himself in so to speak, trying not to soil himself and the Rover. With him, it was a mental thing that had become a physical one: it wasn't simply that he didn't want to piss in another man's bowl, but that he tried and he couldn't. Taut pelvic floor. Lift not going down. Thoughts in his head. *I'm a man, I have children, I can piss with pride. Just a dribble, a dribble would tide me over.* Nope. *Get me outta here!* He twitched. He never soiled himself on the back seat, but he would sometimes cry. He would catch me glancing at him in the rear-view, and he would do that head thing that men do, holding his chin up but pretending he hadn't seen me, as if there is only shame if there is a witness. You're not guilty of the things people accuse you of, just the things they see you do.

'Bobby Tubby. Was he the one who?'

Not an easy name to forget, surprised it took you this long. Before you wonder: no, I was not the driver on that occasion either. Another notch on my stick. I am charmed, see. Not me, it was a Monday, and I didn't work Mondays on account of I did work Saturdays, but Monday was a day I couldn't use the car for myself because Tubby *did* work Mondays, he worked nearly every bloody day, so he would pick a random guy to drive him then. On this occasion, it was, it was, it doesn't matter who it was, you don't know him. The point is it wasn't me. And it was *supposed* to be me. *They* thought it was me. That's the only explanation.

Round my way, driving a racing green Rover is an ostentatious thing to do. A Rover is a *British* car, it's practically at that point in time the only damn car the British build, you might as well be driving a Union Jack as a Rover. It's a big target. There is a lot of chassis you can hide a bomb under, if you are in the car bomb business. I would check under the car every morning, and, on the mornings I didn't, my son did because I had trained him. Everyone did that back then, in particular everyone who drove a Rover. I had no special reason for thinking I would be targeted, just a general impression that, for some, Cullycreggan was not done with, and would not be done with until I had been done with. These people, suspicious, wanted to know why the police knew not to be in harm's way when the Cullycreggan bomb went off, and why Ryan and the driver were.

'And the driver?'

For these people, there's always a tout about, and I—for some—fitted the bill. Word had gotten out that I had passed on the opportunity to drive to Cullycreggan. Ergo. If it wasn't Cash (and it *could* have been Cash), then it might have been me. I might be the. It could not be chance: the security forces could not simply have been having a lucky night. Someone must have informed them. And we know what happens to people who. Not just a finger here or a kneecap there. For a job of this size, reprisal would be mighty. So I— or the boy—checked under the car every time. Except on Monday mornings, when the car overnighted at the firm. That's the sort of minimal information you would reasonably expect a person of criminal intelligence to collect. If you want to get Frank, try a Tuesday. Mr Tubby was setting off early that day, that Monday. He'd had his piss ahead of an anticipated long journey to Dublin. Dublin trips, for that reason, were a nightmare for him. He was in the back, on the phone to his darling wife, fiddling with papers concerning the deal he was set to do with some dodgy Irish minister. The driver, whose name was, whose name doesn't matter, you don't know him, the driver just turned the key—that's all. *He* didn't check under. Which is almost impossible to believe. Part of the job description then. But there it is.

'Do you think it should have been you, Frank?'

Should, as in did I deserve it? No thank you very much. *Should,* as in was I the intended? That's a thought I was not allowed to keep to myself for very long. *That one was for you, Frank,* people were kind enough to say. But, in the first instance, that was not what people were saying. Press attention was on Bobby Tubby and his suspect dealings with the Irish, his suspect dealings with many others besides. He was corrupt, taking backhanders for himself or for the firm, backhanders the government called incentives, incentives to set up shop in Northern Ireland in the first place, to build a technology factory in Northern Ireland when no one in their right mind would do such a thing. According to them—the press—the bomb was right under his seat, blew him out arse first, precious little left of him, or the car for that matter. According to them—the Republicans—he was an economic target, killed for giving financial succour to the illegitimate whatever statelet blah blah. According to them—people—his darling wife heard it all over the car phone. She heard the blast itself or the buzz of interference or the silence that followed. She had the tinnitus still at the funeral.

'You went?'

It's always ringing in my ears, she repeated, *I can't get it out!* She kept ramming the butts of her hands into her earholes, like that would help.

Millions of tiny particles of sound lodged in my ear, she cried. A little tiny woman, dwarfed by the outsized box they had her war-hero husband in and the hulking pallbearers who carried his box away. Quivering, shiny crying eyes like a hamster. People didn't know how to comfort her. Yes, I went. Ahem. I owed it.

'What does that mean?'

Eilis went too.

'What does it mean, you owed it?'

I owe. Do you know Eilis was not well for a long time. She is not her best yet. Better, but not her best. And I know for a fact that Betty, for all that she hated it in Ireland, wanted nothing more than to be back here. And Cash too. The fact that he had left meant that he could not come back: in his case, flight and guilt were the same thing. I am charmed, like I said. I have a notch stick. I owe. I have to at least go to the funerals.

'Who was the driver? What was his name?'

I told you, it doesn't matter, you don't know him.

'I'm not talking about Bobby Tubby.'

You're not talking about Bobby Tubby. I have told you everything about the other, about Cullycreggan.

You haven't.

Did you say something? I haven't? I have.

You didn't drive?

No, I told you. I asked Quinn. He said he would drive.

But he didn't.

He didn't.

Who did?

I can't say, Mandy. Let's just admit that I owe him too.

☙❧

'You should be asleep. You will need your strength.' Mandy tried to pull the pillows from behind her patient.

'Get away, will you, for heaven sake! Strength, my arse! What, I need strength to fall asleep now under general anaesthetic?' Frank straightened his arms outside of his blankets, down each side of his body, as if to pin himself into position. 'You leave if you want to, if you have better to do, don't mind me, I understand, you nurses are worked off your. Get on with, I won't take offence.'

'Will you agree to try to sleep if I leave you?'

'I will not.'

'Then, I may as well stay.' Mandy picked up the clipboard from the end of Frank's bed. That's what a nurse is supposed to do, thought Frank, *that* and not *this*: they were not meant to keep their patients up all night. She checked the upside-down watch at her breast, she licked the nib of her pen, and she made the notes he was never meant to see. What would she write about me? Frank wondered: has she been writing down my statement all along, and I didn't notice? What have I been saying? Have I said more than I should? Me and my loud mouth. I am no informant, but I should have held my tongue once in a while.

I am not a tout. Are you listening, Amanda? *Amundah?* That really is a pretty name, if it's all right to say that. Right now, with everyone asleep, with total silence but for all the machines keeping people alive, I can call you what I like. I am not now, and was not then, an informant of any kind. It's official, in writing, in the records for all to see, beyond doubt for all but the evil bastards who refuse to read or believe what they read. It's a settled affair. I saw to that.

It would be the thirty-year rule—was it thirty years—the time after which it's deemed safe to release documents that are too prejudicial to public safety to release sooner. Presumably they have calculated that all affected parties are already deceased. It's like when your copyright expires and any Joe can publish your stuff without your permission: the Public Records Office can release all this because you yourself have already expired. Or not, but so what. It was this January gone. You won't remember because, like the rest of the universe, your attention was instead on the document dump relating to the Daytona Showband massacre. All that occurred on the same day, don't forget.

The Daytonas were frequent cross-border tourists. They would come in at Derry or Newry, turn up in Armagh or Enniskillen, willy-nilly, like they were keeping people guessing. So far, so very sensible precaution for anyone at that time wishing to avoid being tracked and blown off the face of the earth. There were death threats: in the PRO release, they actually had two of them in full, alongside the recommendation to the band by the RUC to regularly change up their route and check under their bus for bombs. This went on for some months, but the threats kept coming, and so the Daytonas accepted the offer of a discreet police escort, described as 'unmarked', at a distance and 'from the point of crossing to the performance venue'. Some junior in the Home Office questioned the expense of all this but was roundly put down: 'The Daytona Showband in particular and the show band phenomenon in general are essential for our efforts to maintain a semblance of equilibrium in the province.' I have the words memorised. The last thing that the government in Northern Ireland wanted at that time was for the massacre that did take place to take place. On the night it happened, on the night when Eilis was to relive her finest moments on stage with them, when her when she, on that night the RUC escort went missing on the A1 near Hillsborough, 'called to an incident in Cullycreggan'. You heard right: the time the RUC went walkabout was the exact time the IRA decided to make an example of a bunch of popular singers and musicians. The band's bus was blasted into a field. (For all to see, on Gloria's TV.) It took a full ten minutes after an emergency call from the public for the police to show up. The deceased were named as David Black and Seamus McDowell from the Irish Republic, and Sean Hamill from County Londonderry. Cynthia Sorley was listed among the injured, expected to survive. Also in the papers was a letter to the police chief by a civil servant on behalf of the Stormont prime minister, with a sentence underlined by the PM himself in purple pencil: 'I wish for there to be no blame attached to your escort officers for any perceived failings on their part. *Information that may, or may not, have been known about IRA intentions could not reasonably have been acted upon in the heat of unfolding events.*' I have memorised those words too. Paperclipped to this was a memorandum dated one month thence, rejecting the suggestion of an enquiry on the grounds that it might 'diminish confidence in the security forces at a time of heightened tensions'. Do you remember, from January? The nationalist press called it a cover-up: 'Nothing to see here.' The suggestion was that the police knew of a specific plot on that night to murder the Daytonas and that they let it happen. Why that should be was harder to fathom, and the documents in the Public Records Office gave no help there. That the RUC—or elements within—should find common cause with the IRA – or elements within – gave the newspapers plenty to write about, now that in the peacetime we have these days, the police and Republicans give the papers precious little to write about. One theory was that, due to a high-placed police informant at the top of the movement, the IRA had had a few too many of their atrocities foiled, so, to protect this super-tout, they had to be granted at least one spectacular success.

'I don't follow the news quite as religiously as you, Frank,' Mandy said, as if she should apologise. 'Of course, I remember all about the Show band—well, not *all* about the Show band—but I do remember them vaguely, I remember there *was* a show band, and I remember there was an atrocity associated with that—that's the sort of thing anyone of any age here would know about, I should think—but as for the details of that . . . Wasn't Clodagh Rodgers (you said something about her before), wasn't she in that band, one of the Daytonas?'

'Now, isn't that a funny thing?' said Frank, a bit amused, a bit dismayed. 'There was a Clodagh Rodgers connection, but not in the way you remember it. It's a funny thing that you should have a memory of something that was not true, that never. I may have inadvertently. I may have put that in your head when I said Eilis had the look of Clodagh Rodgers the first night I saw her sing in Slieveban with the Daytona Showband. You remembered the association, where there wasn't one. And yet there was a journalist—I knew her even, or I made a point of getting to know her—who did try to connect those two things, who wrote about it in. Colour photos, a Sunday, interview with Rodgers herself, who is still alive, though I don't think she. Anymore. Sings, that is.'

I watched this journalist at work. Emma Cooper was her name, quite well known now, but that's not important. I was in the Public Records Office looking at the thirty-year disclosure of documents related to the Cullycreggan fiasco. Cooper was there, poring over every paper she could find on Clodagh Rodgers. Would you believe. There was I, fretting over the cruel fact that nobody in the world was interested in my Cullycreggan story; there she was—a journalist with the power to exonerate me—writing about the Eurovision bloody Song Contest.

'Exonerate?'

No less. For most of those thirty years, looking under my car or teaching my son to, evading death because I didn't work on Mondays, the fine folk of Suzy's had my name down on the same list as Judas Iscariot and et tu, Brute. I hadn't driven the car; someone else had, and he died along with the criminal mastermind Ryan. Ergo, I must have dobbed them in, or I might have, I had the means. The fact that I never had, and never would do such a thing, was no odds. I stayed away from Suzy's; I stayed away from the town altogether. The fact I stayed away also counted against me, though it was hardly the same as catching a ferry for Rhodesia. I was not number one suspect, but I was on their list. Then, just January past, the British government, in all their beautiful wisdom, decided to release every document on the affair that they had and put them on public display at the PRO in Belfast.

'Frank, you always call it just "the town". Why is that? It's not that I care, but I have noticed you never say: you make a point of not saying.'

And these papers—I have read them, re-read them, memorised them—would put me in the clear. I wrote notes. I would not say my notes were verbatim. But, if no one was going to read the original documents, then they might read my summary of them. I made sure that my notes quite clearly stated that the police had no prior intelligence of the attempted ambush of security forces at Cullycreggan. *The device, had it not been detonated prematurely, could have caused multiple deaths to the border police nearby,* was one. *Contrary to established practice,* said another, *no warning was called in.* Finally: *None of the assets within the Republican movement provided any useful intelligence of this operation.* And did the newspapers splash this all over their front pages? Not a bit of it. The Daytonas and Rodgers got all the attention. From the point of view of the newspapers, if the story from Cullycreggan was 'no information', then it was 'no story'. The *Irish News* readers in Suzy's and elsewhere in the town remained in blissful, prejudicial ignorance.

'What town?'

In steps Emma Cooper. Hair, I might describe as 'dirty black', skin a shade of pencil; with her accent, she had the ability to make her first name and surname rhyme. *Ermerkerper.* She, as I say, was hard at work on the Clodagh Rodgers story. Jesus preserve us. All kinds of everything.

'I know that: Dana.'

Right. The Eurovision was in Dublin because our Dana had won it the year before, and that's the way Europe shares its prizes. Royaume-Uni thought to itself, who better to send over to war-torn Ireland to fly the flag than a girl from Northern Ireland, and a Roman Catholic no less? Clodagh from Ballymena was a perfect patsy. Who cares if she was just a Jack-in-the-box, a toy used up when it stops? In she springs, fringed in pink. Comes fourth. No disaster. But the death threats flood in. That was the point of the thirty-year gag: the Ballymena sweetheart was subject to an ugly campaign of violence-by-letter, which they decided at the time to be quiet about. Who decided, who decides? It could have finished her. Give Clodagh credit, though: she kept working even if the hits didn't follow. More *Seaside Special* than *Top of the Pops*. I think that might have been one of the points Emma Cooper was trying to make: some of the innocence, some of the life—literally—went out of Irish clubland music. Who sings songs about bouncing on their spring when there is a shrapnel-filled box primed under your seat? You don't say your name if you don't have to, Mandy, and you don't say where you are from. 'The town' is fine. It's a habit I have not lost. Eilis and I carved our names on a tree once, leaving our trace, leaving our evidence, saying *it was us*. But, when men in uniform can stop you in the street and demand your name, do people still do that? Did people still carve their name? We all have a bench, a tree, a street where we cherished our dreams: a childhood that has been too short.

'That's sweet. Do you sing, Frank?'

I sing when Eilis sings. And I hum when she's not there. But the sort of innocent, guileless pop that Clodagh Rodgers—and Eilis—specialised in, that the Daytonas were masters at: that was cut short.

'Who won?'

How can there be a winner?

'Who won Eurovision?'

Monaco. I don't always remember the stuff I need to remember, but this shit comes easy to me. Eilis remembers it too. Eilis always had something of Clodagh about her: strong voice, never sweet, clear as a bell, sometimes slipping to shrill; glamorous, not quite sexy—though always, to me, she was. 'If Clodagh can't make it, how can I?' she would sometimes say, somehow still accusing me. I don't think she has ever lost that, that sense of guilt, my guilt.

୧ଠ୨

'Do you want to stop there, Frank?' For the first time, Mandy touched her patient's hand. She noticed he had no tissues by his bedside. No flowers, no card, no bottle to drink from. She felt sorry for this man who had not done wrong. 'It's a shame. About your wife. That she never quite.'

'Did you see Eilis when she came in earlier?' His cheek was still wet, but Frank had stopped crying. 'A fine-looking woman still, don't you think? She never lost that, Eilis, never lost . . . what is that? Self-regard? Self-worth? That makes her sound just vain. But, after all, is vanity such a bad thing? In moderation? She never lost the sense that, however good she looks, she should look her best. She knows what lipstick suits her, what scarf to wear with what. Sometimes make-up is armour, and sometimes it's a weapon, and sometimes it's none of those things. She knows it makes me proud to see her beautiful. That's not why she does it, but she does know it makes me proud. It does. There are worse things.'

'No,' admitted the nurse. 'I don't think I could have been on duty when your wife came in. What time was that?'

'God knows. How long have I been here?'

'Just today, Frank. You were brought in yesterday evening.'

'Really?' Frank dipped his head, aware of his confusion now and ashamed of it. 'I thought it was longer,' he whispered. Freeing his hand from hers, he wiggled his fingers slowly to make a show of counting, but it was no use. 'She must have come in with me.'

The nurse shook her head but said nothing. She had been on duty when her patient was admitted, and he was alone then. It was a thing to remark upon for a man in his state. She remembered the police officer being around. It was lucky that they found an organ donor card on him with an emergency contact on the back. They called his son.

'You were maybe on one of your walks with your male nurse when she came in,' said Frank, now with a smile.

116

'No doubt, you're right, Frank.' That suddenly felt like a thing to celebrate. After a pause, to think, she asked, 'Frank, is there anything you want? Is there anything I can get you?'

Frank did not need to think. 'Mandy, indeed there is! You can help me out of this bed and escort me to the loo in such a way as I don't embarrass myself. Is that too much?'

'No, Frank, it is not! Just swing your legs out, if you may.'

She helped him there, and she helped him back. Back in the ward, there were two unoccupied beds. Frank shuffled towards the one still empty from the patient who died there earlier. Did he think it was his, or was he simply paying his respects? He turned, as if to sit on the edge of this bed. No, no, not there. Mandy eased her patient round, back towards his own bed. Sore, unsteady, he still bent down to check underneath. All clear. With his nurse's help, Frank climbed back into his own bed and pulled the covers up to his chin.

'I'll leave you now to sleep.'

'You will not.'

'But you need your sleep.'

'For what do I need my sleep?'

'For your strength. Like I said before, you need your strength.'

'What do I need to be strong for? Sure, I'm not going anywhere, I'm only staying here. As long as I can afford it.'

'I told you: it's free.'

'Oh, yes. You did. My mind!' Frank knocked the side of his head and gave it a comic wobble.

The stuff I do—and the stuff I don't—remember. Stop—don't say you'll put me down. Love—don't go away. Drop my feet back on the ground. Open your arms, let me stay. She, Eilis, loved that song and she loved Clodagh. *I could have done that song in Dublin*, she said. *Nothing wrong with my voice, or my look. If they wanted an Irish girl, they need have looked no further. But no. Sad Eilis wouldn't do.* She was sad a lot after the *Panadol*. Still. She would sing all the time, my Eilis: arms in the sink, heating a bottle for the boy, all the time. Not quietly, not just to herself, but like she was performing it, arms aloft to encourage the audience. In the bedroom, in the kitchen, in the shops. Sometimes, she would do that in front of other people, which is when. She needed. I had. You can't go singing out loud in Belfast and expect people to. Ha, you can laugh about it now! In front of others, but. We had to have that sorted.

ᕙ⊙ᕗ

That stuff, I remember. So, God help us, Emma Cooper thought the story of the day was the silencing of Clodagh Rodgers after Eurovision and the coincidence of this with the massacre of the Daytonas. I showed an interest. I bought her a coffee, told her about Eilis being a singer too. No, she did not know the name. *That's her professional name*, I added, not wanting to give the game away.

'So your wife was meant to be supporting the Daytona Showband on the night they were killed?'

She was. She was devastated. She was brave, yes. It did affect her, yes, but you know.

'Things move on, I know.' What did she know? 'Did she know them well? Was Sean Hamill as brilliant as they say?'

Cynthia Sorley was her friend.

'I would love to interview Sorley for this piece. Do you think your wife . . . Are they still?'

No. No, they aren't still. Cynthia, I heard, moved back home to Dublin. Santry. Something tells me Santry, Dublin. She lost most of her face. (*Catastrophic facial injuries*, said the records I helped Emma Cooper find.) It's the most important part, isn't it, your face? Worse than a smashed-up leg or a lost voice. Jim Cash had a harelip, which sometimes gave you the impression he had two faces—which is bad, but not as bad, nothing like as having no face. Having nothing to face the world with, no means to face up to the challenge, the years ahead. You remove the face and you remove the possibility of using the word.

'Why don't you go see Cynthia?' I asked Eilis months after Cullycreggan.

'How can I go and see her? How can I . . . her now?' Eilis, applying make-up to her. Putting on her best. Preparing to . . . the punters in the pub she was singing in. I could tell she wanted to. But Cynthia had been so beautiful. That was such a lot to have lost, on top of everything else she had lost. 'Dublin is such a long way to go, for a day,' she reasoned. It is not. 'I don't think I can f . . . crossing the border.'

We dropped it there.

No, they are no longer in touch, I told Cooper. Moved back to Dublin, I assume. You could look up 'Sorley' in a telephone directory, that might be worth a try.

'Are you hungry? I'm starving!' she said. We had lunch, a packet cheese sandwich in the PRO. She had crisps with it. She paused between crunches.

I said nothing, waiting for her to say something, something other than about Daytona Rodgers. That took a while. Crunch, crunch.

'So,' she said eventually, 'why exactly are you here?'

Well, Emma, glad you got around to asking that, because I really need you to do the most massive favour for me, though the favour is more from me to you because—believe it or not—the story that I have that you are not writing is much more important than the one you are writing, if I may say so. I tell her about Cullycreggan. She, naturally, knows nothing.

Two young lads, a bomber and his driver, take a van to the border with the intention of blowing the guard to high heaven. The bomb is defective. It explodes on the lap of the guy in the van. The Guards, who should have been nearby, are nowhere around so get away without a scratch. The bomber, the driver: not a chance.

It's all in those documents, I say, pointing back towards the desks we had been working at before we broke for a cheese sandwich. Released, like yours, under the thirty-year rule. As of routine.

'I see,' Emma Cooper says, clearly not seeing. Then perhaps seeing something after all: 'Did you know these men?'

Did I know them? Would it take this to interest my journalist in my story?

See here? I say, pointing at the notes I have taken into the cafe with me. See: we are from the same town. We would, we would have known each other, of course, it's a small place, a one football team sort of place. You wouldn't know it, I can't even say for sure you can find it on most maps. Even I haven't been there in ages.

'I see,' she said again. 'This was on the news at the time, I suppose?'

Yes, it was, I say, after a fashion because—and this was somewhat the way of things back then—because the event *I* am talking about happened on the very same evening as the event *you* are talking about.

'Eurovision?'

The Daytona massacre. That event, your one, was more of an. Event is a silly, look-away sort of word, it does not say what it is. Your fucking tragedy was deemed to be a greater fucking tragedy than mine. Actually, it was, because your guys—Sorley, Hamill, Black, and McDowell—were talented, beautiful, innocent children singing songs to other children. My guys were stupid, but they were not innocent. I honestly can't tell you how much thought they even gave to what they were doing before they did it.

'What makes you say that?'

The whole operation was so makeshift. The device they were carrying was obviously made by an amateur. *The most homemade of homemade bombs* was the view of the forensics expert who picked over the pieces. (I show Emma Cooper my notebook.) *As if they were carrying their own booby trap*, he said. That's interesting, don't you think?

'Well, it does make them seem stupid, as you say. Unless it *was* a booby trap, unless the man who made it wanted it to go off early. Is that what you think?'

I say this to you, and not to Emma Cooper, Mandy: that is not what I thought. Jim Cash made that bomb; it was the only, or at least the first, bomb he ever made, and I am firmly of the view that he simply made a rubbish bomb. And that Ryan was a fool and almost certainly mishandled it. But why should I not say all this to Emma Cooper if it was getting her interested?

('Because Jim Cash was your friend and you could get him into trouble by talking about him to a journalist,' said Mandy. 'Because, if you didn't think he sabotaged the bomb, you should have told her that, because that's what a friend would have done.'

You are right, Mandy. I am not a good friend.)

I have no knowledge of that, I say to her. Just that the forensics man thought it was shoddy. The police never discovered the bomb maker, nor did they try very hard. They could have found out if they had asked the right people. I mean, that is interesting that they didn't try, that they let that slip.

But there is something else.

The van they drove.

'Why is that interesting?' she asks.

They used it to help identify the driver. He drove his own van, which does not in itself feel like a well-thought-out plan. Don't they usually hijack someone else's vehicle for this sort of operation?

'They do. That's a fact.'

Not this one, as I say. Which may suggest that our driver was not the intended driver, that, in fact, in some way, he was a coerced driver, innocent after all.

('That was a dangerous game, Frank.')

'Is that what you think?' She starts to skim through the pages of my notebook, which, of course, I was happy for her to do, having previously underlined all the points I wanted her to find.

'It says here that the driver was not previously known to the police,' she goes on. 'That's odd in itself, as surely every bloody person is known to the police here. No record of. No known associations with. Not registered as the owner of the vehicle . . . You said that they identified him through the van.'

They did. Read on.

She reads on. 'The van was registered in the name of the parish priest, Fr Vincent McCaul.' She opens a pad and makes her own note. 'I presume that that is the same Fr Vincent McCaul we all know?' she asks.

It is, I say. The late Fr McCaul, who helped broker the ceasefire, the 'priest of peace', the very same, God rest his.

Emma Cooper is, by now, not really listening to me but instead flying through the pages of my notebook while jotting in her own. *Registered to the parish. Football team and scout van. McCaul has unrivalled contacts with all shades of nationalist and Republican opinion. Pressing charges would likely result in an upsurge of resentment against the state. Counterproductive at this stage. The minister is of the opinion. Contrary to established practice, no warning was called in. Tensions are already heightened in the border areas. The minister is of the opinion. The device, had it not been detonated prematurely, could have caused multiple deaths to the border police nearby. The two deceased were the most likely guilty parties. None of the assets within the Republican movement provided any useful intelligence of this operation. Rumours in the town of the involvement of a taxi driver. The minister is of the opinion that nothing is to be gained from pursuing charges against the priest.*

'I think this might be a story,' she finishes. Some colour enters her grey face. 'Ben, our security correspondent, might take this on.'

'Not Ben! Ben—I don't know Ben—Ben will screw this up. This one is for you, Emma Cooper!'

'But I am only the entertainment reporter.'

'You are *not only the entertainment reporter!* You are here, in the Public Records Office, for crying out loud, researching the massacre of the Daytona Showband. Entertainment, my arse! This is *your* story, Emma Cooper.'

I lay it on pretty thick, do a bit of motivational, until she accepts her destiny.

'Did she—accept her destiny?'

She did, after some more hours' chat from me. But she did her job, thank you, *Ermerkerper*. The extra hours were to make sure she understood the part about there having been no informant. It was all there in my notes. She needn't bother with the actual documents themselves. I had done all the work for her. Sure, there would be a splash about McCaul—maybe something on the mysterious bomb maker, a bit extra on the rumours of a taxi driver—but, somewhere in the text, there had to be a line saying that the police had no tout on this operation. You get me, Mandy. There could be no lasting peace for me in this land, if Suzy's still had me down as a turncoat. The line had to be there, however short and unnoticed by the majority. That's why it had to be Emma, not Ben. I had to be sure. And it was there. Fr McCaul had done another good deed for peace.

'Didn't you think, Frank, that dragging Fr McCaul into this was besmirching his name? A bit?'

Fr McCaul is dead, Mandy.

'Could you not have let him rest in peace without informing the press about him?'

Ahem. Perhaps. That was a calculation. Or, rather, as the opportunity presented itself in the form of a journalist, I did a quick sum and reckoned the reputation of the late sainted Fr McCaul was a price worth paying. I see you used the 'informing' word there: you are a clever one, Mandy. Though, under my present circumstances, how happy are you to play around with my psychiatric condition? Your job here, tonight, is reassurance. You needn't worry, Mandy: I have tapped on the glass of my moral compass, and the needle has settled on 'Done nothing wrong here'. The questions asked, the questions asked by Emma Cooper and then all the other columnists that piled in subsequently, the questions were about why Fr McCaul himself had not come forward, or why nobody else from the town had pointed out that it was the Cub Scouts' van scattered in bits around Cullycreggan. Pretty fair questions, I would say—again referring to my moral compass. But these were questions he would never have to answer because he's.

'Dead. Had he no family?'

Mandy, he was a Catholic priest. He did have. 'Have' is a funny word. What does it mean? Does it mean it was something he possessed, he owned? Does it imply love, or does it mean he was saddled with it, like he had it whether he liked it or not? Is 'having' a temporary or an ongoing thing? Is it acute or chronic? He had Alice. She was present, in the picture, around—formally, his housekeeper. Maybe she had him. She certainly looked after him, *kept* him.

'Would Alice have been upset by the papers?'

She would. I am sorry about that. That is not something I would have wished for her. That was not in my calculation. That's a cross to bear, for sure.

'For you or for her?'

Ahem.

For me, as it turns out.

Chapter X

Frank was asleep. Rather than try to lay him out flat, which would certainly have woken him, Mandy pulled gently at his feet to slide him downwards. They don't teach us this kind of thing at nursing college, she thought to herself. She removed his glasses, which had slipped comically down his nose, and put them safely in a drawer.

Nicole looked at her accusingly when Mandy joined her at the nurses' station. You knew where I was, if you needed me that badly, Mandy said. It was a busy night, but they had known busier. Mandy found a patient out of his bed in Ward B, lost and miserable. She took him by his bony arm and led him back to where he belonged. Why do old men have yellow toenails—are they all deficient in the same vitamin? She should probably know. In the bed next door to Frank, Mr Kennedy was groaning with his hernia. He was asleep. It wasn't pain, Mandy decided, it was not that sort of groaning. Mr Kennedy was already well-known for swearing in his sleep. Mandy smiled to herself, sad though it was.

Back at the station, Nicole asked Mandy if she could help Mr Mitchell to the toilet, and try to keep him quiet while he's at it. We don't want them all up! Then Nicole laughed, because she was actually really fond of Mandy and knew she was a proper nurse. Imagine the line of them if they all wanted to go! Mr Mitchell was a large, shy man; he spoke so quietly and strangely, the girls thought he was reciting poetry. If I eat nothing but soup / My clothes will start to droop. He was crying now, and that meant that Mandy would have to help change him. Never mind, Mr Mitchell, it happens to us all. / Let's get you back to bed. Can you help, Nicole?

Would you like some tea, Mandy? I'm making some anyway. You look exhausted. Are you sleeping here tonight?

I am, I am on again in the morning. I sleep all right here. Didn't used to. I have my own pillowslip, which cods your brain into thinking you're at home. Well, it does me. Jeez, would you listen to me! I'm (what age am I?) and I'm practically in my slippers drinking my hot milk. It's like I've been here all my life, or I will be. Surely there must be better.

There's worse, Mandy.

But surely there must be better. Is it not too much to expect there to be something better?

People die expecting, Mandy. I know! This is your home—you oughtn't to knock that.

That bed, in the quarters, with my pillowslip: sometimes, when I lay my head down, I imagine it's my whole home, that everything I own in the world is in that one tiny room without windows, with that one single bed. There's a bed, there's a toilet, food is brought. If you had to, you could survive like that for a while. Do you ever think like that, Nicole? Don't laugh at me. Sometimes I do think that. If I had to, all a body needs is to eat and sleep and occasionally use the loo.

A body needs a home too.

That is a home! A kitchen, a bedroom, a bathroom. We don't need much in the end.

In the end?

I didn't mean that but, yes, in the end. Like Mr Mitchell and Mr Kennedy and the others. That's all they want from us here.

And the drugs, Mandy. You forget the drugs.

Something to take the pain away. Yes, there is that, Nicole. Take the pain away or, if we can't manage that, take the mind away from the pain. I am not knocking it: to be the reliever of pain. That's a good thing to be. But is that what I have come to with my own life? All I expect from life is to have relief, or distraction, from pain? A balm. Is that it?

That Mr Frank seems to be sleeping well. He'll need his strength.

Frank. That's his name.

Has he been talking?

Hardly at all. Mostly he's been sleeping, as you say, but he doesn't seem rested, not to me.

Some people don't know how to rest, Mandy. Some people spend so much of their lives on the run, on the go, they fail to notice when it's time to slow down. Maybe that's the scenario with Mr Frank. Have we had any luck with this family?

His son lives in London. That was an English number we called him on. He'll try to get here tomorrow, says he hopes he is not too late. The son and I must be of a similar age. He has a fancy job in the City of London. That will mean he has an office in a skyscraper overlooking the Thames. Imagine that! From his windows, he could see into the homes of nine million people. Can you picture that, Nicole?

Is that what they call a job in England?

You know what I mean. He can see further than I can even imagine. When did I decide that I didn't need to see further?

Mandy went back into the ward to look over her patients.

CHAPTER XI

Some years ago—and thirty years to the month after we beat Carrigbay to take the GAA County Shield, a match I had retained no memory of—the members of the team organised a reunion in honour of the man, Fr Vincent McCaul, who had made it all possible. The decision was made to hold the reunion in Dublin, for the County team had reached the final of the All-Ireland GAA Football Championship and a certain number of tickets for Croke Park had been acquired. I received an embossed card, inviting me and Eilis to the Gresham Hotel for a night of remembrance and celebration, with a meal, a free drink, and the offer of tickets for the game. Proceeds to the Orphans' Fund.

I had no intention, and certainly Eilis would not be going. Then one of the boys—Quinn, the same—who was the only one who had my number, called and informed me we would all be travelling by hired coach. He said something about neither of us having to drive, despite him being a cabby and me having a library van. I was nervous of meeting him again, but he had given me no option.

The pick-up was at the back of the Europa Hotel. 'No wife today?' Quinn called over his shoulder from the seat in front. 'Good move. Could be a bit of a riot, I reckon.' He was rubbing his hands with anticipation, holding his cigarette loosely in his lips. I could smell that he had laid down a few drinks already. Probably he was nervous too.

'At her sister's,' I said, but the lie was wasted on him. Quinn perhaps made a similar excuse for the absence of his own wife, if indeed he had one. I didn't know him. I didn't really know any of these men, now that they were men and not boys. Most had come with their partners, and it seemed to me, without craning my neck to be sure, that they in the main sat happily and quietly with them. You can rest your head there, if you like, love. Can you see 4 across? I will have one of those cups of tea, if you're pouring. Blind devotion to an image or person—eight letters. The whole journey is only a couple of hours, door to door. Idolatry. That's not the same as adultery.

When you sit alone, clippings from others' conversations reach you unbidden. You make sense of them; you don't make sense of them; they are all the same, one no more important than the other. What route are we taking? Have you never driven to Dublin? Of course, I have driven to Dublin. Why are we going this way? McHugh could not make it to Belfast, so the coach agreed to pick him up in the town. I wish *I* had known that—would have saved me a trip. *McHugh! Stand up straight!* Shut the eff up, you lot. So we are going this way to the border? Michaelstown, Slieveban, Cullycreggan. Jesus, this is a twisty road for a big coach. The driver knows what he's doing; the same man drove us to London last year. Wait, was that Cullycreggan we just passed through? There's literally nothing there to mark the. We're over, aren't we? The road to London is nothing like the like of this, all motorway. *Punts for Pounds*, the road signs in yellow, kilometres not miles. What went on in London? Will you listen to you lot, you'd think you were entering a foreign country. Get your kicks on Route 66. In a sense . . . Don't you feel yourself relaxing a little bit more when you? Nothing happened in London, love; you lot need to pipe down . . . Any of you got a song? *Sing! Sing!* Where's Dynes when you need him? Even his harmonica would do. That's bad taste, to bring him up just here. Fuck, yes, you're right, that slipped my mind, pardon my French. Should be some sort of marker for that too. Not bloody likely, that's one they'd rather forget. Breathe deep, guys, that's proper Southern air.

The detour had added forty-five minutes to the journey. The road from the North was clogged by cars sporting our red-and-black county flags. There was no air conditioning on the coach, and we had to stop outside Drogheda for Quinn to vomit. It all added to the sense of jubilation.

ᘒᙒ

A skinny man greeted us in the reception of the Gresham. *He has a Grand Canyon between his body and his waistcoat, you could fit a whole other one of him in there.* This is what I heard Eilis say in my head. It was the sort of thing that Eilis might have said when she let herself be funny. The skinny man had big spade hands, and he used these to shovel us to the private function room reserved for our party. The way he used that word—'party'—was the way a solicitor does, as in we were *a party to* whatever was about to take place there that night. We had accepted the invitation so must accept the consequences. It was in the small print.

There was a DJ, already playing his *Sounds of the Sixties* LP at his station, coloured lights circling him like wasps. Five round tables were draped to the floor with yellow tablecloths, crimped at the edges like discarded beer bottle tops. Besides our coachload, few had arrived yet other than the staff who would have to put up with us for the evening. A table pushed to the side—wine glasses serried and full—was being ignored for now. I had not yet matched every face to a name, but someone suggested we leave the ladies there while the men explored the lounge bar upstairs. As it was down to the authority of the person who proposed it, this was not an outrageous plan. The order of these things matters, it turns out, even after thirty years of not being the captain or the substitute or the leading point scorer; the order, as in the hierarchy, the position you hold relative to all the others. Left half-back does not even begin to describe it. There are instructions you are meant to understand, which govern this sort of society, that are not made explicit. You can be quiet only if that's the role assigned you; otherwise, you are obliged to chip in with a joke or an insult or another sort of noise—whatever it is that you normally do, even if thirty years have elapsed in the interim. You must not change or forget that funny thing that happened or act out of character, unless you are drunk. Then your behaviour can be dismissed as being 'out of character'. I was one of those who was expected to be quiet.

Smaller groups formed for rounds. I got drinks in just for me and Quinn. 'Lucky, there!' he said. 'Cheap round for you. Worked out well. You didn't think of getting in any crisps?'

'Leave him be, Quinn,' said someone. It was Fox. 'Good you could join us, Frank. It's been a while. Eilis didn't want to come with you today? Mine insisted.' I was surprised that he remembered Eilis.

'She's staying at her sister's, according to Frank here.' For Quinn, it was more fun not to believe me.

'Eilis McClean? I've remembered that correctly, or have I not?' Fox went on. I nodded, not really sure I wanted this to go where it might go but flattered at the same time that he did remember. 'God, she could sing! And she was a fine . . .' He looked to me for permission to continue. '. . . a fine-looking girl too. We always said she had everything it takes.' All of this was said just to me, as if to undo some of Quinn's work. 'Such a shame we couldn't have booked her for tonight!' he finished, casting his arm over the company.

'Just give her half the chance,' I said, telling the truth. She actually would have loved that, rolled a few years back for her. 'Pity.'

Someone said that, in America, they love an Irish girl who can sing.

Fox was in tractor parts, I gathered. He had property outside the town. 'I never moved far!' He imported from Czechoslovakia. 'We'll have to get used to calling it the Czech Republic!' he said, like he was announcing news. Tariffs were a nuisance, but the 'good Protestant farmers of Ulster' could absorb it all with the generosity of the British taxpayer. 'These peace talks had better not end up in Irish unification is all I say!' he declared with irony, without irony. 'Although your view might be different.'

'Wily Fox,' someone said, and that was fine because this was Fox playing his part. I wondered, had he been assigned that role because that was his name. Like a curse. That happens, you know.

'The religion of the cow makes no difference to me.' This was Sean McHugh, who, I recalled, was in the abattoir business. He was answering a challenge from elsewhere at the table. 'A heifer's a heifer, whatever her church.'

'But you put "Genuine Irish Beef" on your packets,' said Shiels. 'Why do you do that, if it's all the same to you?' Shiels got a pat on the back for this provocation.

'I can explain that one,' said Sean McHugh. He was used to having to explain. 'You see, in a manner of speaking, I adopt every one of them cows before I have their throats slit. Their papers say they are mine, it's my name on the slaughter papers, and I'm a "genuine Irishman" so, so are they.' Someone applauded *olé*, or *touché*, or *sláinte*. 'My girls are as Irish as I am, however they were reared.'

'And then you kill them.'

'Then I slaughter them. Same thing, you're right.'

Shiels had flown in from America just to be with us. That sheer fact alone was barely credible. As were his teeth. None of us had good teeth, so Shiels' really were remarkable. Evidently, he had bought and paid for them, his tan and his haircut all in the States. He and his guys went fishing in his boat in Brooklyn Bay. He had a boat to himself or he owned part of a boat with a syndicate. A timeshare, he called it, like in America that was nothing to be ashamed of. His daughter was an *au pair* in Boston, for now. The implication was that she was stopping by there on the way to one of its nearby universities. His wife—an American herself, called Kitty—did charity. 'She loves it here,' he reassured us. 'She has Irish in her too, somewhere, a grandfather, I think. I am vague on the details. She'll know. I'll bring her over to you later. She's excited about meeting Fr McCaul.'

Everyone agreed that that was indeed a thing to look forward to. No one was sure when McCaul would arrive. Back in the day, could you have imagined he would have turned out the way he has? He taught me boxing, for Jesus' sake! He put us all in the cubs, even the girls, and not one of us could stand up straight. ('Not McHugh, for certain.') Great man! Everything I am is because he made me that way, I'm not exaggerating. Kitty wants to thank him for helping them raise money Stateside.

Shiels' accent was relaxed and glowed like even it had a suntan. I wanted to ask him if he knew what a storage leader was.

Quinn asked, 'What's that you say about money?'

'McCaul's been over our way, twice or more, dinners and that. People will put their hands in their pockets just to be in the same room as him. That's Americans for you!' Shiels was ready to leave it there: he had said too much as it was. 'The Irish ones especially.'

Quinn asked, 'Raising money for who? Do I need to ask for what?' He thought he knew, but Quinn, I was learning, was never one for keeping his mouth shut.

'Kitty—she would not like me to say it is her, but she does her bit. One of her charities, let's say. They raise a wee bit of dough where they can, you know, for the effort back home.'

No one, even Quinn, spoke up. The word 'home' seemed a place far removed from here, this hotel in Dublin. Shiels would have dropped it, but, when no one spoke up, the rules said he had to go on.

'Of course, now peace looks set, they may roll back on their money raising. The last consignment of . . . I had better not say. Not that I know for sure what was in it anyway, you'd need to ask Kitty. It's in a dock somewhere in New York State, and my understanding is that's where it will stay. So that all turned out well.'

It did, everyone agreed.

Quinn asked, 'So, before McCaul was negotiating with the Provisionals to put aside their weapons, he was raising money for them to buy guns? That's hedging your bets, all right!'

Everyone agreed to that too, and that that was enough from Quinn.

There was no drink left on the table, and someone suggested we all move back to the private function room, where the ladies no doubt were wondering about us. It may have been O'Rourke—I hadn't heard his name yet, but, of us all, he had the most looked-after hair. It made sense that it was O'Rourke. We found, when we got there, that the ladies had commandeered their own tables and weren't wondering about us at all. They had discovered the free wine, which was now in disarray. Other people had arrived too. There were men in blazers with the insignia of the County GAA, and a woman too in near identical uniform. With the team in the final, they had never felt so central to affairs in all their lives. For the past month, everyone had been tapping them up for tickets, so much so that their own Dublin weekends were paying for themselves. A couple of enterprising young lads in yellow kit from the town's current team, who had been pressed into representing today's generation, had chanced upon an untended bar at the far end of the room. One of them was on crutches. There was a priest also there, presumably appearing as a substitute in case the real thing was unable to show up.

Fox said he would get in a round from the free bar, and I volunteered to help him carry. There were questions about tractors that I might have asked him while we were queuing, but none came to mind.

'You never did have a lot to say for yourself. No offence,' Fox started.

'No, no. None.'

'I see Quinn is still on at you. Back there, Quinn couldn't lay off you. Probably jealous.'

'Probably.' Jealous of what, I didn't know. It seemed to me only that Quinn was in a panic, shooting his mouth off because he didn't know what else to do with it. He was worried about me, worried about what I might be capable of saying about him.

'Wasn't he always like that with you, a bit of a gobshite?'

'I wouldn't say.'

'A gobshite is exactly what he was!' said Fox, warming to his theme already. 'They would call it something else nowadays: bullying, whatever. Sorry.'

'Sorry for what?'

'For bringing it up. No reason why you would want me to. Got your own issues with it without me.'

'No, I am fine.' The queue moved slowly forward. Maybe I could ask him about Czechoslovakia, I thought.

'Do you recall there was that one time? We were getting changed after a game, remember. You had a comb from somewhere, one of those you keep in your pocket, wherever you had got it from you were proud of it because you were—ostentatious like—running it back over your head, and you were never one for ostentation. You were playing to the gallery a bit—a bit Gene Vincent, you were funny—but Quinn could not take it. He snatched the comb out of your hand and threw it to the ground, in the mucky water. You tried to pick it up, but he held you off. So you used your foot, like so, to drag the comb more your way for you to reach it. The players were all gathered around, expecting a fight, picking their own side. Somebody—it wasn't me, I wish I could say it was me—pushed at Quinn's shoulder to get him away from you, so you were able to retrieve your comb. But, of course, it was all scratched and mucky from the water, and you didn't want it any longer, even though this was a really prized thing for you at the outset. So you threw it into the corner, left it there. I remember that time. Do you remember that?'

I didn't, but I said I thought I did.

'He was a bastard for doing that, sorry to say because he's a friend of mine. I hope you got your revenge on him for doing that to you?'

'Oh, yes,' I assured him, not specifying because, apparently, I never did have a lot to say for myself.

'I sure hope you did.'

Back at our table, everyone gratefully grabbed their pints from the trays. 'Is Kitty paying for this too?' O'Rourke wisecracked, catching a glimpse of his reflection in his glass. Shiels puffed himself up, to take the credit. So no offence was taken. There was a separate conversation going on about Fr McCaul and his role in the peace negotiations. He was styling himself as the go-between. I had to wonder, what did the British know about him really, and did any of it make them more, or less, confident he would be able to pull off a deal? I was thinking this and thinking how much of it I would want to divulge in this company.

'Frank is the only one here who would know about Jimmy Cash.' I heard this before I saw that it had come out of Quinn's mouth. 'You were his bosom pal, were you not?' I hadn't been listening to that side of the table. This was one of those moments when two or three or however many conversations that have been happening at the same time all converge into one, and it's like the whole table is tipping towards you, ashtrays and all. There was no way of avoiding it. All ears were on me. When I worked out what they had been saying, I stammered, 'We were friends, of course.'

'Friends! That's one way of putting it,' said Quinn, not quite getting the chorus of support he needed to keep this going. He was that bit more drunk than the rest, which was in character. 'Always into scrapes with each other, you two.' Only O'Rourke found it funny.

'Drop it, Quinn,' said Fox.

'I know he went abroad and that he came back, but not a lot more than that.' Lying to these men was no hardship.

'I recall the day Jimmy Cash arrived,' said Shiels. 'Maybe not the very day, but the day I was first aware of him. He was taller than the rest of us, was he not, and a whole lot better fed! He was from Scotland originally, don't forget. He may have been the first person I ever saw who had ever been anywhere else. That sort of thing makes an impression. Well, it did, speaking for myself.' For a moment, Shiels became shy, as if he were recounting his first love. He blushed a little, became quieter and suddenly less American—by which I mean he looked and sounded a lot more like the rest of us.

'He arrived, as if out of nowhere, on the Gaelic pitch. I'd say it confounded Fr McCaul for a second: he didn't know where to put the fella. So he, Father, made a joke at his expense. Does anyone else remember this? He said Jimmy Cash could be "left back in the corner". Jimmy didn't know what he meant. McCaul wanted us all to laugh, and, of course, we obliged because we were only kids at the time. And then, because he was on a roll, he went one further and said that thing about Jimmy's face.'

'What thing?' someone asked.

'Fr McCaul said that Jimmy McCaul was already so ugly, the other team's players were bound to be frightened of him.'

'Father McCaul had a wicked sense of humour,' someone said. 'That's one way to describe it,' said someone else.

'Not one of us stood up for him.' This was Shiels still. 'Not one of us. Maybe if we had, things would have been different for Jimmy.'

That was almost, not quite, how I recalled it, but I was pleased that Shiels had told this story despite the inaccuracies. Shiels was the goalkeeper in the team. Goalkeepers have got to know something about the game.

'I heard Cash had joined the RAF,' McHugh chipped in, hunched over. Maybe this was to stop anyone feeling too much sympathy for our split-faced Scottish friend. Others expressed no particular surprise. 'Big up in it, I heard,' he added. Then to me: 'You never heard that, Frank?'

Any true friend would know that much, surely, if even McHugh did. How—unless there had been an epic falling out—could I not know at least that about my bosom pal?

'Yes, I did hear that, as a matter of fact,' I offered, although I hadn't. 'In England, I believe, somewhere. Lost track.'

No one said anything, which meant I should go on. Should I say anything about Betty? No one had asked, but I could imagine they would all be curious, because they were always too curious about her.

What would be the way of putting it: that the two are still together, still in love? As if that was the most incredible thing to report. But I had said enough already.

'Still making bombs, then?' This was Quinn, naturally. Nobody was quick enough to move the conversation on, even though they ought to have seen this one coming. 'Bombs that go off just like that. That don't need him to set them off, because he is safe and sound tucked up in bed with that one, what was her name?'

'Pity he could not be here tonight,' said O'Rourke with a tone approaching menace. 'If one of us had known how to get in touch with him. Do let us know, Frank, if you ever hear of him in the vicinity. I know a bunch of people who would love to catch up with him.' O'Rourke was sitting next to Quinn. As if he hadn't made the point bluntly enough already, he added, 'I know for a fact that McCann and her boys in Belfast would appreciate a word in your friend Jimmy Cash's ear. In England, you say? The places people turn up in.'

'Bastards will turn up anywhere,' said Quinn, as if that were his whole philosophy.

'Jimmy was not a bastard!' This was me, barely recognising what was coming out of my own mouth. 'If people at home would still like to have words with him, then they have the wrong man. There are others she, McCann, should maybe speak to first.'

This was the most interesting thing these boys had ever heard me say. I wasn't known as a talker, not in that sense, not in the everyday sense. I saw Quinn look at me, and he was looking at me like he suddenly did see me as a talker, but in that other sense. And he looked worried.

ⵠ

Most of us were nearing the bottoms of our glasses, so a couple were sent to the bar for more refreshment. I'll need to put food down soon on this, one said. They won't start the meal until the guest arrives, another clarified. Seems right. Do you think that DJ will ever give over, who does he think is going to dance to that? The girls will get up after a few martinis, just you wait.

'What time is he due?' McHugh asked. 'Did it say on the invite?'

It did not.

'You would have to say that that is "open",' suggested Shiels with some authority. 'Things are "live" at the moment, from what I am told.'

From what he was told, from what he was hearing, knowing what others know. We boys pulled our chairs in a little tighter. A little tighter around Shiels meant a little farther away from me.

Shiels offered some elucidation. 'Vincent's—sorry, Fr McCaul's—main contacts are within the former prisoner community. Contacts built up over many years but cemented in the time of the hunger strikes and so on. The families, the ex-prisoners themselves, their fathers' generation too: any one of them will take a call from Vincent. We hear that, aside from the political leadership, this is the group with the most sway within the movement. None of this is news to you boys . . .'

. . . Indeed, no . . .

'We hear most of this second-hand Stateside. The moneymen—the people you would say I have most to do with—are largely frozen out at this stage, much to their annoyance. As you might imagine. Ultimately, they will fall in line with whatever is decided over here, but some listen out also for noises from the South.'

The Dublin government?

'No, no, no. The southern Republicans. They are not the force that once they were, but they still get an audience in America.'

'As does Fr McCaul, from what you have told us.'

Shiels left it dangling there, having given away too much already. Kitty would be around somewhere, you could tell he was thinking. Keep her away from O'Rourke, he was also thinking.

'So we may have longer to wait for our meal,' said McHugh reasonably. 'Fair enough.'

Drinks finished, some of the men got up to locate their wives, to check in. I've only had three, love. No need of a driver tonight. Three, maybe four. McCaul's a great man, we've been hearing what he's. Are you having a nice time too? Ahem. Ahem. Well, I can't help much there, I'm afraid. No, I will dance with you later if you are that keen. Have you been talking to Shiels' wife? No? Kitty, I think he said her name was. No, no, nothing, just wondering. Anyway, I'll probably be.

'Seriously, though,' McHugh said again to the two of us still sitting. 'Do you think there's a chance, with all his peace making, that Fr McCaul may not make it at all tonight?'

'You're hungry, I can tell,' said Quinn. 'I'm on these, so I never need for food.' He meant the cigarettes.

'It's not that I have to eat; I just have to know if I am going to eat. Frank will know what I mean, won't you, Frank?'

'Makes perfect sense to me,' I agreed.

'Frank would eat anything put in front of him. You wouldn't turn down free food even yet, would you, Frank?' said Quinn, of course.

What would you know, Quinn? What would he know?

'Not from my recollection anyway. Please, miss. May I have some more?'

'Quinn, shut the eff up now, would you?' McHugh intervened before I had to say something myself. 'And you could get us some drinks in while we're waiting, we wouldn't mind.'

Quinn stumbled off in the wrong direction for the bar. 'Let him go,' McHugh said. He then allowed some moments to pass, in case I was sore and needed to get over it. 'Hasn't changed, that one.'

No, I agreed, though I could not be sure.

'Something remains the same in us all, I would say,' said McHugh. 'I still have this.' He meant his crooked back. 'Quinn is still a fool!' McHugh was not used to talking much, but, with me, he calculated the onus was on him. 'We all have the mark from those days, I suppose, even you.'

That's fair, I thought. Go on.

'I was a bit frightened of Fr McCaul, I don't mind saying. My brother and sister would have said the same. Great man now, of course, but. Others here mightn't say so, but he was terrifying. I can't say how, exactly, as he never raised a hand to anyone to my knowledge. He wasn't that way terrifying, thank God. *Come here, you wee bastard!* he would say to me, offhand like that, to me and even to my sister. *I'm not swearing now,* he would try to say in his own defence, *I'm using the term in its technical sense.* That's because my father had died and Mummy hadn't married my wee sister's father yet. It's not right for a priest to talk like that. I know he ran the scouts and the boxing and the football on top of his parish duties, and he drove that van and baptised everyone and buried everyone all by himself, and he's now saving us all from blowing each other to kingdom come, but he still. You know? Susie wasn't that happy with me coming tonight.'

Your sister.

'Susie, my sister. I had to lie to her, to say there was no guarantee Fr McCaul was even going to be here. Not looking like such a lie now!'

He'll be here. He won't miss the game tomorrow.

'Do you think so? Something remains the same in us all is what I think. *The philosophy of Sean McHugh.* Do you think there's a book in that?'

I drive a library van.

'So you do! Someone said. Good man! That would suit you down to the ground, I would imagine. Very good. Nice and quiet. I'm still in the meat trade, as I said earlier if you heard. No change there. Not that I love it, but it's a good living. I had limited options, with my spinal curvature. Abattoirs it was at first, oh, the glamour, but I was young, so what would I mind. I have slit a few throats in my time, Frank. It's not the messy business it once was, but it's still a life one minute and a carcass the next. I wouldn't say that that had not affected me in some way. The way a cow cries when it knows it's about to die. They don't, for most of it, know what's coming—there'd be shit everywhere, it would be out of control. We have ways of channelling them, so they are calm, so the meat remains tender. But then word gets out, so to speak; they feel it, pick it up from each other; then they start to cry. They have kind, dopey faces, cows. Unworldly black eyes. I have not been in an abattoir in years, Frank, but I still have that crying in me. Do you hear what I am saying, Frank? Some of the things you are and some of the things you do, they stay with you.'

Like it or not.

'That's right. Like people are never forgiven. Guilty or innocent, it makes no odds. Like McCaul calling me a b: a bastard. Or. Or you. We all have our own examples.'

McHugh and his cows—*the philosophy of Sean McHugh.* Just goes to show you don't have to be a book person or well-travelled to be full of shite.

('That's harsh, Frank.'

That is harsh, Mandy. I agree. McHugh was a soft big man. He was too sentimental to be a butcher.)

We all have our own examples. My eye fell on the two young lads in football jerseys, the ones I had spied at the bar earlier, the one of them on crutches. Do you remember that time, it was in the semi-final against Michaelstown, they had a player, a showboater called Simon—although, why I recall his name I have no idea, it makes no odds—he had a tan, this Simon had a tan, and he was taking the mick out of Jimmy Cash the whole game, never gave him a sniff of the ball the whole game. And Jimmy clattered him. He actually smashed him. Leg broken, bone sticking out, there on the pitch. The worst thing I ever saw or heard.

'In the semi-final against Michaelstown?' McHugh asked.

On the Pitches. I bet that boy Simon never walked properly again after that: there'll be a limp in cold weather, he'll be cautious. Not a bad player, after all is said and done, he might even have gone somewhere in the game, but not after that day. It's like you say: some of the things stay with you; they stay in you.

'Do I know a Simon?'

And I doubt that ever left Cash either. You can try to block that kind of thing from your memory or pretend to yourself, but it's there in him yet, I would bet. Something riled him that day.

'Is that the one who runs the Adair now in town?'

Something riled Cash that day.

'I recall it didn't take a lot to get Jimmy riled once he worked out he was bigger than the rest of us. I wonder he never lamped Fr McCaul for all the abuse he took from him. It will have been that, I've no wonder, that got Jimmy going that day you are talking about: it will have been some remark from Fr McCaul that set Jimmy off until he injured one of their players. I shouldn't speak ill of the man, I know, given as he's about to walk in at any minute, but that was the way of him. Shiels said it earlier: it might have turned out differently for Jimmy Cash, if Fr McCaul wasn't such a.'

I promised myself I would ask Cash, if I ever saw him, would his memory of it be the same as McHugh's? There are more details in my recollection; more particles have stuck for me. And that means the pieces fit together differently, have different relationships with each other, amount to something different. An entirely other person could emerge from these events as I have remembered them, set off on another path altogether.

'No, that bloke who runs the Adair is called Eddie,' said McHugh.

'And does Declan manage Suzy's for his dad?' I asked.

'Declan was shot by a soldier, they say,' he said.

'Oh. I hope McCaul gets here soon.'

'Yes. I am starving.' McHugh was always hungry. Some things stay with you.

ᢒᢡ

Many hours passed before a man and a woman arrived. He was wearing jeans and a blue check shirt, which was out of place anyway for the Gresham Hotel, and doubly so because he was Fr McCaul. In all the times I had seen him with my own eyes, and all the times on television, he had been wearing his black priestly gear. Sometimes, he would have his sleeves rolled up, and he might even have dispensed with the dog collar on occasion, but you would always say he was recognisable as a priest. Not this time. He had the same round head and the same round belly, and—when he opened his mouth—he had the same texture to his voice, but other than that, he might have been travelling in disguise. The woman on his arm with the glamorous dress and gold jewellery was Alice, his housekeeper. She was in conversation with the man I took to be the hotel manager, pointing to different corners of the room, nodding her head in a concerned sort of way, checking her understanding of the arrangements tallied with the management's. That was how it appeared. When the manager ran off to respond to something she objected to, she turned her attention immediately to the County GAA people who were talking deferentially to Fr McCaul. Now she was smiles and touches. Her hair bounced. In the disco lights, her lipstick was brown. The little party went to take their seats at the top table, and there was a momentary overspilling of discomfort, and, on Alice's face, there was a fraction of determination, I would say, and the embarrassment was resolved only when the lady committee person took up a spare seat at a table with the young players. Alice assumed her rightful place next to Fr McCaul.

'Who is she? Is that Alice?' asked Quinn out loud.

'She is his companion,' said Shiels from knowledge. 'Now. One hears.'

'There is more said about that than is strictly true,' O'Rourke intervened. 'Or helpful. She checks his diet and his pills. He is high maintenance, with the lifestyle he has to keep. Nowadays.'

'That's Alice?' asked Quinn out loud again.

'Behave yourself!' O'Rourke scolded him. 'Anyone would think you'd never set eyes on a female.'

'Did you know?'

'Did I know what, Quinn? That she was . . . How did you put it there: McCaul's companion? The world knows that.'

'I never.'

I never.

'It's not. I know what you think, and it's not that. McCaul wouldn't last five minutes in the priesthood if there was any of that going on.'

'Look at him,' said Quinn. 'Is he even in the priesthood still?'

'Calm down, would the two of you!' Shiels had his big hand up, like the reassuring goalkeeper he was. 'A man, even a priest, is entitled to a night off now and again. I presume he has chosen to spend that night with Alice . . .'

We broke out into instant clownish laughter as Shiels struggled to complete his thought:

'. . . and us.'

'Fair play to him is what I say,' said Wily Fox. 'And good, so long as he is able to keep any gossip out of the papers. We all know what they can be like, particularly on a Sunday.'

'McCaul will have put the tighteners on the reporters, don't you think?' said McHugh. 'Or the frighteners. There is a lot riding on these secret talks he has been having, the editors will know it. McCaul will make sure they remember that. Somewhere down the line, all these journalists will owe Fr McCaul something. That's just my opinion.'

'I think you may be right,' Wily Fox agreed.

'It's only my opinion, you don't have to agree.'

'No, I think you may be right, Sean,' said Fox again. 'Let's hope anyway.'

A bowl of vegetable soup was placed in front of us. Then dinner. 'Moussaka,' guessed Shiels. A Greek place near him in New York did the best anywhere 'outside the Greek world'. Alice sent away the waitress who tried to offer them bread. Shiels pronounced the moussaka acceptable. Later, we were tantalised with a selection of ice cream for dessert, like we were children. Raspberry ripple. A man cleared his throat and stood up and started burbling on, but we ignored him because he was not the one we were there to hear from. He was just the relief act, as it were. I noticed he wanted to thank our guests, but he could not find the words to describe Alice, so he simply left her out of his remarks.

'I give you Fr Vincent McCaul.'

As he stood up, the disco lights were still revolving, and they dazzled on his shiny head like comic concussion.

'Thank you, Simon. Everyone is looking very smart in their blazers and their dresses, and it's lovely to see you young lads there in your match jerseys.'

'Thanks, Father!' they called back too loudly.

'You may think you have caught me on an off day, dressed like this.' The audience appreciated the self-effacement. 'Quite the reverse, in fact. You would not expect me to divulge any details of my current day job. However, one titbit you might like is that on days when I am to meet representatives of the Provisionals, with McCann and her boys, I always wear my priest get-up, but when I have a day with envoys of Her Majesty, I prefer to turn up as their idea of an Irishman. Sometimes, I make sure I have mud on my boots! It helps that they think they are superior. Whereas with the McCann and her acolytes, I like her to imagine she can confess to me and I won't tell!'

He was promising more jokes than in his usual sermons.

'It's great to see so many of the boys back here this evening and that you didn't all turn out to be the lazy bastards that we feared.' A half pint of beer had materialised in his hand, and he took a sip from that so as to remove any remaining doubt that, for tonight at least, he was not our priest. 'O'Rourke, I'm looking at you!' Everyone accepted it was all right at that point to laugh at O'Rourke, whether they knew him to be or not to be a lazy bastard.

'No, it's a genuine delight to see the boys here, and, if my partner Alice here allows me later, I look forward to catching up with you all.' That was like a little toast to Alice, and some at least raised their glasses. From here on, Fr McCaul read his sort of homily from scripted notes, although he permitted himself the occasional moment off the cuff.

'As you know, not everyone could make it. I understand that Tomas Casey is not with us tonight. Despite his handicap, he was a loyal supporter of the team, and we would have been happy to find an extra seat for him. If anyone is in touch, please pass on our regards.'

McHugh nudged me then and whispered in my ear. 'Tomas Casey died twenty years ago, and McCaul here officiated at his funeral. He said the same about him then, God rest him.'

'Another who could not be here. Many of you will recall the Scotchman we had in our side. James Cash, I'll never forget him, made an impression on us all, and me included. Thought he was better than the rest of us. In some ways, he may have been. Handsome fella!' McCaul gave a wink, inviting another laugh. 'He was not that handy on the pitch, as I recall, but he was strong and brave, and—I will give him this—he had a talent for getting out of scrapes as quickly as he got in them. James would be at the other end of the field before the poor fucker he had decked could pick himself back up again. That's a talent that can see you through life, which, of course, I could not possibly endorse.

'For those of you who do not know, James Cash is a long-time member of British secret intelligence.' Fr McCaul allowed a beat here for anyone who felt the need to boo or hiss. 'It is not the life trajectory that would be expected of many growing up as you boys did, but it is worth reminding ourselves that James Cash was never really one of us. That's not to cast aspersions—as I say, he had many fine qualities— but, *being Scottish*, always did set him apart, and I would add set apart those who most closely associated with him. Morality is a singular and a collective decision, if I may speak professionally for a moment. I am these days in the business of forgetting and forgiving, and, in that spirit, I did attempt to reach out to your friend. I, you will have heard, have my contacts in the British military, and they tried to oblige me by getting in touch with him. I have it therefore on good authority that James Cash is an intelligence officer, stationed somewhere in Africa.' The priest was, at this point of minor climax, suddenly unsure of himself. McCaul paused there, leaned down to Alice, and asked her if she knew anything more precise than that. She was occupied at that moment making a fan of a paper napkin, and, as this required all her attention, the priest continued with an abandoned expression on his face. 'That is, I should add, true as I understand it. However, should you feel inclined to contact him there, I shouldn't bother as all efforts on my part came to nothing. Understandably, they are a bit slippery over there. I got no reply to the missive I sent—my olive branch, if you will—but I accept that a note from a long-forgotten curate from a long-forgotten town is hardly likely to find its way to the top of his in-tray. My purpose here is merely to acknowledge the role James played in our local tragedy while also placing on the record our thanks for the part he played in getting us to the Shield final that year.' By assaulting the star player of the Michaelstown team, the priest did not add.

I noticed that Quinn was missing. He must have left his seat while the GAA blazer had been talking. Maybe he didn't trust himself to behave if McCaul got going on the old boys, those not here, as indeed he was now doing. He didn't want a mention from Fr McCaul in his speech, that was for certain. What would McCaul—who knew everything about everyone—know about Quinn? Quinn didn't want to be there to find out. I wished at that moment that I had made the same choice, to leave my dinner jacket in the wardrobe and not be there. Did Fr McCaul have me in mind when he spoke about those associated with Cash being set apart? He must surely have, and the other players must surely have thought so too. I doubt there was a person there that night who thought of me ever but for my association with Jimmy Cash. Bosom pals we were. And was he semaphoring me there when he advised against trying to contact Cash? That put a shiver down me: McCaul, somehow, knew already that I had tried to find my old friend. As a priest, he likely knew a whole lot more. He was still talking, and, though I would rather have been anywhere else so as to not have to listen, he had picked me for the side, so I had to play.

'There are two men who are not here tonight because of the tragedy I speak of that cut them down in their prime. I spoke at their funerals all those years ago as their priest. Then I honoured them as young men. Tonight, in this hotel, we think of them first as boys, teammates, proud wearers of our yellow jersey, and I talk as their coach. Patrick Ryan. Oh, Patrick, Paddy, Pat! He was, we all know, such an impulsive person. You may not know this, but, in all of my days serving God, Patrick Ryan was the only altar boy I ever had to fire. Believe me, that is saying something. I found boys supping at the Communion wine, I have found boys listening to their Walkmans during Mass, I have seen it all. But Ryan was the only boy whom you could guarantee to . . . I won't swear . . . mess up at some point in every service. He would drop the chalice or spill the hosts or trip on his surplice. Every fucking time. Pardon my Anglo-Saxon. But we loved him for it! I fired him for his sacrilege, but, clumsy as he was in real life, we all knew there was one place where he was truly blessed. Left corner-forward. I say that, for that was his position, but Ryan was liable to turn up in any bloody place on the pitch, and he could score, seemingly, from any of them. Point after point, from either foot. Patrick Ryan: from Carrycreagh to Skerrybeg, Dunaderry to Balnakerry, the county hated that boy. I know that this is not a fashionable opinion, but I have long pondered that there might have been a player, or opponent coach, out there who had it seriously in for our Patrick. One day, not many years from now, the records will be out on this: I would take a read.'

I heard a disgruntled cough from the lady in the blazer.

'And while you are there, in the records, don't forget my Aloysius. I do think, sometimes, that Aloysius is overlooked in all of this. I never heard a political word come out of that boy's mouth, and to my dying day, I will never understand how Dynes got caught up in that Cullycreggan affair. What the effin' hell was that boy doing there!' Fr McCaul wiped an actual tear. Alice touched his fingers, splayed on the table for support. 'Even God himself had no answer for me. I prayed, I swear to God I did, for some inkling: Who put my Aloysius up to this? For it sure to God was not his idea!' Despite all the years that had passed, Fr McCaul was still able to retrieve appropriate emotions for the occasion. His soft spot for Aloysius Dynes was also a blind spot. There was not much going on in his parish that Fr McCaul did not know about, and, if he did not, it was because he had chosen not to know. He may not have been aware of the precise chain of drivers that led to Dynes, but that Dynes, at some point, would have been a driver for someone was not really in doubt. McCaul preferred not to see it. Dynes was no angel any more than the rest of us were.

'He—Aloysius—drove my van.' This was the reason he preferred to look away. 'You boys will remember Pat's bread van, kindly donated by the baker himself for the purposes of the parish. Beautiful smell it had, I recall. Yeast is the agent that turns dough into the bread we eat. There is a metaphor there—I guess I should call it a parable: the catalyst that stays the same when all about it changes. I may have misunderstood what it does—I am no baker!—but that van smelled forever and a day of yeast. I smell it yet, and I bet you can too.' And because he was a performer, the priest took a deep breath and led his congregation in the same.

'I drove that van. The van was mine to drive. No one else was ever registered to get behind the wheel. I drove the cubs and the scouts, the boxers and the footballers in that van. Heaven only knows how I fitted you all in there, but I did. Then you, Dynes and the rest of you, grew up and couldn't fit any longer, and the younger lads who came after you climbed in in your stead. That's the way of it. There is a parable there too, if I could reach for it. You all got older, but some of you were unable to let go of your childish things, if we can think of the van as that for a moment. Aloysius was one who would not let go of the van. James Cash was another. And you!' (He pointed at me; I think he bellowed.) 'You, Frank, were another.' I froze. If I had attempted to talk, I would have found my tongue was tied. That was a power he always had, the power to disable.

A smile, or a sort of smile, appeared on his lips as he turned his mind away for a moment from the bomb that destroyed his van and his boys. He was imagining Aloysius behind the wheel when he hijacked the van for happier purposes. He pictured Dynes, his big hands gripping, his dirty boots slipping nimbly from pedal to pedal. No one taught him how to drive, he just knew in the way that we all knew, or came to know, how to drive then. Fathers showed us or uncles or—for those of us who had neither—friends of mothers or fathers of friends. There were no lessons and no tests, not until well after we knew it all. We could all do the driving, but Dynes was unusual in that he had a way in with Fr McCaul, and Fr McCaul was not particular about where he left the keys to the van when Dynes was around. McCaul was also imagining the boys occupying the passenger seat. The boy in that seat—quite apart from anyone else who might be stowed in the back—was the person being driven. He was the one saying, *Take me to the Palm Beach in Slieveban*, or *I'm on a promise tonight, for sure, Aloysius*. Here was Cash and, undoubtedly, at other times, Fox and Shiels and McHugh and O'Rourke. Cash and Dynes were the first of us to catch the dance hall craze. They knew what villages and venues were on and how to get to them, and they had seen the posters advertising which bands would be playing and who would be their supporting acts. One of them, both of them—maybe another, such as Wily Fox—heard about Eilis McClean, knew of her before I did, got there ahead of me so to speak. In outline, Fr McCaul was picturing that too: then at the time, and now in the hotel. *Boys!* he was thinking. Up to their. Busy getting their. No doubt, he forbade himself from completing his thoughts. Block out what ought not to be there. Cut short, at least. So I don't think he gave a sinful thought to the girls in the back of the van, paid that no heed, though for sure he must have known. That made him an unusual priest, even then. There were many unusual priests then, come to think of it, including those who turned their own parochial halls into venues for chaste dancing and mild cavorting. There was money to be made after all.

'I saw more than you all think,' he was saying. 'I heard more.' He seemed to fumble then. There were some inaudible words spoken and a shifting about of the glasses in front of himself and Alice. It was not obvious to me whether he was praying for or drinking to the memory of the men, or maybe it was like one of those pauses in the Mass where the priest has a rest and the altar boys take over. As he had not sat down, he was not finished.

'Seeing and hearing is half of what a good priest does, more than half. You think it is sermonising on Sunday or commiserating at funerals, but it is really all about the use we make of our senses. This'—he pointed to his temple—'is my filing system: faulty, unreliable certainly, but the place I store the fragments, I see, hear, and even smell. Fragments of what? The things you tell me when you are frightened or elated; the smiles I see at a wedding or the frowns on the touchline in a game; the smell of Pat's bread van: all of it means something, and I do my best to lock away most of it up here. Believe me, a priest sees and hears a lot, and it's not just in the Confessional: a lot goes in here!' And again, the finger on his temple. 'So be careful what you say to me, because I know when you are lying!'

There was a terrified silence in the room. McCaul had something on everyone in there, a grip on each of us. We were sinners again, teenagers and instinctive liars. He glanced down towards Alice and seemed to change his mind about consulting her this time. He, evidently, had control over her too. 'As I told you earlier, I have come to you today after having had meetings with mandarins of Her Majesty's government. Dressed as I am, they do not look upon me as a man of the cloth, but they surely know I am one. I encourage them to call me Vincent, to underestimate me, but secretly I am aware that in the official notes they make, I am only ever Fr McCaul. They know I am watching and listening, *sensing*. They know that I am collecting information from them, filing it up here; in fact, they rely on me to do that, for they want me to pass it all on to Miss McCann and the Provisionals. Through me, they imagine, our Republican friends will learn more about the political—or material—benefits that will come their way once weapons have been put beyond use. The economic investment, an increased say for Dublin, that sort of thing. I can't tell you about that. If I did tell you, I know that there is at least one person here tonight who would feed that back to the British, and my days would be done!'

Again, we were the accused: not we collectively this time but we singly. Every*one*, if you catch my meaning. I thought it, but others did too, I am sure. McHugh certainly did; Quinn, from his hiding place, knew it for sure. McCaul was fingering me as an informant, potential, actual, or habitual. He knew this about me because he sensed it. In other words, he had been watching me, listening out, filing it, and then reassembling all of that until he knew me as a weasel. Stamp, stamp.

'I am the narrator,' the priest continued. 'I talk to the Provisionals and I talk to the British, and I present the point of view of one to the other. Honesty is my trade. Each must believe that equally. I must be expertly honest: that means I must know what honesty, at a given moment, is. Honesty is not, by definition, simply the absence of a lie. There are circumstances when a lie as I know it is not the same thing as a lie as you know it. And honesty is not simply the facts either. A fact, on its own, may be observable and undeniable, but, taken together, the truth is something else. One example of my point can stand for the rest: the very existence of a place called Northern Ireland is a hard-boiled, plain-as-day fact and therefore true; or, if you are of a different persuasion, it is a fiction, a false construct, it is history's bastard: its legal existence is not evidence enough that it is truly there.'

Many in the room clapped, relieved to have heard something they understood and deciding that they agreed with it.

'The facts are not always the same as the honest truth, and indeed they are often not. My role, when I speak to one side of the other, is to present facts in an order and from a selection that conforms with the ready expectations of the men I am talking to. I am a narrator. I must decide, is this a fact, is this the best fact to use, and when is the best time for me to use this fact? These are often subjective judgements. Is it a fact if you do not agree with it, if you do not believe it, if it is contradicted by your other instincts and life experiences? Another man's fact cannot be true, if you know it not to be.

'There is a wealth of information that is told to me by one side in the expectation that I pass it on to the other. They want me to pass on this information because, if they were to do so, it would be like an act of betrayal—they could be killed in their cars for doing it. So they tell me so I can tell the other side, and they leave it to me to decide how much I actually pass on. No doubt they watch me, no doubt they listen in with their spies, but, still, if I have a role, it is to sift through what I am told before I tell another. I am partial—not in the sense that I am representing a party but in the sense that I hold their information in many parts and I share it in part. And I decide when is the most propitious time to reveal these parts, their information, their facts. Do I lay it all out at the start, so there are no surprises? Do I, from the very beginning, reveal *this is the man* and *this is what he does*? Or do I, like a narrator, set the scenes, establish the characters, and, as for plot, lay the breadcrumbs as I go?'

It was a tiny move, imperceptible for anyone not looking for it, but Alice's hand shifted again to touch McCaul's, not now to console him in his sadness but to stop him saying more. The contact seemed to bring him back into the room, where he could see our dumbstruck faces and hear his boys' bemused silence. So he expertly brought his remarks to a conclusion. 'As with any narrator, I have to know when is the right time to stop telling stories, and I think we are there now. But I do have one more request of you: pray for me. Pray that I get this right. Pray for me that I am hearing what I think I am hearing, seeing what I think I am, that I am being honest on both sides. Pray that I am not a madman and not a fool!'

That seemed to be a joke, so we laughed and decided that was the end of it. Fr McCaul sat down, Alice still holding his hand. She leant into his ear, maybe to whisper reassurance to him, maybe to kiss him, the truth of that I could not say and do not care. We clapped.

∞

I would have left then, but that did not appear in the order of service. A queue to the bar formed immediately, and those who did leave only decamped to the lounge upstairs where our evening had begun. Fr McCaul's sermon unleashed an evening of untrammelled hedonism.

('You got drunk?'

Yes, Mandy.

'Did the priest, Fr McCaul, and his girlfriend get drunk too?'

Who can say, Mandy? They left earlier than most, not as early as might have been expected.

'Did Quinn reappear?'

Just as soon as the subject was changed.

'Did you talk to Fr McCaul?')

I spoke to Alice. It's funny, I had no intention. McHugh had gone to fetch me a pint. I was standing therefore on my own, and she came out of the Ladies'. Otherwise, I guess, she would have been with McCaul. She hesitated about two yards away from me, scanning the room for him, looking suddenly more like the maid she was when I last saw her. She was skinny then and wore the simplest of dresses— you would have to call it a housecoat—and I had a vision of her doling out the soup on match days. She really was not a lot older than us. I said hello.

'Sorry,' she responded, still looking about the room for her partner. 'I don't.'

That's okay, I replied. I just thought you were.

'Sorry,' she said again, this time to me. 'Vincent knows all the names, but I am terrible that way.'

I told her who I was. I mentioned the soup, because that was what, in my mind, connected her to us.

'Oh, you were one of our "broth boys"!' she exclaimed.

Broth boys?

'That's what we called the boys we fed. Sorry, that sounds insensitive now. It's impossible to talk politely about charity.'

('Charity?'

Apparently so, Mandy.)

'So you were Frank?' Then she laughed at her own ridiculous question. 'You are Frank? I do remember you, I think.'

It's all right that you don't. Most people have forgotten me or remember me in ways I don't remember myself.

'But you have changed. Of course, you have! Who does not change after all those years?'

Sean McHugh thinks otherwise. What is it, Mandy, what is it really about a person that alters over thirty years? Are the physical changes we see in a person—the thickening of their limbs, the creases creeping on their face—are they, do you think, little more than the outward effects of living a life? That, if it's true, would mean that we could read the life of joy or worry in a person's face. The loss of a parent, the illness of a child, all of it—we would see all of it. That's what Alice was saying here when she said I had changed. She was saying that, in my face, she could see betrayal.

'Yes! Every afternoon, rain or shine, you would trot along to the parish house for a bowl of soup or whatever I could cook out of what was left. You were always very polite and grateful. Your poor mother did her best, I suppose, and she gave you manners.'

('Have you mentioned your mother, Frank?'

I did just once, Mandy. It's not something I talk about.

'I'm sure you didn't, Frank. I would remember.'

Then, Mandy, you have not been listening. I told you I was born prematurely, I told you my mother did not like talking about it.

'Are you sure that was me you told, Frank?')

My mother did do her best.

'That's what I always thought,' Alice continued. 'But you lost your father, didn't you? You were still only very young. You can't hardly remember your father?'

I remember he was tall.

'I can't picture him. Now I remember, you were the quiet one! Maybe that's why I said you were so polite. We could hardly get a word out of you.'

I was tongue-tied.

'Barely spoke up for yourself. I have got that right, have I not? All about you would be hollering and screaming, and you as quiet as a dormouse.'

From being born prematurely.

'I did think—sorry to bring this up, as it hardly matters now—but I did think, Can that boy not stand up for himself and his friends just once?'

('What did she mean, Frank? She sounds like an old witch.')

I was tongue-tied from being born prematurely, and surely you must have known that.

'Because he was mean to you then, you know. Father. He was mean. I couldn't say anything because I worked for him and I was Protestant and didn't know any better: I thought, that's just the way priests are. But he was mean.'

He never laid a finger on us.

'Mean with his words. Maybe not to you—I don't know, I was not there the whole time—but certainly to some of the other boys. That was his way of getting the most out of you, so I thought then. Was there one boy in particular?'

Jimmy.

'There was one boy in particular. A Scotch boy. He was your friend, I think. Vincent talked about him just then.'

Jimmy was my friend.

'Your only friend, at a guess. Sorry to say that, but mute boys don't attract a lot of friends. I'm quiet myself. A Scotch boy, I don't mind his name, it doesn't matter now.'

Jimmy.

'Vincent was mean to him.'

He said he could not be trusted, because he was from elsewhere. He said that he knew nothing about football and might as well not be on the pitch. He said that, on account of his harelip, Jimmy was brutishly ugly and would scare the wits out of the opposition. He said that, for all that Jimmy was useless, he was at least useful for that.

'I thought you could have spoken up for your friend.'

Alice didn't watch the games, but she was at every one. She hid behind that great big soup tureen, in her housecoat, behind a sweet but blank expression. Is that what inscrutable means? It is what inscrutable means. She was that then, more than she was that now. She was more expressive now. Actually, that's wrong—although it hardly matters that I get these things exactly right. She was not more expressive: she was merely expressing more. Her face, even after thirty years of living a life, really had not changed that much: it was still a little sweet, overall blank, featureless you'd have to say, neither careworn nor joyworn. She just *spoke* more. She said more to me then, at the Gresham Hotel, than I remember from a whole boyhood of eating her broth. She was wearing a glamorous dress and had on fancy jewellery, but these were adorning a face and a frame that were the same as they had ever been. Narrow shoulders, sharp cheekbones, betokening childhood undernourishment that the rest of her life never made up for. And, like then, she was still serving the bully priest.

'I thought you were a good boy, deep down.' She said this out of the blue.

I don't know, Mandy. Is it better to be a good person deep down or one only on the surface? She was saying I was not, for all intents and purposes, a good person, except maybe in my quieter moments. Not my "quieter moments": I was always quiet. I was only good when it didn't matter to be good, when hardly anyone was there to notice. The rest of the time, I.

'You went off the rails there, did you not?'

('What did she mean by that, Frank?')

She meant, I went off the rails.)

'Would that be fair to say?' she said fairly. 'People said—I didn't know this for myself—that you suddenly found that tongue in your head and you used it to start fights in Suzy's, the Adair even. You caused a near riot after attacking Declan of Suzy's, the bloody army had to step in. You started talking about civil rights and how the Catholics didn't have any, long before anyone else did and—long before anyone else did—you advocated for violence as the only way. You followed your friend, the Scotchman, up to Belfast and dragged him along to all sorts of meetings. Revolutionaries, I don't know what. You had Vincent worried for you.'

He paid me no attention.

'He was watching, Frank. And he heard what people were saying about you. People came and told him directly. How else would I know about it?'

(Mandy suddenly rose from her seat beside her patient's bed. She wanted Frank not to say the thing that she feared he was about to say; she hoped, by the magic of standing up, that she might change the subject.

'Are you okay, Mandy?'

'I'm okay. Are you?'

'Well, I'm in hospital, if you have to know.'

'I noticed that. I am a nurse. I should take a look at you.' Mandy checked her patient's heart rate and temperature (as it was time) and noted her numbers on the record at the foot of Frank's bed, out of his reach. 'You are sick,' she concluded.

'I had that impression.'

'Well, you are!'

'Sorry, Mandy.')

What were people reporting about me?

'Well, Frank, you know how people are: when they don't know a thing they want to know, they make do with the next available evidence. They could not work out what Dynes was doing in that van, they could not understand why he—who was not political—should have driven a bomb to the border. Ryan was a different case: he was a daft monkey who was capable of anything like that. But not Aloysius Dynes. He was a lovely fella, ran errands for everybody. Why was he? No one could work that out. And then there was big Jimmy Cash. Officially, there was no case made against him, but the whole world knew different. They said—because they didn't know and they wanted to make sense of it all—they said you were the one who put

Cash up to the job at Cullycreggan. That he never would have gotten himself involved in all of that if you hadn't filled his head with a load of nonsense. He wasn't even from here! That's not me saying it. That's them saying it. Jimmy Cash was involved in that, wasn't he? It wasn't only Ryan and Dynes.'

And what do you say, Alice?

'I don't say anything, Frank. I don't talk about what I don't know about. That would be a good policy overall, in my mind. As I say, deep down, I always thought you were a good boy.'

Deep down, where it doesn't count.

෴

McHugh returned then with a pint for me. Alice disappeared. We got drunk. After the priest and his companion left, the whole party kept drinking, and, as Quinn had foreseen, there was something of a riot.

CHAPTER XII

Sometimes, Nicole, when I look at these old men lying here, I wonder if they haven't died in their sleep already. Do you ever think that? I catch myself staring at them, waiting to see their chest rising, reassuring myself they are still breathing. I know that the monitors would tell us if they had passed away, but these old guys are devious, they have seen things, they could trick a heart monitor if they just wanted to slip off unnoticed.

You're a mad one, you are, Mandy.

Mandy stood looking at Frank, waiting to see him breathe. She thought to herself that his skin was dry and textured like the hospital pyjamas he was wearing. There was a crease above his lip, the sort that occurs when you sleep with your face buried in the folds. She touched his arm, and the flesh shifted forward against the bone. Frank looked older in his sleep. We all look older asleep, she decided, being that bit closer to the end.

'Is that you, Mandy?'

She sat down joyfully. 'It is, Frank, sorry to wake you. There's nothing wrong with your memory!'

'I try not to forget a pretty face. And I wasn't asleep.' She saw him grimace and rose to rearrange his pillows. 'Thanks. That's better.'

'Not good, but better?' She thought that sounded like something Frank might say.

'Are you allowed to sit so long with me? I'm not chasing you away, I just don't want any trouble for you.'

'The men are quiet tonight, Frank. It's not always like this, believe me. The other nurses say that the men behave better when Nicole is on. That's our joke amongst ourselves. They think she is more fearsome than she actually is. So, no, it's all right for me to sit here for a bit, if you wanted to go on.'

'Go on? Oh, I see. You mean.' Frank looked to the bedside table. 'Can I have a wee drink of that, do you think?'

The nurse allowed her patient a sip of water.

☙❧

My mouth is so dry. It's so dry in here. Is it the atmosphere? Not my throat so much, but my tongue and the roof are parched; I can feel my lips are cracking. I'll need another sip soon, with all of this talking you're making me do. I thought I had finished with my story: I've said practically everything there is. What everyone thought of me, what they thought they knew about me, that I had put Cash up to Cullycreggan. And Quinn was sure he was on to me for the other thing. If Cash was such a great guy in my opinion, that left me fingering myself for the role of tout. Quinn had it all figured out, unless I could do something about it. There was no one else who could help me, was there?

All I have is.

Frank didn't finish his sentence, for what he had left was either too small a thing or too big a thing to properly contemplate. The dimensions of a mountain or a hollow are much the same. He was in pain, but are you allowed to press the morphine button when the nurse is sitting there beside you?

Mandy could see the colour had changed in Frank's face since his sleep. For some reason, her thoughts drifted to her own uncle and to the fingers of his right hand, whose yellowness had at first fascinated her and then frightened her as a child. He would run them through her hair, insisting she liked it. He would urge her to sit on his lap, then he would comb his yellow fingers through her yellow hair and tickle her. She was the only one, and it made her feel special until the day she noticed the look on her mother's face, the one that told her she was disgusted with her. Then Mandy sat on her uncle's lap only because he liked it. That period in their lives ended when she was tall enough for her feet to reach the ground. No thank you, Uncle. Please. And, because her feet now touched the ground, she ran off. Frank was not like her uncle—and she was not like the girl she had been—but she wanted her mind taken from the pain of that time.

'Cash? What happened to your friend—did he ever make it back from Africa? I'd be interested in how he turned out. Did you ever hear from him? Did you?'

Frank stirred. Maybe, despite the discomfort he was in, he had been about to drop off to sleep again. Drag yourself back awake, get your thoughts in the right order. Had he ever heard from Jimmy Cash again?

I did. I say I did. He said he wanted to meet me one last time. We arranged, all of us, to rendezvous (his word) at a hotel outside Belfast. So that happened. I can tell you about that, if you'd like. That did not turn out as I thought it might. It was like he was a different man. I don't mean that he was different—we are all that. I mean, he was a different man. That was just the strangest day; I can't work it out in my head even yet. It was as if the night I saw them off at the Liverpool ferry was in fact the last I had seen of the old Jim and Betty, and these two were someone else entirely. Betty had even said that would be the case. I will tell you about that.

But you may as well know he is dead now too. He died in an accident in the normal sort of way, I don't know quite how. I only recently found that out; a woman called Liz told me that. Too much life: the body tells you. You are medical, so you might not agree. There is a limit to the number of times you can allow yourself to fall over and to the number of times you can pull yourself together again. Shall I go back?

Jim and Betty were in Rhodesia, but they didn't stay there. Long before I saw him again at the hotel, they were living somewhere in England. I explained it to Emma Cooper at the Public Records Office.

'Why did you do that? How did you get talking to her about Jim?' How many other people had Frank sat on his knee and told his story to? Mandy wondered.

I had to. I didn't have to. It came up; she was a journalist, she asked questions, I had to give her something, she wanted a name, she wanted to know more about me, I didn't want her knowing more about me— that was not the point, that was the reverse of the point—so I had to give her answers, and Cash was on my mind, so I told her about him.

'What's your name?' she asked. She had just been looking through my notebook, taking down all the details of the bomb at Cullycreggan, about the van and who owned it. I had told her that I knew, or did not quite know, Dynes and Ryan. 'Were you friendly with them?' she asked.

I told her—I had the feeling that this was crucial, that she might not be interested otherwise—I told her that I did know the bomber and the driver, that I was or had been their friend, that in fact I knew them well, the driver at least. But you can't use my name, I said. You understand.

'Okay, but what is your name?' She said I was her source, and, although I would be anonymous for the story, I could not be anonymous to her. How odd, I thought, that we had been sitting here all this time, that I knew her name, that I had been calling her by her name all this time, and she—the journalist—did not yet know who I was. I thought, if she doesn't trust me, if she needs a second source, that's easy: all she needs to do is to take a look at the register we all had to sign to get into the PRO. *We had badges.* So then I thought: she has done that already. What she wants from me now is not my name but the name I want her to think I am known by. Is that too convoluted? Is that too conspiratorial a thing for a reporter who came in interested in Clodagh Rodgers from Ballymena?

'My name is Jim Cash,' I told her. She wrote it down in capitals. She flicked through my notebook one more time, checking if my name—JIM CASH—came up. It didn't. She set it down and shook my hand.

'Pleased to meet you, Mr Cash,' she said. Straightaway, just by how she said it or by how it sounded in my ears, we accepted it was false. But she didn't care, we needn't speak of it; it was not important to her to get this most basic fact right. 'Is there still a Mrs Cash?'

(There *is* a Mrs Cash, I reasoned.) There is, I lied. Betty, or Elizabeth. I'm a lucky man. Betty, Betty to everyone.

Emma Cooper looked around in exaggerated fashion, as if to ask, Where is this Betty person now? If you're so lucky?

This is a personal thing, a personal interest of mine. I knew I sounded defensive, and the more I did, the more I had to tell her. These were my friends rather than Betty's. Betty was from elsewhere.

I'll say Newcastle. *Our* Newcastle, not the one in England. That fits. I was from somewhere else too, originally, as a matter of fact, Scotland. You can't hear it in my.

'You can't hear Scotch in your voice at all, Mr Cash.'

No, well, that was a long time ago, I was a wee boy. And we have moved about a lot since then, you'd hardly know there was any Scottish in me at all now. Rhodesia.

'You lived in Rhodesia?'

('You told Emma Cooper that you emigrated to Rhodesia?'

Yes, I did. No, I didn't. I told her that Jim and Betty had.)

Yes, we did. Zimbabwe. As it is now. But we had to leave.

'Had to?'

The guerrillas. Yes, had to. This, you understand, Emma, this . . . this is not what I would like you to write about. This is just because, well, I won't tell you if you're not bothered, but, either way, I don't want—I don't give you permission—to write about me.

'I understand, Jim. And I am bothered. I mean, I am interested.'

I don't want anything by you in the papers about me. That has to be understood. I am actually a very private man, as I need to be. I'm a. Well, never mind that, for now.

'You're a what, Mr Cash? And, maybe, before you answer, do I really need you to talk to my colleague Ben? Would you actually be better off talking to our security reporter?'

I'm an engineer. I build roads. Or I engineer them, if you know the difference. I plan where they go, what needs to be cleared to make way for them, what the optimum mix of materials will be. Then I supervise the team as they lay it down: the precise layering from sub-base to base to sand to asphalt; the geology of the subgrade it sits on and the means of levelling it off.

'That doesn't sound like something you have to flee from.'

It doesn't. When I went there with my wife—with Betty, that's my wife—I didn't expect to have to leave in a hurry. Two basic things you need to understand about roads: they have to go *through* somewhere, and someone has to pay for them. Those are problems beyond the remit of your common or garden engineer. My boss in southern Africa, Danny Simms—she was a woman—she had a particular approach to these problems. I say that she was a woman

---

161

because otherwise you might not assume that, and even people who work for her don't always realise that about her at first. She has a habit of turning up unannounced. In short, Danny Simms' solution to these problems was to sell weapons to one set of insurrectionists to raise the funds to plough a road through the homes of another set of insurrectionists.

('That does sound like something you might have to flee from. You don't want to aggravate your minorities.' Mandy found that she was second-guessing the attitudes she assumed Jim Cash would have. 'He might in actual fact be on the side of the oppressor but see himself on the side of the oppressed.' Mandy felt she was getting to know this man she had never met. 'Try as he might, so far he had failed to flee from that.'

That's interesting. That's exactly what Emma Cooper said.)

'That does sound like something you might have to flee from. You don't want to aggravate your minorities.'

That's interesting you should put it that way, Emma. As you may know, the black population of Rhodesia at the time, taken as a whole, was not a minority in the country—quite the opposite. The whites held their position in government for so long only by dividing the blacks up and setting one tribe against another. It's an old trick. It's exactly this that Danny Simms was attempting to pull off. She was lucky for a long time until, in the end, all the little instances of bad luck were added together, and her good fortune was found to have run out. Other forces were at play. Enough of the separate guerrilla groups realised that together they were the majority and decided to join their forces. My own operation was rumbled. A transport I was trying to get over the border to South Africa was intercepted. The gang took the merchandise for themselves and then turned it on us: they gelignited my road, stole my equipment, and shanghaied my men into their armies.

'I think, Mr Cash'—and at this point, she looked down at her notes, as if to emphasise she didn't really believe the name she had written there—'that you are a gunrunner. Or a failed gunrunner, which is no better, is it? You ran guns to terrorists, just like what used to happen here. I don't like saying this to your face, because you certainly don't look like an active terrorist, but in my book, that in no way makes you a hero. You got caught, and then they ran you out of the country. Am I wrong?'

No, I would say that your last point is correct: I was driven out, or I got out only with help. But—how can I say this without blowing my own?—others, yes, others, *friends would say,* friends who know me would not say I was a coward. You can use a word like 'gunrunner', and everyone would agree that person was on the wrong side. But a gunrunner is a smuggler by another name, and, in some people's eyes, a smuggler is simply someone who supplies what you need without going via the usual authorities. Smugglers brave rough seas in tiny boats, landing them on deserted beaches by the light of the moon. Smugglers are even romantic, or glamorous. Some would say.

('A smuggler handles contraband rum. A smuggler has a family to feed and keeps his trousers up with string. That's not what you were doing. You were running guns to terrorists.' The nurse found herself taking sides with the journalist.

Not me, Mandy. That was Cash. And they were only terrorists if you are a fan of minority, apartheid rule in southern Africa.

'Okay, not you. Cash. But you are saying that Cash is some sort of swashbuckling hero. Is that what you think of him? Is his the life you would really have wanted for yourself?' Mandy was getting to know Cash, but not to love him as much as her patient did.)

I am not saying that's how I saw myself, Emma: I am not calling myself a swashbuckling hero. But I did try to stay on the right side. I was an importer of equipment vital to the construction of my road. Thinking of it as my road meant that I did not have to think about it as Simms' or the government's; I could even tell myself that I might be hastening the arrival of a different sort of government. Even if my part in that was small. But that did imply guns, yes. Running guns to one side, to raise money for the other. It is rather easy, in these situations, to find yourself on the wrong side.

'On all the wrong sides, Mr Cash.'

('Did she really say that, Frank? All the wrong sides.' Mandy wished she had thought to put it that way. She suddenly found herself in awe of another woman, living in the same city as she, perhaps of a similar age, but capable of thinking such a thought and saying it. Where had Emma Cooper been that she, Mandy, had not? What school, what books, what friends, what men in what parks had she agreed to follow to what places? What choices had Emma Cooper made for herself or luck had she had—that ended with her saying such a thing? Had Mandy herself found herself on some of the wrong sides?

'She really said that, Frank?'

She did, Mandy. That's not a line I could make up by myself.)

Emma Cooper picked up her pen and turned a page in her notebook, even though I was not her story. Cash was not.

Well, Emma, morality is both a collective and a personal concern. Just as a person must know right from wrong, so must a people. A person may condemn or take an action, but it's up to the people to know when and how to act.

'That sounds like the opposite of what a great person might say. That sounds like just the thing a person might say if they knew what they were doing was not right. I am sorry to say that to you, Mr Cash, because, like I said just now, you sitting there don't seem to me to be the sort of person to allow himself to be morally compromised like that.'

(What was I to say, Mandy? That she was wrong on both counts—that both the man she was talking to and the man she thought she was talking to were, in their own ways, morally up the creek?

'I expect you defended yourself.'

I didn't. I did.)

Emma, I. Let me. I had a. It was my job to build a road. That meant it became my job to find the money to build the road. It was a road to Nyasaland, which by then already did not exist, so, by definition, it was a road to nowhere, and perhaps I ought to have questioned more why we were destroying villages for a highway that would never be constructed. It was a funny place for a person from Ireland to show up. 'Away! Away!' I once watched on as a priest, a black man, of course, stood in front of a rusty old excavator we were using to destroy his school. He was trying to shoo away my men, white men, of course, because we were specialists, in hard hats—'Away!'—while at the same time urging some stray children to run to safety. Away! They had no shoes. They taunted my men, even climbed up onto the open-backed truck we were using to spirit their mothers and sisters away in. 'Away! Away!' the priest kept calling. It was pathetic.

He had all the moral courage and still he could do nothing. And, therefore, I could do nothing.

'You destroyed his village. You did not have to do that.'

You are right, there is no denying that. But, as I say, it was my job, and at that time I needed to be working elsewhere than Northern Ireland, and that 'elsewhere' was Rhodesia. My boss, Danny Simms, reckoned that selling weapons to the black nationalists in South Africa would persuade the rest of the world to defend the white nationalists in Rhodesia. I thought the opposite was just as likely: to destabilise the regime in Cape Town could topple the government in Salisbury. It would take the people to do that, not me. But I did decide to make it my personal concern. I did take part, and it was the guns I was running that fell into their hands.

'How did they get that information, Mr Cash? How did they know that by stopping your trucks they would find weapons? Did you tell them? Were you a tout?'

No.

'But someone did tell them, right? You know who the tout was, right? You made sure.'

Yes.

'Who told them, Mr Cash?'

(Betty, my wife.

'Why did you tell Emma Cooper it was Betty? Really, why did you have to bring her into it?'

You misheard. I didn't tell Emma Cooper it was Betty. I am telling you, Mandy. You are getting mixed up.

It was true: Mandy had become confused between when Frank was talking to the reporter and when he was just talking to her—and between when he was being Frank and when he was being Cash. There was a difference in the relationship one had with a journalist and with a nurse, and that ought to be respected, she felt. But, however strongly she felt it, she could not quite define what this difference was. You talk to a journalist, you talk to a nurse; to both, you tell them about as much of the truth as you can bear at that moment; it can feel good, even therapeutic, to get it off your chest. There is a difference—where exactly is the difference—there *is* a difference. You talk to a reporter because you know she is going to tell everyone else:

that's her job. You talk to a nurse: sometimes you can just talk to her, and she needn't tell another living soul.

∞

Mandy, do you remember the gardener? What was his name? Jeremy? No, it was Joshua. He and Betty used to drive around to the sorts of places she shouldn't go to, and to which he could only go because she was there too. She asked him few questions, but still she knew things because she listened.

'Over there is a diamond mine, Mrs Cash,' Joshua would say. 'The men you see coming out are local men. They live their days underground. They often work only with their hands or with tools they can carry in their hands. They earn enough money to buy fuel for their stove and to buy enough food so they are fit to do another day's work. Over there'—Joshua pointed to a two-storey, white-painted brick building—'it is the administration. That is where the manager sits and his three secretaries. He eats in there too. I think he never comes out until the end of the day when his driver collects him and takes him home. He is a white man, educated in South Africa. The boss before him was the same, as so will be the boss who comes after him. In the evenings, he goes with his wife to the Balaclava.'

Ahem. Sal, Betty thought: he knows about Sal. And Piet, Diamond Piet.

'It is the law, Mrs Cash. The manager must not be clever or competent or fair; these things are not needed, but he must always be white. We cannot change the law because the lawyers are white and the lawmakers are white. White lawyers and white lawmakers cannot make laws that are against their own interests. One might as well ask the horns of a sable antelope to arch forwards and not back. Nature might one day find a way, but it is too long to wait for evolution.'

Ahem.

'There is a quicker way, Mrs Cash.'

Even if he were not so straightforward, Joshua would have been easy to understand.

And there was also that one time she chatted to Danny Simms. Betty Cash was a hard woman to astonish, and I can imagine Danny Simms wanting to do that. Is that why a person passes on information,

166

is that why they betray confidences—because there is someone they want to impress?

'You are something of a mystery, Mrs Cash,' Simms told her. 'Your husband does not talk about you.' Simms drank from her whisky and looked about the room where the party was being held in honour of some target being met. She had been left alone with this woman. 'How are you not entirely crushed by your existence here?'

'I am sorry, Miss Simms.' Betty wanted to leave, but this was her house. 'If you like, I can find you more stimulating company.'

Simms laughed. 'I like that! No, don't go. I am provoking you. I just can't imagine you wanting to stay here, in this house with its housekeeper and its . . . whatever else the company gives you to keep you from doing anything useful.'

'It's a nice house.'

Simms laughed again. 'What do you care about that? What do you *do*?' But she looked away, or drank from her whisky, so that Betty did not have to answer. 'There is so much to be done here. There is so much to do for a person who does not need a home to sleep in at night, right? I wonder, were you the person we ought to have employed?' This time, Simms did expect a reply.

'Are you unhappy with Jim?'

'Your husband is perfectly satisfactory, Mrs Cash.' And now, if she looked around or drank from her whisky, it was to open a space for some jealousy to enter. 'He's a good boy who does what he's told, right?'

'My husband is a good man,' Betty tried.

Simms continued to laugh at her hostess. But there would have been other people there at the party that she ought to speak to, however unattractive she found them.

'My husband . . .' Betty may not have gotten to the end of that line, if that was the way she had started it. I say it no more strongly than this: Danny Simms—to impress the woman, shock her, or merely to move away from her—may have told Betty Cash that her husband was running guns over the border to South Africa.

Ahem. Betty, because she could listen, knew that Joshua was in the same but opposite business, supplying the Spear of the Nation, the youth wing of the ANC in South Africa sometimes called MK.

Maybe her intention was to take her husband out of harm's way: after all, why should Jim do the gunrunning if Joshua was prepared to do it? She knew when her husband travelled south of the border because he used to invite her along, and she knew he told her only because she always declined. So, if Danny Simms told her about the guns and Jim told her his travel plans, Betty would have been able to put the two together. She formed a plan.

'All the wrong sides.'

Yes, Mandy.

Jim's team was to cross the border at the bridge over the Limpopo River. The MK would have travelled up from Messina. Jim's truck had the guns and his construction workers in the back; he drove because everyone knew that the guards on the border asked fewer questions when the driver was white. They never got that far. Two miles short of the border was a roadblock. Cash would surely have recognised it for what it was, but he pulled over obediently; he would have had no option if he wanted to live. A paramilitary, in mismatching uniform and brown beret, poked the nose of his Kalashnikov through Jim's window and used it to force him from the cabin. He handed over his driving papers.

'Why are you driving to the border, Mr Cash?'

'You have no right to ask me that. You are not a border guard.' One protests one's civil rights with such trite recitations. You have no right to know where I have come from or where I am going to.

The paramilitary landed a rifle butt to the side of Jim's face, as was his right.

'Mr Cash, whether you choose to tell us or not, you are going no further tonight.'

He had a split lip. Sorry, but I cannot dislodge this detail from my image of the scene: Jim's lip, split already, would be bleeding from the blow, bleeding prodigiously. What's in his head right now? Is he afraid of permanent damage to his face, enraged by that? Is he still scouring his brain for technical defences?

'I am chief engineer for Nyasa Communications. I am on legitimate business.' Maybe he tried to scare his attacker with a name, Simms, Douglas.

'We want what you have in the back of your truck, Mr Cash.'

Under these circumstances, why would Cash still continue to stick up for himself? If he put up a fight, I prefer to think it was for a cause other than himself. Did he know what this paramilitary wanted the guns for, that they were destined for just the same group—Umkhonto we Sizwe—that he was trying to reach? If so, the fight he put up was simply over who should profit from the sale.

'You can't have what's in my truck.' The truck belonged to Nyasa Communications, the workers in the back were its employees, and the profits from the sale of the guns were to go to funding the road to Nyasaland, a place he was aware did not exist. That was the fight he chose.

Another man in brown beret stepped up and forced his enormous fist into Jim's solar plexus. The same fist then came down on his neck like a pile driver, and instantly Jim was powerless, as if his arms and legs had been switched off. He would already have been beyond feeling the boots kicking into his back and his ribs, yet these would have delivered the injuries he would need to nurse for the next four months.

The workers scrambled mutely out of the truck, hands aloft. They lined up by the side of the road. The crates they were sitting on were then lifted out and piled up, also at the side of the road, two miles short of the border and the armed presence of the Rhodesian army. If Cash had been able to call out, would they have heard him? And, if they had, would they have come? The paramilitaries—Joshua, perhaps, among them but not declaring himself—drove off in their own truck, with Jim's men and the crates of guns and ammunition. Jim lay gasping at the side of the road, wondering if he would live and at what a strange place it was for him to be.

That's what I think happened.

'Or not?'

Or not.

'What makes you think that's what happened, Frank? Who told you, or why have you decided that's the way things happened?')

I can't tell you that.

'Why can't you tell me, Mr Cash?'

I can't tell you that either, Emma.

('Are you talking to Emma Cooper now?')

'Why don't you let me write *your* story, Mr Cash?'

('Because it wasn't true!' Mandy raised her voice, as if she expected Emma Cooper to be able to hear. Come on, Emma, she seemed to say: make the connection.

Yes, Mandy, as I understand it, it *was* true.

'What makes you say that, Frank? How do you know that's what happened to Jim Cash unless he told you himself? Did he tell you?'

He couldn't tell me. He was not at liberty to talk to me about those things. That's what I believe. But I could not tell Emma Cooper about all of that.

'Because you were making it up?'

No, because it was true, only not of me. But, as I had used my real name—no, no, I had used *Jim's* real name—I had to steer her away.)

Because it's an official secret. Emma, I have already told you more than I ought to have.

She was less impressed by that excuse than I might have imagined. Then I remembered what kind of journalist she really was.

'Then tell me about your wife. You said she was a singer, that she sometimes sang with the Daytona Showband?' She flicked through her notebook. 'Eilis is her name, or Betty? Is that the same thing? Which is it?'

Had I already told her that, or was she simply moving too quickly for me?

I told you that Eilis was a stage name, I said.

'You did! You did tell me that. And you told me also how lucky you were to have her as a wife.'

I did. Where was this going? Was this the sort of conversation that was going to just stay a conversation, or was it going somewhere else, for example, into one of her articles? How much of my wife would I have to throw into this to get Emma Cooper to write the ruddy story for me?

I *am* lucky, I am very lucky. Isn't any man who? She was in a book. There was a book about the show bands, and Eilis featured in that. We had that book once. The blonde songstress from Toberlough. She was in that book as Eilis. But she didn't use her stage name after. Betty didn't have use of her stage name after that night, because it was very soon after that we went to Rhodesia and. There was no call for it there. Maybe that's when we lost the book.

'Did Betty want to go with you to Rhodesia? Would she not have preferred to pursue her career here?'

Sometimes, sound travels at very slow speeds. I was nodding, with no words coming out.

I recall very well the night we left, I said at last. A good friend had seen us off. A good. Was he such a? He. He was. Frank was there. With Betty and, with Betty and me, and he even brought some Guinness, which was peculiar. There was a family of boys lying on the floor of the waiting room, waiting for the ferry to England. Frank was the only one who. Emma, that's hard for me to say right now, but I am sure he saw himself as a good. Yes. Sorry, that's not what you were asking. I. How can I? *I* have not thought about *him* in this way for.

'How did Eilis feel about leaving?'

We *had* to leave.

'Because of the Daytona massacre? Eilis wanted to leave?'

That's right. Betty, her name is Betty. It was for both of us, really, but yes. We. Betty and. What you've got to understand here, Emma, is that Betty and I make decisions together. I might be the one who, but she is the one who. See what I mean? It's always been that way. People can say things, people can say all they like, people—you couldn't credit people, Emma—they said things when we lived over here, and they said things when we lived over there, about Betty in the main, but I never listened, or I did listen but I ignored them because. Because you're right. Just as you said it: I am a lucky man.

What I recall is. Just let me get this straight, Emma, before I. Yes, funny thing is I recall very well, as if it were. Have you ever taken the ferry to England, Emma? I am sure you have. Isn't it marvellous? That's what we did, my wife Betty and I, we had our own room like we were in a hotel, because that's a long crossing overnight to England, or at least it was in those days, I have no idea nowadays. Clean sheets, your own sink, the lot. A window too, but not a porthole as you might imagine, a square one, but a view by anyone's definition. Not of the front—that's a thing to appreciate here—not of the direction you are actually headed in (nor, for that matter, the view of what you've left behind) but of the *side*. The side is just sea, with no land to catch a grip of. Port and starboard. It means you arrive before you see you have arrived. That's what I recall that time, in our cabin. England was somewhere off there, over our shoulder—and Rhodesia and—round a corner we couldn't yet. And our view was of the side horizon, which we drew no farther towards or away from. We never stopped, but we got no farther.

'How did Betty feel about leaving?'

Did you hear me, Emma? I wanted to say. Moving, moving but making no progress. We never stopped, but did we get anywhere?

'Was Betty happy about leaving Africa? It's hot there, I bet.'

Yes, it is hot, I wanted to say. But there is enough rain for there to be golf courses, if that is something you would want to do.

'Would it be fair to say your wife was bored?'

It would be fair to say that Betty repeatedly made the mistake of following her husband. She went wherever he went, so consequently she never went anywhere at all. I wanted to say.

'Mr Cash?'

The truth is, Emma, I never really took into account how my wife felt about living there, or leaving. It's odd, I know, to say that about someone I love. It is only now that I know the truth about it myself. I remember once, watching her at a party in our house. She was talking to my boss. I couldn't hear what they were talking about; I was too far from them and it was noisy. But I knew that they were talking about me—they had to be, there was no other subject they had in common. I looked at them: my boss, dressed as if she could immediately go into combat, as hard and as squat as a bullet; and my wife. As I say, I could not hear her. Somehow—and I had this feeling *then*, you understand—the sight of her without the sound of her, I could not *see* her. I could have looked from the front or the back or any of the sides, and I would not have been able to fix her in my vision. The particles were all there, arranged as they always were, but at a length from me; and the vision of her, the vision in my eye of her, was also at a distance from me. Blurred, I was drunk. Maybe. But, Emma, I do wonder how well we see the people we see all the time.

Chapter XIII

After Rhodesia, we went to England.

'Who are you saying this to?'

I am saying this to you.

'Frank? You mean me? Are you looking at someone else?' There was no one else. 'There is no one else.'

I am saying this to you. There is no one else.

'And you said, "We went to England".'

Easy mistake to make; I have never been. Cash and Betty went to England after Rhodesia, although where to exactly is a matter for Sherlock Holmes.

'Not Newcastle, then?'

Why would they have gone to Newcastle? What put that notion in your head? Who have you ever known live there?

'Nicole lived there, remember? I told you. Met the footballer with the legs.'

And Nicole. Nicole is. The girl here with the thighs is called Nicole. Nicole, the nurse.

'Remember I told you about Nicole living there, Frank?'

This is a hospital. Nicole is a nurse here. This nurse is called. You are Mandy. I am in a hospital, and you are starving me and stealing my yogurt nuts.

'Are you okay, Frank?'

Fine, Mandy. Mandy! There, you see. I had a wee . . . there: a wee head stagger. They come and go. Too many names. Too many sides.

'You don't think they went to Newcastle, in England?'

No, I don't, Mandy. I don't really know how Newcastle comes into all of this. I do know that there is more than one of them, and that makes life more complicated than it need be. However, having said that, they might well have lived there. Official secrets. I was not meant to ask. We got one postcard, with a picture of Westminster Abbey.

> *Look where we have landed up!*
> *How's Eilis and the boy? Would love to*
> *see you but looks like we will be stationed*
> *here For a while. Don't ask!*
> *Contact me through M.*

'M?'

Moira.

'Moira?'

Moira is Jim's sister.

'Did I know that already?'

If you were listening. Obviously, you will miss some things. I try to repeat.

'I am sure you did not say anything about a sister: I would have remembered. That's okay, Frank. You can't be expected to keep a track of everything you have ever said to me.'

Are you sure I never mentioned Moira?

'I'm sure.'

That she was affected?

'No, you never said a word about her. Affected. Did she also have a harelip?'

Soft in the head.

'You can't say that, Frank!'

I knew you would tell me off, but there it is: she was dropped at birth, some said, and she was never right again.

'She was vulnerable: that's what you call it.' Mandy visited the end of the bed and recorded another misdemeanour on Frank's chart. 'Are you going to tell me more about this sister?'

Not yet. It's not her turn. You asked about her before I was ready.

'You called her "M". The postcard said "M". I wasn't going to let that pass, was I? Not since you made Cash out like a spy. Cash. James Cash.' Mandy laughed.

You laugh, Mandy.

'Should I not?'

I'm not sure I would. I mean, what was I to make of that postcard? I'd show it you if I had it on me still. Someone here will have stolen it. A beautiful picture it had of the Abbey, from the outside, I have never been to London. Actually, the Abbey is at the end of the view, you look down a line of trees at it, it's autumn I assume, there are statues to left and right, only one do I recognise. Not because I have seen it; I have never been to London. It's a statue of Lincoln, Abraham, unmistakeable, though it's odd as he is standing with a chair behind him. It drew my eye, although I very much doubt that was on the photographer's mind when he took it. Bronze and twiggy like the trees it's in line with. The postcard was regular size, but the photographer was clever with their perspective, so the scene was . . . what you could see was *longer* than. It made you look *into* it. You see all those trees and statues of leaders, and you are meant to look beyond them to the Abbey at the end, and you have to conclude that the church is superior to nature and politics, that it trumps the here and now or the merely living. And, by the look of it—I have never seen it for myself, I have never been to London—it, the Abbey, is certainly impressive. But that was not what Jim intended *me* to see: he wanted me to see Abraham Lincoln. I wish I could show you the card.

This is what I think.

Jim was intercepted before he could run his guns over the border to South Africa. But if his intention was to hasten the end of the white regime in Rhodesia, he got his wish anyway. During the months of his convalescence, the government was dragged into talks with the insurrectionists, with the British in the chair, and soon enough a way was found to allow the white leadership to walk off. Zimbabwe was born. Nyasa Communications did not fold straightaway, but they did insist on the repatriation of their overseas staff. That must have made an interesting departures lounge, full of diamond smugglers, neo-Nazis, and mercenaries. My thinking is that Jim and Betty did not associate themselves with that bunch, even if they were on first-name terms at the Balaclava. They would therefore have avoided the first plane out. Betty did not necessarily come quietly: she had not entirely been crushed by her experience there. How crushed can one be in spaces so large? The distance from her fridge to her cooker was a small walk; her garden would be better classed an estate. There is something to be said for being able to stretch out your arms when, for years, you have been taught to pull in your elbows to sit on your own living room sofa. Isn't that what we do—don't we learn how to sit neatly, to use up less room? We could make do with smaller lungs, to take smaller breaths. I do wonder—I *did* wonder: would the excess of space cause her the opposite problem, would the air suddenly be too thin for her? You can stretch your arms out, but, after all, you can get stretched too far. Simms may just as likely have asked her if her life there was not disintegrating her. By my reckoning, however, her answer would still have been no. Betty learned how to drive. A car can cover any journey in Rhodesia, with Joshua beside her, and time is no factor when Cash is good with telling her when he is—and when he is not—expecting to be home that night. She can stare at the sable antelopes for herself.

What would happen to Joshua, she would want to know. 'Never you mind about the gardener,' the reply might come. 'He is one of the winners out of this. Zimbabwe under Mugabe will look after the likes of Joshua. At least he will live. There is no certainty that we would be so lucky: look at me! It's the Danny Simms of this world who have to look out.' Not that anyone had seen recent sight of her. Danny Simms can go fuck herself, for all I care, Betty thinks. She will find a way of disguising or reinventing herself, grow a beard or a set of. *Away! Away!* Simms was not the issue. Not even Joshua, the gardener. But what about the men that were already missing before the engineers reached their villages, and the priests and the children? They watched their schools be pulled down, then climbed up on the tyres of the trucks. Away. Nothing could stop the children from playing.

'You should come away with us.'

I can't really hear the conversation that must have taken place or picture the men and women in the room when it occurred. What I am saying is this: the British Secret Intelligence Service offered Jim and Betty Cash a way out of Rhodesia, which avoided them sharing the departures lounge with assorted white supremacists. *Don't ask*, said Jim. 'You should come away with us.' I can't really hear this conversation. I can see the twitches, I can see Betty's facial muscles constrict as she tries not to cry, or cry out, or be sick. What effort would it take her just to clear her throat? Ahem. She would be back in her home-made dresses (lemon, peach, baby blue), her suitcases packed with not a lot more than what had come in them. An extra box for her Dansette, unless she left this for Maisie. I can't hear. Maybe there is a smell in the room, the one with the spies, combining cigarette smoke and poorly masked perspiration, a stink like sex. (But how could a stench like that linger in my nose, if I was never there?) The men, the women, the spies would be explaining the deal, where the couple would go to next, where they could wash what secrets they would be obliged to keep: but I am assuming all of that, because, as I say, I cannot hear them or see them. Jim must be there too. He must be because he *must* be, but I confess I have struggled also to put him in that room. His face, when I try to reconstruct it, is blank: as in, it is pale and it has lost all of its features, even its harelip, as if he had left them in a mess by the roadside near the border. It has no expression. I wonder (since I am the one attempting to make meaning out of this) what this may mean. Is blankness synonymous with ambivalence? He could come or go, live or die, he would not care. Or is it indecision that it signifies—panic, inertia at having to choose? Or, Mandy, I think you might be drawing a different conclusion from my inability to describe my friend. You are thinking that this scenario is simply beyond my imagination. You are thinking that my friend—who could break a child's leg playing Gaelic football and could put the intellectual case for civil insurrection in Northern Ireland—could not also dally with British spies, or that I could not hold such a thought in my head. Yet, Mandy, you are surely forced to concede that it was I who told you it in the first place: the SIS offered my friends a route to escape.

And then they went to England and sent me a postcard with a view of Westminster Abbey.

ⓧ

Then M contacted us.

Jimmy was throwing a wee party for Betty, and she—Moira—was invited. A big number, a round-numbered birthday, M not sure which, forty for sure. More, because Betty was a good bit older than Jim. This was Moira telling us after the fact; we were not invited.

They told me to go to RAF Aldergrove and present this letter they sent me. Then they flew me to somewhere, must have been Scotland.

That will have been Prestwick, Moira.

I didn't even get into the whatchamacallit, the terminal. A fancy car, a Rover or whatever, picked me right up off the plane. Its own driver and all.

They drove the rest of the way. A Rover's a good car for a long journey.

We drove the rest of the way. I am no good with directions. Even if I had been able to read the road signs, I couldn't because we had those shady window things—there's a word.

The car was fitted with tinted glass, to ensure the passenger would not know where she was going. They were heading to England.

We were heading south, that I could tell. How could I tell? That's just a feeling you get. You get that? Like you can tell if your blood is rushing to your head or to your toes, upside down or right side up. England is south; we were going to England for sure. I've never been.

I've never been.

They have ever so long roads over there. If we had a road here as long, you would drive off the end of it. Jimmy laughed when I said that. 'You didn't see any signs on the way?' he asked, and I said, No, of course not, when was I ever one for that? I had to say that. Such long roads, I had to get them to stop so I could be sick. Do they have a Newcastle over there, like we have over here? I wanted to hold it in my mouth, but it explodes when you try that, so I was forced to beg the driver, ever so embarrassing. Pull over, please, I asked, I'm going to boke. He understood me. Drivers with caps on are a bit house-proud, I discovered. He pulls in sharp by the side of the road and runs around to the back where I am to open my door—it was locked; I didn't know—and lets me out and stands over me while I vomit everywhere, missing my good shoes, thank God. I think he stood there to make sure I didn't wander into the road and get run down. There are an awful lot of cars on their roads in England. There was a road sign right behind him. Newcastle, Sunderland, some other places, would that be right?

The road from Prestwick to Lincoln would pass Newcastle, Sunderland, and some other places, yes.

There was still light in the day, which came as a surprise after being in that car. Ever been to the pictures in the middle of the day, or a pub, and you come out? Like that. The sort of light that makes you not want to look at it and leaves you dizzy. That might have been the carsickness too.

By the time of year, the time of day was maybe six o'clock.

They had beautiful clouds. Does that make me sound mental? I admit, before that, I would have been prejudiced against English clouds, all high and mighty. Ha, that does make me sound mental! Clouds are the same everywhere, you say. But these—once I had brushed my hair away from my mouth after I had boked—these clouds were in chaos, like hospital cotton wool and bandages, with grey tattered edges and the sun behind them like a huge red blood-drop smeared across the sky like someone had slipped in it. There was a rusty smell, which was the sky; and a grassy smell, which was the verge I had been in. The driver gave me a tissue. I felt a whole lot better.

Darlington, Leeds, Doncaster, Lincoln.

We landed up in a forest, one of those they plant rather than one of those that's always been there. Not in the forest, as such. The gate to the base was in, but as we drove, we drove out or. What am I saying?

It was an RAF base: whatever trees there had been had been cleared to make way for the runway. There would have been hangars of huge corrugated iron semicircles. Control towers, UFOs on a stick. Semaphore and windsock. The whole thing camouflaged by a pine wood. Or perhaps the party was off base, in another secure place.

The party was in a bar on the base. The bar was built like one of our Housing Trust houses, pebble-dashed on the outside. Inside was like Spain. I haven't been to Spain, my friend Alice has been to Spain, I've seen her slides. Little archways made from red brick, with things made from straw such as baskets and donkeys hanging, and wine bottles on the wall for no reason. Ladies in hoop earrings and buns on the side of their heads dancing with men dressed like snooker players. There were nuts and a free bar before they brought us our dinner. I don't know what I had: is moussaka a thing? I had that.

Cash wore a red shirt. Betty's dress was yellow, slit, silk to the ground.

I thought they would be in uniform, but this was their night off. They gave me a wee man to talk to, because I knew no one else and Betty and Jimmy could hardly stick with me all evening. The wee man was called. He was called. Now, why can't I remember a thing like that? It was something like Dennis. Did he even tell me his name, now I think? Dennis will do. Wee bald man, who was only about thirty, who kept saying the British should leave Ireland alone, if it was up to him, and I kept thinking: it is up to you! Drives me mental, that. I have been there x times (he was telling me), lovely people, salt of the earth, no argument with the ordinary people. Then he does an accent, which is nothing like how we talk: if we got out of your way, you would settle your differences in next to no time. Then he tells a joke—it's the way I tell 'em. Jesus wept. He was all right, I suppose. I think: this is the one that they gave me to talk to. What would the others have been like? I promise, I told him nothing.

For dinner, Moira sat at a table, which included her brother and Betty.

It was nothing formal, no speeches nor. Trestle tables and paper cloths. They sat me between the two of them, giving Dennis a rest no doubt.

What did they talk about? 'What did you talk about, Moira?' You must have had questions about Rhodesia and how they had come to leave it. Was it true they had been spirited out by the intelligence service? When did the Royal Air Force come into the picture? Did Jim actually go to the Falklands to fight?

I thought Jimmy would have been full of chat—what he had been up to and whatnot—but maybe these are not people he can be frank in front of, not his friends yet if ever they will. He was full of questions instead. He asked after you, of course, and.

Eilis.

Your wife, and was she singing still. How was it in town, were people curious about him, and so on. He was asking the wrong person. I said to him, 'Jimmy, you're speaking to the wrong person.' When was I ever aware of all that? Poor Moira, I know that's what people say. I mightn't know much, but I know that. Poor Moira. You're asking the wrong person, Jimmy, I said. People never shut up about politics, wherever you go and on television, especially after all the hunger strike business. I can't make head nor tail of it all, it's all noise in my head. Wasn't Fr McCaul up to his eyeballs in that, wasn't he, wasn't he something there? Did I know that already, or was that one of those things Jimmy put in my head? Do you ever see Fr McCaul, he asked me, did Fr McCaul ever drop in on Suzy's, what were people saying about him now that the hunger strikes were past?

Moira didn't know what she knew.

What I knew about all that wasn't worth knowing, though I had my own views as everyone did. Alice was the font of all. Though she likes to keep up the pretence, what's the word I am after? What's that word she uses? Discretion, is that it? Sometimes, I reckon she thinks she is the real priest in that relationship. Ooh, did I say 'relationship'? I should wash my mouth out. You know what I mean. Sometimes, it's like she wants you to do all the talking, as in the Confessional, and she will suck it all up and say precious little back to you. Not that I go to Confession. And she says such things as 'My lips are sealed, Moira,' and 'What I could tell you, if I could tell you.' That sort. I prefer not to ask, I don't want to give her the satisfaction, even if she is my friend.

Moira didn't know what she knew.

I call in on her in her little house the first Friday of every, I don't know who is doing who the favour: I like the company well enough, but I think she really needs it more than me. Although, it's all, 'What can I do for you this time, Moira?' and. I don't mind. I let it all wash over. I think she is lonely. A priest is not hard to keep, and she only has one, and he's not often there, what with all his peacekeeping. She likes stout—you would not know this about Alice to look at her, but she is fond of Guinness. Not 'fond', as in raving alcoholic! That's how rumours get legs! I mean, I bring a couple of bottles with me I have bought in the Mace, and she likes to share them with me. She pours them into nice glasses. She says she has to keep private business to herself, that people don't expect to hear their priest's housekeeper spouting all about, but I have another theory. My theory is she can't help herself.

Moira didn't know what she knew.

Especially after a glass of Guinness.

What did Alice tell you, Moira, about Fr McCaul?

'He tried ever so hard,' she says. 'What do you mean, Alice?' I ask, since she knows, the world knows I know nothing about all that. 'During the hunger strikes,' she explains, 'there was the British on the one side—the bastards—and then on the other side, there were those poor boys only in there because they had done things for the Republicans. And now the British had taken their food away.' Now, even I know that's not the way it was, and I says so to Alice so she would know I was not a total fool. 'Okay,' she admits, 'the prisoners stopped eating as a protest. They wanted to be treated as ordinary prisoners.' I told her I knew that too, and why was she talking to

me like an idiot? What did she mean to tell me? She pretended she couldn't say, before she went on to say that Vincent was in there every day, with the prisoners and with the families, and with that woman McCann—who Alice seems to imply is top of the tree now—and Vincent had been one who had passed news between them and the British. She used a word.

Conduit.

Vincent is Fr McCaul. The British needed to know what the prisoners would accept before they went back to eating, and the prisoners needed to know how long they would have to go on before the government would cave in. Those cells they are in are disgusting. Everything you might need for a home, they have taken that out: it's the opposite of a place you should keep humans in. I said, 'Alice, sure everyone knows that already. That's been in the news, has it not?' That offended her, it did. Clammed up, she did. Not for long, though. 'Let me tell you, Moira—and I am only telling you, mind—the British didn't know the half of it with my Vincent.' That's what she called him. 'He's much more in with your woman McCann and the Republicans than they realise. Much more. Money for the families is only the start of it. I will leave it at that. Arranging places for boys to stay. I'll say no more. Passing on information of a security nature, when he catches wind of that from people he knows in the police. I will leave it at that. You'll get not a word more from me, Moira, on the subject.' Had I even asked her? No, not I. I wouldn't know what she was saying to me, even as she was saying it. The only reason she tells me this is because she is convinced I am half stupid.

But she forgets about the other half.

But she forgets about the other half!

And this is what Moira talked to Jimmy about at the birthday party in England. Moira didn't know what she knew.

'Frank, do you think the British government knew all of that?' Mandy interrupted. 'When Fr McCaul was their go-between over the ceasefire we have just had? Did they know what they were dealing with, with him? Were they manipulating him, or was it the other way round?'

Not now, Mandy. Moira hasn't finished yet.

I watched them dance.

She watched Betty dance with Jim. She wanted to talk about this.

They looked so grown up. I know that's a silly thing to comment on. Of course, they are grown up—it was Betty's whatieth birthday. It's just, when

I last saw them dance together, they were no more than children and they danced the way children did in those days. And now, although the dances were the same—I mean, it was a party for people who liked music from the old days—the dances were the same, but the dancers weren't. Children dance and they bounce a lot and sweat, their hair jumps, they shout in each other's ears because the music is too loud. Grown-ups don't. Betty and Jimmy didn't. The music was just soft enough to hear their feet shuffle on the dance floor. They kept contact the whole time, sometimes both hands, sometimes right hands only, sometimes only the tips of their fingers. They had eyes on each other, never off even when Betty passed under Jimmy's arm. They would get really close then, smiling maybe just a little—her to him, him to her—easy not to see, they would ease apart. Him to her, her to him. Jimmy's red shirt clashing with Betty's yellow dress until—it was dark in the room—his shirt was a little less red, her dress something deeper than yellow. I was not around, they were not around, when they became adults: I don't know when that happened, and I don't know how. They were children, and then the next minute they weren't. That was missed. I missed the fact they had fallen in love.

'Is that what you would have said, Frank? That they were in love?'

I watched them dance, Mandy. In my mind's eye. It wasn't a wedding, so, despite the way Moira tells it, they were not the only ones on the dance floor: there would have been numerous other señors and señoritas. And everyone, without exception, would have been blind drunk. The man in the red shirt would have done most of the dancing with the lady in the yellow silk dress, but others would have requested a turn. It *was* her birthday. I had my own dinner jacket and dress shirt back then, I would not have been out of place, and I could dance a little. Betty would not have turned me away. In her heels, she would have looked tall against me; she could have easily rested her chin on my shoulder if she needed to whisper a word. I can't hear what she might have said. I can't hear the song we might have danced to either. I can't hear a song, because there was no Eilis then. I feel her fingers splayed on my shoulder, I see her knee through her dress, I smell the hairspray and cigarette smoke of her hair. I feel and see and smell all of that, all those particles are still lodged in my senses even though I was not there; but I hear nothing. It didn't happen, if you can't hear it, Mandy. I wasn't there.

Yes, they were in love. Even in the hotel, when we met again outside Belfast, they were in love then too. Does that come as a surprise to you, Mandy? It shouldn't, if I have told you right. *When Raj met Amundah* is not the only love story in town. You, by the way—and it's none of my business—should not let that. Why would you. No, we'll let that pass, you can make your own mistakes. Eilis and I . . . no, we weren't on that subject. Betty and Jim were in love the first time we met them. It was more obvious the one way than the other, so to speak, more obvious that Jim had fallen for her, but. I'm not going back over that: if you missed it the first time, you weren't listening properly.

I danced with Eilis. For years we didn't. I went dancing when she went singing, that's the way it went. Then the show bands stopped, then Eilis stopped, then she stopped. We got there in the end, though, Mandy. The end is the wrong word: we did get there again for a while.

CHAPTER XIV

I danced with Eilis. For years we didn't. She would sing and I would dance, that's the way it went. Then the show bands stopped, then Eilis stopped, then she stopped. We got there in the end, though, Mandy. Not the end. The end is the wrong word: we did get there again for a while.

It's a long road. That's what they say: it's a long road, but you get there in the end. However, someone's got to build the bloody road. I tell you, Mandy, it can feel endless, I don't want you to. People do, you know. Judge. It can feel like the road to effin' Nyasaland. *You just wish you had gotten away with Jimmy Cash when he did. As if they would have any need of you over in Africa!* Eilis was certainly a judge.

Where was I? Betty and Cash were still in Rhodesia: we are back there. I was driving for Bobby Tubby. Mrs Tubby, at this point, was free of tinnitus. On Sundays, the Rover was mine so long as I got it back to the firm by the evening. Somebody else drove on a Monday. But on Sunday afternoons, Eilis got to sit on the back seat. She did that—she sat in the back, wearing her fake fur bomber jacket, playing with the fridge and pretending to make calls on the car phone. I was her driver. It's a long road, however you get there in the end. But someone's got to drive on the bloody road.

'Do you remember that book, Frank?' Eilis asked me.

Which book?

'That book they put me in.'

The Show on the Road.

'Do you remember what it said?'

You could have had your pick. You could.

'I could.'

Yes, you could.

'And do you remember Aloysius Dynes?'

Of course, I do, love, I would say on Sundays when this came up. Why did she keep bringing Dynes up.

'Remember when he was my driver?'

Of course, I do, love.

'Do you know, he used to say to me I was better half the time than the band I was meant to be supporting?'

No, I did not know he said that to you.

'He was the only one to say that to my face.'

I did not know that. (That's the sort of thing I should have said. What was Aloysius Dynes doing, coming out with that sort of thing.)

'He was a singer too, I remember.'

I remember. He could have been more than the occasional player of the harmonica.

'Where did he *not* drive us to in Fr McCaul's bread van? Any night of the week? Tullymourne, Glencort, Michaelstown, Ballytor, Toberlough, Carntasie, Shesk, Beagh. Arse-end places like that. Remember?'

Of course, I do, love.

'The Palm Beach in Slieveban: that was an arse-end place too. A carpet bloody warehouse in normal times!'

Where you first played with the Daytonas.

'I remember, of course, love,' she said.

Where we first met.

'I remember, love. And Aloysius too. We got swankier after that. The Mecca in Belfast and the Arcadia on the coast.'

(The Panadol.)

Eilis would take an empty champagne glass from the fridge and toast the cows and the tractors as we drove past. 'Happy days,' she would say. And then, 'Did you ever hear what happened to . . . ?'

She had forgotten. Of course, only for a moment. Most Sundays. Most Sundays, we drove around in Tubby's Rover, wearing fake fur and toasting from empty champagne glasses, trying to remember happy days, trying to let the other forget.

Sometimes, Eilis would allow Odette to take the boy, and she would pack him off with sandwiches. Sometimes, he would take the passenger seat beside me. He was little. The seat belt would have chafed. And you have no idea how difficult it can be to strap a boy of that age and energy into a seat for even an hour. He would lean forward on the dashboard to get a view of the white lines disappearing under the car; or he would sit in the gap between the seats, talking to his mother behind him in the back. *Sing! Sing!* He would demand. Eilis had a way of blocking that out, as if she could not hear him, as if when she smiled she was smiling at her own thoughts and not the child in front of her, as if actually the boy were muted or not there. As if she were smiling at a totally different child.

Sing! Sing! Leave your mother be, I would tell him. I would go to turn on the radio, but Tubby's car had no radio. Sometimes, we left him with Detty. Sometimes, we left him with Gloria. We had people who were helpful.

Carrickfergus, Larne, Carnlough, Cushendall, Ballycastle, Ballintoy. Our favourite place then was the East Strand at Portrush, and we would get there the long way round, by coast. On a Sunday, there'd be hardly any other cars, it being frowned upon to do things on a Sunday. There would be Mass traffic or Church traffic, or, around Cushendall, we would sometimes run into a hurling game with cars parked along the roadside, but, aside from that, we would have a clear run to the Port. You can stop at certain viewing points, and, if the weather is right, you can see Scotland and, a little further on in the other direction, if the weather is right, you can see Donegal in the Republic. Those are the views that fathers point out. From that distance, they look similar: two-dimensional hills unfolding blue grey on the horizon. All our dads say that, don't they, Mandy? From a distance, on a clear day. Pretending they know some geography or maritime lore. What's that about? What if they are really saying: take a good look, sonny. This is as close as you'll ever get to anywhere, princess. Why would you ever go there when you've got all this here? On a clear day is one thing, but how many of those are there when you count them? Over there is a long way. Stay here, we have all this green, the people, forty different shades of. All our dads say that, trying to hold us back. I mentioned, I was eight when we buried my dad.

The East Strand, Portrush, on a Sunday could be deserted in those days. I doubt it's the same now. The shops and pubs were closed too, but we had a café, which, it seemed, was open only to us, and it looked over the strand. They did burgers and chips and had those squeezy tomatoes you don't see anymore, which had sauce in them, and a choice of vinegar. The boy liked it because he said the plastic scoop seats reminded him of a spaceship. And we liked it because the boy could run down to the beach and play in the sand while we watched him over our teas. While he played, we tried to talk about the future.

Should we try for another child. *Not a great world to bring a baby into.*

What would you think about taking on a full-time job. *The boy still needs me at home.*

We could do with the money. *If you let me out to sing, that would help.*

Where shall we drive next weekend. *Oh, you know I don't mind, I like it here.*

The chips are good. *Always.*

The boy was wearing a startling yellow T-shirt (easy to see from a distance, on top of his froth of white hair). He was sitting all alone on the beach on a blanket his mother had given him, sharing a one-person picnic with a stuffed rabbit. It was the purest concentration of happiness I have ever seen. And I was happier at that moment than I had been ever since I first set eyes on his mother. Was it my eye or his mother's he caught as he waved up at the couple having tea in the café above? At that age, did he even distinguish between the two as our heads moved closer to talk? Did he see us as anything other than his parents—did he, for example, look at us as people? And, when he sat on that sand and looked out at that sea, was he seeing only his sand and sea, or was his mind able to perceive the world they were a part of? At what age can a person start to generalise?

We tried to talk.

We don't have to stay. Really, what's keeping us here. *You can't keep running: you've got to reckon with what's coming to you.*

But you could be better somewhere else. We could all be better elsewhere. *What does better mean here.*

Better! However good good is, better is better than that. You think this is good, that I am good. This could, you could be better.

This was our usual conversation. We rarely got much further than this. It seems so little, doesn't it, Mandy? How could we get by for so long on so little? You know already, of course, that our problem was that the little we had to talk about was huge. Cullycreggan, what I had and had not done, Aloysius Dynes, the Daytonas, the effect this had on her. For now, we had no way of getting around any of this. But these coastal, indirect roads we drove, the chats we tried to have, they did—for a while—seem to make things just a little better.

'This is peaceful,' she said.

'You look at peace.'

She took an extra breath, just deep enough to make some sort of decision. 'Do I?' she said. 'It's not peace you see, but fright. I'm on stage, Frank. There, you reach behind the fear. I push aside the panic, because panic is self-indulgent—you won't allow that. I push to a space, a wide-open space of calm and peace. I fight my way there. Can you imagine peace like that, Frank? Does that seem like peace to you?'

It sounded like remission. The respite was soon shattered.

It was a kid's blanket, about a metre square, green tartan. The clouds crossed the sun, and the green turned black. The wrappings of a discarded snack rolled aimlessly this way and that. I stood at the café window to see if the boy had wandered to the water's edge. I was looking for toddling black dots, straying between the red and yellow beach warning flags. Black dots flapped their wings and rose into the air about the rolling waves. There (my eyes shot farther to the right) was a couple with a dog; a lone woman, large, with a swimming cap, ran gamely up to and into the ocean. No one else. I could see no one else. You have seen the East Strand at Portrush, Mandy. It is vast. It's about a mile deep, and it stretches out of sight around the coast, yellow and flat. At that moment, it was as empty as the Gobi Desert. My fingertips tingled; there was an ache in my gut like shit, and I felt the cold patch on my forehead, which turned out to be the window I was pressing it against. Then my thoughts flicked from, Where's the boy? to, How can I conceal this from Eilis? I wanted to do that. I wanted not to have to utter the necessary words to her, and I wanted not to have to witness their impact on her; I wanted, if I am honest, not to have to gather in again the broken pieces of her. I could only save her if I could see the boy, and now, suddenly, the glass of the window was an impenetrable barrier between him and me. I had to be the other side of it. *Darling, I can't see the boy.* I was forced to admit it; I could hide it from her no longer.

She was outside the door of the café before I was. (I had to pay. Eilis had left her fur jacket on the back of her seat. The girl in the café was slow with her numbers, I had to leave her with my fumble of pound notes.) Outside, Eilis was running down the ramp from the promenade to the sand, almost tumbling over her own momentum. She stopped twenty metres short of the picnic blanket to scan the whole of the beach and sea and dunes. I caught up with her, passed her, collected in the blanket and rabbit and the boy's rubbish as if these might be vital clues. He had finished his biscuit and crisps and left only the core of his apple. He had not been snatched, I reasoned. I turned, like I might report this good news to Eilis, then knew how ridiculous that would be. Instead, I ran towards the sea as the next hopeful, practical thing to do. But, as you know, at Portrush, the tide can go a long way out. I ran, then I jogged, then strode quickly. You can only run quickly, I discovered, if you are actually running towards something, a point. I was running towards the whole sea; I didn't know where within that vast ocean my son might be, if he was there at all. I might be running away from him right now, I thought, slowing to a stride and catching my breath. Where was Eilis now, where was she looking? Don't lose her too! The sea: the sea, when I got there, was a mile from my wife. The sea was a million white heads of bobbing foam, dark bodies of indifferent water. How do you see the smallest, most important thing in that? What is the strategy for that? Do you look first among the shallows, along the breaker line, or do you reach out as far as you can see and trace your way back? When is the right time to give up? What do you do with the thought that you have given up already?

I waded in up to my ankles shouting his name. Behind me, a mile away, I heard the echo of Eilis also calling his name, along the beach or among the dunes. Eilis had a voice that carried to me, even against the sea breeze. She was calling his name, calling his name, calling his name, without letting up, but she was calling to me. My shoes, my socks, my trousers up to my knees were sopping with seawater, but I ran (I ran quickly) back to her, and when I reached her, I embraced her as hard as I thought she could bear and held her to me lest she should break apart.

The swimming lady with the cap, the couple with the dog: none had seen our boy, nor any other person on the beach. 'Wee blond boy, in a yellow T-shirt? No, love. He was on his own?' Yes, he was, we were watching from the café above. 'You can't take your eyes off them even for a minute these days.' Thanks for your help. 'Have you looked in the town? The wee boy may have gone wandering there.'

The pair with the dog said they would help us look. The swimming lady in the cap said she would have to dry and get dressed first but would keep an eye out too. 'He'll turn up somewhere,' she said, like he might be a slipper we lost behind the armchair. I'm sure you're right. That's what I said, as if it was my duty to console the other people, to reassure them. It'll turn out fine, once we get past this. And, in that spirit, I told Eilis to wait in the café, have another tea. 'He'll probably show up there. That's where he will go when he decides to come back.' She did as I told her.

It was a Sunday. Most of the town was shut. The shop with the angling supplies was shut. The general store that sold cheese sandwiches and towels was shut. The Harbour Bar was licensed to open later, and the receptionist in the neighbouring hotel said the only people she had seen all day were a couple walking a dog. She asked me if she could help me with anything else.

The amusement arcade was open. The dodgems had been chained up and the one-armed bandits arrested. Gypsy travellers, because they run the show, were sitting in the cars of the waltzer, frozen mid-spin, facing away. Three—they must have been brothers—were camped in one of those booths. I approached slowly, even though I was in a heart-pounding hurry. In my sodden, sandy shoes, I looked comical.

'In a yellow T-shirt? Did you see anything, Billy?'

'Can't say I was looking out for that, Willy. Did he have a name?'

I told them his name, not that that would make a difference.

'I might have seen him,' said the third, who was called Dominic. 'Wee blond boy, you say? Now, let me think here. We have hundreds come in like that all the time. Blond boys, dark boys, ginger boys. What else can you tell us about him?'

I told them everything. He was as high as his great-grandfather's armchair. He had a voice like birdsong. His hair was the colour of pampas plumes. All week his head would smell of the family shampoo we used. He never cried, but sometimes tears would melt from his eyes. His ambition was to be a spaceman because, he said, he wanted to live among the clouds. He had never before walked off on his own.

'Hold on, that's a lot of description,' said Dominic. 'Willy, take a run round the back there, to see if you find anyone matching all that.'

They were playing with me, I thought, but I thought I had no choice but to wait for Willy to take his run and come back. In the booth with Billy and Dominic, it was as if the subject had to change: we couldn't keep talking about my boy until we had more news. 'This weather's wasted on a Sunday,' one of them said, and the other agreed.

Willy came back at last. 'I found this,' he said. It was a toy car, a VW Beetle. 'I bet that's no good for you?'

I swear the gypsy brothers were laughing at me as I stepped back onto the pavement, trying to decide which way to run in now. I had wasted so much time. The street was empty. Was it always this deserted, or was it mocking me, like the gypsies? And I had told them so much. The street gave me no clue as to which way to turn. The bank was shut, and so was the post office. The charity shop, the department store stocking cheap clothes for old people, and the Christian bookshop were all closed. A stray dog sniffed at the piss left by another dog. A mass of newspaper, smeared with ketchup but looking like the detritus of a hospital in crisis, was blown by the breeze against the window of the fish and chip shop, closed since late last night. A homeless woman sat like a statue on the kerb, clad in brown rags and verdigris. I approached her with a penny but left it with her without asking her thoughts.

I called his name, I called his name, it echoed off the shutters of the shops. It was a hot day, but the street had captured the shade and it was chilly. I stepped off the kerb, wobbled, and realised I was dehydrated. I needed to drink but told myself I had more important things to worry about.

The newsagents, Scappaticci's, were open, selling ice cream in tubs. I went in there. The boy liked ice cream, but he had no money, and he had never in all his little life paid for anything himself. The lady was delighted to see me, having no other custom to stay open for or customers to gossip with. She wanted to talk about all sorts, and, at first, I had to let her. There was political stuff in the news she tried to express an opinion about without expressing it too strongly for fear of alienating me. 'Power sharing, my arse. They're all as bad as each other,' she concluded, because in her book, to offend everyone was to offend no one.

'How can I help you? Vanilla?'

I said that sounded grand, but I had no time for ice cream now, I had to find my son.

'Ah, you should have said,' she said.

I gave her a description (this time, just his height, hair colour, and the clothes he had on).

'We have children come in here all the time. Some are right tinkers, God forgive me. Let me ask my husband if he saw anyone matching your description. He was out here earlier. Hold on there.' And she left me standing there alone among her newspapers and ice creams for what seemed an age as she consulted her husband. The headlines were much as they always were back then. The Forum Hotel had been bombed again, the bottom three floors fire damaged, but no residents harmed. A joint RUC-Army patrol had rounded up some suspects in the Falls area and come under an impromptu petrol-bomb assault. About an hour's drive away from here. When a lit petrol bomb lands, the shatter is of the most brittle glass, and the fire sizzles almost pleasantly, but the blaze catches hold to the road, to the uniform, to the hair. It smells of stock cars at Nutt's Corner. The shop door lay open, and I could hear the sounds of the breaking sea and the angry squawks of seagulls. I wondered, had I ever spotted a seagull in Belfast? Would their curiosity ever take them there? Better off flying in the other direction, to Scotland. She must have been doing other business at the back of the store, because she had been a good five minutes. I thought, maybe she is getting her husband's dinner on, the useless bastard, having me mind the shop for them. What if someone came in, would they expect me to know how to serve them?

I could be off with the merchandise, paper folded under my arm, and they would be none the wiser.

I abandoned the newsagents. How long had the boy been missing already? Was it an hour, or nothing like that? I began to wonder how much longer we had. How long could the boy last on his own, was one thought; another—crowding this out—was that I needed to get Tubby's Rover back to the firm tonight. He would not be sympathetic if I tried to explain my situation. He had seen orphaned and abandoned and dead children in Italy in the war, and no other trauma compared to that for him. I'd be out on my ear. So I would, at some point, have to get the car back to the firm. Me driving, Eilis in the back. I'm a monster, I know, for even imagining that. Don't think it was because I didn't love the boy. But sometimes your mind forces other, inappropriate subjects to the fore; sometimes it diverts your energies away from where they should truly be. Mandy, when you lose your son, you have no control over your mind.

I saw the police station, and I knew that, whatever day it was, it would be open. I didn't want to go in there. That's normal for someone like me, even in these circumstances, having through life been trained to fear the questions they would ask and the information they would require. The fence around the station was the green of the boy's tartan blanket and as high as the dunes. It was the sort of double-fronted house priests from a wealthy diocese might live in, if you can imagine that. I couldn't find the way in, and the longer I spent walking up and down the fence, the more culpable I felt. Then I spied a box with a button, a buzzer, and before I could stop myself, I pressed it.

A woman police officer escorted the two of us back to the café, where we found Eilis still waiting. The owner had stayed open for her. Somehow, Eilis was angry at me. She hummed the whole way. We drove back to Belfast, and I dropped the Rover off.

☙

The following Sunday, we were in the car again, me driving, Eilis in the back in her fake fur. The boy with Gloria or my cousin.

'Do you remember that book, Frank?'

Which book?

'That book we were in.'

The Show on the Road. You could have had your pick.
'And do you remember Aloysius Dynes? Lovely singer himself.'
Of course, I do, love.
'Remember when he was my driver?'
Of course, I do, love.

ೲ

This all had to stop when Tubby was killed. Mrs Tubby decided she had to go back to America to try to get the ringing out of her ears. The firm went with her. Whatever sweet deal her husband had been making with the Irish government went up in smoke the same time as he did. Five hundred of us lost our jobs. Detty was offered a job in the States, and then so was I, as a storage leader. I never found out what that meant.

I think we were in the living room of our house and it was daytime. The sunlight had a way of falling only on the fireplace and the dusty television set, leaving the rest a shade of grey. The window had those dapples of grime you often see after a rainfall, like a thousand tiny puddles. Toys lay round about.

America, we could go there, I suggested. They love an Irish accent in the States, I said. They love an Irish girl who can sing.

It was a change of subject for her, away from the dust, the grime, and the mess. She paused for a moment. For a magical moment, I thought it might be to consider the idea; instead, it was to measure out the degree of her abhorrence. 'I'm going nowhere. I have enough to do here. You go if you want to,' she said. 'You should take what's coming to you.'

Remember, we were sitting in our living room in daytime, not busy, not doing anything in particular. Remember, too, that she said this after Tubby and his stand-in driver were blown to smithereens. I had lost my job.

Would you rather that had been me in that car? I asked her. Do you think that's what I deserve?

I knew she did not actually want me dead. There was some metaphorical atonement that she wanted meted out to me, a fair reckoning for the man for whom other people suffered. What she really meant was that these people were better than me. Dynes, the band members, even Tubby's driver did not deserve to die, whereas I.

'No, dear. I mean, you should take up the offer. You have it coming to you. With all the terrible things that have happened to you, you deserve some luck. But I can't go with you: my career is here. I can't quit, not now when finally I am beginning to get some decent work. You said Odette was going? You should go too.'

Ahem.

('Did she really say that?' asked Mandy. 'Did she really? That's not the impression you gave me before. The impression you gave me before was that she would rather you had traded places with all of those other drivers. Did she really say you should go to America?'

Ahem.)

Sitting in the armchair in the bright-grey side of the living room, I said, Your career here is over, Eilis. Face up to it. An occasional singing spot in a bar in north Belfast is not a career. You won't now ever cut a record. Even Clodagh Rodgers can't sell records, and she is famous. You still have a voice, I grant you—if anything, it's stronger than before—but no one wants to listen to what you have to sing. Your style has passed. It passed with the Daytonas and the rest of the show bands. On stage, you don't tell jokes, you can't engage, you are too sad. You are miserable, even when you paint a happy face on. You could, if you want, sing sad—that's a register that could suit you, accompanied by an effin' harmonica. But here you are, always singing other people's songs, and, for you now, they are all the wrong songs. Go to America: no one knows you there, no one would be reminded of the past when you stepped behind a microphone; they have no memory of you there. Come with me.

('I cannot believe you would have said those things, Frank,' said Mandy, checking her patient's monitors once again. 'I can't believe you would have blown up like that. You didn't, did you, Frank?')

She heard me say all of these things, whether or not I spoke the actual words. Do we need to speak the words for a person to hear them? Maybe it's a talent reserved for the special. Some people can hear a thing into existence. For some people, the very sensitive, the speed of sound has no barrier: they slow it down, speed it up, bypass it; they engineer it. She was a singer after all. Through music, a singer invents reality; she conjures music and joy and sorrow out of the thinnest air. People can make peace because of a song or go to war. Even a singer such as Eilis, who sang the songs of other people, through her nuance and inflection she makes something out of nothing. Do-Re-Mi, Every Good Boy Deserves Fruit. Accidental reordering is all it takes to bring a new sound into being. She heard me, even if those were not the words I spoke or the order I spoke them in. Accidental reordering would be all that it took.

('I cannot believe you would have said those things, Frank,' said Mandy, checking her patient's monitors once again. 'I can't believe you would have blown up like that. You didn't, did you, Frank?')

She heard me say all of these things, those were my actual words. My son was sitting there too. Years on, with his head in the clouds, he would accuse me of being mad, of us all being driven mad by the sheer fact of our existence in that time and in that place. I could not listen to her and watch her in that dusty spotlight of our living room and think she could still be serious about singing. Tubby had been murdered in his car (in our car) along with his driver (who should have been me), and she wanted to sing 'Yakety Yak (Don't Talk Back)'. I had to fight my way through to the space, the wide-open space of calm and peace. It's a long road, Mandy.

☙❧

I don't think they had any need of me in America. Can you just imagine that? How totally irrelevant and meaningless would I be there. My van among millions. Do you not think that a person must lose all sense of their own dimensions on such an enormous plane, that at the very least a person must lose their depth? There would be no notice taken of me there. I would be a storage leader, whatever that is. I would be there on paper, but turn me sidewise and I would vanish. But if I ever planned to motor west, I would certainly take the highway that's the best. It may not have been so bad.

Instead, I got a job with the Library Board, driving a book van around to people too infirm or living too far away to get to the real thing. Monday to Thursday, my beat would be a different compass point of the city, and on Friday I would venture to some of the outlying villages and small towns. A library van man could go anywhere, even in the days when it wasn't always safe to drive an ambulance or fire engine. To be diplomatic, we didn't carry a dedicated 'Politics' section, but we had pretty much anything you could want in 'Biography', 'Fiction', 'Children', and 'General Interest'. I was the driver, but I was more: I stamped out the books and issued fines at my own discretion. I was not expected to dispense advice the way a full-blown librarian would, but I pitched in anyway. For that, I needed to know not just where the books were but what was in them. That meant reading them, which I could do because one thing I discovered in this job was that the readers in Belfast don't make many demands on your time. The South read the most; the East think they know books already so don't need to read them; those in the West and North manage at most one book a week each and have already decided what they want to borrow next before you have even parked on their street. So I would sit an hour or so and improve myself. That's when I started wearing glasses. Geology, colonial history, a little relativity: the van didn't normally carry these subjects, but I could order up what I liked on inter-library loan. I would say pretty much my whole education I got in there. Ask me anything. You can travel anywhere in a book, around the world, into space and out. All the great thoughts and all the trivial ones too. Books—please tell me you read them, Mandy.

I didn't have it all my own way. If the boy was at school, Eilis would often ask to come along. 'You can concentrate on your driving and your reading, and I can serve the customers,' she reasoned. 'Slip the wee cards out, *stamp! stamp!* Look at them sternly over my glasses, if I can find a pair, but not *shh!* them overly. I won't read the books: I won't disturb you.' Occasionally, if I thought it less likely she would break out in song, I would let her, and then it was like we were a team. The seats in a van are highly sprung, and, to be fair, we both enjoyed the elevated view and the comical bounce when I drove over a pothole. We would see one coming aaaaaand *bump*. She would make a flask of tea and wrap some biscuits in paper towel, and we would park up with a view over the city and pretend we had grown old together, sharing a bag of yogurt nuts. The van radio was fitted with an 8-track cartridge tape deck, so when the mood was right, we would sing together on the way home to Charlie Pride or Nat King Cole. I thought I had met pretty girls in my time, but that was before I met you, I'd tell her, brushing the hair from my eyes.

Often, I could not allow her to come. This was my workplace after all, and it is not a given that you bring your wife on the job with you. 'We've had complaints,' the head librarian warned me, putting it no stronger than that but making clear that these 'unusual practices' needed to stop. Eilis would have to stop singing in the library van. When it was just her and me, it was not a problem: Eilis just sang the way a normal person would. When there was maybe just one other person there, say browsing in Biography, Eilis might start up a gentle hum, the way you or I might do that in an absent-minded sort of way. But when three or four turned up—and, I add, the van was just a van—there was a fair chance that Eilis would break out a full performance. Books would rattle on their shelves; small children would cower in the corner. Some liked it. Some turned up every week to witness the funny lady. They might gather outside the van, children, of course, and call on the lady to sing them a song. 'Sing "The Sash", lady!' they would request, or 'Do you know "The Soldier Song"?' There is a narrow path to tread politically between these particular anthems, as I don't need to remind you, Mandy. Unfortunately—thanks to her days in the clubs and dance halls, where she would be required to please the locals whatever their stripe—Eilis did know these songs, and sing them she did, giving them full voice in the housing estates of East Belfast and the two up-two down terraces of West. We acquired notoriety. Behind Eilis' back, I turned down numerous offers from the TV and radio people to do a feature on us. Eilis might love the publicity, but the Library Board would not. Already they had noticed we had fewer borrowers than before—many stopped coming entirely or dropped off their books and ran away. 'Perhaps, if you just asked her to stop, Frank?' my head librarian suggested.

'People like it,' Eilis reasoned.

'Some do,' I conceded. 'But it's not what a library van is for, love.'

'It should be! Songs and books: why am I the first to hit upon that concept?'

'You're just too far ahead of your time, Eilis, at least from the point of view of the Belfast Library Board.'

Let me go out on my own for a while, that'll be best. I'll take my own flask and biscuits.

Eilis took that like a slap. But she did not argue back.

ᏉᏇ

In any case, she found all of a sudden that there was plenty for her to do at home, with the boy and. She found her ancient Singer sewing machine and started making clothes for him out of the old clothes she used to wear on stage. She made a cowboy waistcoat out of a suede skirt, complete with leathery tassels. He loved that. She had a silver-sequinned blouse, which, with the addition of a belt, she convinced him could be a space suit. He loved that. Then she gave him her boa for a walk in the park, paired with pink-framed sunglasses. The boy did not mind, naturally: his mum was making a fuss of him, and together they were making strangers laugh. I found out when a neighbour called me over his fence.

'You want to watch that one, Frank,' he counselled.

I didn't ask him what he meant—I knew what he meant.

'What did he mean, Frank? Which one were you to watch, Frank—your son or your wife?'

That was the beauty of it, Mandy. Sammy left that unsaid so he could not be accused. I knew what he meant—he meant the both. If I wasn't careful, Eilis might turn the boy, if he wasn't turned already.

'Turned? What's turned?'

Don't make me say it, Mandy. You know rightly. My neighbour Sammy thought that Eilis, with all her dressing up of him, might make my son into a gay. And before you start protesting there, Mandy, let it be said I am on your side on this one. Just because I am doesn't mean I have to be. If he was or if he was not would not have bothered me one way or the other, even then when it was not so. Pardon me, easy. And what Eilis dressed him in had no bearing on it. You don't need to convince me. But.

'But?'

The boa in the park was a lot to take.

'Did you have to give him a feather boa, Eilis?' I asked. 'The cowboy suit, the spaceman—that's one thing, but?

'Has the boy complained?' she asked.

No.

'Well.' She won that one. 'Sammy can go eff himself.' She was correct there too.

Do you have any sisters, Mandy? It's not what you're thinking. I am not asking for the usual reasons. That malarkey is long past me. There was a time I might have been tempted, but fortunately the opportunity never coincided with the instinct. That never happened. Why do I ask if you have a sister? I ask because I don't, and neither did Eilis. I think that might have helped us then. When it came to Eilis, who was I to speak with? Sammy, you can gather, was worse than useless. Betty and Jim were *incommunicado*. Odette had skipped off to the States. A sister—mine or hers—would have been of some use to me. I often think that; I might have acted differently. In the end, you do what the doctor tells you to do.

In the meantime, I went back to driving alone and stamping out the books by myself. That was no hardship. Back in the day, after there had been trouble the night before, you could feel like a hero driving a van round the deserted streets of the scabbier parts of the city. There might be the odd patrol, you'd see a soldier kick a broken bottle to the side of the road. I might have been Charlton Heston as the last human being in *The Omega Man*, driving around his open-topped Cadillac to the tune of Ron Grainer's 'A Summer Place'. I have it in my head now. I tell you, after the humans have gone, there'll only be those women in headscarves, snatching their milk from the doorstep or hunting for tinned fruit at the corner shop. They weren't bothered about books. They looked at nobody and watched everything, like proper spies. To me, they were entirely adapted to their environment, but maybe you would say they were psychiatric cases too. They could not get away. When Charlton Heston is driving around Los Angeles, he takes right turn after left, and he never seems to get anywhere. Belfast was a bit like that then. You could get a roadblock and have to turn back on yourself; there would be no right turn followed by no right turn, so, if you weren't careful, you would end up where you started or at the wrong end of the wrong sort of street. When you did break free, you put your foot down, nervously checking your rear-view in case there was one final grab at you. Okay, so nothing like Charlton Heston. But I could still get that open-topped, elbow-out-the-window feeling once I got the van onto the country roads. Now I was an aid worker, convoying supplies of vital books to readers in remote villages. Sometimes, in my head, these were war-rutted tracks I was on; oftentimes I was instead on a great American highway, a Route 66, sun visor down, one hand on the wheel, with a continent to traverse. Hitchhikers, roadside motels, drive-in diners all flew by my window. In real life, it was not at all like that. In Northern Ireland, you are never much more than an hour and a half from anywhere else, and you bounce off the border like it's a rubber guard rail.

Eilis never let off the singing in public. There was never a chance she would. She would lie on in bed until after I had left for work; then she would get up, fix her own and the boy's breakfast, and spend the next hour putting her face on and assembling her wardrobe for the day. This was in preparation for going to the shops. I know she did this because the boy told me she did; he touted on her. She would take the bus and get off where the permanent police roadblock was, just short of the centre. I have to imagine the rest. What did she do? With the boy, she would allow her coat pockets to be wanded by the security lady, by those gates that are like the cages they trap cattle in before they slaughter them. That's a thing you will have no memory of, Mandy. With her coat, for example, or her hat—did she lay them on the ground in front of her like a busker and sing for money? That, that might have been okay, for buskers are an acceptable feature of public entertainment; ignore them, reward them as you wish, drop a few coins in there, no harm done. This, though, is not how I imagine it being done by Eilis. For one thing, the police would have had none of it. For another, I have seen my wife sing a hundred times, and one thing she was not was a singer for cash: she got paid, not tipped. That's the sort of distinction one's dignity and psychological stability rest on. There is a line there. She would sing all the day long just for the opportunity to sing, to perform for an audience. The audience needn't pay her much notice; that was not essential to the deal. Remember, when I first saw her, she was the relief act for the Daytona Showband, and you're looking now at the only living person in the whole of the Palm Beach dance hall that first time who paid her the blind bit. The crowd could walk on by, turn their back, and Eilis would not drop a note. There just had to be people there milling about, in the vicinity, keeping her company. She would hold her microphone a bit like the way an old man might hold a cigar and have her spare hand out holding up the folds of an imaginary skirt and then belt it out. I can't hear the songs now, I was not there.

Keeping her company. That's funny. Until now, that thought had not occurred to me since. Do you think that could have been it, Mandy? Company? You see, a sister would have helped in more ways than one. A sister might have forced me to get my act into gear a bit sooner, if all she needed was some decent company.

'That's not all it would have taken, Frank.'

What's that, Mandy?

'I said, if Eilis was experiencing trauma, it would take more than a friend calling round, or a sister, to help sort it. I am not psychiatric, Frank, you know that. But it does not take a lot of medical training or experience to know that your wife was post-traumatic.'

Ahem. Perhaps so. I don't remember those words being used. I remember sad and lonely and in need of rest. I remember that she was unusual, she was a funny lady, and that I had to watch her. I remember the GP said that the tablets he prescribed her would help for a while, and that, for a while, they did. This was the pause in time when it was possible for her to ride again with me in the library van without embarrassing herself. In this period after the doctor helped her out, she could take the boy shopping in the bus and come back, and she would not in the meantime have broken out into song. We could share a flask of tea and yogurt nuts and pretend we had gotten old together. We could even do a dance. That felt like an achievement. Gently, we started having conversations about the future again, not about America—there was no point in risking that—not about going anywhere else, but about how we might live out our lives exactly here in this place, or back in the town.

We might open a shop. *A bookshop maybe.*

I can get the boy interested in football. *I think he might have a musical ear.*

We could take a Sunday out to Portrush again. *I hear Newcastle is nice this time of year.*

You seem better. Better is good. *Those tablets are a lifesaver.*

The GP doesn't think it's a good idea to stay on them. It's not recommended practice anymore. *We'll see how that goes, then.*

ⲟⲭⲟ

I don't remember the names of the medications she tried, and it's not important. I don't remember how many months she was off and then on again. I don't remember who had the thought first, or who made the suggestion first, that Eilis needed a rest from being off and then on. I do remember the word 'rest'; in fact, the word is practically all I remember from that time. The GP dropped it into conversation, or he would whisper it sometimes like a promise or a secret, and it did begin to feel like this rest was magical. Even the word—'rest'— might be spoken by a hypnotist as they send you under, lingering on the long *s*, not quite making it to the *t*. Rest is not a place (although we all know the name of the place); rest is a prolonged state of being, like unconsciousness. Rest, even when it is involuntary, is salutary: you are just being rested.

Hotel. That was the word we chose to use. There is something of the workhouse about the other words people use, a condemned place, a place for the condemned. I am not saying anything original here, I realise. I am not the only husband who sent his wife away and preferred to call it by another name. I told the guys at the reunion we held for Fr McCaul that she had gone to her sister's. I told Sammy the same thing, who said, 'That makes sense. I didn't know Eilis had a sister. She left the boy with you, then?' Sammy was a slabber. I didn't have a car at that time, and the Library Board did not offer their drivers the loan of their book vans at weekends, but there was a bus I could catch to the hotel and back. I went as often as I could. Explaining to the boy what was going on was harder than to Sammy, the neighbour: Why could we not all stay with Mummy in her hotel, he wanted to know. It's not easy being a mummy, I tried. Am I the reason Mummy has to stay away, he asked. No, that's not why. I am the reason Mummy has to stay away.

Long after, when we stopped talking about these times, the boy had not forgotten. He accepted the blame for this thing that was no fault of his. Eilis would come out of her hotel then, when she felt she needed another rest, she would check herself back in again. She did this by herself—I didn't have to suggest it or get an order for it—and still the boy thought his mummy was taking holidays away from him. When she was home, he would do extra things to help out, and he would wear the pink sunglasses to make her laugh and to tell everyone that he had no problem with wearing pink sunglasses. He was a fine boy. Then he got older, and he reached the point where he could start blaming me too. Years passed like this.

CHAPTER XV

When I checked out of the B&B on Gardiner Street Lower, I hadn't decided that I would spend the day looking for a book. I was looking for a coffee, something strong to lift my hangover from the night before. I didn't know where I might get a coffee, but, like everybody else in the world, I do know about Bewley's on Grafton Street, so I headed in that direction, safe in the knowledge that, if I crossed the Liffey at O'Connell Bridge and kept going south, I would come to it eventually. Our County boys had let themselves down in the night; we had not had a good night sleep, and it was showing on Dublin's streets. The bars I passed had the local sky-blue flags fluttering in the pristine morning sunshine, young and confident and well-slept. Dubliners who lived in the flats two, three, four storeys up had opened their windows to let out their flags and let in the fresh air. In contrast, a damaged man, alone with a beer can and asleep in a doorway, was using our County flag for a blanket; we had bruised the capital's premier streets red and black, their gutters were sore with piss and beer. I nursed my coffee in Bewley's Oriental Cafés, hoping I could contain my hangover in the mug.

Mandy, so you know, this was the hangover after the night before, when Fr McCaul had (in front of the whole team—but not Quinn, who had hidden himself away somewhere), on account of my association with Jim Cash, as good as accused me of being an informant for the British. We in general, but me singly. Me, whose tongue was tied and could barely even speak up for himself. After McCaul left with Alice, there had been a lot more drinking, with only the lucky ones hauled off to bed early by their wives. For the rest of us, there had been something of a riot. All I knew was that I could not face Quinn or the rest of them, and I most certainly would not be going to the match.

'That's a nasty one,' the waitress said to my black eye in admiration. Bewley's Oriental Cafés, Grafton Street, Dublin.

I could only say, 'Yes, thank you.'

'Here for the game?'

'That was the plan.' Yes, I had come for the game.

She checked her watch, maybe thinking to herself that, until throw-in, my plan was to sit in her café drinking from my one mug.

'I'll be heading after this,' I assured her.

'My favourite thing to do on a Saturday morning, when I am not working here, is to sit in St Stephen's Green with a book.' Then, reading my thoughts, she added, 'No one bothers you to move on.'

I liked that she had looked at me and seen a reader, despite my black eye. 'I came without a book, for some reason I can't fathom.'

She liked that. What sort of a football fan brings a book to the big game. She pointed vaguely out of the window. 'The Dublin Bookshop is where you want to go, then. Wilde, Joyce, Beckett, Shaw. Strong on Irish interest—if that suits you.' Maybe, in her mind, there was always going to be an *if* when talking to a northerner: is 'Irish interest' the same as our interest. 'History, biography, music . . .' She walked off to her next customer, still reciting the categories the bookshop stocked. I shook the paper tube of sugar from one end; I bent it stiffly at its knee. My mind was not yet on the book, but absent-mindedly I allowed my waitress to narrow down my choice. We once owned a book of history, biography, music; it had a green cover but with black and white panels bearing the faces of some of those featured within. The last mouthful of coffee was cold but gratifyingly bitter. I scooped the sugar, split at the knee, into the empty mug.

Before I stepped into the Dublin Bookshop, I had decided I wanted to buy *The Show on the Road*. I had forgotten the book's secondary title—something about the show bands, the life of, the joy of—but I could still name all the figures on the cover. Brendan Bowyer, Joe Dolan, Tom Dunphy, Sean Hamill, Dickie Rock, Twink. When had we lost our copy? Was it when we had been forced out of our first home in Belfast, the one given us accidentally by the Housing

Trust? Had Eilis binned it around the time she was cutting up her old stage clothes to dress the boy? I would like to have that book again. I will sit with it in St Stephen's Green, so long as the weather remains fair. I will find a place for lunch, let those teammates still standing meet up and make their way without me to Croke Park. McHugh might ask after me, Shiels might suggest a delay, but in the end they would take the bus they had hired for the weekend.

ᏋᏇᏋ

They didn't have the book. They had a memoir of Joe Dolan, but I had never been a fan. The shop assistant thought me ungrateful for I was sure never to find my particular book unless I trawled the charity shops, and there was never any telling what I might find there. You can try, but Waterstone's won't have it.

Waterstone's, on Dawson Street, did not have it, but I stayed in there a while because it felt like a library. They had a huge oak refectory table just inside, piled six deep with *Captain Corelli's Mandolin* and John Grisham. They had Mandela's book, one on the border by Colm Tóibín, and a whole section for Edna O'Brien. I picked up a Pat Barker and took it to the till (I had read her other two) and then changed my mind. You have got to be in the mood to read about war. I could take to St Stephen's Green a history of the Easter Rising; there was no shortage of those. But reading a book in public is an invitation to passers-by to question you on its contents. I've noticed that even in the library van. A borrower might only just have lifted *Birds of the UK and Ireland* down from its perch, and Johnny Nextdoor will be quizzing her on her ravens and starlings. Dublin is a city of experts on the Rising—do they even have another subject? I'm barely qualified. It may be the best, and the worst, place to learn. I know that something happened on St Stephen's Green. Was that where Countess Markievicz was? Do you know your history, Mandy? Is it your history, Mandy? Sorry to ask. It's meant to be mine, for sure. There was definitely a gunfight or standoff at St Stephen's Green, just around the corner from where I was standing in Waterstone's. They dug themselves in. The British shot at them from the Shelbourne. Did I read that, or is that just the sort of thing that you are meant to know if you are born on this island? That's such a weight, even for someone like me who does read: the burden of having to know or, rather, of already knowing without having to ask. I'm expected to be able to criss-cross this city and know that the Volunteers stored guns in that bank, that they were imprisoned in that old workhouse, which is now a hospital, that those are bullet holes and not just pockmarks from acid rain. To sit in St Stephen's Green with a book on the Easter Rising means I must have an opinion on the wisdom of occupying a post office or a biscuit factory. That's my history. I suppose you have an A-to-Z knowledge of every highway of every Orange Order march of the past two hundred years. Don't answer; it wasn't meant to be a question.

I came out of Waterstone's empty-handed, with no better clue what to do next. There was another bookshop opposite, with a name—Hodges Figgis—like a packet of biscuits. I thought, maybe, if they don't have *The Show on the Road*, I would just give up. In any case, the longer I took to find it, the less time I would have to read it. Inside, it looked as if Figgy Hedges had been there forever. A woman was on the floor, righting the books along the bottom shelf of New Arrivals.

'Do you want one of these while I'm down here?' she asked, catching me looking at her. I must have looked like one of those customers, happy to carry away any book so long as it had a famous person on the cover. 'I have football managers and ex-football players. English too. Is that the sort of thing you are after?' She had seen my black eye.

I assured her I was not.

'Ah, you're from the North.' She looked about her dismayed, at a loss as to what to recommend.

'I have a book in mind.' I gave her the name. Then (because this meant nothing to her) I told her the subject matter.

'You want Irish history.'

I doubted it, but I followed her direction to the back of the shop. There were all the twentieth-century themes you might imagine. There were the wars: the First World, the Second World, the independence, the civil. They covered the Troubles from every angle. They had books about the Volunteers—those that called themselves 'Irish', those who thought they were 'United', and those that trooped only for 'Ulster'. The Land League, the Gaelic League, the Irish Justice League. They had books about boats, books about prisons, and books about boats that were also prisons. I had read some of those. I had already read the books here that I would want to read. There was nothing here on the show band era, as I knew there wouldn't be.

There was a person standing behind a computer. He was typing with one hand; without looking at the screen, he was leaning into a box of books at his feet. I stood in front of him, hoping he would consider it his job to help.

'I think I must be in the wrong section,' I said to him eventually.

'This is "History",' he said, implying the inverted commas. 'We have separate sections for ancient history and pre-history. Sometimes, people stray here when it's really mythology they are after. The times that has happened! Any of that any good to you?'

I told him what I was looking for. 'Maybe you don't stock it. Waterstone's didn't.'

'In that case . . .,' he mumbled nonchalantly, and he lost himself a while in his screen. 'The show . . . A show . . . Road . . . The Roads . . .' His frustration showed. 'Sometimes, these machines they make us use are . . . We are talking *in Ireland* here, right? I made that assumption.' He bashed away a few more seconds. 'Nope,' he concluded.

'You haven't got it?'

'No one's got it. It doesn't exist.'

'It's out of print, you mean?'

'No, that's another category: books we did have but have no longer. Your book's another sort: books we don't have and never have had.'

'I had the impression it was quite an esoteric book, if you know what I mean. I mean, its subject was quite a popular one, but the writing itself was on the academic side. Have you a category for that?'

'If that was all, it would be no trouble. Your book presents a challenge of another order: it doesn't exist.' I thought then there was a change in his tone. 'Let me be clearer still: it never did exist.'

'You are wrong there.' I said that with all the respect due to a person with a computer working in a bookshop with at least two storeys. 'We had a copy of it once.' I thought about adding that I drove a library van.

'Independent production, minority imprint. That's been known. The National Library could settle that. But they wouldn't be free to sell you a copy.' He bashed some more at his keyboard. 'Does it have to be *that* book?'

It really did have to be. Other books would feature the Freshmen, the Plattermen, and the Drifters. Other books would cover the tragedy of the Miami. Surely only *The Show on the Road* had an entire chapter devoted to the Daytona Showband; surely only that book paid tribute to the relief bands, looked down upon by most of the paying public. *The Show on the Road* was the only book in existence to carry miniature biographies of the lesser celebrities, including, in the back pages, one of Eilis McClean.

Eilis McClean, the blonde songstress from Toberlough, sang with the Dulcettes, a relief band for the Clipper Carlton before going solo at nineteen. Thereafter, she supported the Atlantic Sound and, at her height, the Daytona Showband. Of her singing ability, Cynthia Sorley of the Daytonas said, 'Eilis could have the pick of the show bands. She has it all.'

Present tense. It did have to be that book.

'Yes, it does have to be that book,' I said.

Then the man rotated his blank screen to face me. The book did not exist.

I left Hodges Figgis empty-handed. I walked, not knowing where I was walking, imagining I had time on my hands. Men, dressed in County colours, had woken up and found their way back to the pubs they had left disgracefully the previous night. They called each other Mickey O' and Paddy Mac, whatever they were called in fact. I had noticed that before—it is a known thing—but never before like I noticed it now: they appeared like and sounded like strangers to me. They had descended upon this city and attacked it like a what, like a bacterium. Of course, they had nothing in common with the sky-blue people of the city, but I felt I had nothing in common with them either. That made me stand out, I realised. I was the one who—if anyone were looking—would be the spectacle. If I raised my hands and spread them, if I opened my mouth and my lungs, they would stop and stare. Not knowing where I was walking, I walked, time on my hands. A group of men, caped in flags like superheroes of my County, staggered up the centre of the street I was on like they could cast cars left and right with a flick of a wrist. One crusader caught my eye and struck out his arm to halt the others, ironically giving me privileged passage because he had spotted something exceptional about me, my damaged eye. Paddy Mac, let the man past. It was my mistake to have caught his attention. 'Up the red and blacks!' I said, searching for the right password. That sparked something in them, made them drunk all over again. One produced a spare flag, insisting I wear it, and the group jigged around me until I joined in. Luckily for me, I knew the songs they needed me to sing. The ordinary people observed a quarantine around us, stepping well back from the spectacle I was now in the middle of. Men—in this form, at times like this, when they are banded together drunk—have a herd shape and an undifferentiated smell. There is beer and sweat, and they come on at you incessantly. They overwhelm. Or subsume is a better word: it's the crowd you disappear within, which insists you submit yourself as a part of it. I sang one of the songs, joined in the chorus. I wished I had somewhere else to be, I wished I had some business to be about, even a book in my hand to have an excuse to be somewhere else. I hoped the waitress from Bewley's would not see me. If Quinn saw me, or O'Rourke or one of the others, what would they make of this performance? One song ended and another was about to start up, encouraged by the crowd. I slipped away from the arm on my shoulder. 'My wife's waiting for me,' I pleaded, adding, 'She's waiting for me in St Stephen's Green.' I felt shame at telling the lie because I knew no one would believe it. This man is down for the match, he has not brought a wife with him, if he even has a wife. I was ashamed too for not being more at ease. It was like I had lost the knack for it; suddenly I was not at home with them. How would it have been at Croke Park, at the game itself—would I let myself sway with the mass? In my experience, only in a football crowd—or a music concert—can you allow your body and your voice to be lost in a larger body and voice.

I walked away from my new friends, but I still had the flag that one had given me to wear. I judged I might stand out less if I kept it. Not knowing where I was going, I walked straight past another bookshop called Fred Hanna's. They won't have it; you can't have what does not exist. The shape and the feel of the book took form in my head as I wandered, not as it was when we last had it in our hands, but as it must appear now if we found it in a box in the attic. The cover would have faded from high gloss to matte by now; the pages (once nimble and whispery) would have stiffened with age. I was sitting on a bench. With its cover on, *The Show on the Road* belonged on our coffee table alongside others on football and *The Atlas of the World*. It was a used book, a loved book, a useful book. Once, I was clumsy and the book slid downwards, out of its jacket onto my lap. Its character was immediately altered. Without its flashy jacket, it was now a plain tome from a private collection, easily misplaced in a library of other lost books. I was sitting on a bench, and there were trees and birds and tiny indestructible insects. If our book had slipped out of its jacket, that could explain why it had gone missing. It had become anonymous in a mass of other books, its smell and shape indistinct from the rest.

I was sitting, I supposed, in St Stephen's Green. How long could I stay there before someone asked to share my bench with me or inquired—because of my bruised face—how I was or, because of my superhero cape, was I on my way to the final at Croke Park? How long do you think, Mandy? How long do you imagine your friend Mr Raj was sitting alone in that park in Belfast before you came along and altered the course of his life? I don't know how long I sat there. Trees don't count their hours in human time. Birds don't observe our geography. We are so puny by comparison. Not long, I would say. St Stephen's Green is a pleasant enough space, but I never entirely lost myself to it. I could still hear the clank of kegs being rolled up to a pub somewhere near and could still sense the delivery vans and taxis circling.

It was always a mad plan, Mandy. Where, in this city, might Cynthia Sorley be living, if she were alive at all? I decided to look for her.

The GPO on O'Connell Street had telephone directories for every district of the city. I stood up and cleared the birds and the trees from my head. I walked back towards the river, in the same direction as other fans who also had flags hanging down their backs. They were making their way to the stadium—time had passed while I had been sitting on the bench. The city traffic was busy now, making me stop at lights and wait at the bridge. I had the absurd idea that the GPO might be closed, it being a Saturday afternoon and a post office after all. So I lengthened my stride. I took the steps two at a time. I can't recall what it looked like on the inside—I was not there as a sightseer, but my memory tells me the light was yellow and it was spacious like in a train station. I found the directories where there was a line of booths. 'Sorley' was the only name I had; if Cynthia had married, I had not heard about it. Eilis had said nothing to me on the subject since last I had suggested she try to track down her friend. Sorley, Sorley, Sorely. Cynthia had an address in Santry, and there was a phone number. I tapped my pocket for coins. I would have to explain who I was. You knew my wife when she was Eilis McClean, when she was a singer. She sang that night in Belfast (they made her) when your bus was attacked. She was the relief act that night. You once said she could have had her pick of the show bands, she had it all. There was a book: perhaps you have it? I should like again to have a copy. That's a lot to say to a stranger on the phone, so I didn't place a call but wrote down her address instead.

A little way up O'Connell Street, I found a taxi. The Gresham Hotel was opposite, so I suppose taxis are easy to find. The driver was surprised when I read out to him the address in Santry. My flag, my black eye, the smell still on me from last night.

'An old friend,' I explained.

'For sure,' he replied, seeming not to believe me.

'I don't think it's far.'

'Not far at all,' he confirmed.

'Spare of the moment.'

'For sure.'

The roads were not busy here, but the footpaths were crowded with men and women and children all heading for the game. The red and the black mixed easily enough with the sky blue, I noticed. To my ear, the songs from one county mingled with the songs from the other. Through my driver's window, Croke Park stadium appeared fantastically huge, but real. He slowed. I felt I could touch it. All I would need to do was wind down the window.

'You can drop me here,' I suggested. Cynthia Sorley would not be at home. There was no longer any point in pretending. She would not be there now, if ever she had been. The woman who came to the door would not know me, she would not want to know me, she would not want to face me, and she would not have the book. I gave up on it. Books cannot simply disappear, whether you burn them or lose them; if they ever were, then somewhere they still are. My book, *The Show on the Road*, never did exist, the man in the shop said it: that was the only explanation for its non-existence now. It did not matter that I could quote what it said about Eilis or that I could recall the slip of it through my fingers. And so for the smell of piss in Dublin's gutters and Mickey O's singing on Dawson Street. These were mere sensations to me now. The smell that lingers in the nose and the sound still ringing in the ears long after are inadmissible evidence of a thing happening. The bruise on my face—that was real enough; the empty seat beside me in the taxi was truly empty; that was Croke Park ahead of me, if I just wound down the window.

'For sure,' he said.

Chapter XVI

When Frank went to see Jimmy and Betty, he went alone. He no longer made the excuse of Eilis being at her sister's. Years had passed. She never did have a sister, which, for Frank, was a pity.

That fact did not spoil his excitement. He lost sleep the night before, plotting the route his taxi would take from his house to the hotel, wondering whether he would eat there or whether the rendezvous would be over before dinnertime. How many years had it been since he had been with the great man. Would he even recognise them. How much of what they had been—how much of their glamour—would remain. Would this turn out to be the last time he ever saw them. That last thought, more than the others, was the one that had kept him awake: it crept under his skin and spread like a non-specific bruise. He felt sure that Betty and Jim would see it in him, the physical effects of his submission.

Cash was excited too to meet his old friend again. He had put that off for too long. He and his wife had come back to Northern Ireland when they had both decided it was safe. For a while, they had struggled to sell their place in England. In the meantime, they rented a grubby property in a former Housing Trust estate, and, before they knew it, this had become their home. It was his wife's idea to get back in touch with Frank. *You will regret it, you know you will, if you leave it any longer.*

She was also looking forward to the rendezvous. She had remembered her husband's friend as a manipulative sort of man, but she had since learned to respect that as a quality in a person. Manipulation is what is left to the lucky one who has no natural advantages or who has already cashed in all their favours. It is a psychological disfigurement that, like the physical kind, can mature into something more beautiful. Straightforwardly, she would rather have seen Eilis again, but according to Jim, Eilis was not to be spoken about.

⟨⟨⟩⟩

I had never moved, my number had never changed, Jimmy had no trouble finding me. He named a hotel he knew, I said that was great, I never mentioned Eilis, and he never asked. There was an exchange of how are yous, of proper replies deferred to later. We were two close friends who could not get started on the conversation we had put off all our lives. Even on the phone you could hear he was looking over his shoulder, monitored by Betty, expecting her to chip in. Perhaps he detected the same in my voice, constantly speaking up so I could be heard by the person in the next room. Neither of us had spoken to the other in all that time, and it was as if our underused voices were still too sore. He was more Scottish than I recalled.

We met in the hotel carpark. I got out of my taxi as they were parking their car. Betty was on the driver's side. She had learned to drive since last we had met. Fancy meeting like this, here, after all these years. I can't remember if someone actually said that or if I only thought it. Carparks are such provisional places, neither coming nor going. The only people who actually choose to meet in carparks are up to no good. There was certainly a handshake and a kiss with Betty, but I don't recall how we got started. How we started to, as I say. So inside I bought a drink, I bought pints of stout for Jim and myself, that's how we started and Betty said, No thanks for me, just a cup of tea if they do that. You're looking well, said Jim, which made me look back at him. Thanks, and yourself, I replied. I'm keeping well, I said, although that wasn't true as I was already having problems with this, my heart.

'You are rushing this. Slow down.'

Sorry, Mandy. I am missing details now, because I missed them somehow then. Did we shake hands, was Betty driving, what did we all drink. Does any of that matter? If the handshake or if the drink was what it took to get us started, then it mattered. There were conversations we needed to have and others—like about Eilis—we needed to have but couldn't. They wanted to ask about Eilis but had probably rehearsed beforehand, making themselves promise not to mention her. I wished they would ask, as that was the most natural thing to do. I missed her, as I hadn't in a long time: my one being outweighed by their two. You know those see-saws, like that: they were anchored to the ground, while I dangled sky high; none of us was all that comfortable on our own side.

'You're looking fabulous, as ever, Betty,' I said instead.

'Betty? Wow! No one has called me Betty since I was a youngster! Call me Liz.' She announced it like she was introducing herself to me anew. Pleased to meet you, call me Liz, I don't believe we have met. I don't know this Betty person of whom you speak. You must be mistaking me for someone else—someone else who slept her way around the local police force, who got a man in trouble in Rhodesia, who turned every head in every room she ever entered. All of that was mistaken, this Liz was saying.

'Sorry, of course. Jim never said. Liz!'

In the silence that followed, I could see now she looked like she had always been Liz, never Betty. Liz, not Betty, wore the glass beads and the bare feet. Liz danced in the yellow silk dress. She, not Betty, drew the attention of Danny Simms—if ever there were a Danny Simms.

'It's been a long time, Liz,' Jim interrupted the silence. 'It's not as if Frank's life here has been on hold while we were away. And it's not as if we have been good at keeping him up to date with our own to-ings and fro-ings. There are worse crimes than calling you Betty!'

I wonder, had they rehearsed that line too?

It was a sunny day; it was warm. It was the sort of day we have very few of here. Nothing about the day was normal. Normally, you can be glad of an afternoon pint in a hotel bar as a chance to get out of the rain or the drear. Maybe a peaty fire blazing and the glasses of a dozen or so strangers knock, knock, knocking on mahogany. That's the setting you would choose. That wasn't this. The sun cast a sharp triangle of hot light across our table like a cinema projector, funnelling motes of trapped dust and cigarette ash our way. The windows had been painted shut in less optimistic times, so there was no route in for fresh air and no route out for the stuff we were left to breathe. The steam from Liz's tea left a wet film along her hairline, which she ignored but which made me feel ill. Something rose in my throat. I had no taste for my Guinness. Jim was already two-thirds down his glass.

'Tell me at least that you are still Jim.'

'Jim, or Jimmy. Cash a lot of the time. Liz tries out James from time to time, but I get jealous because it feels like she is talking about someone else.'

'You have your limits?'

'I have my limits, I do!'

Even yet, we hadn't started. Liz and Cash both dragged on fresh cigarettes, which brought a pause. Were they regretting having asked to see me? We had, after all, in Belfast dock—many, many years before—said goodbye for the last. That had been Betty's instinct at the time. (Was it Liz who had changed her mind?) She had thought it then a precious moment: it is a valuable thing to recognise when the end has arrived, the pivot point after which nothing will ever be the same again. And it's a mistake—were we all starting to think this?—to turn back on that moment.

'Do you remember, you all, where we were when we last all saw each other?'

'Is this a quiz question, Frank?' asked Cash. 'Right, I've got this one. We were at the bar in the Adair. We wanted a quiet drink, and you couldn't get one of those in Suzy's in those days—maybe it's different now. It was the. Four of us, if I'm right. You, Liz, had those check trousers on that I liked, and your eye make-up that made you look like Dusty Springfield.'

'That's not it,' said Liz between sips. She was remembering many joyful, illicit occasions in the Adair when she was Betty, none of them with me present, many of them without the presence of her husband. 'I told you earlier that wasn't it. Frank was making sure we got on the ferry to England—that's when we last. We had said we wanted no send-off, but you couldn't help yourself, you had to come anyway. Bottles of Guinness in your pockets, if I recall.' Steam rose desultorily from her cup, tracing reluctant time and no certain direction, allowing her to rearrange the thought and, maybe, change the meaning of the moment for her. 'It was good of you to do that. Jim was grateful for that. You were the only one after all. A small gesture, maybe, but.'

She completed the sentiment in her own head. It seemed that she had surprised herself.

'He was my best friend.' This was simply the truth. 'Don't you see, he was my only friend, really. I was sorry to see him go. The both of you, of course. I was sorry about it all.'

Why had we started without Cash? He was sitting back, content to let his wife and friend do most of the talking and ready to run to the other end of the field at the first sound of cracking bone.

'There was a lot for you to feel sorry about, Francis. But Jim—ever the saint—never felt that way.'

'No, indeed, that's correct!' Jim announced, reaching the bottom of his cigarette and glass simultaneously. 'I'm having another, to get this sing-song started. Frank, I see you are still with that one: can I fetch you something else, perhaps a whiskey? That's that decided! And a gin and tonic for Liz, I don't know how you're drinking that tea in this heat. I'm stifled!' Cash sprang to his feet like a much younger person, eager to get to the bar. It was easy to subtract the years, to see him as I might have seen him had he not left the country all those years ago. Liz was smiling, looking at him, looking at me.

'One of his few pleasures,' she said, under cover of her smoky breath, explaining nothing. But the look she then flashed me was one of her old ones, showing there was no concern. 'We are so glad you agreed to see us, Francis.'

You don't have to say you love me.

I had the feeling she was really speaking for her husband. Jim had missed me. Jim, had he stayed, might have stayed an engineer, and they—had she changed—might have had children. They were so glad I had agreed to meet them. Somehow, she judged, it would do Jim some good to catch up with me. You don't have to say you love me. Was that what her Dusty smile meant?

('Maybe you got that wrong, Frank,' said Mandy, beginning to piece together what her patient had been telling her. 'Isn't it just possible, Frank, that Betty—or Liz—was glad you went to the hotel because it would do *you* good?'

The thought does occur to me, Mandy. It does now.)

'I have been looking forward to it for a long time,' I agreed. I wanted to say her name, but 'Liz' was still foreign to me. I paused then—not sure of the code words for Cullycreggan and the rest—and I held my breath. First, it—the holding of breath—was a metaphor: while waiting, our lives had been on hold (the metaphor meant), but, inevitably, one has to let go and breathe again. Then, the more it became uncomfortable to hold my breath, the more it seemed necessary to do it: I had been waiting a very long time, long enough to cause me actual damage; some reckoning of that was essential, they ought to at least see that. I let out my breath in a rush.

'Waiting for circumstances here to be right.'

Liz frowned.

'Waiting for the politics to be right for you to come home.'

She was still not playing along.

'Peace here, the dust settled, bygones. The past in its rightful place and no one asking questions that take us nowhere.'

'Questions, Frank?' Of course, this was *Liz*. The Liz who had lived in Rhodesia, in England, did not know the questions, or have the questions, that Betty would have. She had willed those away. Or, simply, she had let time pass in the way that it does.

Still, all I had been attempting to say was that I understood why it had taken them so long to take up their friendship with me again. It was politics, it was beyond their control. It was typical of Betty not to allow a simple statement to go by unproved.

'It was me,' she said, finally. 'Jim would have come back at the drop of a hat: he had no worries. There were no circumstances. I was the one. I hated it here.' As matter of fact as that, no attempt to smooth it off for the benefit of the one who had had to live here all along.

Of course, it wasn't news to me. My son was always on at me on the same subject, how hateful a place it is to live here. He finds it easy to look down at us from his office in the skies above London. I wanted to tell Liz that I understood and that I agreed that people here had not been kind to Betty, but she—Betty, Liz—didn't expect me to talk.

'I hate it now, Frank. People want you to be so happy all the time. *How are you?* Grand. *Are you liking it being back home?* Oh, yes, it's grand. *Isn't it marvellous, all this peace we've been having?* Just marvellous. Everything is just so bloody marvellous. But not everything is marvellous all the time, you know that, Frank. A lot of the time, life. There's a. There's an impact on it, on your psychology. It's lonely, on your own.'

But you are not on your own, Liz.

'Are you sure, Frank? Isn't everyone?'

It could have been my son talking.

'What can I *do* here? Jim suggested we move near to my folks in Newcastle. Did you know that's where I was from? It might be lovely there—mountains, sea—but do I really want to see out my last days back in the exact place I tried all my life to leave? How could I ever convince myself I'd ever actually done anything?'

Standing outside our house, you can watch the boats row one way up the river, and if we stand there long enough, you can watch them row back past you in the other direction, having gone exactly nowhere.

What have you ever done, Liz? Whatever that is, do that. You will be fine.

'I can't stay in the one place all my life, like you can, Frank. I'd leave tomorrow, if it weren't for Jim. He's like a pig in. He really is happy to be here, so I do my best to be happy for him. He claims the air is good for his health. I say, *that's Lough Neagh over there, Jim, not Lake Geneva!* But these days, we can just laugh at stuff like that, or he can. If he can, I can. It could be a whole lot worse, I recognise. I am not ungrateful. Oh!' It sounded like chronic, irremediable pain. 'I wouldn't want to leave you with that impression.'

The impression she left was murky, clouded in her cigarette smoke and the dusty sunlight. Maybe she did want me to talk, maybe I had gotten that wrong. She was not happy; there was room on her scale to be unhappier still: that's what this amounted to. She didn't need me to counsel her.

'Where would we be without Jim to lift us! Am I wrong?'

No, you're right there, Liz.

Jim arrived back at that moment with a tray of drinks. 'What say we get totally bollocksed?' he said. He was pleading. 'I don't remember the last time we all got hammered together. What's there to lose?'

Liz offered no objection. 'Francis—over to you. Get that whiskey down you, and we'll get you another.' Thank Christ for Jim and taxis.

At one point in the proceedings, a family—a mum, a dad, three grown-up sons—came in. They had not all been together as a family for some while. The sons, I imagined, had travelled, lived abroad, so this was a special occasion for them, planned some considerable time in advance. What must they have thought when they saw us? We would not have been a handsome sight, Mandy. Three middle-aged people getting drunk in the afternoon is no advert. The headache it gave me after can still bring a tear to my eye. The Guinness was off—I was ill in the gents'—but I never let up drinking the whole afternoon. How I got home, I don't know; I think the taxi driver must have put me to bed. We can't have been all that discreet. Anyone listening— those parents, those sons—could have called the police and had us arrested. For historic crimes, if nothing else.

At some point in the haze, we started. A hotel, it turns out, is a good nowhere place. It's nobody's home, although the armchairs they have could belong in your living room. In a hotel, you are safe enough to speak your truth, before everyone leaves, goes home, and forgets all about it. Like hospitals and hospital beds, they aren't real solid places, they are temporary. Provisional is the word I want again. Say your piece, be party to whatever takes place, there are no consequences. It would be a good sort of place to reveal that the British Secret Intelligence had airlifted them out of Zimbabwe; that the two of them—in their own ways—had been running guns; that they had been set up with nice posts in the RAF in England. With my eyes dazzled by the trapped sunlight and my head woozy with whiskey, then would have been a good time to reveal what they had been party to. They were looking good, the two of them, I thought—I could not take my eyes off them. Liz had on a pair of open sandals. They suited her. The buckle of one was bust. When had that happened? She had only noticed as they were getting ready to drive to meet me, and, rather than switching shoes, she pulled the pink band from her hair and improvised a buckle from that. The RAF, said Jim, had always found someone else to promote over him, 'someone who didn't have a dodgy history to run away from'. The cuffs of Jim's smart shirt had frayed to the quick. But it was a smart shirt, it showed off his tan, he looked good in it. The engineering firm he worked for in Rhodesia— that had paid him handsomely and supplied his wife with a gardener and a maid—wanted no more to do with them once independence had arrived, and the UK government hid their shame by sticking them on the last commercial flight out of the country. 'Basically, we left in the clothes we had arrived in.' I could not take my eyes off them.

I don't know, Frank, what you imagined we got up to all of those years: you always had a talent for invention, for narration.

You could fill a library.

You could fill a library with your stories.

And drive them around in a van.

A van smelling of the words of every book that had ever been in it.

Words linger in the mind, they leave a trace there, tiny particles of the thing itself.

Start.

'Why did you do Cullycreggan, Jimmy. Why did you do that?'

'Let's not do that, Frank. You know why.'

'How would I know? You never said. You were my best friend, I can tell you that. But you never said.'

'You were my best friend too. I don't have to tell you.'

'You two are like a pair of boys.'

'What do you mean you don't have to tell me?'

'I mean, you know you were my best friend. You know the whole thing, I don't have to tell you.'

'The truth is, Jim, I don't know. Patrick Ryan put you up to it, that is all I heard. But why you would, I haven't the.'

'Well, Frank, you ought to know, an intelligent man like yourself. Calling yourself my friend.'

'I do call myself your friend.   If that's all the same to you.   So, why?'

ℭℓ

Another drink. No route in for fresh air. No route out for the stuff we were left to breathe.

'Do you remember that time, Frank, when you played in Fr McCaul's football team? Now, that man was a fucker, I don't care what he's done for world peace.'

'You played too, Jim.'

'I was hardly ever on. There was a wee handicapped boy he would rather have put in the side before a Scot like me.'

'Casey?'

'No idea. I don't remember the names. Why would I, anyway, that doesn't matter. McCaul had me on the pitch this one time, whatever the game was, he must have been desperate.'

'Semi-final of the County Shield. V Michaelstown.'

'Fuck, the shit you remember—it doesn't matter! McCaul put me on, and he says to my face, "I know you know fuck-all about the game, Cash, so do just one thing for me: that guy you're marking—break his leg." This man—this man I am talking about—was a priest, Liz. And not just any sort of a priest.'

'Did you do what he told you, Jim? Did you deliberately break the boy's leg?'

'No, that's the whole point of this story, Liz: I did not. Frank, here, did the honours for me. This guy I was marking, he was a bit of a fancy Dan, I couldn't get near him to break his leg, even if I'd wanted to. McCaul kept up his abuse from the sideline, you never heard the like. *Smash him! Show him your studs, Cash.* Worse, I'm sure, I forget now. I never laid a finger. Then—I don't think I could have seen it happen, I only heard it—there's this stomach-winding crunch, *oof!* and the guy is a heap of bones on the grass, with Frank standing over him. You practically maimed him. And there is nothing of you, remember, you were so scrawny in your sharp shin blades and borrowed boots. Players vomited there on the pitch at the sight of it. I was sick too. McCaul pulled me off, like I had the job done, not before you ran the length of the field so the referee might forget about you in the mayhem. Did you get away with it? I think you must have.'

'I'm sick now even thinking about it. Why did you do that, Francis?'

'Don't say, Frank.' Jim lay his hand on my arm. 'And, Liz, you should not have to ask that. He did it for me, pure and simple. Frank committed an act of unequalled violence, so I would not have to. It was the most brutal thing I ever saw; I thought you'd killed him. When I had done vomiting, I realised you'd done it for me: you had crucified this guy so I wouldn't have to.'

'I'm going to be ill, I really am.'

'You're missing the point, Liz. The point is Frank had done this for me because he was my friend, because he knew I was not up to it. I saw all of that straightaway, sitting on the wet ground pulling off my boots. I saw exactly what this meant: it meant that whatever Frank would want me to do in the future, I was honour-bound.'

'That's ridiculous!'

'Is it, though? Maybe so, but I knew it nonetheless. Remember, we were just kids.'

What would I want you to do? Honour-bound to do what, Jim?

'I didn't know at first. What am I saying? I wasn't *looking out* for opportunities to do your bidding. That's not how our friendship worked. What demands will Frank make of me today? Not like that. But in Belfast, when I was studying and you were working, if you were going to a meeting, say, then I would go along with you, whoever the crazies were who were at them. Maloney, McCann, the Irish Justice League—do you remember all that?'

'Ahem, I do!' cried Liz.

'You were mad for all that, Frank. Going to the library to fill up on books, attending public lectures with people in damp duffel coats. Of course, being you, you were too self-conscious to speak up at any large gathering. You thought people would laugh at you, like my university friends did. You wanted me to speak for you instead. You thought, if you filled me with your ideas and I did the talking, people might sit up. You said that we weren't living in a democracy, because defeat for one side had been engineered in. *Minoritarianism* was the word, and it was logical not to engage in a contest you were bound to lose.'

'Ahem!'

'So we had been holding and watching, you said. I carried this all for the rest of my days, Frank. The strategy of watchful disengagement had run its course is what you told me. Do you remember all that McCann, all that IJL shit? I do. That's where you got it from. Hours you would spend filling my head with it. There was plenty of that chat to be heard all around in those days, not just in Northern Ireland. That made it all the more. What do I want to say here? It made it all the more true. The times they were a-changin'. The theory met with the facts that we knew for ourselves, and that made it true.'

Then I told him Patrick Ryan needed a bomb maker.

'I was no bomb maker. I mean, I hadn't the first clue, but I did know how to make an electrical switch, and it turns out that that—and a bit of explosive material that can easily be found knocking about the building industry—is mostly all you need to make a bomb. Not a very good bomb, as it turned out, but we weren't to know. Ryan needed it, you told me, and you told me you were going along as the driver. You didn't instruct me to do anything—there was no *instruction*, Liz—I was not obliged, I wouldn't go unless you were going. But it's also true that I would not have gone anywhere near that whole business but for the fact that you were. Or so was the plan.'

Neither of us followed through.

'I let you down, Frank. I could not go through with it. I sat at home with Liz, watching the television. That stupid song contest was on. Then there was a newsflash: the Daytona Showband had been attacked, and all we could think about was Eilis, lovely Eilis. Only later did we learn that you had also backed out, that you had set Aloysius up instead.'

I did not set up Aloysius Dynes. I did not do that. I would not have done that to him.

'I could not blame you for that. I was in no position to after I had let you down.'

That's not how I saw it. At least that's not how I see it now.

'Even then, Jim was going to stay,' said Liz. 'I persuaded him otherwise. I told him, "Fuck Frank, we're leaving!" I practically had to push you on to that boat, didn't I?'

'Ahem. No, it was Frank's idea to leave.'

'Up the bloody gangplank. You would have stuck around with your wee friend Frank had I not forced you.' She turned from Jim to me, to Jim to me. 'I convinced him you'd be all right, that others— the dead, principally—would be held responsible. No one would be interested in the guy who did *not* drive the frigging car, but the guy who had made the frigging bomb had a good reason to get away.'

'As I recall it, it was Frank's idea to leave. Our life might depend on it, you said.'

They *were* interested in the guy who had not driven the car, or the van rather. I was the one who was left behind after all. I ought to have followed my own advice and left at the same time as you. That's a regret, for sure. Eilis was not keen, so that was decided. I wasn't going anywhere without her.

Another drink. Breathing in our breathing out.

'You wouldn't go without Eilis,' Liz and Cash both said. They stole a glance at each other, for permission to say the next thing. 'Have you heard much, or at all, from Eilis, Frank? In London.'

That was the wrong thing to say then. I was drunk. I chose to forgive them. That turned out to be easy to do. They might have been telling me there that they had been down to London. That's where my son lives. I have never been. Getting annihilated was the plan now. We were, all three of us, quite drunk. We had reached the state where we could have started a fight or fallen in love. I looked at Cash. Betty was always beautiful, so was Liz. It was that capability you talk about: you always had the sense with her that she had a power, a force to seduce or compel. Partly it was to do with what we all thought we knew about her but didn't in fact. Aside from all of that, she was simply attractive. I didn't need to look twice at her to know that. I did look twice at Cash. There was something missing about him, a thing not there that could almost persuade me that he was not the same man—or the same boy—that I had known. He had reinvented himself again. His ugliness had gone. The disfigurement that Fr McCaul was convinced would scare the opposition, which he turned into a joke at the boy's expense: it had gone. I could long look at Jimmy's split face and see the ghoul that everyone could see and then see the other side, the side that was always soft and appealing. I looked again; I looked for as long as a drunk man is permitted to look. His harelip had vanished. There was no sign that it had been repaired, there was no scarring or telltale lopsidedness. He had no good side or bad side, just one face intact. Cash must surely have seen me staring, but he showed no sign of suspecting what it was—or what it wasn't—I was staring at. It was as if he had a different version of this story too, one in which he was never crooked-faced. In this story, I had not become his friend just because no one else would: I had simply, through the breaking of bones, become his lifelong friend. I looked at his face, and it broke into an even smile, one you could fall in love with.

Chapter XVII

I have been back home, Mandy. I have been back to the town where it all began, and which I have been avoiding lest it bring about my end before I am ready. I guess that must mean I am ready now. Maybe I shouldn't have, but I did. It was Eilis' idea. You saw her earlier, I believe. From where, I don't know, but somehow she heard about the area championship match taking place at the Pitches, and she says, Frank, shall we go? It was a beautiful sunny day, a bit chilly, but what can you expect at the time of year, so I say, Wrap up warm, love, wrap some biscuits and let's go. She sang in the car on the way, a modern song, I don't know how she keeps up. It's a pleasure to hear Eilis sing nowadays when she is so much better. Eilis did the driving. Her own car. I only have the library van, which is not mine to use at the weekend. The van—like an actual library—is a quiet place. And it moves on quiet wheels, with no siren or jingle to announce it.

We got there early before the game so, on Eilis' suggestion, we took a saunter around the Diamond, skirting Suzy's for now, and into the churchyard. Cemeteries are hard places for me to be, I've been to too many, and I oughtn't to have gone to this. But, Mandy, I couldn't come all this way and not call in. Fr McCaul's gravestone is a bit of a landmark: a huge block of rough granite, black and sparkly, flanked by guardian angels, decked out in green ribbon. I hadn't known it would be there. That's a lie: I knew it was there, but I hadn't prepared myself to see it. Had I not gone to his funeral? I went to every other bloody funeral. There's a stick for this sort of thing, with notches so you can count your way down to your own grave. There are those who ought to go before you, and there are others—too many others—whom I survived. If I had gone to McCaul's funeral, I may not have come out alive.

Fr McCaul heard my sins as he heard everyone's when I was a lad, and the feeling I had then—of being rebuked by him, of him knowing my crimes before I had told him them—was the same feeling I had now facing his gravestone. He was inscrutable as granite is, hard and impossible to impress. He could swear, Fr McCaul could swear. He was saying, *You, you wee fucker! Coming into my puddle of a graveyard now that you have buried my reputation along with my corpse. Couldn't wait to do that, could you? Just to save your own skin.* That's what his block of granite was saying while his angels flapped their heavenly wings. Lucky for me and my mental health, I was alone and only I could hear them.

Then the angels spoke. 'You haven't got one of those freedom fighter wreaths, I hope? We are always lifting those off, ruddy nuisance they are, even now.' They spoke with gravel voice. Then I saw another appear from behind the granite, and I could see it was Alice.

'No, no!' I said, recovering quickly, avoiding the impression of having communed with the cherubim and seraphim. 'Just paying our respects to the great man.'

'Bit late, he'll not hear you.' She rearranged one of the green ribbons around an angel's wing, in no hurry to leave, not yet really seeing me.

'We were sorry to hear it, when he passed away.'

'Ahem. Aye.'

'Very sorry.'

That's when she looked up and recognised me. 'Broth Boy,' she said simply, taking her time over the cruelty. 'Why did you come? Are you hungry?'

'We've come to watch the game.'

She didn't say much more, but she seemed to say plenty. You said you are very sorry, she seemed to say. You've come here to say sorry to Vincent or sorry to me? You've come here to atone for setting the newspapers on to a dead priest who could no longer defend himself? You've come here because you feel guilty that a van—his van, the van in his name—that you both got so much fun out of when you were young was used at Cullycreggan? And that it killed Ryan and your friend Aloysius Dynes? Do you feel guilty about that, Frank?

I thought she said all of that, but she said none of it because she knew none of it.

'Did you see the papers, Frank?' She was blushing now. A blush means shame, but it also means rage.

She had recalled my name. 'I did,' I admitted. 'Terrible what they said about.'

'What they said about what, Frank? Are you still tongue-tied after all this time? Do you mean what they wrote about Fr McCaul?'

'Of course, that.'

Her hand rested on his gravestone. 'They can do him no harm.' Then she looked straight at me. 'What about what they wrote about me, Frank? Did you read that? Did you enjoy reading that?' Did you enjoy the way the papers trashed Fr Vincent's reputation by writing about me—his housekeeper, his partner, his *fancy woman*?

'There was no call for all that, Alice. You weren't deserving of that. I am sorry about that.'

She was looking at me now, as if I were singly capable of wreaking all the harm that had befallen her. And this surprised her. I was, after all, to her, a pitiful, mostly mute boy she knew only from the queue for broth. Where had I found the tongue to disgrace her and her Vincent? What, indeed, was I sorry for?

'We've come here to watch the game,' I interrupted. It sounded like an interruption even to me. I couldn't bear to be in that graveyard another minute with her. 'Will you be going up?'

'I never watch the game. As you know,' she added, looking away and somehow receding. She became smaller, younger. 'I just feed the boys and then stay in the background. Or I did. They don't seem to need that from me now.' Nobody needs me now. 'That's what they call peace.' Even the press stopped hounding me, when I became less interesting. I didn't look the way they would have preferred me to look. 'Why is the ground in this churchyard such a bog,' she asked herself suddenly, as if the thought had only just occurred to her, 'when the town generally has wonderful drainage? Why is that, do you think?'

'It's the sandy soil, Alice.'

She accepted that explanation; she knew about the sand, though still could not see why, of all places, the churchyard should be the one without. She shuffled off without saying another word. She had held her tongue. We watched her move round the side of the chapel towards the little house that she used to keep, when Fr McCaul was alive in it, and which she appeared now to live in alone. The new priest, whoever he was, had evidently decided to reside elsewhere.

'She has no curtains,' said Eilis. 'Why would they take her curtains away? Anyone can just look in: that's not right. She has the right to at least that much privacy.'

'She could have been much worse,' I said to Eilis, who didn't really know what I meant, who thought I meant one thing when, really, I meant another. Then I stood with my head bowed at the gravestone so she would not disturb me to ask.

Like you hear at the end of a minute's silence, we heard a whistle blow, and we followed it up to the Pitches. Eilis held my hand because, despite the sandy soil, it was slippery from all the rain we have been having. I got the pain in my side at that point, just a discomfort, but I was already out of breath. I should have turned back right then, shouldn't I, Mandy? The signs were right there. Eilis must not have noticed; I hid it. I mean, I felt her holding my hand, but she was actually somewhere else. We're playing Michaelstown, she reminded me on the way up. They hate us. It's mutual. We are in yellow; they are in red.

I didn't know any of the boys playing, and it's not as if there is a programme or anything, we are not talking Croke Park here, but I wouldn't be surprised if many of the players had the same names as in our day. Sons. Then again, maybe not. I ran the names through my head. Not Casey, he was disabled. Neither Ryan nor Dynes. Not Cash—he and Betty had no children. No son of ours there. Perhaps there could be a McHugh or two. Stand up straight! Shiels, moved away; O'Rourke, God only knows. 'Is that Hughes boy the son of Declan Hughes?' 'Aye.' 'He can play.' 'Aye.' 'May he rest in peace.' I found I wasn't really watching the game. ('You missed that point!' I felt Eilis shout in my ear.) Over the back of the Pitches where, before, there was nothing at all, there were houses: identical, individual houses, red brick and white ledges all in a row. Down below, past Fr McCaul and

Alice and the churchyard, there was the Diamond and the four streets running to it as before, but at the top of one was a petrol station that was new—or it was new up until the time they shut it down. ('Ouch! Did you see that, Frank? That poor boy is in trouble. He won't get up from that, he must have broken his leg.') The housing development where Jim had lived with Betty was finished at last and looking like a proper part of the landscape, mossed over like the rest like it had always been there and had never been a half-built place where daring Catholic children might run into daring Protestant children. ('I could hear it from here, Frank, could you? That break won't mend any time soon.') I heard someone on the touchline say my name, but when I looked, I couldn't see who it was, so I paid no attention and started watching the game again. Eilis told me we were losing and that the referee was a joke. An old guy too fat to run the length of the pitch and back, he pretended he could see everything from the centre. He waved his arms a lot to keep the play flowing, ignoring all the fouls even when they were actually dangerous. Two players contested the ball near the sideline, and someone raised a flag and called, 'Out!', but I thought I heard 'Tout!' underneath. Then I seemed to hear it every time the ball left the pitch. People were looking my way—people I only recognised when I subtracted thirty years from their faces, smoothed out their lines, and darkened their hair. 'You knew that big shot.' The guy was no more than a youngster, never knew Cash, Cullycreggan was something only his old man could have spoken of. 'That one who told the police about the thing before the whole thing went up.' I had other, better, friends, I said. But that was a lie; I never had. Then just at that moment, like I was Peter hearing the fucking cock crow, there was a grip at my chest. Eilis gripped my hand and asked me was I feeling all right and had I seen enough and would I rather head down to Suzy's, perhaps they do food there these days? I must be hungry, so that's where we went.

I have a memory for some things and none for others, and I can never be sure whether something I remember is a thing that has happened or a thing my mind is telling me must have happened. That, I have been assured, is entirely normal. Suzy's was not as I remembered it. I had in my head McAllister and his old mates huddled around little round tables and then going for a piss against the wall out the back. It's not like that now. In a fairground, the seats on the rides, side by side, face away from all the others; they move in and out in their pairs, taking sideways glances but never actually confronting each other head-on. The same person designed the interior of the new Suzy's. Each snug had its own walls, its own opaque windows, its own turning-away from every other snug. Only the mahogany bar was the same as before, dulled by generations of fingerprints, traceable back to the great-grandfathers and great-grandmothers who had also leaned there. In the meanwhile, the landlord had found and laid a new carpet, which was too bright red and too . . . what's the word? Nap? Pile? At each step, your foot would land and slide forward an inch like you were walking in shoes too big for you, knocking you off your balance and timing, upsetting your stride, making you spill your drinks.

'You don't look good,' I heard Eilis say to me.

'It's the place,' I said. 'I'll be all right.'

The bar served beer. I wanted a coffee, so I had half a Guinness. And a selection of crisps stood in for lunch. Proper food would have helped. Do you know, Mandy, I have been starving for bloody ages. Can you believe, all this was only yesterday.

There wasn't much chat in the bar; whatever people there were hidden mainly out of sight. You could hear glasses touching tables in other snugs, and I could hear the sound of crisps crunching—always louder in my own head than in anyone else's. I was just beginning to think, this is uncomfortable, but it is all right: I could have come here anytime over the past thirty years, and I would not have enjoyed it, but I bet I could have nipped in and out and it would have been all right. And, besides, these people will have read Emma Cooper and will know now for sure that no one from their midst had warned the police that Ryan was coming for them at Cullycreggan. I decided there had been a cessation of hostilities at Suzy's.

Then I saw Quinn again, and I knew that the peace was over. Not since Dublin had we met, and that was a thing I'd rather have forgotten. He was breathing heavily from an oxygen bottle, gulping air through his mouth in a technique not recommended by his respiratory nurse. He was smoking too, so that the tank beside him was a danger to life for all around. Sometimes, sound travels faster than light: I heard him before I saw him. But before all that, he saw me.

'There's that fucker again,' he said, no names necessary. 'They let you back in then, did they?'

You needn't get the impression he was being jovial. 'Here on my own accord, Quinn,' I said. 'Just having a quiet drink with the wife.' Eilis, accidentally introduced, felt obliged to say hello.

'That's a bad business about Dynes,' he said, deciding to ignore her. 'You know anything about that, seeing how he was your friend?'

'Aloysius Dynes? No idea what you mean, Quinn. He's dead these years. What would I know of his business?'

'Thirty years, Frank. As you and I both know only too well.' Quinn was maudlin now and, for a matter of a few blessed seconds, seemed to forget about us. The background music was turned up. 'I'll never forgive myself, and I will never forgive you either for that.'

'What's he on about, Frank?' Eilis turned away from our friend to talk to me privately. She looked at me like she had me covered from every angle, so comprehensively it was impossible for me to turn away. Her eyes were fierce and defeated and desperate for hope, all at the same time. All I could think was that I loved her, but that Quinn was looking on, spectating as my wife and I had the conversation we had started—and then dropped—in our bedroom thirty years ago, on the night of Cullycreggan and the Daytona Showband. We, Mandy—you and I—have talked more about this than ever Eilis and I have. 'What's he on about, Frank?' she asked, but she already knew. 'What will he not forgive you for, Frank?'

You know, Eilis. You *do* know, I said—or I pleaded, hoping she would will herself to knowing again. I let you have the car, remember? So you could drive to the Panadol, so you had the car for your big night in Belfast, so you would not have to take a bus back from singing with the Daytonas. That was as it should be. But I was also meant to have the car that night, to drive Ryan to Cullycreggan. I never wanted to do it, it was never my, I, but I let myself be talked into it.

'What will he not forgive you for, Frank?'

Jesus, Eilis! It's not hard. Quinn was the one I called to take my place. Then—I don't know why—he couldn't or wouldn't drive either, and so he called Aloysius.

'Dynes took the fall for the both of us, wouldn't you say, Frank?' Quinn still ignored Eilis, like she wasn't there. 'Just because I wouldn't drive anywhere with that fool, Ryan. Just because you. You will have your own reasons for not. We have had all this out before,' he went on. 'We've had our words. Only now the newspapers think the story is worth going over again, and I, for one, am interested in why that should be. Are you interested in why that should be, Frank?'

Eilis, God love her, butted in. 'I don't know who you are, but you are upsetting my husband, so I would thank you to leave us in peace.' Or words to that effect.

Quinn, it seemed for the first time, turned his gaze on my wife. He was trying to work out who she was and why he didn't know her before remembering he probably did know Eilis McClean and did know why they had not met before. But he left all of that unsaid. He chuckled instead. 'I will. I will do just that.' Every move he made after that was slow and effortful. He screwed the remaining life out of his cigarette. He finished off his drink in one but by glugging in the smallest possible mouthfuls. That alone left him breathless, but he disconnected himself from his oxygen supply and slid the bottle further below the table of his snug before raising himself onto his unsteady legs. Trying not to stumble on the tricky carpet, he exited by a door near the bar.

'Loo,' I guessed.

'Nasty frigger.'

'Maybe, Eilis. Maybe not.' The truth was, for thirty years, Eilis and I had been having this same conversation, but never once after that first night had we actually spoken about it. She held me guilty for everything bad that had ever happened to her since; she never let up especially in the early years; she knew all about Dynes—that he had been the driver, when I was meant to be—that he had died on the spot; she knew this all about my friend, her friend, our driver in the dance hall times. But she never once said, You killed him, it was your fault. That was never a part of her illness, even though she could have made it a part and blamed that on me too. She spared me that. She was gentle with me there.

'Do you know why the papers are interested in all of this again, Frank?' she asked me.

I do.

'Is it because it happened on the same night as the Daytonas?'

Partly.

'Is it because they confirmed that no one was an informant to the police, when local people had suspected otherwise?'

It's because I told Emma Cooper to say there was no informant. It's because I gave her the quotes to put in the newspaper.

'Is it because of who owned the van?'

Yes, and because I told her who owned the van, even though in no fair sense could it be said by then that Fr McCaul was the owner of the van. Just like it could in no way still be said to be a bread van, even though the smell of bread lingers.

'Is it because they connected the van to Fr McCaul?'

Yes, and because I wanted them to make the connection, I wanted them to get that bastard even if he had nothing to do with it, because in life none of us stood up to him. Not one of us. Maybe if we had, things would have been different for Jimmy.

'And why does Quinn care?'

Because he is the only one who knows as much as I do. He can take everything away from me and throw it in the mucky water, as once he did a comb I owned. He can do that.

She left me, there and then, or long before then. 'I'm going to the ladies', Frank. You should maybe get yourself a drink of water.'

That was a good idea, I thought. I went to the bar to attract the attention of the barman. Quinn came back from wherever he had been, and shortly after that, we were in another fight. He accused me again of harbouring Cash.

'Shame about your friend, the Scotch man,' he prodded, 'after all that looking after him you did. The papers come out, and he has his wee road accident. That's a terrible coincidence, Frank. Do you think McCann's boys had anything to do with that? Had it coming, naturally, but you've got to feel for a guy who thinks after all those years he has gotten away with it.'

Even though Emma Cooper had been careful to say there was no informant, the thought remained firmly ingrained in the bar at Suzy's. Thirty years on, it just got them talking again. Cash made the dud bomb, placed a call to the police, and then booked his tickets to Liverpool or wherever: that's the story that made the most sense to them.

'I always thought it was Cash,' Quinn went on. 'Cash ran away, it was obvious he was the one who touted. But then, in Dublin, when we all went for that reunion with Fr McCaul, you put up such a defence of him. I could not work it out: sure, he was your friend, but he was also your get-out-of-gaol-free card. Why would you defend him? Then it hit me: you were going to fit me up—you were going to put it about that I was the one. For ages, I could not work out how you would go about doing that. Then, in January, the papers all came out again about the Daytona Showband and about Cullycreggan. There was that line, confirming that the police had had no prior information but suggesting there had long been rumours in the town that it might have been a local man who drove taxis. That was as good as naming me: it's a small town, and no one only me drives a cab. But it wasn't me. In this whole sad business, the only thing I knew for sure was that I had not been a tout for the RUC. On the night of the bombing, you called me. You said you were meant to drive the car to Cullycreggan, but you had changed your mind. Could I do it for you? Before I could say no, I had said yes, but I never wanted the job. When I saw Aloysius Dynes early that evening in Suzy's, I took him outside, and before long, he had agreed to do it. Poor, stupid Aloysius, his life had already run out of useful road.'

I could feel the sweat forming on my brow. I took a drink of the water. The barman was nowhere to be seen.

'So I knew it wasn't me. But whatever the papers might be saying, it was plain as day that there had been a tout. The only way the police and border guards could have avoided going up in smoke with Pat Ryan's bomb was if they'd had a tip-off from someone who knew. Who else did know? Cash knew. Cash: the perfect fit for the job. Except you, in Dublin, had been adamant that Cash had nothing to do with it. That left only one person. It was you. All along, I knew in my bones it was you. Now I know for sure, and now everyone is going to know. McCann's boys are going to know, I will make sure of it. I know people who can put a call straight through to her. Your time is up, Frank.'

This was the last clear thought that I had. Maybe I ought to have given *his* name, Quinn's, to the police when I had the chance. So, what if he had done nothing. Doing nothing is not enough.

Watchful disengagement was no strategy at all. I thought all that, then he knocked my glass of water clean out of my hand. The glass bounced on the carpet, and the water formed a neat puddle. I pushed him instinctively with both hands on his shoulders, and he stumbled back onto a bar stool, and then he fell over the bar stool and was on the floor, on the thick red carpet, gasping for breath like a pathetic old man. I think that's when I must have lost my glasses because, for the life of me, Mandy, I can't find them anywhere. I was very fond of those glasses, and I do need them.

Quinn was fragile to begin with, I'll say in my defence. His dentures fell out and lay beside him grimacing. His oxygen tank was below the table in his snug, but I said nothing about that at first (why should I have?), and the barman, who was pretty frantic having just shown up, couldn't find it, and then finally I said, The bottle is under his table. The barman called the ambulance. I wanted to leave, but they would not let me, and the barman too said, I think, mate, you should hang around. Quinn's head's cut. The barman was about twenty. The ambulance came. It wasn't quick, it was at least thirty minutes because the town is in the middle of nowhere, but they put Quinn in the back and tried to settle his breathing and check for fractures. He had a gash over his eye, however that happened. The paramedic—Indian bloke, Ray: a funny name for an Indian—had questions for the barman, but soon his questions were for me. *Had I struck the man? Had he attempted to assault me? Where had I pushed him? Was I aware of his pre-existing respiratory condition?* The paramedic would be obliged to report my answers to the police, his statutory duty in cases of possible GBH. I said, *That's a ridiculous exaggeration*, but he saw me wince. Wince is such a fairy word, as if it is a light, inconsequential thing. However, I winced hard, I winced tight, I winced into a tiny, muscular knot around my heart. So Ray hoisted me into the back of his ambulance alongside Quinn with instructions for us not to hit each other.

Mandy, you would have to agree that it has been my cross to bear.

And now I can't find Eilis. Was she here earlier? You say you didn't see her, but I am sure I remember her coming. You put her sweets in your tabard, yes! But why is she not here now? Why am I talking to you when it should be her?

Chapter XVIII

'Geriatric fisticuffs,' explained the paramedic, wheeling his patient up to the hospital admissions. His colleague was still at the back of the ambulance, loading another man into a wheelchair. 'Can we put that on the report?'

The police officer who was already standing there lifted her cap off, pulling with it a strand of her hair from her ponytail. Music from the hospital radio station jingled in the background. 'Depends on whether this one survives the night.' She was pointing at the man on the trolley. 'Or we might be looking at aggravated.' Then she thought again. 'If anyone thinks it's worth while pursuing.' A nurse had come out to meet the paramedics. 'Are you the one I need to talk to—are you in charge? Sorry, I need your name?'

'Jeremy Black. No, I am not in charge, but I have beds free in my ward. What do I need to know?'

The police officer explained as far as she had been able to gather. The two men had been in a fight in a bar. The barman reported that the two of them had been having a row. This one had pushed that one; that one had fallen over a stool; this one then bent down and gave that one a good beating and cracked his head open. There were no witnesses, only the barman. 'I have their names here,' she finished, showing her pad to the nurse for him to record on his admissions notes.

The nurse rested his finger on one of the names. 'And Mr Quinn has COPD, or similar?' It was not a question for the policewoman to answer. The oxygen bottle beside the gurney was evidence enough. 'Okay, Mr Quinn,' he said, changing his tone to address the patient, 'we'll patch you up and have you in a bed right away.' The nurse called for a colleague to find out where the hell the registrar was. He rolled his eyes at the police officer, as if to say to her, *A fine lot of good the registrar will do.*

The second paramedic, the one with the wheelchair, had caught up. 'Where do you want my guy?' he asked breezily. He had done this before.

'Good evening, sir. You are Mr . . .'

'Frank.'

'Mr Frank? No, just Frank.' Jeremy added the name to the surname he already had in his notes.

'There's nothing wrong with me. I don't know why they had to bring me here. Eilis will be wondering.' Then, 'Where's that music coming from?'

The second paramedic jumped in. 'You didn't look right to me, Frank, did you? Your heart giving you a bit of a scare.' Then, as if the man were not there at all, the paramedic continued. 'He may have a touch of vagueness too.'

'Do I need to put them in separate wards?' the one called Jeremy asked the policewoman. 'We are short-staffed tonight.'

'I shouldn't think either one will be fit to lift a hand to the other, do you? But do keep an eye on them. I'll be away now. Another officer from the station will be along shortly. But call us if he—the other one—crocks it. Let's hope not.'

The policewoman left. The paramedics had another call to respond to. Jeremy himself wheeled the patient called Frank into the main ward. In a private side room, a teenage boy, his leg in full-length plaster, was entertaining some other boys in football kit. 'Quieten down, you lot!' the nurse shouted in. 'I have sick people here.' In the main ward, nurse Nicole had already transferred Mr Quinn into a bed and connected him to his oxygen and to a heart monitor. The registrar would take it from there.

'Nicole, could you help me assist Mr . . . Frank into this bed, please.' Between them, the two nurses dressed their patient in hospital pyjamas and made sure he was comfortable. They placed his wallet and his glasses—the only things he had—on his bedside table. The registrar would be along to see him shortly also. 'Can we get you anything, Frank?'

'Yes! There's nothing wrong with me. I want you to call my wife. Eilis will be wondering.' Frank pointed with his head at the small pile of personal effects that had been placed on the stand beside his bed.

'Is there a phone number in your wallet, Frank? Is that it?' Jeremy picked up his patient's wallet and found in it a donor card with details of next of kin.

Together, the nurses went to their workstation and placed a call to Frank's son.

Mr Quinn died in the night. First, the curtain had been pulled around his bed, and then the nurses and orderlies, quietly so as not to disturb the other patients on the ward, had lifted the body onto a trolley and wheeled him out of sight to where they go.

'That's an awful shame about that man,' said a nurse, tucking the sheets in again at the end of Frank's bed. 'We haven't even found out who he belongs to yet. It's hard enough as it is, but that makes it so much worse for us when we don't know who to call. I wish families could bear that in mind.'

'I'll try to remember that,' said F4rank. 'I haven't lost that yet,' he added, tapping the side of his head.

The nurse was inspecting her patient's notes clipped to the end of his bed. 'Sure you haven't, Mr . . .'

'I'm just Frank,' he insisted. 'By name, by nature. Eilis tried out *Francis* for a while, maybe a day, maybe the day she showed me off to her parents, but it felt to us both like she was referring to a totally different man, so she dropped it. She will be in later on to see me.'

'Are you sure about that, Frank?' the nurse asked, puzzling over the man's notes. 'Maybe your son will make it in? That'll be nice for you.'

'No, my son is in London. He's just had a child of his own. They will hardly bring him over from England to see me here, now, in this state: a baby can catch things in a hospital.' Frank watched the pretty nurse, who was busying herself around his bed and the bed next to his. 'What do they call you?'

'I'm Mandy. Sometimes Amanda.'

Frank thought she said *Amundah*. 'That's a lovely name,' he said.

'Is there anything I can get you, Frank?' Mandy believed she knew the kind of man that Frank was. 'You have a heart scan this afternoon, which I will get you ready for. Nothing to worry yourself about.' Like a magician misdirecting her gullible audience, she slipped her hand into the pocket of her tabard and popped something in her mouth. 'Or will I wait for you to give me a shout?'

'Am I here for an operation? Is that why they brought me in?'

'If you need one, and if you're lucky and there's a cancellation. Only if. You'll be fine. I'll get you a newspaper to read, if you like.'

Mandy pulled the curtain around her patient and left him to sleep for the rest of the day.